Miss Peachy and the Daughters of the Narodniki

GORDON JOHN THOMSON

Copyright © 2016 Gordon John Thomson

All rights reserved.

ISBN:
ISBN-13:9781519021656

DEDICATION

For my mother, Jean Thomson, who still loves a good story

Miss Peachy and the Daughters of the Narodniki

An exciting historical crime thriller set in Paris and Switzerland in 1902 – the era of *La Belle Époque* and the *Entente Cordiale*.

This is the first instalment in the adventures of young American detective, Joseph Appeldoorn, and Miss Amelia Peachy, Edwardian actress and athlete, British secret agent, and mistress of disguise and intrigue...

In this first episode, which takes them from Paris to Bern to Lake Constance, the pair encounter beautiful courtesans, deadly assassins, anarchist plots, Russian revolutionaries and royalty, as well as both the young Picasso and Albert Einstein...

The time is March 1902. The Boer War is coming to its conclusion in South Africa, while turn-of-the-century Europe is beset with political rivalries between imperial dynasties, and the threat of violent anarchist groups. Paul Kruger, former President of the Transvaal Republic, has hired a deadly assassin, codenamed "the Butcher", to kill Edward VII, the new King of England, in reprisal for British action against the Boers. Joseph Appeldoorn is a young and rather naive American, a scientist turned reluctant detective, sent to Europe to find a missing Connecticut heiress, Eleanor Winthrop. Joe's search for the missing girl takes him from Paris to Bern where he finds a murdered woman in a hotel bath and is, himself, nearly murdered by a mysterious German, before being rescued from the River Aare by the young Albert Einstein. Joe follows further leads in his search for the heiress that take him to a political meeting in Zurich addressed by Lenin, and on to an infamous bordello, *Le Royale*. Here he encounters the enticing British agent Amelia Peachy...

Joe and Miss Peachy soon come together in their bid to both find the missing heiress and to foil this dangerous assassin, but must face many new and dangerous challenges on the way. In particular they discover that Germany now has a new and potent weapon to use against the British Empire – a giant airship called a Zeppelin...

CONTENTS

Prologue   Pg 1

Chapter 1   Pg 5

Chapter 2   Pg 18

Chapter 3   Pg 30

Chapter 4   Pg 44

Chapter 5   Pg 54

Chapter 6   Pg 64

Chapter 7   Pg 74

Chapter 8   Pg 84

Chapter 9   Pg 95

Chapter 10   Pg 107

Chapter 11   Pg 118

Chapter 12   Pg 129

Chapter 13   Pg 139

Chapter 14   Pg 153

Chapter 15   Pg 161

Chapter 16   Pg 169

Chapter 17   Pg 183

Chapter 18   Pg 194

Chapter 19   Pg 202

Chapter 20   Pg 210

Chapter 21   Pg 218

Chapter 22   Pg 230

Chapter 23   Pg 236

Chapter 24   Pg 243

Epilogue   Pg 248

PROLOGUE

January 1902

Stephanus Johannes Paulus Kruger had reached an age, with the grave looming ever larger in his thoughts, when a man becomes obsessed with consideration of his legacy to the world. This was especially true of statesmen and politicians, of course, and Kruger, formerly President of the Transvaal Republic - "*Oom Paul*" (Uncle Paul) to his Afrikaner people – was, despite his lowly origins, the ultimate politician.

He stood in the grounds of a villa on the northern shore of Lake Geneva, feeling the cold morning air ruffling his wispy strands of grey beard. The French Alps to the south of the lake were draped in glistening snow; it was two hours after dawn, and the mid-winter sunlight added diamond glints everywhere to facets of rock and ice. Kruger shivered despite the bright sun, his weary old Afrikaner bones unused now to this kind of cold.

He blew his nose with a handkerchief and wiped his rheumy eyes, before turning his head reluctantly to look at his companion again. Not many men had ever frightened Oom Paul but this German standing alongside him did. Kruger didn't know his real name; in fact, given this assassin's mysterious personal history, he wondered bleakly whether the man himself could even recall his original name any more.

Van der Merwe called him simply "*de Slager*"- the Butcher – and that seemed an appropriately grisly epithet for such an individual. The man's features were unremarkable but not unpleasant – apart from his eyes, anyway. Those were the emptiest and most disturbing eyes that Kruger had ever seen in a human being. Like a wild beast's almost…

Could those strange amber eyes be concealing an equally disturbing soul? Kruger wondered. Were they a glimpse of the savagery beneath that mundane exterior?

It was certainly hard to guess the Butcher's age – he could have been anywhere between twenty-five and his early forties. He spoke good English, but with a distinct Prussian accent – or was that perhaps simply another pretence put on for his benefit? Kruger couldn't yet decide the full depth of this man's duplicity and fakery. What Kruger did know for sure was that the man had used many different personae in his murderous trade and had a distinguished list of victims. According to van der Merwe's informant (who was a most reliable source) this unremarkable looking individual had been deeply involved in both the attempt on the life of the Prince of Wales in Brussels Central railway station two years ago, and then the assassination of King Umberto I of Italy a few months later. That former enterprise had apparently been one of the few failures in the Butcher's distinguished and murderous career.

But *de Slager's* latest coup had more than made up for that disappointment - the assassination of no less a personage than an American President. Last September, President William McKinley had been shot and mortally wounded at the opening of an exhibition in Buffalo, New York, supposedly by a lone crazed anarchist. But Kruger's information was that this man standing beside him had masterminded the whole thing, pulling the strings of the mad Pole, Leon Czolgosz, who had actually done the shooting.

Kruger couldn't avoid asking the man a direct question. 'When and where will you do the...err...*deed*?'

The German stared at the lake. 'There is no need for you to know. Be assured, though, that the plan is ready and will be put into effect as soon as I have your down payment.'

'You will receive a banker's draft, drawn on a Zurich bank, before you leave here this morning. At least tell me where it will be done.'

The Butcher glowered for a moment, then said reluctantly, 'Paris. It will be done in Paris. Our mutual friend will arrive at the Hotel Bristol on Thursday, March the sixth, according to my informants.'

'How...?'

The man raised a warning hand. 'No more questions.' The tone was imperious and icy; Kruger had never been spoken to like this since he was a child.

The former President of the Transvaal Republic was too astonished at his own timidity in the face of such arrogance to speak for a moment. That was the worst of losing political power; it allowed every guttersnipe to treat you as if he was your equal. In his anger, he couldn't help blustering, 'You do understand that we require not just his death, but his public humiliation.'

The man closed his yellow eyes and gave a languid nod of his head.

'That will certainly be achieved.'

'Who else knows the plan?'

'One person only. A woman, absolutely trustworthy.'

Kruger strove to assert himself again. 'An agent of my own, a woman operating here in Europe, has also offered her services to you in this endeavour. She is very accomplished and therefore may be of some help to your enterprise.'

The man raised an inquisitive eyebrow. 'What is her name?'

'Ma'mselle Cecile Flammarion.'

'Am I expected to trust an unknown Frenchwoman? I think not. Where do her loyalties lie? Purely with the highest bidder?'

Kruger almost laughed at the man's hypocrisy – *this was fine talk coming from him*! 'Ma'mselle Flammarion's father was French, but her mother was an Afrikaner from Stellenbosch in the Cape, who died in one of the British concentration camps. So her loyalty to my cause is unquestioned.'

The man sniffed coldly. 'Where is she based?'

'Currently in Zurich, where she collects information and passes it on to my government in exile.'

The Butcher shrugged his shoulders. 'Then it is unlikely she can be of use to me. However, give me details of how and where I can contact her, should the need arise. It's important to have contingency plans, should anything go awry in Paris.'

Kruger cleared his throat with a harsh cough. 'You do realise that the final and main instalment of your fee – *ninety five thousand pounds sterling* – will only be paid on successful completion.'

The man finally turned his yellow eyes to Kruger's, who felt like prey himself under that implacable stare. 'Yes, I understand perfectly. I will not fail. You have my promise that I will persevere until I succeed. *Nothing will stop me, except my own death...*'

*

After the man had left, Kruger waited in the garden until his aide-de-camp and friend, Hennes van der Merwe, returned from seeing the man to his carriage.

Kruger watched Hennes with affection as he approached; his long-time comrade-in-arms was balding, bearded like a patriarch, lined of brow, even widowed twice like himself – they had so much in common. Hennes had the eyes of a farmer too, wrinkled from forever staring into the dusty immensities of the African landscape. Kruger knew that Hennes too, like himself, longed to smell the crisp air of the High Veldt again, see a huge honey-coloured African moon float above the horizon, hear the calls of the African night. Even the taste of *biltong* was a forgotten pleasure for both of them now.

'Perhaps Switzerland would suit us better as a permanent place of exile than Utrecht, Hennes,' Kruger suggested as van der Merwe drew within speaking distance.

Van der Merwe looked at the snow-capped mountains to the south. 'Well, they're not the Sabie Gorge or the Drakensburg, but the mountains do lift my spirits, compared to the flatness of Holland.' He paused as if embarrassed. 'Did you give that man Ma'mselle Flammarion's name?' he asked Kruger curiously.

'Yes, I did. She did volunteer to help, after all...You don't think this is a wise thing to do, do you, Hennes?' Kruger had sensed the younger man's disapproval of this move into the shadowy world of espionage and political murder.

Van der Merwe frowned. 'No, sir, I think it's a huge mistake. If that man succeeds, it will come back to haunt us.'

Kruger was shocked by the sudden contempt in Hennes' voice – something he'd never heard before. 'It's too late to stop him now.'

'I understand that, Mr President.' Van der Merwe was sombre and suddenly contrite at his previously harsh tone.

In the uncomfortable silence that followed, Kruger felt distinctly like a man who had unleashed a wild dog to hunt a noble animal, and now regretted that decision and wished he could recall his monstrous servant...

CHAPTER 1

February 1902

'Relax yourself, Joseph. Just let things run their course, and your little Yankee belle will soon reveal 'erself again to ze world. For ze moment, why not just let Paris work its magic on you?'

Sitting in front of their usual rendezvous - a café on the Rue Lepic in Montmartre – on a chilly late February afternoon, Joseph Appeldoorn wrinkled his brow and mentally translated René Sardou's garbled pearl of wisdom into something approaching understandable English. Joe had done his damndest to get René to speak only French to him, but the four months that M Sardou had spent in New York City fifteen years before (most of which had been spent in gaol as it happened, Joe had since found out, before René had been finally deported as an undesirable) had convinced the diminutive Frenchman, for some unknown and entirely erroneous reason, that he had formed an exquisite intuitive facility with the English language.

Joe Appeldoorn pondered his slightly depressing situation. He had been sent to Europe at the behest of the Pinkerton Detective Agency in New York City to find a missing heiress, an assignment which had seemed a straightforward enough one at the time since there was no suggestion of anything sinister or criminal in the disappearance; Miss Eleanor Winthrop appeared merely to have run off somewhere with a young good-looking Frenchman – an occupational hazard for a young, rich American woman in Paris, no doubt. Yet the assignment was turning out to be much trickier than expected, Miss Winthrop proving surprisingly difficult to find.

So could René be right in his badly expressed sentiment, Joe asked himself. Perhaps he was expecting results too quickly; maybe he should simply sit back and enjoy being an American in Paris for a while, and hope that Miss Eleanor would eventually turn up again of her own volition.

He reminded himself, with a touch of resignation perhaps, that there certainly was a lot to be said for being in Paris in the early spring, *and* at this particular moment in its history. Paris was (undoubtedly) one of the great capitals of the world, a beautiful and historic place, but also a city looking boldly to the future. The architecture of the Second Empire and the broad boulevards of Haussmann were now presided over by the futuristic wrought iron tower of M Eiffel, while the new century had brought a tumult of fresh ideas in art, literature and science. Paris undeniably made the young United States seem like a parvenu still – here paintings were vibrant with impressionist colour, people travelled in electric underground trains beneath the city, elements were being discovered that gave off mysterious radiant sources of energy, a whole modern new world was being created.

Yet, to tell the truth, Joseph Appeldoorn *had* become disenchanted with most of the attractions of Paris, even after only a month or so. Joe had been given a generous allowance in expenses yet he was reluctant to be lavish with other people's money. He had discovered in himself – rather unexpectedly – a streak of Puritanism when exposed to the fleshpots and temptations of the wickedest city in the world. He avoided the best restaurants – Magny's, the *Voisin*, the *Bignon* or the *Café Américain* – in favour of working-class diners. He did not go dancing the fashionable new craze, the Cakewalk, in smoky late-night clubs, or indulge himself nightly with prostitutes in Montmartre.

Neither had he chosen to stay in one of the best hotels in the Rue du Faubourg St-Honoré or Place Vendôme, nor do his shopping in the swanky *magasins* in the Rue de la Paix - nor even patronise the *Théâtre Français*, the *Vaudeville*, or the *Nouveautés*. He had instead elected to lodge quietly and anonymously in a fleapit of a rented room in the Rue de Babylone in the 17th *Arrondissement* in the Northwest of the city (a street which he'd found, to his slight disappointment, to be not nearly as wicked as it sounded.)

So far, though, this self-imposed Puritanism, while good no doubt for his soul, had not seemed to have any beneficial effect on his mission. A month had slipped by with surprising celerity since his ship had berthed at Cherbourg on Saturday, January 25th, and little seemed to have been achieved...

Joe wondered again at the combination of circumstances that had led to *him* being selected for this particular assignment. The fact that he spoke fluent French and German had clearly been a major factor in the decision when so few other people in Pinkerton's New York office could even speak passable English. It was also the case that he was young and personable, as well as tall, dark-haired, and muscular, although Joe doubted whether these were critical factors in his boss's – John Kautsky's – decision to send him

(although, saying that, his looks *had* certainly helped in getting Kautsky's blonde and well-endowed secretary, Angie, on his side at least, and *she* had a lot of "influence" with the old man.)

So all of those things had been factors of a sort in why he, of all people, had been chosen to track Miss Winthrop down, and why he found himself, one misty Sunday morning in mid-January, on board the *Kaiser Wilhelm der Grosse* of the North German Lloyd Line, steaming out of New York Harbour, destination Cherbourg. Yet his most significant advantage over his rival candidates for the job, Joe guessed, was that he knew both the lady in question (slightly), and her extremely wealthy grandfather, James D. Winthrop (rather better). (Joe had heard a long-standing joke that old Mr Winthrop's middle initial stood for "dollars", although it could equally well have stood, in Joe's opinion, for "devious", "dour" or "determined".)

During the six days of the voyage from New York, Joe had researched everything he knew about his – for want of a better word - *quarry*. The most noteworthy fact about his search for Miss Eleanor Winthrop, though, was the promise made to Joe by her steely-eyed grandfather – that, if he, Joseph, did manage to bring his granddaughter back safe and sound to the United States, he personally would receive a reward from the Winthrop family for *twenty five thousand dollars* – enough to pay off the business debts left to him by his father, almost to the cent, and escape being declared a bankrupt. It was an incredibly generous reward to offer, and Joe was sure that the amount was no coincidence: Winthrop was probably as well acquainted with the details of his depressing financial situation as his own bank manager. Joe suspected however that there was more to this offer than first appeared. James Winthrop had certainly had some dubious personal business dealings with Joe's late father in the past, and had perhaps even taken advantage of his father's weak position when the Appeldoorn business had been getting into financial difficulties. So Joe guessed that there might be an element of recompense and making good an old debt in Winthrop's generous offer of a personal reward.

Yet, whatever degree of guilt James Winthrop might be feeling over his previous cavalier business treatment of Joe's father, it was also clear to Joe that none of the reward would be forthcoming if he failed to deliver his side of the bargain. Joe couldn't help but remember the sobering caveat to this fabulous offer from Eleanor's grandfather. 'Don't dare come back until you have found her, Joseph,' Winthrop had warned, as he and Joe stood together in the offices of the Pinkerton Detective Agency, looking out over the wintry rooftops of downtown Manhattan. As he offered his hand in farewell, Winthrop had added softly, 'I want my granddaughter back, and in good health, so *don't fail me, Joseph...*' It seemed an innocuous enough comment the way it was made, yet the understated tone in the man's voice belied the hard glitter in his clear grey eyes.

Joe had swallowed nervously and nodded, finally realising what the steel magnate's middle initial really stood for: *Dangerous*...

Yes, James D. Winthrop was a man used to getting his own way, and would undoubtedly be a *very* dangerous person to make an enemy of...

*

Miss Eleanor P. Winthrop had sailed for Europe in June the previous year, and Paris had been the first leg of an extended Grand Tour of European cultural centres, designed to broaden her mind and lift her spirits after the tragic early death of her father a few months before. Her grandfather had been reluctant to let her go at first but had been persuaded by the fact that Eleanor would soon turn twenty-one anyway (in November) and would then be in control of a considerable fortune of her own, left to her by her doting dead father. And being confident and forceful also no doubt helped Eleanor carry the day with her doubting relatives. In her grandfather's eyes, at least, she was far from being naïve or unworldly – he'd been particularly pleased to discover that Eleanor, as she got older, was developing both a surprisingly good brain for business and a natural distrust of handsome young fortune seekers. He'd even heard Eleanor described, by those casual acquaintances who didn't like her much, as a "level-headed young woman" - "level-headed" being a synonym for "dull" in their vocabulary, no doubt. But James Winthrop was more than happy to have a quiet sensible young woman for a granddaughter rather than an empty-headed flirtatious girl.

At first everything seemed to have gone well for Eleanor in Paris. She rented an apartment in the Rue de la Boétie, close to the Avenue des Champs Élysées, and hired a paid companion, a young Frenchwoman called Monique Langevin, to teach her the language and show her the cultural sights. James Winthrop had received long weekly letters from his granddaughter extolling the splendid time she was having. Funds had been sent to the American Express Company's office in Paris to take care of her needs. James had been informed by a friendly director at American Express of the amount Eleanor was spending and, although high, he had anticipated that – a young woman exposed to the temptations of European style and fashion for the first time could hardly be expected to be thrifty. But the warning bells in his head had only turned to alarm when he discovered that Eleanor had gone to the American Express company office in the Rue de Rivoli on Thursday, December 5th, in company with a young Frenchman, and withdrawn *thirty thousand dollars in gold and cash* – the cash mainly in French and Swiss Francs.

And Eleanor hadn't been seen or heard of since that day. Her apartment was empty, the maid and kitchen staff paid off, while the French companion and language teacher, Mlle Langevin, had also conveniently disappeared.

*

During the month he had been looking for Eleanor in Paris, Joe had constantly tried to focus on his own recollections of the girl.

Five years before, after finishing high school, he'd taken a summer vacation job in Hartford, Connecticut. His own circumstances were different then, of course, and he'd got introductions to a lot of Hartford high society, including the Winthrops, father and daughter. Eleanor's mother was already dead by that time; Franklin Winthrop, Eleanor's newspaper-owning father, had turned his palatial Connecticut mansion into a mausoleum to her memory. During that summer of '97 Joe had escorted Eleanor once or twice to social events, including a fancy dress ball at the Old State House. She'd made no great impression on him, though, until the night of the ball when she'd appeared in a voluptuous and particularly fetching Marie Antoinette wig and costume. It was only then that Joe had noticed her considerable attractions for the first time: a lot of Titian hair, milky-white skin, an encouragingly large bosom for a sixteen-year-old. He had, naturally enough, soon begun having certain youthful male fantasies about releasing her spectacular bosom from the confines of that tight pink corset. This, combined with the reputed vast wealth of her family, had persuaded him to battle away gamely all night, trying desperately to charm her.

Yet she'd remained cool and aloof throughout that evening, as she had throughout their whole brief acquaintance. Her general aloofness might just have been shyness, he thought, or perhaps his own gauche tongue-tied manners at the time might have been partially to blame — he remembered that he did have some trouble that night preventing his eyes from straying occasionally downwards from her face to her wonderful breasts. But after he had slipped on the marble floor in front of her and ended up upsetting a bowl of fruit punch all over himself, he'd realised, from her startling explosion of laughter at his *faux pas*, that his mission to win her was probably going to be a wasted one anyway...

*

On arrival in Paris, Joe had naturally consulted the Prefecture of Police about Miss Winthrop's disappearance, but they'd been frankly unhelpful. Joe had been forced to deal with a morose middle-aged detective inspector called Louis Le Boeuf. It was an appropriate name for a man who seemed as unresponsive as a cow.

'Take my word for it, M'sieur Appeldoorn. Miss Winthrop has run off with this man, Paul Gaspard.'

'Has this man, Gaspard, got a criminal record?'

'Not to my knowledge, M'sieur.'

Joe's jaw dropped. 'You *have* checked, haven't you?'

The French detective gave the kind of Gallic shrug that Joe was beginning to detest already. 'He is not known to the Paris police at all, but I haven't checked elsewhere. I don't have time to check the identity of every gigolo in Paris – and Gaspard may not even be his real name anyway. In any case I don't think it's necessary. Believe me, your American lady will return to the bosom of her family when it suits her. Hopefully not in a pregnant state, M'sieur.' Le Boeuf smiled salaciously. 'That may be one souvenir too many to take back home with her from France. *Un bébé français...*'

*

Joe had spent most of his time in Paris talking to American expatriates and neighbours who knew Eleanor, even if only slightly. The wife of an official at the American Embassy, Mrs George Freemont III, was the most helpful of these, even though Eleanor seemed to have gone out of her way to avoid official American Embassy functions. It was Mrs Freemont who had revealed to the police, and Eleanor's family, the identity of the man Eleanor had apparently been seeing. And, at her extravagant apartment on the Avenue Matignon, she seemed more than willing to talk to Joe about Eleanor and the mysterious Monsieur Gaspard.

'Oh, she was totally smitten with him.' Jane Freemont was fifty if she was a day, powdered and painted and thirty pounds overweight. Yet she crossed her legs beneath her muslin skirt like a twenty-year-old vamp, and fluttered her eyelashes coquettishly in Joe's direction. 'A very good-looking young man. I saw them together for the first time at the *Gymnase* during the interval. Some dreadfully depressing Russian play; I forget the author's name. Why are Russians so relentlessly gloomy about everything?' She paused in mid-sentence and studied him closely. 'You're not one of the Newport Appeldoorns, Joseph, by any chance, are you? No?...Where was I? Oh yes! At the theatre. Eleanor introduced her companion as a friend, a M'sieur Paul Gaspard. I seemed to bump into them a lot after that. A few weeks later, George took me to the theatre to see one of those new moving pictures made by Georges Melies, "*Voyage a la Lune*", and I met the young couple again as we were going in. I could see things between them had moved on by this time, and that she was simply besotted with him. Oh, have you seen any of Melies' films? Absolutely incredible...*incroyable...*' She savoured the sound of the French word as she gazed intently into Joe's eyes.

It was a superfluous question, of course, since everyone in Paris was talking about Monsieur Melies' films, which had amazed Joe too. Particularly *The Indian Rubber Head*, in which Melies appeared himself, and in which his head seemed to blow up to twice the size of anything else on the screen.

Unfortunately Jane Freemont knew nothing concrete about the young Frenchman, Gaspard, even though she was sure that Eleanor had simply run off with him somewhere for a few months of passion. It was clear to Joe that Mrs George Freemont III was the source of Le Boeuf's conviction that Eleanor's disappearance was nothing sinister, but only the result of *une affaire du cœur*. Joe was far from convinced himself, though.

Mrs Freemont barely paused for breath. 'Well, it's probably what she came to Paris looking for, after all...*love with a beautiful man*, I mean...' she added with heavy emphasis, '...although I doubt she is even in the city any more. Gone to Biarritz or Baden-Baden more likely. It was very foolish of her family to allow her to come here on her own, if they didn't want this sort of thing to happen. I'm sure, though, she will come back when she's good and ready. Eleanor is not silly enough to marry such a man, no matter how handsome he is.'

Joe had finally managed to extricate himself from Mrs Freemont's clutches only with the greatest difficulty. Even so he had been forced to accept an invitation to one of her musical soirees, an engagement which he intended immediately to forgo.

*

The concierge in Eleanor's apartment block in the Rue de la Boétie in the 8th *Arrondissement* was a woman of similar vintage to Mrs George Freemont III, but made that lady appear a model of decorum by comparison. The Widow Signoret was a voluptuous baggage with a leery grin, who looked as if her carnal desires might have been a major contributing factor in her husband's early death at the age of forty-five. Certainly M Signoret's photograph, standing alongside an aspidistra on a dusty piano top, revealed to Joe a man prematurely aged and with a slightly nervous half-smile of anticipation.

Joe could see that the widow was taken with him and, if he'd thought she had known anything worthwhile, he might even have indulged her need to prattle a bit more. But she clearly knew remarkably little about the American woman who had lived in the top apartment of her building, or of her maid, or even the increasingly mysterious Monique Langevin. And yet Mme Signoret could describe them perfectly; Joe could judge that from her physical description of Eleanor and how well that fitted with his own recollections of her. For some reason the widow had almost an artist's eye for the detail of faces.

'You speak very good French for an American, M'sieur. And I thought Americans were all rough men with guns. Why, you don't even have a moustache or beard. Such fresh pink cheeks! Your face looks quite as soft as my...'

Joe did his best to retain his dignity under this onslaught. 'Beards are no longer fashionable in New York City, Madame,' he interrupted stiffly, 'although I can grow one perfectly well, if I wish.' He got back to the reason for his visit. 'Is there nothing else you can tell me about Ma'mselle Winthrop's personal maid, or the companion, Monique Langevin.'

'I'm afraid not, M'sieur.'

Mme Signoret had an encyclopaedic memory of the Franco-Prussian war, though, and seemed determined that Joe should discover every last detail of her ordeal during the siege of Paris thirty years ago, before he could be allowed to leave. 'I was a beautiful young virgin then, of course, not yet married. Why, you won't believe this but Louis Napoleon himself once smiled at me as his carriage passed me in the street...'

As she finally did show him out, after her seemingly endless reminiscences, a wistful note entered her voice. 'I'm sorry I can't tell you more, M'sieur. I promise, though, I shall do my best to think of any other information about Ma'mselle Winthrop that might help you...' and here she gave him a naughty smile and a wink, '...but only if you *promise* to come back and see me!'

*

So now, on this Tuesday afternoon in late February, sitting together with René in a Montmartre café only a few doors from René's own sordid little apartment in the Rue Lepic, Joe was forced to concede his complete failure to himself.

Yet René had probably been the best decision that Joe had made since coming to Paris, he had to admit. After his first week here, and seeing that he was going to get no significant help from the French authorities, Joe had hired a private French detective, René Sardou, to help him find his way in this bewildering city. René was a former thief, police informer and ex-con who now ran a small detective agency of his own, mainly dedicated to finding the absconding husbands of middle-class women. He seemed to be able to make a living out of it, although Joe was unsure to what extent he still subsidised these legitimate activities with other more dubious ones. René was in his thirties – an ugly little man, and one certainly loud-mouthed and sometimes crude – yet Joe had formed a strange affection for him and his constant lascivious stream of observations on life, love and happiness. *Especially* love...

Last night, Joe had finally given in to René's pestering to join him for an evening on the town, ending in a particular *boîte de nuit* in a Montmartre backstreet where René had promised him something special. And the exotic dancer performing there had certainly lived up to his promise. Joe's heart beat faster under his starched shirt as he thought about her again now: a beautiful and willowy Creole from the island of Martinique, divinely lithe, the colour of glistening honey. Vivacious and exuberant, and clad only in sequins and see-through silk gauze, her name was Corazon. After her performance she had come and sat on his lap - a great honour - and the feel of her lovely bottom on his knee, and her delightful smile, had certainly relieved the tensions and frustrations of the last few weeks. But he'd not had the nerve to take her home afterwards (even though she was clearly willing to be taken) - his straight-laced Philadelphia upbringing just winning out over overwhelming lust. René had been frankly bemused at his reluctance to sleep with the magnificent Corazon at the first opportunity; he, himself – as he told Joe later on the way home – had become almost hypnotised of late by Corazon's dusky beauty and had been desperately thinking of some way to get into her (no doubt) silken drawers. Yet, being the person of generous spirits that he was (in his own modest estimation at least) – or, more likely in Joe's opinion perhaps, because he was also generously filled with spirits at the time too - he made it clear to Joe with a drunken embrace that he held no grudge against him for attracting the wonderful Creole's attention...

Still nursing this hangover from the night before, René nudged Joe now, his eyes following the slim and graceful shape of a wasp-waisted beauty dressed in red, as she walked with a swaying motion along the Rue Lepic. '*Oh, quel cul t'as, Mademoiselle!*' This was René's favourite line to passing girls. Inexplicably to Joe, this bold approach seemed to work with everyone from lady's maids to the ladies themselves. René, for all his simian looks, seemed to have an endless stream of pretty and willing girls (Corazon excepted) at his beck and call. Joe could see that the girl in red had heard perfectly well what René had said and, with a ghost of a smile, twitched her bottom a little more in response before crossing the street with style.

Despite all the exhortations from suffragettes and other women's groups for women to abandon corsets as their mothers had abandoned crinolines and bustles, the young women, even in a city as sophisticated as Paris, seemed reluctant to change. Hemlines were only slowly creeping up above the ankle but no one appeared to be willing to abandon their long skirts for knickerbockers quite just yet.

Joe finished his glass of wine with irritation. 'There's only one *derriere* that I want to see at this moment, René, and that is Miss Eleanor Winthrop's.' He instantly made a wry face; that wasn't *quite* what he'd meant to say.

René leered, and mercifully spoke in French. 'Then we really must find her for you, *mon ami*. And then perhaps you can persuade her...'

*

Finally - on Wednesday February 26th, to be precise - Joe had some luck. Or rather René had.

René Sardou had reluctantly decided to try his own chances with the Widow Signoret - something above and beyond the course of duty in Joe's opinion since he had fully warned René what to expect. It certainly wasn't a task that Joe would have relished taking upon himself, to go back to

Eleanor's apartment building in the Rue de la Boétie and try and weed some useful information from the sex-starved concierge.

But proving that timing is everything in detective work, René marched into the lioness's den at just the right time, the widow hinting heavily to him that she had discovered something new and highly relevant to the search for Miss Winthrop since Joe's visit. The widow initially insisted that the young American would have to pay her a return visit before she would consider revealing what she knew, but René talked her round, using all his lascivious charm and a full range of blatant sexual innuendoes to prise the information from the extravagant bosom of the voluptuous Mme Signoret. It seemed that, while visiting her sister, Amelie, in the Rue Lamarck in Montmartre the previous Sunday, the widow had happened to see a young woman leave the apartment block opposite her sister's. This apartment building, with a red marble foyer and hanging flowers on every balcony, was near the bottom of the Basilica steps. The Widow Signoret told René that she had been almost convinced - despite the fact that the woman had been wearing a dowdy maid's uniform - that it was *Monique Langevin*...

The widow was clearly expecting some kind of reward in return for this information and, from the significant body language and coy looks she was giving him, René soon realised with slight misgivings what sort of "reward" that might entail. In the next hour, though, he actually ended up enthusiastically "rewarding" Mme Signoret *three* times in total, after discovering that the experience with a woman of mature years and generous curves was a surprisingly pleasurable one. So it was an unusually fatigued but satisfied M Sardou who eventually retraced his weary steps to Montmartre later that afternoon to find the apartment that Mme Signoret had mentioned. Living in the district, René knew the streets around the Basilica intimately, of course. The Rue Lamarck lay almost under the shadow of the *Basilique du Sacré Coeur,* much closer to the famous white domes, in fact, than René's own home in the less fashionable Rue Lepic.

René found the building without difficulty from the widow's description of it, and asked the ancient crone of a concierge whether any single women were living there answering to Monique Langevin's description. It seemed, to René's disappointment, that there weren't – all the apartments were occupied by families; yet there *was* an unoccupied apartment on the top floor owned by two sisters with a strange Russian name – Melly something or other. The old woman was only a temporary replacement however (standing in for the real concierge while she visited her daughter in Amiens) so she didn't know the sisters at all by sight. But she'd been told both had left Paris for a while - perhaps to return to Russia, she added helpfully with a gap-toothed smile. The woman wasn't aware that either of the sisters would be back soon; the apartment was still closed up, and the furniture covered with dustsheets, as far as she knew.

René didn't take the *in loco* concierge at her word, though, and, with the help of two of his part-time assistants (an eleven-year-old street urchin called Pascal, and his equally snotty-nosed younger brother, Thierry) had the place watched continuously for a week, twenty-four hours a day, until, on the morning of March 5th, he himself, in company with Pascal, eventually saw a young woman in a maid's uniform arrive at the building. She fitted the Widow Signoret's detailed description of Monique Langevin perfectly – one metre sixty tall, good figure, long chestnut hair, brown eyes, a mole on her cheek, a large sensuous mouth. (Mme Signoret had been particularly good on such details.)

When the woman left in a cab an hour later, still dressed in the maid's uniform, René followed her in a hired two-wheeler cab of his own.

*

That evening, at their usual rendezvous, the café in the Rue Lepic near his home, René reported his findings to Joe. 'It definitely *was* her.' He hesitated. '*I zink zat yes, anyway,*' he added in English.

'*Parle Français*, René!' Joe growled at him, but was still unable to hide his pleasure at this unexpected stroke of good fortune.

René was about to continue when a young artist friend of his brushed past their table and slapped him playfully on the arm. Joe had met the man here a few times - a Spaniard called Pablo, visiting from Barcelona, who had an even more disreputable reputation with women than René had. Despite his unprepossessing appearance - bearded and shaggy-haired – he did apparently possess a little talent, and his art was becoming quite well known in Paris. Because of the Andalusian hat he habitually wore, though, he was known in the café – disparagingly - as "*Le Petit Goya.*"

René nodded to his friend as the man passed him, clutching a large canvas to his chest. 'I like Pablo, you know,' he confided *sotto voce* to Joe. 'But have you seen his pictures? Really *merde!* He can do three of them in one day. Whoever heard of great art being made in three hours? I keep telling him no one in Paris will pay real money for crap like that. But what you can do? You have to try and make a living somehow, I suppose.'

'Tell me about Monique, René.'

René smiled complacently. 'Don't worry. I didn't lose her. I'm sure she must be one of the sisters who own the apartment in the Rue Lamarck. Perhaps she needed something she keeps there – clothes possibly. She had a suitcase with her when she reappeared, anyway. I followed her and she took a cab to an address in the swanky 16th *Arrondissement*. It seems she is now working as a lady's maid for a woman in the Boulevard Suchet, next to the Bois de Boulogne, and using the name, Joelle Loubet. The Boulevard Suchet is a very fancy street, full of rich people in silks and satins and smart carriages. It almost made me wish I was still in the thieving business! Such easy pickings...' René clicked his tongue against the roof of his mouth and tried a sentence more of English. '*I exerted my charms on a maid, Madeleine, in ze next 'ouse who very well acquaints 'erself with "Joelle". Zey walk wiz ze doggies in ze park all togezer.*'

'Speak French! And?'

'And what a woman "Joelle" works for! I caught sight of her myself, returning home in a liveried landau. Apparently she is the Polish-born widow of a recently deceased Russian exile, Count Igor Alexander Petrovich. She now uses the title "Comtesse de Pourtales", although no one quite knows how she came by it. A very beautiful woman of about thirty-five - tall, slim, blonde. *Magnificent* colouring...!' René smiled indulgently and made a crude clutching gesture with his fingers. 'Magnificent breasts too, from where I was looking. Usually dresses in white satin but on certain days, when she is receiving a "particular visitor", wears black.'

'How did you get all this?'

'I told you. The maid next door, Madeleine, is an observant girl.'

'And who is this "particular visitor" the comtesse receives?'

René smirked. 'An eccentric English milord, the Duke of Lancaster, who visits Paris regularly and normally stays at the Hotel Bristol on the Rue du Faubourg St-Honoré.'

Joe was thoughtful for a moment. 'Monique Langevin was a language teacher and companion. So why is she working as a lady's maid, a job of a much lower social standing? I don't want to approach her directly just yet, though; it might frighten her into disappearing again. Let's just keep her under close observation for a few days to see what she gets up to in the employment of the Comtesse de Pourtales. I think I detect the faint aroma of performing seals in all this.'

René nodded sagely and sought a meaningful English phrase to match. '*Yes, good point, Joseph. I smell ze fish too.*'

*

René continued to watch the home of the Comtesse de Pourtales for the next few days. He saw Monique Langevin again walking a white poodle in the Bois de Boulogne on Thursday, in company, as on the day before, with the delightful and ever-talkative Madeleine. Madeleine's charge was a black poodle so the two dogs together resembled a couple of giant animated chess pieces. On Friday "Joelle" was on her own though (Madeleine apparently having being detained by more important things than walking the black poodle) so René tried to engage his quarry in conversation. But he was rebuffed with only an icy stare when he tried his usual line; clearly Mlle Langevin was not impressed by having the shape of her bottom complimented in such a familiar fashion.

On Saturday "Joelle" didn't appear at all, but René didn't panic. Instead, a manservant on his own walked the white poodle belonging to the

Comtesse de Pourtales, a middle-aged man called Jacques, later identified by the ever-helpful Madeleine. However it didn't need a great feat of skill on her part to identify the man; the manservant in question had the broken nose of a bad boxer, a hairline so low it threatened to overwhelm his brow, and was almost two metres tall.

The following day, Sunday morning, March 9th, when "Joelle" failed to appear again with the dogs, René did panic though, and rightly. A calamity had occurred.

René spoke urgently to Madeleine at the basement door of her apartment building who in turn spoke to the towering Jacques next door. It turned out that "Joelle" was gone! She had quit the employment of the Comtesse de Pourtales the day before – packed her things on Saturday night and walked out the door with hardly a word. René immediately returned to Montmartre and the café in the Rue Lepic, telling the driver of his horse-cab to use the whip on his lazy nag, as he wondered how on earth he was going to break this news to Joseph Appeldoorn...

CHAPTER 2

Sunday March 9th 1902

The Boulevard Suchet was even more select and refined than Joseph Appeldoorn had imagined - a wide tree-shaded avenue bordering the emerging spring greenery of the Bois de Boulogne, lined with sumptuous town houses and grand four-storey apartment buildings. The tall rows of lime and plane trees were just budding into life, daffodils waving golden heads in swathes along the pavement verges. The clip-clop of hooves echoed on cobbles as corseted ladies in elaborate feathered hats and fine silk and sequinned dresses took the spring air in polished carriages of black lacquered wood, the serene calm of the street disturbed only by the occasional rattle and belch of a motor car – a Renault, Lanchester or Benz.

A sleepy Parisian Sunday afternoon for everyone, except Joe, who was in turmoil as he imagined the consequences of losing his one good clue in the search for Eleanor Winthrop. A crestfallen and subdued René had met him at lunchtime in their usual rendezvous in the Rue Lepic and admitted his *faux pas*. Joe had immediately sent him back to keep a watch on the apartment in the Rue Lamarck, in case Monique/Joelle returned there, while he went to call on a comtesse.

On noting the style and wealth of the neighbourhood in which the comtesse lived, Joe was glad that he'd gone home and changed first; he was now dressed in his best blazer and white drill trousers, polished shoes, silk cravat and straw boater, and carrying a cane. On arrival in Paris, he'd had visiting cards printed just in case he had to visit anyone important. These were miniature works of art: embossed in gold, with slanting copperplate writing on the most expensive cream-white paper, they announced confidently to the world his true name and address in New York, as well as the famous name of the Pinkerton Agency.

The comtesse lived in a grand corner mansion, built in the Louis

Napoleon-style, set behind a high laurel hedge and a formal French garden of box parterres. Two stooped and elderly gardeners in smocks were lackadaisically clearing the borders of winter detritus and weeds as he walked up the drive to the portico entrance.

A huge manservant (presumably the infamous Jacques) answered the door and read the proffered card with suspicion. From his great height he inspected the visitor disdainfully as he listened to the polite request to see his mistress, the Comtesse de Pourtales. Joe had been given some warning by René of what to expect but, even so, was quite unprepared for the spectacular ugliness and size of the man. His face was certainly memorable: this was a nose not so much broken as completely devastated, and a hairline so low that it barely left space for eyebrows. Joe was six feet three inches tall, yet this man seemed to tower over him – it was an unsettling experience for Joe Appeldoorn to have to stretch his neck to look up at someone for a change.

Jacques went away with the card, and Joe somehow expected to be turned rudely away, with a contemptuous gesture of the huge man's thumb. But perhaps the comtesse was intrigued by the card and by the New York address; although Jacques didn't seem happy about it when he returned, he announced that the comtesse was prepared to see M Appeldoorn, *if* it wouldn't take too long. Joe followed the massive figure up the curving stairs to the drawing room on the first floor...

*

Joe had found himself immediately disconcerted, both by the woman's extreme beauty (René had not exaggerated her charms) and even more by her sophisticated manner. Joe had read of such women, of course, but his knowledge was limited to the academic and theoretical – he knew them only through the lens of various playwrights' probably fevered imaginations. Yet he had no doubt in his mind that the Comtesse de Pourtales was a courtesan of the highest class – sultry and sensuous, and as different from a common prostitute as the work of Michelangelo was from the street daubings of a pavement artist.

She made Joe feel every inch the colonial dullard as he tried to make small talk with her.

They were alone in the drawing room on the first floor, Joe standing almost to attention in front of her, like a recalcitrant pupil called before a teacher. A zephyr wind stirred gossamer curtains. Chandeliers gleamed above his head, a gilded ormolu clock ticked loudly. His gaze was drawn to a marble chimneypiece decorated with carvings of statuesque bare-breasted female angels who seemed, from a quick surreptitious comparison, to have been modelled on the comtesse herself. The comtesse too was dressed in angel white, so clearly wasn't expecting her English milord today, which was probably why she had found the time for him.

She reclined on a *chaise longue* and seemed to be enjoying his discomfiture; from across the intervening space, her eyes sparkled with secret amusement. Joe had soon understood why he, a stranger, had been given the privilege of access to her company – she was bored on a Sunday afternoon and needed a diversion. And he was it.

She had obviously been reading *Claudine à Paris* before his arrival – an open copy lay on a card table at her side. This new novel by a mysterious author known as Willy was a sensation at the moment in Paris, not least because many suspected – perhaps because it captured the thoughts and secret desires of a woman with such intimacy - that it had to be in reality the work of a female writer. A rumour was even going the rounds that it was actually the writing of a girl of barely twenty, called Colette.

The comtesse stood up gracefully and moved over to the window and balcony. Yet she didn't walk so much as glide; Joe felt his throat tighten just at the sight of that delightful motion.

She had offered him coffee and cognac, which he'd refused politely, but hadn't pressed him so far about the reason for his visit. But now she turned to him, her back to the window and the sunlit view of the Bois de Boulogne. 'So, to what do I owe the pleasure of this visit, M'sieur App-le-doon?'

Joe had never heard his name pronounced so badly, or so charmingly. 'Madame, I wish to know what has happened to your maid, Joelle Loubet. I believe she has just left your employment.'

The comtesse seemed only mildly curious at his question. 'Why do you wish to know about Joelle, may I ask? Has she done something wrong?' Her splendid figure was outlined dazzlingly against the afternoon sunlight spilling into the room. She turned her body a little to the left, then to the right, studying her own silhouette on the opposite wall. This was done quite deliberately, Joe thought, to show off her figure to best advantage, although it was hardly a necessary tactic in his case. Yet this was a woman who clearly craved to be admired, Joe realised intuitively, someone who needed constant approval from whoever was at hand - which suggested that even a woman as beautiful as the Comtesse de Pourtales was not entirely immune to feelings of insecurity.

Joe forced his mind back to the reason for his visit. 'I can't be sure if your maid has done something wrong or not. But I do believe she has been masquerading here under a false name, which makes me suspicious.'

The comtesse was moved sufficiently to raise an eyebrow slightly. 'Her references were impeccable.'

'Did you check them personally?'

She gave a pretty little snort. 'Of course not. My manservant, Jacques, did.'

'Then not very well.'

'Will you tell him that? Or shall I?' the comtesse asked dryly.

Joe tried to look as if the thought of Jacques didn't worry him at all.

The comtesse came and sat down on the chaise again. Every movement she made seemed choreographed like a dancer's; Joe was beginning to envy the Duke of Lancaster who apparently had such a woman at his beck and call. 'Are you really American?' she asked, picking up his visiting card and holding it to her retrouché nose. 'You speak French extremely well.'

'I was born in Philadelphia but I have lived in Europe. I spent three years studying at the Polytechnic in Zurich.'

'Oh? And what did you study, M'sieur?'

'I studied physics, Madame.'

'So, another budding Becquerel or Pierre Curie? How interesting. I meet so few physicists. And even fewer as handsome and well-spoken as you. So how did the study of physics lead to a career in detective work, M'sieur App-le-doon?'

'It didn't. My circumstances changed: my father died, and his company was left with huge debts, which I found myself liable for. So I had to find a new career and make my own way in the world.'

'Oh, I'm sorry to hear it. But to speak French so well, though, you must at least have had a French lover. Oh, my apologies again. I have embarrassed you.' The comtesse looked anything but apologetic, though.

Joe's tight collar was beginning to feel like a noose around his neck and he longed to tear it off. 'You have not, Madame. I am here in Paris trying to find a young American woman called Eleanor Winthrop, who disappeared three months ago – on December the fifth, to be precise. A Ma'mselle Monique Langevin had been working for her as her companion and language teacher. I believe this Ma'mselle Langevin and your former maid "Joelle" are one and the same person.'

The comtesse smiled complacently. 'Then I'm afraid you have made a mistake, M'sieur. Joelle joined my employment in November. And she was living full-time in this house, so it is quite impossible for her to have been doing another job at the same time.'

Joe was embarrassed now. 'Are you absolutely sure?'

'Yes. She came to me on my birthday, November the seventeenth. That's why I remember her arrival so well.'

Joe calculated quickly. That was over *two weeks* before Eleanor disappeared so it did seem impossible that "Joelle" and Monique could be one and the same woman. *Had that damned Signoret woman sent him and René off on a wild goose chase?*

The comtesse studied him curiously. 'This American girl...is she perhaps your sweetheart? Is that why you came all the way from New York to find her?'

'No, not at all. I do know Miss Winthrop, but only slightly. She travelled here to Europe on her own.'

The comtesse looked scandalised. 'How shocking! You mean her parents actually *allowed* her to come here alone?'

'Her parents are both dead. But perhaps I have misled you. Miss Winthrop is not a child; she is over twenty-one so no one could stop her if she really wanted to go. American women can be very determined.'

'So it would seem,' the comtesse agreed dryly before continuing, 'I'm sorry, M'sieur, but I really don't see how I can help you when Joelle is obviously *not* this Langevin person you are looking for: this must be a case of mistaken identity. But even if it isn't, I don't know where Joelle has gone, or why she departed so precipitately - she left my service without even leaving a forwarding address. It was annoying because she was quite an accomplished girl in her way – much better than the usual silly girls I am forced to employ.' The comtesse stood up abruptly, suddenly business-like again. 'Now you must really excuse me, M'sieur App-le-doon. I have another visitor soon. Jacques will show you out.'

This was stated politely enough but was still a firm and unequivocal dismissal. Joe could see that she was now thoroughly bored with him, and with this conversation. The comtesse offered him her hand briefly, then glided away to another room.

Joe wanted to say something more, but the retreating figure smiled demurely and closed the door firmly behind her. He could still smell her perfume lingering in the air – a ghostly trace of lily of the valley.

The giant Jacques appeared from nowhere at his side; he moved very quietly for a big man. 'If you're ready, M'sieur.'

They walked down the stairs, the giant leading the way. Being a little higher than Jacques on the steps made the manservant seem less physically daunting and Joe felt confident enough to ask him a pertinent question. 'How well did *you* know the comtesse's maid, Jacques?'

The giant stopped and turned, his face expressionless. 'Not very well, M'sieur.'

In view of that answer, Joe's next question seemed even more hopeless, but he asked it anyway. 'Would you have any idea where she's gone, though?'

The manservant leaned forward belligerently. '*Non, M'sieur!*' he said with what seemed like unnecessary violence.

Joe had the distinct impression by now that the man was hiding something so, despite Jacques's formidable appearance, he continued to press him. 'Did you know her real name wasn't "Joelle"?'

The giant regarded Joe with icy contempt and shook his head.

'Her real name was "Langevin" – did you know that?' Joe persisted, and caught a gleam of response in the manservant's porcine eyes for the first time. That name had meant something to Jacques...

'You *do* know that name, don't you?' Joe insisted.

'What name, M'sieur?' The man's eyes were blank again.

'Come on! You can tell me! You know her real name is "Langevin". *How* do you know?'

The giant hesitated fractionally, a gleam of avarice finally appearing in those dull black eyes. 'Perhaps I do know something about Joelle,' he finally admitted. 'Is it worth fifty francs to you to find out, M'sieur?'

That was at least a week's wages for a servant like Jacques so Joe was wary of being swindled. 'Yes, it's worth that much to me if you can tell me how you know her real name is "Langevin".' Joe counted out the bills from his billfold and offered them casually.

Jacques pocketed the money deftly before Joe could change his mind. 'All right. I do know "Loubet" isn't her real name. I saw her receive a letter once at the post office addressed to a "M. Langevin" and with a post box number on it. I don't recall the number, though.'

'You're sure about this?' Joe asked, his pulse increasing.

'Yes, I met her by accident that day as she was leaving the post office, and I saw the letter in her hand. What's more, whatever Madame la Comtesse says, she also knows that "Loubet" wasn't Joelle's real name.'

Joe considered that for a moment as he also wondered just how Jacques had managed to overhear his supposedly private conversation with the comtesse. Joe decided it was time to take some bold and assertive action to get at the truth of this matter. Before Jacques could react and stop him, Joe turned suddenly and ran back up the stairs, where he quickly locked the drawing room door behind him. Then he went over to the far door where the comtesse had gone and opened it abruptly. 'Now, Comtesse...'

Joe's jaw dropped as he realised he had walked into her private boudoir. There were pink satin sheets on the double bed and risqué pictures on the walls. The comtesse herself was in a state that could only be described as *déshabillé*, reclining on a similar *chaise longue* to that in the other room, but now clad only in silk drawers, with a gauzy robe open to her waist and brandishing a Japanese fan...

*

She seemed remarkably unfazed by the impromptu return of her visitor. Joe had guessed by now, with an embarrassed glow spreading across his cheeks, that he had walked in on what the French would call *"un cinq à sept"* - even though it was still only three in the afternoon.

But then Joe heard a discreet cough, and turned to see a familiar figure standing in the corner of the room, brandishing brushes and a maul stick in front of a large canvas and easel. Joe recognized the bearded, long-haired man immediately, and even the familiar Andalusian hat on the table by his easel.

The comtesse seemed more amused than disconcerted, and didn't attempt to cover herself. 'Do I take it that you two gentlemen know each other?' she asked, apparently trying not to smile.

Pablo, the artist, looked sullen even though he had clearly recognised Joe as René's friend. '*Oui, Madame, je connais le monsieur très bien.*'

'A gentleman friend wants a permanent souvenir of our friendship,' the comtesse explained breezily. 'A portrait. And young M'sieur Picasso was recommended, although I'm not sure if his distinctive style will appeal to the gentleman in question.'

She had to be talking about her patron, the Duke of Lancaster, of course. '*And even if he does like it, where on earth will he find a suitable private place to mount it?*' Joe thought idly, thinking as much about the generous size of the canvas as its intimate subject - then flushed even redder when he realised that in his confused state he'd spoken his private thought out loud...

But the comtesse responded only by hiding the briefest of smiles behind her fan, before saying, 'Pablo, will you please excuse us for a moment.'

Young Pablo did go eventually, but clearly didn't appreciate being dismissed like a servant, giving Joe a dark look as he passed him, and mumbling whispered obscenities into his dark beard in a language Joe didn't recognize, but was presumably Catalan.

The comtesse stood up and put on a light kimono, of red silk decorated with chrysanthemums, over her gauzy robe. 'Now see what you have done. You have upset my young artist. He *is* even younger than you, M'sieur App-le-doon, after all, so I put up with his sometime surly manners. One has to make some allowances for youthful genius.'

Jacques suddenly pushed his way angrily into the room, glowering at Joe, but the comtesse dismissed him with a cursory cutting motion of her hand. Jacques retreated tamely, like a well-trained poodle.

'It seems you have made yet one more enemy, M'sieur App-le-doon. What a talent you have for annoying people!'

'Why did you lie to me, Madame?'

Her cheeks flared as red as the silk of her kimono. 'How dare you! I didn't lie to you.'

'Joelle's name was really "Langevin", wasn't it, Madame?'

The comtesse shrugged prettily. 'Perhaps. I can't be sure.'

'Yet you told me she wasn't the woman who worked for Eleanor Winthrop.'

'I told you the truth – she can't have been. She did join my staff on November the seventeenth last year. She simply cannot be the woman you want.'

'You could have let me discover that for myself, rather than trying to protect her.'

'She was a good maid. I saw no reason to get her into trouble, even though she did walk out on me so suddenly. It is not in my nature to make trouble for people unnecessarily.'

Joe braced himself for a difficult question. 'Forgive me for asking this, Madame. But was her leaving your employment anything to do with your liaison with the Duke of Lancaster?'

The comtesse seemed truly annoyed for the first time by one of Joe's questions. But she answered it anyway. 'Not to my knowledge. But, my word! You are a forthright young man. How old are you?'

Joe shrugged uncomfortably. 'Twenty-three.'

She came closer until her magnificent jutting bosom, straining at the red silk and gold chrysanthemums of her kimono, was only a few inches away from his own chest. 'The duke left Paris yesterday morning, Saturday, after only arriving here on Thursday. Normally he stays several weeks when he visits Paris but clearly something important had come up to make him change his plans this time. Joelle left my employment and walked out on me yesterday too, for no apparent reason. Perhaps there was some connection between the two events. I don't know, to be honest.'

'Did "Joelle" ever have any personal dealings with the duke or his entourage?'

'Do you know anything about the duke?' The comtesse's momentary anger had passed and she seemed highly amused by something again.

'No, nothing at all, apart from the fact that he's English.' Joe saw the comtesse's bemused shrug in response and wondered what it could mean.

'Joelle did visit the Hotel Bristol on Friday to arrange...a liaison...for today,' the comtesse finally admitted. She coughed dryly. 'But then, I could hardly send Jacques on such a delicate errand. The liaison had to be cancelled however, because of the duke's early departure for Switzerland.'

Joe thought for a moment, not sure whether this information was helping him or not. 'And you really have no forwarding address for "Joelle"?'

'No, she left me nothing apart from a scribbled note apologising and saying she had to leave immediately. I do of course have the original address she gave me when she joined my staff, but it will probably be as bogus as her references, if you're right about her.'

'Very possibly, but could I have it anyway?'

She went to a drawer and copied an address on a slip of paper, then handed it to him. He saw that her writing was as graceful and accomplished as everything else about her.

Joe nodded gratefully, folded the notepaper, and placed it carefully into his billfold. 'Thank you, Comtesse. This may help. Now, if it pleases you, I will leave you in peace to continue with your sitting.'

The comtesse's eyes glittered. 'No, Monsieur App-le-doon, it does not please me. Now that you have forced your way into my boudoir, you will stay. I absolutely insist -' she smiled like a cat - 'and so will Jacques insist,

I'm afraid. Still, I hope it will not be *too* much of an ordeal for you to keep me company while I am painted. It is very dull having no one to talk to. Pablo is so intense and so young; yet he has no agreeable conversation at all. And it seems the least you can do, to tell me something of your fascinating country and keep me amused. If not, then, perhaps *I* can keep *you* amused...'

*

The woman was indeed charming, sophisticated, and with a fount of amusingly risqué anecdotes that entertained Joe despite his pressing wish, even on a Sunday afternoon, to get back immediately to the search for Eleanor Winthrop. The comtesse talked entrancingly about art, the state of the world, her Polish homeland - even her late Russian aristocratic émigré husband (who, Joe gathered, had been at least thirty years her senior.) The Comtesse de Portales was undoubtedly a remarkable woman, and showed no concern at all about being near naked in front of two young men.

At one point, though, Joe realised something about the comtesse. It was when he was recounting a story of his own life growing up in Philadelphia, playing baseball in the park with friends, and she interrupted softly, in perfect English, 'How lucky boys are. Yes, I loved playing ball too, but my father would never let me, a mere girl, play...'

Suddenly Joe knew exactly why he had been allowed to see her today. *Where are you really from, Comtesse?* he wanted to ask her. *Are you really Polish? Or could your origins be closer to St. Petersburg, Florida than to St. Petersburg, Russia...?*'

The comtesse recovered well from her little lapse and reverted instantly to French without a falter. Yet Joe could see that he had crossed an invisible boundary, exposing a side to her she didn't want revealed, and that he was consequently now no longer welcome.

'I think it's time I allowed you to leave, M'sieur Appeldoorn.' This time he noticed – regretfully – that she pronounced his name perfectly.

The temperature in the pink boudoir seemed to have dropped twenty degrees. And Joe found himself within a minute back on the sunlit Boulevard Suchet, wondering just who the Comtesse de Pourtales really was...

*

Joe returned home to his fleapit two-room apartment in the Rue de Babylone in the 17th *Arrondissement*. It seemed even more sordid than usual by comparison with the luxuries of the Boulevard Suchet.

At just after seven, as he was eating a fondue of Emmental cheese delivered by the restaurant next door, and washing it down with a bottle of Chablis, a knock came at the door. Joe didn't have too many visitors apart from René, the four flights of steep rickety stairs and threadbare carpet deterring most people.

Wiping a dribble of hot cheese from his chin, he opened the door casually, half expecting to see the familiar figure of René, but was surprised to find instead a young woman standing in the shadows at the top of the landing. She moved forward into the line of the dim glow of gaslight coming from his room, and spoke in a low husky voice. 'My name is Joelle Loubet, M'sieur. I believe you wish to speak to me.'

Joe was both elated and a little wary at this unexpected visitation. 'How did you know about me?' *And how did you find me*? he wanted to add.

'Jacques Boursin let me know that you called at the Comtesse de Pourtales's home today. He is a good friend; he knew where I'd gone, and he came and told me that you'd asked about me.'

So Jacques had lied! - he knew a great deal more about this woman than he'd let on, even for fifty francs. Joe was thoroughly nervous now, expecting the hulking manservant to appear from the shadows any moment to threaten him too. But he relaxed a little when he realised that the woman really did appear to be alone. 'That still doesn't explain how you found me here, Ma'mselle.'

'Oh, I have ways,' she said airily. It was clear to Joe that she, or perhaps Jacques, must have followed him home from the Boulevard Suchet.

'May I come in?' she went on with a faint smile. 'It's cold out here on the landing.'

Joe finally remembered his manners. 'Yes, of course.' He stepped back to allow her to pass. 'I'm afraid the room is a bit of a mess.'

'No, it's very nice,' she commented, as she walked in and looked around casually; it gave him the opportunity to study her at close quarters in a good light for the first time. She was twenty-two, or twenty-three perhaps, and with the usual self-confidence of young Frenchwomen. Did any Frenchwomen lack that certain "je ne sais quoi"? he wondered. She was quite tall, at least one metre sixty, with a shapely figure, chocolate-brown eyes, a large mouth, and, yes, a mole on her left cheek. The Widow Signoret had got that latter detail slightly wrong - she'd told him that the mole was on Monique's *right* cheek as far as Joe could remember - but otherwise the widow had described everything else with remarkable precision. "Joelle" wore her hair pinned up under a delicate chapeau, and an imposing head of rich chestnut hair it was, with a slight curl to it that he thought might even be natural. Joe would have described her as pretty but perhaps unremarkable, if he'd seen her in the street and not known anything else about her. *But something about this woman now set warning bells ringing in his head...*

For one thing, she was dressed rather too well for a lady's maid, or even for a lady's companion and language teacher: black silk stockings and patent leather shoes, tiny corseted waist, a tight bodice of red water silk, and a fashionable striped skirt of lemon and cream.

Joe now had not the slightest doubt that this was Monique Langevin. If anyone knew where Eleanor Winthrop had gone, it was this woman...

She turned to face him. 'Why have you been trying to find me? Who are you working for?'

Joe sniffed suspiciously. 'I think you know very well why I'm looking for you.'

'No, I don't, M'sieur. I swear it.'

'Is your name really Joelle Loubet? Or is it...' he hesitated momentarily, '...*Monique Langevin?*'

She came closer – so close in fact that he could feel her breath on his face – but Joe stood his ground, refusing to be intimidated by this woman's odd and forward behaviour. 'It is not, M'sieur,' she declared boldly. 'I'm afraid Jacques should *never* have told you that my name was Langevin.' She put her hand out towards the nearby table and fingered the top of the empty Chablis bottle with what seemed deliberate suggestiveness. She licked her scarlet lips slowly, revealing a perfect row of even white teeth, then leaned her face further forward, bringing her tempting lips even closer to his. 'Actually my name is *Martine* Langevin,' she whispered conspiratorially. 'It was very naughty of Jacques to betray my confidence for a mere fifty francs. Although he must be regretting it now...'

'Why, Ma'mselle?' Joe asked, almost mesmerised now by her provocative beauty at such close quarters.

She smiled dangerously. 'Because I had to slit his throat, of course, *before I came here to do the same to you...*'

And with that, she coolly picked up the wine bottle and, with bewildering speed, smashed it viciously over his head.

Through a red haze, barely conscious, Joe sank to his knees. He saw the woman, as if in a nightmare, calmly take out an evil-looking knife from a fold within her skirt. Then, with a snarl, she yanked back his head by the hair to expose his neck, and he saw the blade flash down towards his exposed jugular...

*

René Sardou was grumbling to himself, his breath wheezing from his forty-cigarette-a-day habit, as he mounted the last flight of stairs to Joe Appeldoorn's apartment. He preferred not to come to this dingy area of the 17th *Arrondissement;* too many people around here remembered him and his past dealings with the police. He had watched the apartment in the Rue Lamarck all afternoon without success, then left Pascal and his evil-smelling brother to keep watch in his place. And since Joe hadn't appeared tonight at the café in the Rue Lepic, as was his habit, René decided he'd better visit Joe to see what he might have discovered at the Comtesse de Pourtales' home.

The door of Joe's apartment was open to the touch. René saw a strange tableau unfold as the door swung slowly open: a young well-dressed woman crouched above the kneeling figure of Joe Appeldoorn, a knife raised, about to cut his throat from ear to ear. A pretty face transformed into a mask of evil, yet René recognized Joelle Loubet, otherwise Monique Langevin, at once.

René had a soft spot for this young American even if he was a naïve fool about most things – and perhaps he also saw the opportunity of making a lot more easy money about to fly out of the window if "young Joseph" was to end up as "dead Joseph". Whatever the reason, he threw himself instinctively across the room at the woman and tried to block her scything blow with his arm. But he fumbled his attempted block badly and instead saw the gleaming knife arc downwards to end up thrust savagely into his own upper arm. He felt the blow like a hammer hitting home, but surprisingly no pain. Yet before he could do anything else - before he could even scream at the sight of his own blood pumping in vast quantities from his ruptured arm - the woman had turned and, despite the restrictions of her skirt, bounded away athletically through the open dormer window and across the garret rooftops into the Paris night.

*

Amazingly both of them were still in one piece.

Joe was dazed – perhaps slightly concussed - but otherwise apparently unhurt. And René's only problem, despite an initial conviction that he was destined for the morgue that very night, was a velvet jacket whose thick padded sleeve had been ruined beyond repair by Mlle Langevin's exquisite knife work.

'*Quelle femme charmante*! I didn't like the sting in that one's tail one little bit,' René commented sarcastically, as he sponged Joe's head down with cold water to ease the throbbing headache and ringing in his ears that Monique Langevin's visit had left him with.

'No, nor...did I,' Joe responded haltingly. In truth, he felt far more shaken up by the experience than he was prepared to admit to René.

But even so, he couldn't help wondering why his murderous visitor had been so insistent on calling herself "Martine", when it seemed she had no problem at all in admitting to the name "Langevin".

It didn't make any sense...

CHAPTER 3

Monday 10th March 1902

Sheet lightning flickered, briefly turning the sky ghostly white and illuminating in stark detail the busy preparations on Platform 10 at the Gare de Lyon. The station was a bustle of activity as the night train to Zurich made ready to leave, the drama of the event being heightened by the violence of the accompanying thunderstorm.

On the glistening platform Joe and René stood like a couple of bedraggled alley cats in the shelter of a tall hoarding advertising Pernod, keeping discreetly out of sight. Joe watched and shivered as porters in blue dungarees, uniformed guards, stewards in immaculate white coats, and some late passengers, rather more wet and unkempt than the employees of the railway, rushed to get on board in time.

The hiss of gaslight and the gentle panting of the great gleaming locomotive at the platform were almost drowned out by the thunderous rhythmic beating of rain against the splendid wrought-iron roof. Water gurgled down drainpipes, splashed in gutters from the liveried wagon-lit coaches, and dribbled in little jets from the edge of the platform, like a line of ragamuffins peeing on the track. Joe listened to the deluge and wondered nervously about the challenges ahead and what surprises this night journey to Switzerland might bring...

*

Joe and René's presence at this main railway station was a result of the persistence and initiative of René's urchin detectives, Pascal and Thierry. Pascal, in particular, had had the foresight to keep watching the apartment in the Rue Lamarck through the whole of Sunday night and early Monday morning, even though René had given him no clear instruction to do so. He and his emaciated-looking brother had shared the long cold vigil, waiting patiently within sight of the white domes of the *Basilique du Sacre Cœur* for something to report.

Their patience had been rewarded at five on Monday morning, still an hour before dawn, when the deadly Mlle Langevin reappeared briefly in the Rue Lamarck. Now dressed in a shawl and long woollen coat, this disguise did not fool Pascal, though, who instantly recognised her as the same woman he had seen here the previous Wednesday. The woman crept into the red marble lobby of the building, past the ancient sleeping concierge, and spent half an hour inside, apparently collecting some personal things, before she finally reappeared, carrying an even bigger case than the one she'd had five days before. She walked through the silent cobbled streets of Montmartre, struggling with her case, and the two boys dutifully followed her at a safe distance. Monique walked only as far as a small hotel three streets away (not surprisingly since her bag looked so heavy and unwieldy) and entered the gas-lit foyer on tiptoe. The boys saw a light come on in a fourth-floor room after two minutes or so; then, ten minutes later, the light went out again.

Pascal, the intellectual leader of the surveillance team, ordered his brother to go and fetch M Sardou, while he continued to watch the fourth-floor room with typical Gallic concentration. In a few minutes, Thierry returned with a rumpled, bleary-eyed and wheezy M Sardou in tow...

*

At ten that Monday morning, Joe had been woken up by a persistent banging on his apartment door. Given what had happened the last time he opened this door to a stranger, he answered the knock rather nervously, but this time was relieved to find only the diminutive Thierry standing on the landing, in a positive fever to drag him over to some seedy hotel in Montmartre. 'M'sieur Sardou suggested you pack a suitcase and bring your passport with you too. *Il croît que votre petit oiseau prévoit de voler.*'

Your little bird is about to fly...

On arriving outside the hotel, René had soon apprised Joe of the situation. Monique (or was her name perhaps "Joelle", or even "Martine"? - even Joe was thoroughly confused by now) was still in her fourth-floor room as far as anyone could tell. 'I haven't called the police yet, Joseph,' René warned him. 'Shall I do it now?'

'No, don't. I need some time to think.' In his heart Joe Appeldoorn knew it was the last thing he intended to do. If he'd been willing to call the Prefecture of Police, he would have done it last night, immediately after he'd had his throat nearly slit open by this woman. Whatever else Monique Langevin was – and she was a murderous harpy at the very least – she remained his only slight hope of finding Eleanor Winthrop.

Miss Winthrop was clearly involved in something much deeper and more sinister than a love affair gone wrong.

Joe could see from the frown of concentration on René's face that he was concocting a sentence of sorts in English – and he didn't disappoint. '*I think, Joseph, Miss Langevin might try and jump over ze ship,*' he suggested, while Pascal looked on in surprise, suitably impressed at M Sardou's unexpected command of the English language.

Joe thought he might be right in his opinion, even if badly expressed: Monique Langevin could well be about to jump ship and make a run for it.

But they waited several hours in vain in the cold Paris spring drizzle for her to make a move. The day went by with excruciating slowness, Joe and René escaping to the shelter of a nearby café whenever they could. Then at four in the afternoon, with black anvil-shaped thunder clouds building up ominously over the southern Paris skyline, Pascal rushed into the café with the news that the "little bird" was finally on the move. Joe and René got back just in time to see the back end of a horse cab disappearing down the steep cobbled hill at the top of the Boulevard de Magenta, heading south. In that direction the sky was now a bubbling black cauldron of cloud, riven by streaks of lightning. Joe looked around the corner for the cab that he'd kept waiting the whole day for just such an eventuality, only to find the driver had chosen this inopportune moment to disappear, presumably to the *pissoir* at the bottom of the hill.

'Go and run for the cabby, Pascal,' Joe ordered in a panic.

Pascal smiled smugly. 'Don't worry too much, M'sieur. I heard the lady give a destination to her cabby...the *Gare de Lyon*...'

*

In the booking hall of the imposing Gare de Lyon, Pascal had watched Monique Langevin claim her reservation and ticket for the overnight sleeper train to Zurich, just as the thunderstorm finally broke and the rain began to fall on the station roof in torrents.

After Pascal had reported that Monique was safely out of sight, Joe went to the ticket office himself and tried to do the same. René had already made it clear that he couldn't drop all his other work immediately and go chasing off with him across Europe tonight. That disappointing announcement had given Joe pause for thought – *could he really do this alone? Follow this woman God knows where...?*

At first he thought he might even have to settle for a non-sleeping compartment in second class: by the time Joe got to the front of the long queue in the booking hall, he found that the overnight train bound for Zurich, with intermediate stops in Chaumont, Dijon, Geneva, Lausanne and Bern, was already fully booked in first class. Yet just as he was leaving the booking hall, he had a stroke of good fortune when an irate and florid-faced Swiss woman with a noisy child in tow marched imperiously to the front of the queue and cancelled her sleeper reservation for the Zurich train for that very night. Joe, on hearing this, promptly barged his way deftly back to the front of the dripping queue again and – with muttered calls of

"Well, really!" from a group of drenched English tourists offended by his direct American manners - managed to change his recently purchased second class ticket and get the newly available first-class sleeper compartment for himself...

Now, as he and René waited in the shelter of the Pernod hoarding on Platform 10, the rain was getting even heavier, if anything. From the sound of the rain impacting on the soaring iron and glass roof of the station, it felt to Joe as if the whole of the Gare de Lyon had been mysteriously relocated to the foot of the Niagara Falls. He turned to René, having to shout to make himself heard above the antediluvian deluge. 'I'll send you a telegram or letter from Switzerland if and when I do need your help. And you can always telegraph the Central Post Office in Zurich if you have anything important to tell me. I've already wired my boss at Pinkertons in New York to inform him where I'll be for the next few days.' Joe hesitated awkwardly. 'I haven't thanked you properly for saving my life last night, René. That was a very brave thing to do. Brave, but also a little stupid, my friend.'

René made a deprecating face. 'Oh! *Ça ne fait rien.*' Then he smiled crookedly. 'Well, perhaps it was a *little* brave, and very, *very* stupid. But Corazon would never have forgiven me if I'd allowed you to be killed, and I still have high hopes of helping her off with her sequins one day.' His eyes became serious again. 'I'm sorry I can't accompany you tonight, but it's impossible for me to leave Paris this week.' Joe wondered if some of René's more dubious activities might be catching up with him finally, or whether he was simply making excuses not to go. 'But are you sure about trying to follow this hell-cat alone, Joseph?' He showed Joe a copy of the evening newspaper, the *Paris Soir,* and made a wry face at the front page. *Murder in the Bois de Boulogne!* the banner headline screamed. 'The victim's throat was cut from ear to ear,' René said matter-of-factly. 'And it was the big throat of a big man – a *huge* man, in fact. Now I never thought I would hear myself say this...' there was a note of shame in his voice, 'but perhaps it *is* better if you go to *les flics*.'

If the truth be told, Joe *was* wavering slightly in his determination to follow this dangerous woman alone, still unsure if this was the most sensible course of action. *What should he do?* The train doors were slamming like a drum roll in preparation for departure, and his luggage was already stowed in his sleeping compartment on board, so he had no more than a few more seconds to make up his mind. Yet there was no conceivable way he would go back to Le Boeuf and entrust his knowledge of Monique Langevin to that clod of a policeman. Once the search for Eleanor became linked to a murder investigation by French police, his own chances of finding Eleanor Winthrop – as a private agent in a foreign country - were as good as over.

And with that lost opportunity went any hope of claiming James

Winthrop's reward and escaping his present financial insolvency - Eleanor's grandfather would hardly honour his promise if all Joe had done was simply to pass the case over to the French authorities. If Joe wanted that money, he knew he would have to demonstrate that he had earned it, and that was a powerful incentive for him to keep working on his own, even if it meant following a woman as dangerous and unpredictable as Monique Langevin halfway across Europe....

Joe finally made up his mind. 'I'd better go now before I miss the train.'

René shrugged ruefully. 'Then watch that hell-cat, my friend. She has sharp claws...' From long experience now, Joe recognised the contorted expression on René's face and waited expectantly for him to dredge up yet another bit of excruciating English.

And as usual, René did not disappoint. '...*Zat is certainly a pussy ze most dangerous...*'

*

Joe already knew (courtesy of Pascal's spying mission in the booking hall of the Gare de Lyon) that Monique Langevin had bought a ticket all the way to Zurich and was travelling alone in a private first-class sleeping compartment in Coach F, two coaches further back than his own coach, D. After checking his own compartment was secure and his luggage safe, Joe proceeded cautiously back along the corridor of the train as it finally rumbled out of the station.

He had reached the corridor at the front of Coach F, where the sleeping car attendant, a young man of Romany looks, was checking bed linen in a storage compartment, when Monique Langevin herself poked her pretty head out of a sleeper compartment door only a few feet further down the corridor. Fortunately, though, she turned first to look backwards in the direction of the disappearing vault of the station roof - not surprisingly, since it was an impressive sight, bathed in arc light and a cascade of falling water. So Joe was able to step back quickly out of sight into the utility space between the lavatories, before she twisted her neck again to look in his direction.

'*Qu'est qu'il y a, M'sieur?*' the coach attendant asked Joe, puzzled by his odd behaviour.

'*Pas de quoi.*' Joe cautiously craned his neck around the corner to see along the corridor; Monique was just closing her compartment door again, which he heard her lock behind her with a distinct click.

The attendant clearly thought he understood now what might be going on, and gave Joe a knowing look. 'Yes, a very pretty lady, M'sieur. But I'm afraid she is not having dinner tonight,' he said. 'She is fatigued and has asked not to be disturbed. So if you were hoping perhaps to encounter her later in the restaurant car for dinner, then I'm afraid Monsieur will be disappointed.'

Actually it was good news, although Joe tried to look suitably chastened at having to miss the opportunity to get to know his pretty fellow passenger at dinner that night. It meant that the chances of running into Monique accidentally on the train were considerably reduced and that Joe could therefore probably afford to have dinner in the restaurant car himself tonight without fear of being spotted.

'Does the monsieur wish to have dinner in the restaurant car tonight anyway?' the attendant asked solicitously. 'I can make a reservation for you.'

'Oh, I am in Coach D,' Joe said apologetically.

'*Oh, ça ne fait rien,*' the man smiled expressively. 'I can still make the reservation for you.'

Joe had eaten hardly anything since that interrupted cheese fondue the night before. 'Then yes, certainly,' he confirmed.

The attendant nodded encouragingly. 'And, since you are travelling on your own, M'sieur, I shall do my best to find you a suitable dinner companion to make up for the disappointment of losing the mademoiselle in this coach. My name is Guy, M'sieur. Leave it to me...'

*

A few minutes later, after changing for dinner, Joe made his way forward along the train towards the restaurant car, lurching from side to side as the coaches followed a long curve through the south-eastern suburbs of Paris. Because of the curve, he could see the whole length of the train ahead, the locomotive breathing fire as the man on the footplate funnelled coal into the hungry furnace, a long plume of steam and smoke rising from the stack, torn and shredded by the squalling rain. On the tables of the long coaches ahead, lamps were lit and glowed blue, so that the train resembled a necklace of glass beads retreating through the southern reaches of the great city. Joe saw a signal lamp ahead wink from red to green as the train finally left the long curve and the grind of the wheel flange plates against the bullhead rails changed to a quieter rhythmic rattle.

The suburbs of Paris were thinning by now, dingy tenements gradually replaced by streets of houses, green spaces appearing between the townships. Joe gained an impression of the changing scene through the corner of his eye as he progressed along the corridor: rain-glistened streets, stagnant water, liquid pools of light, a wilderness of allotments - while through it all, the black monster roared on, sparks flying, trailing its ragged curtains of steam.

In the corridor on the way he encountered a sea of faces: middle-aged English ladies clutching shawls and rugs and sketchbooks, a French clergyman with the face of a roué studying a Baedeker of Switzerland. A plump clean-shaven German of indeterminate age, and with the look of a commercial traveller, was clearing a circle in the condensation on the glass to peer out into the darkness. The coaches still held the persistent damp chill of a late winter evening. Passing a non-sleeping compartment, Joe saw an elderly woman turning the heating wheel to raise the frigid temperature, while a middle-aged man with a grey moustache and a shabby hat regarded her sullenly from the opposite corner seat.

The restaurant car was warmer than the corridor, at least, or perhaps it just felt that way, with the partly-curtained windows faithfully reflecting the mauve lamps standing on the tables and the cutlery shining on the starched white linen. Joe searched for his table number and saw that the attendant in Coach F had been as good as his word and placed him on the same table as a single young lady who was already tucking in to her *hors d'oeuvres*.

Joe excused himself and sat down opposite her. When she looked up from her bouillabaisse, though, he saw that Guy, the attendant, clearly had a sense of humour, or else had little choice in available female passengers. This was about as plain a girl as Joe had ever seen in his life – in her mid-twenties, toothy, a little plump, and with ugly, frizzy red hair badly in need of the restraining influences of either a hairdresser or a ribbon. Her eyes were concealed behind round wire-frame eyeglasses that didn't help her other disadvantages. She had governess, or school ma'am, written all over her.

Joe guessed from her unfashionable clothes and her slightly reddened complexion that she was also English, a guess that was confirmed by her accent when he introduced himself and she was forced to respond, if begrudgingly. 'Miss Cordingly. Charlotte Cordingly.' She spoke hesitantly, with a slight stammer, and seemed distracted by Joe's arrival, almost as if she'd been expecting someone else entirely to sit at her table.

Joe was immediately aware of her discomfiture. 'Miss Cordingly, if you'd rather be alone, then I'm sure I can arrange to go to another table.'

She looked up sharply, her voice and her manner cool. 'You can see for yourself – everywhere else is fully occupied.'

'Then perhaps I can change places with a single lady on another table.'

'I believe we are the only passengers taking dinner at present who are travelling alone, Mr Appeldoorn. Therefore there is nothing to be done and we must accept the situation. In any case, I don't object to your presence.' Her icy tone suggested anything but that, though.

Joe was beginning to think this might turn out to be the longest dinner of his life.

But he was wrong, as it happened. Miss Cordingly did not prove to be quite as severe as she seemed upon first acquaintance and, as the minutes went on - after he had ordered his choice of *hors d'oeuvres* and main course - she even thawed enough to take the initiative and engage him in conversation.

'I deduce from your accent that you are an American, Mr Appeldoorn.'

'Born and bred in Philadelphia, although I now live and work in New

York.'

'And yet you speak French and German. Those are unusual talents in a continent where the universal language is English.'

'How did you know I speak other languages?' Joe, his natural suspicions heightened by his circumstances, found himself speaking brusquely.

Miss Cordingly seemed surprised by his tone. 'I have a compartment in Coach F, and I heard you speaking French with the wagon-lit attendant. And then later I heard you say something in German to a passenger in the corridor. Your accent seems very accomplished in both languages, although I am perhaps not the best person to judge.'

Joe had never noticed this woman consciously before he sat down opposite her, but clearly she had been paying him some close attention prior to that. He chided himself for the lapse; he'd been so busy watching out for Monique Langevin that he'd not taken care to notice if anyone else was watching *him*. He studied the girl across the table with deeper interest. The light from the lamp revealed a good bone structure to her face. Take away the awful teeth and hair, and perhaps this wouldn't be such a bad-looking young woman.

'My maternal grandmother was French, from Alsace,' he explained, studying her reaction carefully. 'It was she who taught me French as a child. And I studied physics for three years in Switzerland, so that's why I speak German...and Swiss German.' Joe smiled ruefully at the memory. 'It wasn't until I got to Zurich that I realised that the language they spoke in Switzerland – *Schwyzertütsch* - was entirely different to the German I'd been taught up to that time by an immigrant teacher from Berlin.'

Miss Cordingly accepted the story without comment. 'Your name, "Appeldoorn" – is that German?'

'It's Dutch, I believe. But the family origins in America go back a long way - to the seventeenth century.'

'Was your ancestor perhaps the Dutchman who bought the island of Manhattan from the Indian inhabitants for a few beads and trinkets?'

Joe smiled. 'I wish he had been. I might have been a Rockefeller or a Carnegie by now. But you're English, I think, Miss Cordingly,' he said, deflecting the subject away from himself.

She pushed her empty plate away and signalled the waiter to take it. 'You're correct, of course. I was born in the village of Elstead in Surrey, a few miles southwest of London. Do you know England at all, Mr Appeldoorn?'

'I once visited London as a tourist – but for a few days only. And I'm afraid I played the colonial visitor and only saw all the usual tourist things: Big Ben, Westminster Abbey. I never got to Elstead. What's it like?'

Miss Cordingly made a wry face. 'Oh, very English. Perhaps *too* English, some people might say. Situated on the River Wey, with woods all around.

There is a five-arched stone bridge over the river, a fourteenth-century church, the ruins of Waverly Abbey nearby – the inspiration for Sir Walter Scott's novel, *Waverly*. Elstead is very green and quiet: rose-covered cottages, thatched roofs, dog carts in the street. I suppose you would find it quaint, and condescendingly admire its Lilliputian scale compared to American things.'

'Not all American things are gargantuan, Miss Cordingly. We do admire sensitivity of scale in some things. And what do you do for a living?'

She smiled deprecatingly, but seemed determined to make him struggle. 'I have heard that Americans are perspicacious people, so perhaps you can tell me.'

'Are you a schoolteacher on holiday perhaps?'

She shrugged, and almost laughed. 'Ah, now I feel entirely demoralised for being so transparent. And I had thought myself quite the lady of mystery. Perhaps you're wondering how I come to be here in term time.' Joe was a little puzzled at her apparent need to explain herself in such detail. 'I left my previous employment at Christmas and I have been enjoying a few months of leisure and study before I take up the cudgels of education again in September. I was determined to do some travelling in Europe, although we English are hardly the most popular people on the Continent at this moment.'

'You mean because of the South African war?'

'Yes. We've had a very bad press, from the French and Germans particularly, because of our treatment of the Boers.'

'Putting them in concentration camps, you mean.'

'Yes, I was just reading a French newspaper article about it. Apparently we have incarcerated nearly a hundred thousand people in camps in the Transvaal, Orange River and Natal, where we've treated them with neglect and brutality. Many have died in a measles epidemic. We even serve goat dung tea to Boer children, which sounds less than delicious, although it hardly justifies the degree of censure that we have received from the French government and press.'

'You don't believe these accusations of brutality against your fellow countrymen?'

'Oh, there must be some semblance of truth in it, perhaps, although all of our sins will be exaggerated by our European rivals, I'm sure. But it is the hypocrisy of the Germans, French and Belgians that irritates me most, when they butcher the black Africans in their own colonies with such senseless disregard, and receive no similar censure from anyone.'

They'd left the city far behind by now, and even the remnants of the rainstorm. Out in the darkness nothing was visible, except their own colour-muted reflections. Joe had ordered veal and – deliberately - a cheap medium Burgundy. In his experience, no wine bouquet survived the shaking of an express train so he'd never seen any point in ordering anything expensive to drink on a train. Miss Cordingly seemed to agree – she was drinking only water.

'And what do you do for a living, Mr Appeldoorn? And please don't make *me* guess – I have no talent for it. Why, for all I know, you could be a dangerous anarchist or assassin.'

Joe forced a laugh. 'Well, perhaps I could be. But I'm afraid that the more mundane truth is that I am simply an electrical engineer visiting Switzerland again on business.' That didn't even feel like a lie to Joe, more a subconscious wish on his part to begin again a career that had been on hold for too long.

The train was slowing down to a crawl as it rumbled through a station. By now Joe too had finished his main course and was on a final coffee and liqueur. An industrial town unfolded to view between dark hills, a steel blast furnace glowing like a vision of Hell in the night. They passed under an iron girder bridge studded with rivets, clanged over points and crossed an empty street that intersected the track diagonally. Joe saw a drenched boy and girl walking arm in arm along a gas-lit canal towpath, a pair of star-crossed lovers happy to be together, even in the rain. A lamp shone on a café door and illuminated a young woman standing smoking in the entrance, looking directly at him, her cigarette a glowing red ember, her attitude one of a quiet despair that Joe could almost sense even in that briefest of encounters. Joe wondered about the figure at the door, and their momentary half-meeting. *Who was she, this silent figure standing in the doorway?* Life was a long series of such transitory human encounters, a deep perpetual mystery.

Miss Cordingly seemed to sense his slight melancholy. 'Tell me about America, Mr Appeldoorn. What do you think of your new president, for instance?'

Joe sipped his coffee. 'Teddy Roosevelt? I know little about him, to be honest.'

'Well, how about American writers then? What do you think of them? Melville, Jack London, Mark Twain, Henry James?'

'I think Mr James is one of yours now, isn't he?'

She wasn't to be denied, though, in her quest to learn something about America. 'Then tell me about New York at least. Or about American women – are they really as glamorous and liberated as they are portrayed in literature?'

Joe gave her a wry smile. 'I suspect they're not nearly as liberated as you, Miss Cordingly, if you want the truth...' Joe stopped short in his deliberation, suddenly aware that a young woman had just brushed past his left shoulder. With alarm he realised that it was *Monique Langevin*...

She had clearly changed her mind about not having dinner in the restaurant car and was about to sit down at a table facing Joe, not five feet away.

Fortunately Monique was rummaging for something in her bag so wasn't paying much attention yet to her fellow diners. But Joe could see that he only had a moment to act before he would be discovered. Getting up from his seat, he apologized breathlessly to a surprised Miss Cordingly, before retreating rapidly from the restaurant car, his *Cointreau* still untouched on the crisp white tablecloth...

*

Joe had considered employing the services of Guy as an extra pair of eyes to watch Monique's movements, but decided against it in the end, keeping an eye himself on Coach F for Monique to return from dinner. Which she duly did, after an interminable hour and ten minutes in the restaurant car, following which Joe retreated to his own coach and compartment for the night. Joe had caught sight of Miss Cordingly returning to Coach F too – in fact she was only two compartments away from Monique – and she gave Joe a very old-fashioned look of displeasure as she spotted him loitering at the end of the corridor, before almost slamming her own door behind her.

Obviously she'd been a little put out by his hasty departure from the restaurant car, but Joe had more problems on his mind at the moment than soothing the wounded feelings of a plain English spinster.

Yet there had been something odd about Miss Cordingly – something he couldn't quite put his finger on...

What with the constant rattle and lurch of the train, Joe didn't sleep well – perhaps also because of a growing suspicion that this was too easy and that Monique Langevin, instead of travelling all the way to Zurich, might choose to sneak off the train at any one of the half dozen stops on the way. So, at every station stop through the night, Joe had dutifully roused himself and watched from the corridor outside his compartment for any sign of Monique Langevin getting ready to leave Coach F on the quiet.

At Dijon, at three o'clock in the morning, the platform seemed completely deserted, though, no one getting on or off the train. But Joe continued to watch from the dimly-lit corridor until he was absolutely sure that Monique was not quitting the train surreptitiously.

It was only when he glanced around that he became aware of another figure, standing at the misted window further along the corridor. The man moved towards him and Joe recognised him from an earlier encounter: the plump German – the man he had instantly categorised as a commercial traveller of some sort.

'Is this Dijon?' the man asked in German, after a long yawn.

'*Ja.* I can't see the station name board, but I think so. Can't you sleep either?' Joe answered in German.

The man smiled faintly in the glow from the dimmed coach lights. 'No, I never can. *Ah, Entschuldigen Sie bitte.*' He held out his hand and then offered Joe a business card. *Karl Jurgen Blumenfeld. Direktor. Howaldts Machinenwerke, Augsburg.* 'We make internal combustion engines for motor cars,' he explained.

So, rather more than a commercial traveller, but still not a bad guess, Joe thought complacently. He introduced himself in return to Herr Blumenfeld, but didn't offer him his Pinkerton card, saying only instead that he was an American on vacation. The German company director seemed a harmless enough fellow, but hardly one to reveal a confidence to on such a brief acquaintance.

He seemed determined, though, to engage Joe in further conversation. 'You seemed to be looking for something, or someone, on the platform?'

Joe shook his head. 'No, not at all; I'm just passing the time. And where are you heading, Herr Blumenfeld?'

'Only as far as Bern. And you?'

'Oh, I'm a tourist, as I told you. So I shall get off wherever the urge takes me.'

'For an American, you speak very good German, Herr Appeldoorn. What are you planning to do in Switzerland? Have you ever been there before?'

'Yes, I have. In fact I studied in Switzerland - at the *Eidgenössische Polytechnische Schule* in Zurich.'

'Ah, the Zurich Poly. An excellent institution. And what exactly do you do now for a living?'

Joe decided to employ the same cover story he'd used with Miss Cordingly. 'I'm an electrical engineer. I'm planning to start my own company in time, so right now I'm looking for a suitable financial partner in Europe to provide the necessary investment. Mark my words, Herr Blumenfeld - electricity will completely change the world in the twentieth century. It will transform communications, entertainment, business – in fact it will revolutionise just about every aspect of the way we live.' It was a sentiment his father had expressed endlessly to him, and Joe was happy to repeat it word for word, as if it was his own.

The German nodded faintly in agreement. 'You must have many friends in Switzerland if you studied there. I suppose you will renew old acquaintances.'

'I will – if I have the time.' This was the truth; Joe would certainly take the opportunity to look up his closest friends - but only if he managed to track Eleanor Winthrop down first...

*

Dawn brought the first exhilarating sight of the Alps, draped in snow and skeins of mist, and then an early stop when the locomotive was changed after crossing the French border into Switzerland.

Geneva came and went, yet Monique Langevin seemed determined to stay resolutely in her compartment for almost the whole journey.

Joe was beginning to feel uneasily that she might have already given him the slip, and even the sight of the glistening blue water of Lake Geneva didn't reassure him. The train followed the north shore of the lake, past picturesque wine-making villages, moated castles, Gothic fortresses, steep hillsides topped by limestone cliffs, to Lausanne. Then the train climbed away from the lake into the mountains of the *Mittelland*.

Joe was up, shaved, washed, and packed by this time, ready for a quick departure.

As they progressed further east through the morning, the Swiss mountain landscape revealed its full majestic scale and detail; they traversed long tunnels cut through the heart of the limestone mountains, followed foaming rock-strewn rivers in twisting gorges, emerged onto snowy ridges cloaked in forest, while, far below, green valleys bathed in clean windy sunshine were erupting into spring flower.

At 10.30 local time, the train finally eased its way, with a tired exhalation of steam, into the *Hauptbahnhof* in Bern.

Joe watched the scene on the platform, still only half-awake after his mostly sleepless night. Then he was jerked back to full consciousness when he saw a slim figure moving quickly down the platform in the company of a porter. Monique Langevin was finally making her move and, whether this was predetermined or not, she was clearly leaving the train *here*, not in Zurich.

Joe was galvanised into activity and, not waiting for a porter, dragged his own two bags onto the platform. At the door of the coach, he almost bumped into Charlotte Cordingly who was also hurriedly leaving the train.

'I thought you said you were travelling all the way to Zurich, Mr Appeldoorn,' she declared, almost accusingly.

Had he said that to her? He couldn't remember. 'I changed my mind. I've decided on a short intermission here.'

With that he excused himself and charged away down the platform, leaving Miss Cordingly staring in his wake.

He was just in time to see Monique and her porter going through the platform barrier and taking the stairs up to the main station concourse on the level above. Glancing along the length of the platform, Joe saw that the German company director, Blumenfeld, was also getting off the train here, as he'd said he would.

Blumenfeld called across to Joe, as he waited for a porter for his own bags. 'So, you have decided to see a bit of the capital city, Herr Appeldoorn.'

'I have,' Joe admitted, keeping a wary eye on the slender figure of Monique Langevin disappearing into the distance.

Suddenly, it seemed everyone wanted to enjoy the hospitality and sights of the city of Bern...

CHAPTER 4

Tuesday 11th March 1902

It seemed abundantly clear that Monique Langevin had no idea she was being followed, judging from her casual behaviour in the forecourt of Bern's Central Railway Station, the *Hauptbahnhof*. She was behaving exactly like all the other tourists and visitors to the city, waiting patiently in line for a two-wheeler cab to take her into town.

Watching her closely from just inside the main station concourse, Joseph Appeldoorn had found time to leave his own bags at the left luggage counter while he made ready to follow her cab on foot if necessary. In trying to keep tabs on Mlle Langevin, Joe had a big advantage here compared to Paris: Bern was a much smaller and more compact city than the French capital, and also one which he knew reasonably well from his student days in Switzerland.

It was after eleven o'clock by now, a fine late winter morning in this city ringed by the green mountains of the *Mittelland*. In the dry smokeless air, the distant peaks of the Bernese *Oberland* to the south seemed much closer than in reality, their snowy forested flanks fading away into remote vistas of snow and cloud along high ridges.

Joe hadn't seen what had happened to either of his companions from the train, Herr Blumenfeld, or Miss Charlotte Cordingly, but his attentions had, naturally, been more occupied with Mlle Langevin.

Now, just for a second, Joe took his eyes off his quarry as she was finally getting to the head of the queue for the horse-drawn cabs, and glanced back briefly at the station concourse for any sign of Herr Blumenfeld or the enigmatic Miss Cordingly. But he was immediately punished for his lack of attention because something inexplicable had happened in the brief second he had looked away: Monique Langevin had somehow contrived to disappear completely from the queue waiting for a cab! For a moment Joe blinked in astonishment, refusing to believe the evidence of his eyes, and then began to panic at the thought that he had lost her: she was the key to everything...

In his more optimistic moments on the journey from Paris, Joe had been hopeful that Mlle Langevin might simply lead him directly to Eleanor Winthrop's hiding place. Certainly the Swiss destination seemed plausible at least because one of the few clear things Joe could remember about Eleanor – apart from the extravagant size of her bosom perhaps, and the memory of how nice she had looked dressed as Marie Antoinette at that fancy dress ball in the Old State House in Hartford, Connecticut - was her enthusiasm to see *this* country in particular. If she'd been duped into going anywhere voluntarily with someone, then it would be to Switzerland, the country of her girlish dreams. In a quiet moment together on that evening of the ball, over a glass of lemonade on the terrace, he remembered that "Marie Antoinette" had grown quite dewy-eyed as she'd sipped her drink and confided to him her wish to see the Alps one day. Lemonade was hardly the most appropriate drink for a girl dressed as a queen, Joe had thought at the time, but then Eleanor was, despite her wealth, a sweet and down-to-earth girl at heart who did truly prefer lemonade to champagne...

Perhaps she really was seeing the Alps now – Joe could only hope that by doing so, Eleanor wasn't going to end up sharing the violent fate of her role model that night in Hartford: the tragic Austrian princess cum French queen.

Joe dismissed these fresh morbid thoughts about Eleanor from his mind as he ran out into the forecourt of the *Hauptbahnhof*, looking around wildly for some sign of Monique Langevin. But then, with a sigh of relief, he caught sight of her again, crossing the square in front of the station, the *Bahnhofplatz*, at a leisurely pace. No longer encumbered with his own luggage, he was able to move quickly in pursuit of her before she disappeared into the narrow streets of the *Altstadt*. He didn't run, though – that would have made him far too noticeable, so he limited his pace across the square to a fast walk that still kept her comfortably in sight.

Monique had no heavy bags with her either, he now noticed. It seemed she had changed her mind about taking a cab herself – or perhaps it had always been her intention to walk through Bern's Old Town, and that she had simply entrusted a cabby to take her luggage to her hotel while she walked somewhere else first. That seemed to suggest – reassuringly – that she wasn't going to be staying very far from the centre of town.

Joe recalled that Bern's Old Town – the *Altstadt* – was set on a narrow rocky ridge defined on three sides by a U-shaped bend in the River Aare, almost like a natural moat. The railway and the *Hauptbahnhof* were on the neck of land that connected the *Altstadt* to the suburbs of Bern built on the surrounding hills to the west. The Old Town, perched on this stony ridge above a swift-flowing icy river, did feel almost like an island still; steep-sided rocky banks fell away to the Aare, which was crossed by several arch bridges, exactly like the approaches to the gates of a fortified medieval town. Two landmark buildings dominated the wintry skyline of the old city: the *Münster,* the Gothic cathedral, and the *Rathaus,* the Town Hall.

The morning, though fine, was intensely cold, with the bite of an Alpine winter still prevalent in the air, particularly in the heavy shade between the distinguished old buildings of Bern. Several men's eyes turned admiringly to follow Monique Langevin's progress through the town, but she seemed either not to notice, or to be unmoved by their attention. Monique *was* looking extremely elegant, Joe had to admit, her slender figure dressed to advantage in a long flowing skirt, blouse, and velvet overcoat of dark green. A modest feathered hat was perched charmingly on her head. It still required an effort of will on Joe's part to remember that this attractive-looking young woman was the same homicidal maniac who had tried to shred his throat with a knife less than two days ago.

It did occur to him in a renewed moment of suspicion that this was all far too easy, almost as if Monique *wished* to be followed. *Had she spotted him on the train, after all?* Was she perhaps leading him on deliberately now, spinning her black widow's web, luring him into another deadly trap?

But Joe, putting aside these new doubts, continued to stalk Monique as she carried on down *Spitalgasse* towards the *Käfigturm,* the Cage Tower - once the city's western gate - and then followed *Marktgasse,* the main shopping street. The city was all as Joe affectionately remembered it: long cobbled snowy streets, old houses converted into shops, painted facades above. Because of the picturesque arcades that lined every street, he'd found in the past that it was literally possible to walk through Bern's *Altstadt* without ever getting wet, even on the rainiest day. If he'd had more time, Joe would no doubt have enjoyed again the architectural details of the old red-roofed buildings of this delectable city: the leaded windows, the graininess and patina of old stone and timber, the panelled doors with their exquisite ornamental metalwork.

But the need to keep his quarry in sight, and the worry of losing her, nullified any fresh enjoyment of the sights of Bern for Joe Appeldoorn.

Monique stopped at a colourfully painted fountain and dipped her hand to drink from the water; then she disappeared into a shop apparently to buy herself a new pair of shoes. She seemed almost playfully relaxed, like a schoolgirl allowed out of class for the first time in days.

The *Zytglogge* – the Clock Tower – was just ringing twelve noon when Monique reappeared from the shoe shop and continued her journey, carrying her purchases in a bag. At *Theaterplatz,* she finally left the main shopping streets and turned left into *Kornhausplatz,* a quieter cobbled square leading north to one of the main bridges over the Aare. She walked on, crossed the high new steel bridge, the *Kornhausbrücke,* over the steep-sided course of the blue-green river, then followed a long scenic driveway up a hill through an area of woodland and cherry trees, and entered the lobby of a hotel perched on the hillside above the Aare. The Hotel *Landhaus,* screened by tall cedars and pines, was one of the most select and expensive in the city. Certainly Joe had never stayed there before, even when his finances had been in good order. The exterior of the building was an interesting mix of architectural styles, but predominantly designed to resemble a Renaissance palace, with limestone walls and arcaded courtyards like a Florentine *palazzo,* which seemed to exude an aura of Mediterranean warmth even on a cold Swiss day.

Joe walked up the snowy sunlit driveway through the woods to the entrance too, from where he saw Monique check in at the reception desk in the sumptuous lobby. Standing just outside the main revolving door, Joe got a glimpse inside of the hotel's mid-European nineteenth-century style: crystal chandeliers, oil paintings of Alpine landscapes, mounted heads of deer and ibex on the walls. Judging by the hushed tones of the hotel staff and their quiet decorum as they went about their various tasks, the lobby seemed to have the rarefied and stilted atmosphere of a London gentleman's club. (Joe admittedly had to use his imagination to make that mental comparison, never having actually crossed the threshold of a London gentleman's club.)

A porter was dispatched to a two-wheeler cab parked on the driveway - presumably the one to which Monique had entrusted her bags at the station. Monique seemed to be planning a stay of several days at least, judging from the amount of luggage that was unloaded from the cab and brought inside. Somehow she seemed to have acquired far more baggage than Joe had noticed she'd had at the Gare de Lyon in Paris last evening.

Through the glass-panelled entrance door, Joe eventually saw her get in the open grille wrought-iron elevator, accompanied by a white-haired porter. The birdcage elevator disappeared from sight as the counter moved from ground to four, the top floor. All the best rooms were likely to be on the south side of the hotel, Joe surmised, with balcony views of the *Altstadt* and the backdrop peaks of the Bernese Oberland. And Monique looked like a young lady who was unlikely to settle for anything less than the best, so this seemed like the likeliest place she would take a room. So he quickly retraced his steps down the driveway through the woods, and found his way to *Schänzlistrasse,* a street at the top of the steep wooded north bank of the river, from which he thought it should be possible to get a good view of the front of the hotel.

In this he was proved correct, although at first he saw no sign of any activity on the top floor to suggest that Mademoiselle Langevin was being shown a room on that side of the building. Joe was just beginning to think that he might have been wrong in his assumption about which side of the hotel Monique would choose to stay, when he saw a window open and a curtain flutter as the white-haired porter showed a hidden hotel guest the balcony. Joe was just mentally counting the number of window balconies between that room and the lobby – one, two, three, *four* - when he thought he detected a flash of colour inside the room – a suggestion of a woman dressed in green perhaps, turning her head of lustrous chestnut hair...

*

There was a restaurant in *Schänzlistrasse* with a high garden terrace that offered not only a picturesque view of Bern's *Altstadt* but - better from Joseph Appeldoorn's point of view - an even more useful one of both the main entrance and side entrance to the Hotel *Landhaus,* even if partly obscured by a large deodar tree. (It was true that he couldn't see any staff or tradesmen's entrance from here, but it seemed unlikely to him that Monique Langevin would use either of those, unless she suspected she was being watched.)

Despite the biting wind, Joe found himself a table on the outside terrace, and ordered *Kaffee* and *Bernerplatte* - green beans, chops and sausage and bacon – while he debated what to do next. It occurred to him that perhaps he should have already had a plan thought out of what he intended to do when he got to Switzerland. His mentor, John Kautsky, the head of the Pinkerton Detective Agency in New York City, would have been bitterly disappointed with him if he'd known how badly prepared he was for this first bit of real police work...

He was out of his depth, he knew. Should he simply confront Monique? Threaten her with exposure to the Swiss police if she didn't tell him where Eleanor was? He had a revolver - an English-made Webley-Fosbery automatic revolver, thirty-eight calibre, eight-shot - in his baggage left at the *Hauptbahnhof.* Perhaps it was even a big enough gun to frighten a woman like Monique Langevin...although, with his personal knowledge of this formidable mademoiselle, Joe rather doubted that premise somehow.

Should he instead just go and tell the Prefect of Police here in Bern that a probable murderess was staying at the Hotel Landhaus? Joe could imagine the response if the local police were anything like the unhelpful Monsieur Le Boeuf in Paris. *Who do you say this woman killed, Mein Herr? And what proof do you have of this? And you say she tried to kill you too? Then why did you not report it in Paris, if that is where this supposed event took place...?*

No, that would not do. Therefore a direct confrontation with Monique, backed up by threats, seemed to be the only sensible course of action. Perhaps he could think of something subtler, though, than simply pointing a revolver at her head...

It was then that Joe saw another familiar face and figure – that of Miss Charlotte Cordingly – stepping down from another two-wheeler cab newly arrived at the entrance to the hotel. Joe was nearly fifty metres away but still quickly held up a menu card to conceal his face. Miss Cordingly got down from the cab and marched through the main entrance door with surprising vigour, before the surprised doorman even had time to react, in fact. The *Landhaus,* it seemed, was clearly a popular destination with the passengers from the Paris train.

The distant clock tower was just striking two when Joe decided it was time to confront Mlle Langevin; this time, though, he would be prepared for whatever dangerous or lunatic things she might do. If she was willing to co-operate and reveal to him what she knew of Eleanor Winthrop's disappearance and present whereabouts, then he, on his part, was quite prepared to overlook her other transgressions, even murder.

He breezed confidently into the lobby like a guest; he was dressed well enough to be taken for one, in a fine worsted English suit and bowler. He avoided going to the reception desk or consulting anyone, and instead marched straight over to the elevator. The hotel porter did stare at him for a moment as Joe asked the elevator operator for the fourth floor. But Joe looked back and nodded perceptibly as if he knew the porter, and the man seemed to relax his gaze and did not challenge him.

The top corridor had gilt wall gas lamps, gold-embossed wallpaper, and a deep blue shag pile carpet that must be hell for the staff to keep clean, Joe thought. A bright shaft of sunlight pierced the tall window at the end of the corridor. The view through the window - brilliant blue sky, snow-covered forested mountains of the *Mittelland* - seemed more like a painted stage backdrop than reality.

Joe counted off four doors from the elevator on the front side of the building and found what he believed to be Monique Langevin's room. He had a plan formulated by now; he would knock, pretending to be room service and, when she answered, he would force the door open and quickly overpower her. Provided she was disarmed of any pieces of sharp steel, Joe was sure that he could deal comfortably with Mlle Langevin, notwithstanding her previous violent conduct.

He put his ear to the door, but could hear no sound from inside. Yet that didn't mean she wasn't in there; Joe wasn't sure any sound would penetrate two inches of solid mahogany. He saw that light was issuing through the keyhole so, after a quick look up and down the corridor, he dropped to his right knee to put his ear to the hole. But it was his eye rather than his ear that was drawn naturally to the keyhole as he found he could see a surprisingly large amount through the wide aperture.

Someone *was* inside. He could see her only from the chest down: a young woman, partially undressed, wearing black stockings, a white cotton blouse, corset and tight cotton bloomers. She was standing in a casual pose, probably admiring her own figure in a full-length mirror. She turned a little and then wiggled her bottom in the mirror – and a delightfully curvaceous rear it was, displayed in those bloomers, Joe had to admit, even if it did belong to such a poisonous creature as Monique Langevin. She was holding something in her right hand, something burning; Joe could smell it even through the keyhole. Then her hand dropped and the article came into the view of his restricted window - a smoking black cheroot held casually between two fingers. He couldn't see the woman's face, though, until she bent down to straighten a wrinkle in her stocking and he caught a brief view of her face in his line of sight.

Joe had been sure the woman had to be Monique Langevin and the cheroot had seemed almost confirmation of that. Yet his surprise was total when he recognized the face and, more particularly, the teeth...

It was Miss Cordingly from the train...

Joe was busy wondering both how he had managed to miscount the number of doors along the corridor and find the wrong room and - an even more perplexing conundrum - just how a woman as plain as Miss Cordingly could contrive to look quite so enticing in her underwear, when he heard a loud cough at his side.

Somehow he found the resolve not to jump to his feet like a small boy caught doing something unmentionable. His gaze turned first to reveal a dark skirt, white apron and a pair of perfectly polished laced black shoes, and then upwards to confront a pretty face and a pair of cornflower-blue eyes. The eyes, Joe noted, were icy with indignation and suspicion.

Joe finally eased himself slowly to his feet. '*Gruezi,*' he said sheepishly. '*Entschuldigen Sie. Ich habe mein Schlüssel vergessen.*'

For a moment the girl's face seemed to relax, but then reddened again with renewed suspicion. 'Are you staying here, sir?' she challenged him in Swiss German. 'I haven't seen you here before. Even if you are a guest, this is not *your* room, I think.' She began to back away slowly. 'I am going to call the hotel doorman, and he will call the police...'

Joe remonstrated with her. 'No, please...Yes, you're right. I am not staying here. Not yet anyway. My name is Ernst Bergmann –' the name of a friend from the Zurich Polytechnic had popped immediately into his head – 'and I've just arrived from Zurich this morning.' Joe knew his accent and his looks were both authentic enough to fool even a Swiss, after three years of living and studying in Zurich. 'But my fiancée *is* staying on this floor.' He shifted his feet and tried to look like a forlorn suitor. 'Look, we had a row before she left Zurich so I followed her to Bern hoping to find her and make it up with her. I knew she was staying here but I wasn't sure which room. I don't want to lose her,' he added hopefully, when he saw that the girl still seemed undecided about whether to call the police or not.

But that last bit of improvisation seemed to have done the trick; the girl's face softened as Joe put on the most honest expression he could manage. 'What does your fiancée look like, *Mein Herr?*' she asked.

The polite form of address from the girl encouraged Joe further. 'She is French, quite tall, very elegant and pretty. Her hair is a beautiful shade of chestnut brown.' The young chambermaid's expression melted even more. 'She was wearing green, I think, when she arrived today. Her name is Monique but she may be using another name, Martine or Joelle.'

The chambermaid giggled. 'Then you're peering into the wrong room, *Mein Herr*,' she said dryly. 'The lady you want is in the next room. This one has just been occupied by an Englishwoman, I believe.' She studied Joe's face with seeming admiration for the first time. 'Not your type at all, I think.'

Joe smiled at her, and wondered what he should say or do next.

'Perhaps I should knock at the right door for you, *Mein Herr*,' the girl suggested diffidently

'No, don't do that,' Joe said hurriedly, beginning to wish the floor would swallow him up. All it needed now was for Miss Cordingly, or Monique Langevin herself, to poke either of their respective heads out into the corridor and inquire what was going on outside their doors. 'Perhaps it's better if I just wait for her in the lobby. I'm sure she will be down soon, and then I can take her for a walk and apologise for my behaviour.'

'Perhaps that would be better,' the girl agreed. Joe could detect a trace of suspicion still in those baby-blue eyes so he moved quickly towards the elevator before she changed her mind.

When he returned to the lobby he did not take a seat under one of the potted palms, though, but walked straight out into the street with a long sigh of relief.

*

Joe hadn't learned his lesson, though. Twenty minutes later he was back inside the hotel. This time he used the fire escape at the concealed rear of the building and climbed it cautiously, after a nervous look around the backyard. Like everything else in Switzerland, even the backyard was a masterpiece of cleanliness and organisation, surrounded by a clipped berberis hedge, the garbage cans in straight shiny rows, the paving slabs swept clean by industrious Swiss hands. If the Swiss had chosen to carve out a foreign empire in Asia and Africa like so many other European countries, would that empire have ended up all looking as orderly as this, Joe wondered. Yet, of course, the last thing the Swiss would ever aspire to would be a foreign empire dominating other people – their own history of being the frequent pawn of powerful neighbouring empires made such an ambition impossible to an amiable race like the Swiss.

Joe rapidly climbed four flights of stairs and squeezed through an accessible open window at the top landing, where he found himself in an inside service staircase which led eventually to the same blue and gold corridor as before. This time he moved immediately to the right door; clearly he had somehow miscounted from outside, and Monique Langevin's room had to be the *fifth* one along from the elevator, the last room but one on that side.

After checking up and down the corridor for any sign of the chambermaid, Joe tried putting his eye to the right keyhole this time. This one too had no key in it but the room itself, unlike Miss Cordingly's, appeared to be empty. He then tried his ear against the keyhole and got a similarly blank result – not the slightest sound from inside.

He finally knocked on the door to see if that provoked any reaction from inside. But no one came to answer, and the door clearly was locked.

So it seemed, to his chagrin, that Monique might have given him the slip after all, and gone out again without being seen. In desperation Joe decided to pick the lock. In his first week with Pinkertons, a retired old Irish cop from the Lower East Side called Mickey McGuckin had taught Joe the intricacies of lock picking, and he'd proved himself a willing and natural pupil. Even the best Chubb locks were no match for his skill now - after a year of practice only the complexities of the devilish Bramah locks could defeat him still.

This elderly and cumbersome Swiss lock was child's play; in half a minute he was inside the room. Although he saw, looking around, that it wasn't actually a single room, but rather a suite of rooms: sitting room, bedroom and maid's room, with even its own private bathroom. Luxury indeed... This suite could have housed a family comfortably, never mind a single lady's maid or teacher. Even Monique's former employer, the Comtesse de Pourtales, would not have been ashamed to stay here, Joe reflected.

Everything in the suite was one shade of blue or another – bedspread, wallpaper, even the upholstery to the chaise longue. The bed in the main bedroom was made up, and had not yet been slept in, or even reclined upon, apparently. Some clothes – Monique's presumably – lay draped over the back of a chair. The French window to the balcony was slightly open, fresh wintry air wafting the lace curtains.

Joe walked tentatively into the bathroom and stopped in his tracks as suddenly as if he'd walked into a solid wall. Time seemed slowed to an uncertain crawl as his mind groped with the unexpected scene before him. Here, the blue theme of the suite was replaced by a more jarring white and red.

The wall tiles and enamel of the bath were white, but speckled randomly with red; while the water in the bath was a uniform red throughout. But not the comforting colour of rose petals – the water was coloured a rather more sinister shade of red than that.

Monique Langevin lay naked in that bath of red water, saying nothing at all in response to the arrival of her visitor. But this reticence to speak was not entirely unexpected, since her throat had been cut from ear to ear...

Was that a look almost of aggrieved surprise on her white waxy face? Joe wondered, his stomach threatening to heave. She was after all a nifty girl with a blade herself, as Joe could testify, so perhaps she had reason to feel aggrieved at meeting such a fate...

Was that truly the reason for her surprised look? Had she in those last few moments of her existence been able to appreciate the supreme culminating irony of her life...?

CHAPTER 5

Tuesday 11th March 1902

In a dazed state, Joe Appeldoorn retreated from the bathroom to the relative normality of the sitting room, and sat down on the chaise longue.

He struggled to think what to do; the certainties that underpinned his world had been shaken profoundly by the brutality of this murder. Until two years ago he'd been a cosseted college boy, cloistered in his own secluded privileged world, with little or no experience of the seamier side of life. And while it was true that he had been hardened to some extent by those two years of detective work in New York City and its environs, he'd never before had to deal with the sight of a young woman in a bath with her throat cut. For the first time since coming to Europe, the thought of Eleanor Winthrop – or, more accurately, the reward for finding her – had slipped completely from his conscious mind.

Part of him – the regular law-abiding citizen part - wanted to walk straight down to the lobby and inform the hotel manager what had happened here. Yet another part of him, though – the former college boy - only wanted to get as far away from this room as possible and forget this had ever happened – perhaps the same part of him that realised *he* personally would be in big trouble with the police, given his unexplained presence in the hotel and his previous odd behaviour. He reminded himself that he'd given a false name to that chambermaid, had returned up a fire escape illegally, and then broken into this suite.

And yet another part of him – the aspiring detective – wanted to know who'd done this terrible thing. If he had been a real Pinkerton Agency man, with far more than two years of experience behind him, he knew this would have been the time to start sifting the room diligently for clues. This room, and the bathroom, must certainly contain the *fingerprints* of the person who had killed Monique Langevin...

*

John Kautsky, the head of the Pinkerton Detective Agency in New York, had been a close friend of Joe's father; it was he who had persuaded Joe to try a career in detective work, after the Appeldoorn family engineering business had collapsed, and his father had died suddenly, leaving massive debts. Kautsky had always been keen to embrace new technology in the fight against crime, to use the study of science to improve levels of proof and prevent miscarriages of justice. Kautsky had entertained high hopes that Joe Appeldoorn - with his first-rate scientific education in one of the best institutions in Europe - would perhaps bring the agency radical new ideas and methods.

Science was, it seemed, already making a big difference in police detection work. 'Back in 'eighty-two,' Kautsky told Joe one night over a couple of beers in a smoke-filled Irish bar on East 47th Street, 'this French guy, Alphonse Bertillon, a clerk in the Prefecture of Police of Paris, came up with a system of classification of measurement of various parts of the body, that he called anthropometry, or some such fancy word. But nobody in the Paris police found it that useful in practice in helping to identify criminals. Then, in the nineties, an English guy working out in India, Sir Edward Henry, also experimented with the idea, and he came to the conclusion that *fingerprints* were a much more reliable and practical means of identifying individuals than anything else. No two humans have the same fingerprints – not even identical twins. Now it seems like the British police have followed Henry's system and are introducing the use of fingerprinting into New Scotland Yard. I tell you what, Joseph, we've got to get ourselves some of that know-how, *and quickly...*'

*

Joe wished that John Kautsky were here in this Bern hotel room right now, because his boss had soon become quite an expert himself with the new-fangled science of fingerprinting to identify criminals. And this room was probably wall-to-wall fingerprints...

But there was no point in wishing for what he didn't have. Joe hadn't expected to need scientific skills like that for this assignment so he would have to make use of what his eyes and instincts could tell him had happened.

He forced himself to return to the bathroom to examine the victim in more detail. Monique Langevin was - not unsurprisingly perhaps - entirely naked in the bath, but the viscous red water mostly preserved her modesty from casual gaze. The small mole on her left cheek was more noticeable now, set against the dead whiteness of her skin.

The weapon had probably been a cutthroat razor, Joe decided from an inspection of the wound; that suggested a man had done this terrible thing - presumably a man she'd trusted intimately. Women, after all, did not as a rule allow strange men to walk in on their bath without making a fuss about it. She must have been taken by surprise because there was barely any blood or water on the floor around the bath. The visitor to her bathroom had sliced cleanly through her jugular vein like a surgeon, and she'd died in seconds, unable to scream for the volume of blood gushing up through her throat. Although the whole act had been quick and efficient, it still seemed unlikely that the murderer could have managed it without getting *some* blood on himself in the process - but perhaps not enough to call attention to himself when he was getting away.

Joe went back to the sitting room, immersed in thought. Monique's long green skirt and cream-white blouse lay on a chair, together with her underwear and stockings. The cotton of her drawers still felt warm to the touch. That briefly affected him, knowing the woman had been dead for fifteen minutes or more, and yet the scent and warmth of her body was still retained slightly in these scattered bits of clothing. He saw the new pair of shoes she had bought barely two hours ago, still pristine and untouched in their box - a stylish pair of patent leather shoes for evening wear that were destined now never to be worn properly by Mlle Monique Langevin...

These personal and intimate mementoes of the dead woman were almost enough to make Joe Appeldoorn feel some pity for her.

Almost, but not quite...

He opened the French windows and walked cautiously out onto the balcony. He saw there was a good eight-foot gap between the balcony and the fire escape at the front corner of the building. Yet Joe thought it was possible for an athletic person to jump that gap and escape that way – in fact, Monique Langevin herself, judging by the athletic manner of her escape from his own apartment in Paris, could have probably made it fairly easily.

But it seemed more likely to Joe that the murderer had simply used the front door and locked it behind him on leaving. Monique had been taking a bath, so must have deliberately left the door to the suite unlocked because she was expecting someone...

And that same person was almost certainly the man who had killed her, for whatever reason...

Her luggage – all high-quality calfskin - had been delivered by the porter to the room, but had not yet been opened or unpacked. Joe would have liked to search through it all but he knew it would take hours to do properly, and he could feel a knot of tension building as his instincts started telling him it was time to get away while he still had the chance.

He hadn't yet given up all hope of finding a clue to the whereabouts of Eleanor Winthrop, though, and he went quickly around the suite again looking for anything unusual, anything that jarred. On a bedside table in the bedroom, he found an open Gideon's Bible, which stirred his interest a little.

Perhaps Monique had been a good Catholic girl after all, he wondered dryly, despite her hobby of slitting throats. Yet, even for a good Catholic girl, it seemed unlikely to Joe that she'd been browsing through the bible for spiritual inspiration while running her bath. He picked up the book and shook it out; a folded printed sheet of paper fluttered to the carpet. He retrieved it; it was disappointing, though – merely a pamphlet advertising a meeting of the Social Democratic Federation of Zurich on Friday, March the 14th. That was this coming Friday, and the main speaker was going to be one Vladimir Ilyich Ulyanov, presumably a Russian émigré. It didn't sound to Joe like the most exciting way to spend a Friday evening - to be forced to listen to the ramblings of earnest young socialists - but each to their own. On the back of the pamphlet, he found something moderately more interesting though: someone – Monique presumably - had scrawled a cryptic word in the Cyrillic Russian alphabet. Joe knew just enough Russian to recognise the word as "*Narodniki*", although the word – or was it a name? - meant nothing to him.

He folded the pamphlet again and replaced the sheet in the bible. Then his heart jumped as a loud knock came on the outside door to the suite.

Joe was already on his way out to the balcony, still holding the bible, before the knock was repeated rapidly several times. He got onto the balcony and was just slipping the bible inside his undershirt for safekeeping when the door was opened with an apologetic cough from the person outside. Joe got the barest glimpse of the pretty chambermaid with the baby-blue eyes, with the hotel porter from the lobby standing just behind her, before he ducked out of her sight on the balcony.

The thought of how he was going to be able to explain his presence in this room, and, more especially, that of the dead woman – his "fiancée" - in the bath, made the decision for him, and he jumped on top of the stone balustrade of the balcony without delay and launched himself across the eight feet of intervening space to the fire escape.

His right foot landed on a narrow ledge of ironwork on the fire escape landing, his hand grasping for a vertical stanchion. But he lost his grip on the slippery iron when he heard the girl scream from inside the room - he guessed she had just walked into the bathroom...

Joe slid earthwards as his hands slipped down the stanchion, but he was able to arrest his fall using the steel toes of his shoes as brakes against the iron bracing, and then grabbing a horizontal rail. In a second he was on the fire escape proper and taking the steps three at a time on the way down. As he got to the bottom, he heard heavy steps already thudding on the ironwork above him.

He stopped for a second to think. *Why on Earth was he running?* Innocent men don't run, do they? Yet innocent men with this much circumstantial evidence against them did...

Joe quickly ran on and found himself in a cobbled stable yard at the side of the hotel, lined with horse stalls on three sides. The horses continued to munch hay and regard him from their comfortable stalls with a typically equine lack of curiosity, as he looked around desperately for an exit. Fortunately there were no grooms or stable lads about.

Joe finally found a narrow straw-covered alleyway leading out into the grounds of the hotel. From there he walked briskly down a curving track through the snowy woods to *Schänzlistrasse*, then back to the *Kornhausbrucke*, which he crossed to get back into the *Altstadt*.

Trying hard not to break into a run, he turned briskly into *Kramgasse* and then continued east along *Gerechtigkeitgasse* as if he was merely in a routine hurry. Finally he slowed to a normal walk, then to a saunter to match other pedestrians, as he began feeling relatively secure again. He could feel the weight of the Gideon's Bible still safely lodged inside his undershirt, and was about to surreptitiously take it out to inspect it again in more detail, when he felt a firm hand take him by the shoulder...

He spun around in anguish, then tried to relax his face as he recognised the man accosting him.

'Why, Herr Blumenfeld. I'm sorry. I didn't see you there.'

Blumenfeld smiled. 'No, *my* apologies for the rude way I attracted your attention. Forgive me. You do seem nervous, though, Herr Appeldoorn.'

'You did make me jump,' Joe admitted.

'Sign of a guilty conscience, perhaps.' Blumenfeld smiled guilelessly.

'Perhaps.' Joe tried to smile back, but his face felt as stiff as cardboard.

Blumenfeld narrowed his eyes and studied him closely. 'Where were you heading, Herr Appeldoorn?'

Joe's mind was a blank. 'Oh, I was planning to take a walk up that hill there, on the other side of the *Nydeggbrucke*.'

'Oh, do that later. Why not indulge yourself and join me first for afternoon coffee and some cake? They bake the most delicious Black Forest cake in the world here in Bern, and I know a little café just along here where they do the best even in Bern. And they also have the prettiest waitresses, better even than Bavarian girls.' He lowered his voice to a conspiratorial whisper. 'As a good German, I shouldn't say such things, but it's true.'

Joe accepted the invitation for the simple reason that it seemed like a useful time for him to have a companion. If the alarm had been raised by now, they would be searching the streets of Bern for a lone man matching his description. Better too to hide among a crowd of shoppers and tourists where he wouldn't stand out.

What was clear was that he couldn't afford to be caught and questioned; Joe wasn't sure if the porter from the Hotel *Landhaus* would be able to identify him - but that pretty chambermaid certainly would...

*

The café in G*erechtigkeitgasse* lived up to Herr Blumenfeld's promises, both with regard to the quality of the *Schwarzwälderkirschtorte,* and to the pink-cheeked beauty of the blonde-plaited waitresses.

The coffee too was excellent. Joe might even have been enjoying himself, if he hadn't spent much of the time nervously looking for signs of uniformed policemen searching the streets. So far, though, the response of the Bern Prefecture of Police to the murder of a woman in their city appeared to be nil.

Joe had taken off his jacket and bowler hat by now, though more to change his appearance than because he felt warm.

That seemed to concern Herr Blumenfeld considerably. 'Aren't you cold sitting like that, Herr Appeldoorn? It's hardly spring weather yet.'

'No, I'm not cold at all. Quite the opposite.' Joe looked around in alarm as he saw a uniformed policeman in the street for the first time. But from the casual manner of this young officer, it seemed clear that no general hue and cry had been raised just yet.

'Have you travelled widely at all in your life, Herr Appeldoorn?' Blumenfeld asked. It seemed a harmless enough question but Joe felt uneasy with the man's strange-coloured eyes fixed on him. Or perhaps it was just the reflection in those eyes of the sun, now settling low over the snow-covered western hills

'Only the eastern United States and a little bit of Europe, I'm afraid. And you?'

The German shrugged. 'As a matter of fact, I *have* travelled to some interesting places in my time. Let me think: Russia...Italy...England... Turkey...*amongst others*. I was even fortunate enough to visit your own splendid country last year.'

'Oh really? Where exactly?'

'Let me see...New York. Vermont. Oh, and the city of Boston too.'

Joe raised an eyebrow. 'Selling automobile engines?'

'No, that American trip was for pleasure only. But seeing your country did teach me much about the contrast between the Old and New Worlds. I greatly envy you your detachment from the rest of the world, Herr Appeldoorn. Your country is a continent in itself, after all. I wish we had such luxuries of space in Europe. Even our great German literary figure Goethe said, "*Amerika, du hast es besser als unser Kontinent.*" So many powerful nations sit here cheek by jowl on our small continent. Europe now stands at a crossroads in its history, I feel. Industrial power and wealth have created intense rivalries between the great empires of Europe. In the last twenty years we Europeans have carved up Africa between us, all in a bid to outdo our neighbours. But where do we go from here? And now there are even greater threats to stability from *within* our own societies: Anarchism and the growth of Socialism. Compared to your youthful country, we European powers are like ageing aristocrats with all our vigour gone, yet still bickering among ourselves even when suffering from an incurable cancer.'

'Cancer?'

'Yes, the cancer of the proletariat, who seem determined to take over the reins of power by sheer weight of numbers, if not talent or ability. Why, even *women* in your country want the vote now. What do they call themselves again...? *Suffragettes*, that's it.'

Joe felt his hackles rising. 'You don't think ordinary people have a right to share in the prosperity that they create?'

'A right to share in prosperity, yes. But not to usurp power completely. I think one man, one vote – or rather one *person*, one vote – while it might work in America, is a very unappealing idea in Europe - and intrinsically unfair, I would say. Are all men really equal in talents, in their capacity for hard work, in their genius? Despite what your own Declaration of Independence says, I think not. Although even that – please correct me if I'm wrong - only says that men are "created equal", not that they have to "*stay* equal". If political power falls into the hands of the proletariat in Europe – or rather the people who control them – then we shall sow the seeds of our own destruction. The old imperial order is dying, that is inevitable. Even your own poet, Kipling...'

'I think you're confusing me with an Englishman there, Herr Blumenfeld.'

Blumenfeld smiled. 'Perhaps I am,' he said mysteriously. 'Although Kipling *is* married to a countrywoman of yours, I believe, and you and he do speak the same mother tongue. Whatever...Kipling has recently written a poem foretelling the end of the British Empire. How does it go again...?' In perfect English, Blumenfeld began to recite, '...*Far-called, our navies melt away; On dune and headland sinks the fire: Lo, all our pomp of yesterday, Is one with Nineveh and Tyre!...The tumult and the shouting dies; The Captains and the Kings depart...* Splendid language, but that is the reality of what's happening in Europe now, Herr Appeldoorn - not just to the British, but also to France, Austro-Hungary and the Ottoman Empire. The old empires are fading into history and the question is: what kind of new political order will replace them?'

Joe objected. 'Surely Kipling isn't just foretelling the end of the British Empire, is he? Isn't he saying that all human enterprise is a vanity, and that everything crumbles to dust in the end - everything except the spiritual world?'

Blumenfeld conceded that point with a veiled smile. 'Well, perhaps.'

'I notice you didn't include the German Empire, or the Russian, in your list of doomed empires,' Joe went on.

'Well, the Russians are certainly doomed. They will be destroyed from within by their own ill-disciplined peasantry in time. That is inevitable. Then they will degenerate into barbarism.'

'And Germany?'

'Ah, the old imperial order in Germany will end too in due course, even though my country was only unified quite recently. But perhaps Germany will evolve a more sensible form of government for itself than the mindless whims and platitudes that democracy and universal suffrage would bring. I sincerely hope so, anyway.'

Joe had finished his coffee by now, and was sufficiently reassured by the lack of any serious police presence on the streets to believe that he might have shaken off any pursuit after all. 'Well, that's all very interesting, Herr Blumenfeld. I shall wait to see if your predictions about the future of Europe are fulfilled. But I'm afraid I really must take my leave now. I have to go and retrieve my luggage from the station and then find myself a hotel for the night.' He stood up and put on his short English jacket and bowler hat again.

Blumenfeld held up a restraining hand. 'Don't worry, Herr Appeldoorn. I know an excellent hotel nearby with rooms available, up by the *Rosengarten*. Let me show it to you. The manager is a close personal friend of mine...'

*

Blumenfeld stopped Joe when they were crossing the *Nydeggbrucke,* to admire the brown bears in the nearby pits.

'You must know those,' he said, pointing. 'The *Bärengraben,* the famous Bear Pits. Bern's symbol.'

Joe didn't know what he was supposed to say to that. 'Yes, I've seen them before. I don't know when their connection with Bern began, though, or how long they've kept brown bears here.'

'I do,' Blumenfeld volunteered. 'Actually from the city's beginnings in the late twelfth century. But I think it's cruel to keep such magnificent animals in such a squalid state. Don't you agree?'

It was nearly five by now and the sun lay on the snow-dusted rim of the western mountains. The last tourists were disappearing from the bridge, and Joe was becoming impatient. 'Can you show me where this hotel is now, Herr Blumenfeld? Otherwise I shall have to go looking for it myself.'

'Why are Americans always in so much of a hurry, Herr Appeldoorn? Enjoy the sunset over the mountains. You are a tourist after all, aren't you? And you never know when it might be your last one...'

Joe was becoming suspicious now. 'I didn't know there were any hotels up on that hill by the *Rosengarten*. Are you sure about this?'

Blumenfeld smiled amiably. 'Yes, there is one.' He held up his arm and pointed to a distant roof above the treetops.

Joe, with a shiver of apprehension, noticed for the first time a speckle of red on Blumenfeld's otherwise spotless shirt cuff, and backed quickly away from the man...

Too late, though...

A flash of steel glinted in Blumenfeld's hand and Joe sidestepped desperately to avoid the thrust of the blade directed straight at his heart. But he couldn't move fast enough to evade the lighting fast blow completely, and he saw the short blade plunge instead deep into the left side of his abdomen with a force that propelled him backwards. The impact threw him violently back against the top coping stone of the low limestone parapet to the bridge, but the loose coping gave way and Joe found himself unbalanced and toppling over backwards into the blue-green water.

The drop was twenty metres or more, but seemed even longer as he floundered in the air like a stricken albatross. As he struck the water his head found something hard and rocky, and blackness closed over him...

*

Joe re-emerged from a dream, not quite knowing whether he was alive or dead. He tried to remember what had just happened but his thoughts were as jumbled and confused as the rocky bed of the Aare.

Every instinct told him he should be dead, yet he clearly wasn't. *Death couldn't be like this, though, could it?* The world was reassuringly solid and three-dimensional around him. The water felt icy, the rocks hard and jagged against his belly, the thorns in the palm of his hand painful. Then he had a vague memory of coming to in the freezing water and trying desperately to stay afloat. Something particular jarred in his mind – he seemed to remember someone wading into the water to pull him out...someone quite unexpected...

He looked around as best he could with his stiff and sore neck. He lay sprawled on a rocky ledge, his legs still half in the glacial water of the River Aare, a hundred metres or so upstream of the bear pits and the *Nydeggbrucke,* where an area of thick woodland covered the steep eastern bank right down to the water's edge. With an effort he dragged himself further ashore and into the shelter of a buckthorn bush. The sun had gone down by now and the river was darkening in the twilight hush. A blackbird was singing from the branch of a nearby rowan tree. He peered through the bare twigs of the thorn bush and could see figures – official-looking figures – *policemen!* – on the bridge.

With his head aching fiercely, he remembered a little more about what had just happened. He felt his forehead gingerly and found a bump the size of a hen's egg on his right temple. He couldn't understand how he had survived that sixty-foot fall from the bridge, and still couldn't recall much about swimming ashore afterwards. But he must have swam, and not been simply swept along by the current, since somehow he'd managed to move against the fast flow of the river.

Why wasn't he dead, though? That thrust from Blumenfeld's knife should have killed any mortal man. He felt for his abdomen and then understood what had saved him: *the Gideon's Bible had taken the thrust* - the blade had gone right through the covers and the pages but had barely nicked the skin beneath.

Joe now remembered the speckles of blood on Blumenfeld's shirt cuff. *Did it mean that he, of all people, had murdered Monique? If so, in God's name why?* And why in the Hotel *Landhaus* when he could have killed her more easily perhaps on the train from Paris?

Joe had more immediate problems to think about, though, than why Blumenfeld might have slit Monique Langevin's throat. He was cold, wet and exhausted, a fugitive from the police himself; also he had no place to stay, and his bags were still in the left luggage department at the *Hauptbahnhof...*

He was trying to think of any way that he might be able to recover his luggage and get out of Bern without being apprehended, when a fierce rustling erupted in the nearby bushes.

A voice called out softly, 'Joseph! Where are you?'

Joe wondered if he was hallucinating from the effects of being struck over the head and nearly knifed to death twice in two days, when a figure crawled through the buckthorn and wild roses into the space beside him.

Joe recognised a familiar face in the twilight gloom. A large young man with strong features, a shock of wiry black hair, and a raffish moustache.

'That was quite a spectacular fall from the bridge, Joseph,' the man said conversationally. 'What an extraordinary person you are, as always! I must say you are still clearly just as unpredictable now as you were in Zurich.'

'Albert!' Joe remembered the voice now too — the one person at the Poly in Zurich he was never likely to forget. A highly gifted student of science but also a rebellious type, sarcastic to his teachers and an all-round pain in the ass — a little like himself in some respects.

'Can I help you, Joseph? You do look like you could use some assistance. And my little apartment is very near here,' Albert Einstein offered with a shy smile.

CHAPTER 6

Tuesday 11th March 1902

For the first time in several hours, Joseph Appeldoorn felt safe and able to relax. He sat on a sofa by a hot and crackling log fire, dressed in an old bathrobe of Albert's, while his clothes lay drying on a wooden clotheshorse nearby. Night had fallen over the city of Bern; outside, streetlights cast a muted gaseous glow over the street. A string quartet in the café below was playing a lilting Viennese waltz, and the sound carried through the window, which was slightly open despite the cold outside. The curtains to the apartment stirred fitfully, almost as if moving in time to the music.

Albert had always been a slob in his student days, Joe remembered, and graduation and the responsibilities of having to make a living didn't appear to have changed his approach to life as yet – he was still the Bohemian bachelor to the core. God help the woman who would end up with him, Joe thought, regarding the quiet devastation around him.

Einstein's second-floor, one-room apartment at number 32 *Gerechtigkeitgasse* had probably been a nice enough room a few weeks before when he first moved in, but now it resembled a bric-a-brac shop of the seediest kind. A sofa and six upholstered chairs were the main soft furniture, but were mostly occupied by precarious piles of books and dusty journals. The two wardrobes were already jam-packed with anything *but* clothes, which were instead scattered in untidy heaps around the room like molehills. A sickly spider plant by the window struggled to stay alive without the benefits of either light or water. A violin was perched on a small marble bust of Mozart; crumbs covered the carpet in a fine till that looked ready to sprout seedlings.

And everywhere there were books - more books than you could count. Heavy tomes on philosophy by Leibniz, Hegel and Kant; long scientific tracts by Maxwell, von Helmholz, Boltzmann, and Mach. Joe was glad at least that he could also see the occasional novel too among the heavy reading: the odd edition of Balzac and Dickens, and, in particular, Dostoyevsky's *The Brothers Karamazov*.

Albert hadn't put any serious questions to Joe since finding him half-drowned on the banks of the Aare, and Joe, in return, certainly hadn't volunteered any information. Albert hadn't chosen to lead his old student friend back into the *Altstadt* across the *Nydeggbrücke,* which was still swarming with policemen, but instead via the less busy *Kirchenfeldbrücke*, and then through small alleyways to the discreet rear entrance of his modest apartment building. It turned out that Albert lived close to the café where Joe had enjoyed his Black Forest cake with the treacherous Herr Blumenfeld. *Had that been meant as a condemned man's last meal?* Joe was now beginning to wonder.

It was Joe Appeldoorn himself who got the first serious question in, after they'd arrived at the apartment and he had taken off his drenched clothes. 'So what are you doing here in Bern, Albert? Are you doing research at the university?'

Albert made a rueful face. 'No, not at all. I wish I were. I couldn't find a *Privatdozent* place at any university in this country. Weber made sure of that.'

Joe nodded sympathetically: he had never got on particularly well with Professor Weber, but Einstein's relationship with the man had been a personal disaster. Professor Heinrich Weber, head of the physics department at the Poly– the *Eidgenössische Polytechnische Schule*, the Polytechnic school in Zurich - had been Albert's *bête noir*. Joe had once overheard Einstein being castigated in a corridor by the stern-faced Weber. "You're a smart boy, Einstein, a very smart boy. But you have one great fault: you never let yourself be told anything...!" In return Einstein had always addressed him cheekily as "Herr Weber" rather than the more polite "Herr Professor".

Joe glanced around the apartment. 'So what *are* you doing here?'

Albert shrugged his broad shoulders. 'I'm *trying* my best to forge an academic career for myself, Joseph, despite the hindrances of my former professor. I have already published a paper about the thermodynamics of liquid surfaces - surface tension.' He twisted his face and gave another self-effacing shrug. 'It's an ordinary piece of work, I realise, but I have to start somewhere.' His voice brightened with more enthusiasm. 'But I'm now busy with other more demanding papers on statistical mechanics and thermodynamics to try and prove the Second Law from first principles. What I'm really hoping to do is to produce a piece of work that's good enough to get me an external doctorate, so I can climb on the academic ladder that way. I did try submitting one paper to the University of Zurich recently but it was turned down as being of insufficient quality. So now I'm making a start on a more original thesis that might be good enough to get me a PhD.' His eyes gleamed briefly. 'You see, I've had an idea for something that I don't believe has been done before. I think it should be possible, by applying statistical techniques to solutions of sugar molecules in water, to find a new way to calculate Avogadro's Number, and to estimate the size of molecules.'

'Sounds interesting.' Joe was intrigued with the notion, despite everything else he'd gone through today.

'It is, because it might prove once and for all to the doubters that atoms and molecules really exist. So many chemists still don't believe in the reality of atoms and molecules, you know, but we physicists all do.'

'*I* was never a real physicist, Albert,' Joe denied ruefully. 'I'm only an electrical engineer, a mere technician, who was here in Europe trying to learn the basics of the new science.'

Albert scratched his thick curly hair. 'No, I think you are doing yourself an injustice there. You were always more than just a dabbler, Joseph. You might be mathematically naïve but you have a real physical insight into electrical phenomena. In that respect, you always reminded me of the young Michael Faraday...'

'*I* remind you of the young Michael Faraday?' Joe asked with a disbelieving smile. Despite knowing that such an assertion was nonsense, he was nevertheless deeply flattered by his friend's unlikely comparison. But he was suddenly tired of dissembling and wasting time with all these polite discussions about science, when what he was really impatient to discover was how Albert had stumbled so mysteriously on him today. 'How did you happen to find me today down by the river? How did you know where I was?'

Albert rummaged for his pipe among piles of papers. 'I saw you earlier, from the window here. It was about four this afternoon and you came down *Kramgasse,* almost running. I waved and shouted to you as you passed my window but you obviously didn't hear me. So I descended to the street to find you. But, by then, you had met someone. Who was that – for want of a better word - *gentleman*?'

'A German businessman called Blumenfeld. I met him on the train from Paris.' Joe felt disinclined to say anything further about Blumenfeld, but Albert clearly expected more. 'Why didn't you come and greet me then?'

'To be honest, I'm not sure why I didn't.' Albert filled his pipe from a tobacco pouch and lit it, with a sigh of satisfaction. 'Something in the unspoken language between you and your companion suggested something...' He seemed to be groping for the right word.

'Sinister?' Joe said, twisting his face.

Albert gave him a wry look. 'I was going to say...*puzzling.* Whatever the reason for my reticence to make my presence known to you immediately, when I saw you walk off with this "gentleman" to a café, I decided to follow.'

'Why didn't you join us at the café?'

'Again, I don't know. I decided I would wait until you were finished, and then invite you back here. You don't know how pleased I was to see you here again in Switzerland, Joseph. There are so many things I have to tell you.' Albert smiled sheepishly. 'I really didn't mean to, but I confess I soon found myself eavesdropping on your conversation. But, my word, your companion does have profoundly depressing and disgraceful political views. I was sincerely glad then that I hadn't introduced myself to you and your companion earlier, otherwise I might have been forced to box the ears of such a rascal as your Herr Blumenfeld.'

'He's certainly not *my* Herr Blumenfeld, Albert. That was only the third time I'd ever spoken to the man.' Joe studied Albert's face and decided to tease him a little. '*So...*you played the spy, did you?'

Albert nodded eagerly. 'Oh yes, gladly. To be frank, I was enjoying the feeling of intrigue. Childish but extremely satisfying. I followed you when you left the café too – rather expertly, I feel. I saw you and your obnoxious companion reach the *Nydeggbrücke* and stand looking at the bear pits. You both seemed to be waiting for something. I was even more curious by this time so I crossed over the *Untertorbrücke,* the next bridge downstream*,* and found a place on the east bank below the *Nydeggbrücke* to watch you.'

Joe held his breath as he remembered the terror of that moment when Blumenfeld had suddenly turned on him. 'And what did you see?'

'I can't be sure what I saw. I was concealed partly behind a tree, and you and your companion were standing on the far side of the bridge from me. But it looked to me as if Herr Blumenfeld deliberately pushed you over the south parapet of the bridge.'

'And what happened to my friend on the bridge?'

Albert grinned ruefully. 'I was hardly paying attention to him by this time, was I, with you dead or drowning in the river! I could see no sign of you being washed under the bridge in my direction so I thought you must still on the upstream side, perhaps clinging to one of the stone bridge piers. Assuming you weren't dead, of course, which also seemed a distinct possibility given the height of your fall. I ran along to the bear pits to see if I could catch sight of you, and was lucky enough to see you trying to crawl ashore further up the eastern bank. Then I lost sight of you in all the thick vegetation along that bank of the river. So I made my way down through the woods on the steep eastern bank, and was able to find you. I waded in and pulled you fully out of the water.'

'You saved my life then.' Joe shook his head in disbelief: lots of unlikely people were saving his life these days...

'No, I believe you saved yourself, Joseph. You were dazed and semi-conscious but you still had enough control of your limbs to keep yourself afloat, and even swim upstream against the stiff current. I checked you when I dragged you out; you'd obviously hit your head and swallowed a lot of water but you were breathing all right. So then I went for help.'

'Yet you didn't bring any,' Joe pointed out.

'No, I didn't.' Albert gave him a significant look but didn't elaborate why not. 'And worse, when I went back for you, I couldn't find you again in those thick bushes. That's why I ended up calling out your name in that ridiculous fashion.'

There came a sharp knock at the door that made Joe jump involuntarily. 'What's that? Are you expecting a visitor?'

'Don't look so worried, Joseph. It's just turned seven. That will be Maria Goppert, the woman from next door who cooks an evening meal for me every night. I ordered Raclette tonight – that's a cheese dish, if you remember. Maria always gives me generous portions -' Albert patted his rounded stomach with a grin -'...so you are welcome to share it with me. You look like you could use something warm inside you...'

*

'So, if you are not a *privatdozent* at the university, how have you been supporting yourself while you write your thesis?' Joe asked, as he finished off the last of his dinner.

Albert relaxed in a chair after clearing it of a pile of books. 'Since last year I've been teaching in high schools - first in Winterthur, and then, last winter, in Schaffhausen. But Marcel – you remember Grossmann? – has helped me find a more permanent job in the Civil Service here in Bern. At least I hope so. It hasn't been confirmed yet.' Albert frowned expressively. 'But I expect it will be in the next few months. Patent Officer Second Class, I hope, but I will settle for Third Class if I have to. Beggars can't be choosers, after all.' He hesitated. 'As soon as I have the job confirmed, Mileva will join me here in Bern. We are planning to marry.'

'Ah yes, Mileva.' Joe recalled her, a fellow student of theirs at the Poly- a quiet girl from Titel in Hungary. He could imagine that her Greek Catholic background wouldn't go down too well with Albert's parents, though, if he really was planning to marry her. Joe had not known Mileva Maric all that well but remembered her mass of dark hair, invariably tied up in a bun, matched by dark intense eyes. She'd struck him sometimes as being a little severe and humourless perhaps. But then it had taken an immense struggle over male prejudice and other obstacles for her to even get to the Zurich Polytechnic, when it was so unusual for a woman to study science at all. Even so, she didn't seem the *most* obvious choice as a prospective wife for Albert, who'd been popular with a lot of pretty girls, as Joe recalled, because of his sarcastic wit and sheer physical presence.

Joe studied his old friend again. He had changed hardly at all in the last two years – still the same pale brown skin, sensuous mouth, black moustache, the slightly bulbous nose. And especially the same pleasant voice.

'Perhaps I should get a doctor to have a look at your injuries, Joseph?' Einstein suggested. 'That was quite a bang you took on the head.'

Joe was bruised and battered by the experience, but knew enough about his own physical condition to realise that he hadn't done himself any permanent harm. 'No, I don't need a doctor, Albert.'

Albert gave a mighty yawn and leaned back, replete after his dinner. 'You always were an enigmatic person, Joseph, even as a student at the Polytechnic. You were the first American I'd ever met, and I admit I was a little nervous of you at first, not knowing quite what to expect. Before I met you, I was under the impression that America was a place with no culture at all, and almost no scientific endeavour. I had the image that all Americans were cowboys, or desperados. So, when I got to know an American like you, it was a little disappointing at first. It was difficult imagining someone like you in the Wild West, shooting six guns.'

Joe smiled wryly. 'Actually I've never been west of Cleveland in my entire life.' Nor had he ever fired a gun in anger, he could have added, although he had been taught how to shoot the Webley-Fosbery with reasonable accuracy.

Albert nodded thoughtfully. 'I've actually heard of this city of Cleveland, but only because a man called Michelson once tried to measure the drift of the ether there. A foolish notion, of course, yet the null result was very interesting.' Einstein grimaced. 'Are you going to tell me what really happened on the bridge between you and this Herr Blumenfeld?'

'Nothing. It was a stupid argument, that's all. You saw what sort of man he was. I just want to forget it.'

Einstein reached over for the evening newspaper and threw it on Joe's lap. 'You may not be able to forget it quite so easily.' The headline read: *Woman murdered in the Hotel Landhaus*. 'A young *Frenchwoman*,' Albert said with heavy emphasis, 'but unnamed so far.' He watched as Joe read quickly through the story. 'Joseph, you didn't ask me the reason why I didn't fetch help for you after I dragged you onto dry land.'

'All right. Why didn't you?'

'Because when I went for help, I saw there were a lot of policemen milling about in the area. At first I thought it might have been because someone else had reported your fall from the bridge. Yet the number of policemen seemed disproportionate if that were the case. As it happened, I knew one of these young policemen slightly so I asked him what all the commotion was about. He said a woman had been found murdered at the Hotel *Landhaus*. He asked me if I'd seen anyone answering the description of the main suspect: a young man of twenty to twenty-five, one hundred and ninety centimetres tall, dark hair, blue eyes, worsted suit, bowler hat.

Speaks Swiss German well but may nevertheless be a stranger to Bern. It occurred to me immediately that it could have been a near perfect description of my friend, Herr Joseph Appeldoorn of the United States.'

'So what did you do?'

Albert pursed his lips. 'I said I hadn't seen anyone like that...'

*

'I haven't killed anyone, Albert.'

'If I thought that for a minute, I would have handed you over at once, even though we are old friends.'

A long reflective pause ensued, then Albert said, 'The man who pushed you off the bridge – this Herr Blumenfeld – could he be something to do with the murdered woman?'

Joe nodded reluctantly. 'Perhaps.'

'Then my advice is: go to the Prefecture of Police, Joseph. They are quite reasonable people here, unlike the militaristic police force of Germany.'

'It's difficult for me to do that, Albert. No matter how reasonable the police are, they will suspect me. Even *I* would suspect me on the evidence! I was seen in the murdered woman's room. I asked a chambermaid about her. I gave the maid a false name and pretended to be the woman's fiancé. No, Albert...it's much better if I *don't* talk to the police.'

'Then I won't ask any more,' Albert said stiffly. 'You are welcome to stay here as long as you wish, though.'

Joe sighed in exasperation, but couldn't leave things in this unsatisfactory state, with Albert's suspicion hanging over his head. 'No, you're protecting me, so you deserve to know what's going on. The woman who was murdered is called Monique Langevin. I had followed her here from Paris.'

'Why? Are you a detective now?' Albert chortled at his own bizarre suggestion.

'I'm afraid that's exactly what I am. I now work for the Pinkerton Agency in New York.'

Albert was clearly disturbed. 'And what was your interest in this woman, Monique Langevin?'

'I thought she might be able to lead me to a missing American heiress called Eleanor Winthrop. And I have *twenty-five thousand reasons* for wanting to find her...'

*

Joe told Einstein more or less the whole story to date.

Albert had been silent for a long time, but finally stirred in the glow of the fire. 'I don't know what to say.'

Joe could hear a certain degree of bafflement in Albert's voice and wanted to explain the circumstances that had forced him to take on mercenary work like this. 'Your father was in the electrical engineering business like mine, wasn't he?' Joe asked him.

Albert nodded. 'He still is – and still financially unsuccessful, so that's why I feel such a burden on him. I've always felt guilty at not being able to help the family's finances.' He looked at Joe. 'But I thought your circumstances were different – I heard your father was a rich man.'

'He was at one time...not that I knew him that well as a kid, though.'

'Why was that?'

Joe grimaced. 'Well, I was an only child and, after my mother died, I was mainly brought up by my maternal grandmother and various governesses.' He paused, the memory of losing his mother still a real and painful one. 'Not that my father didn't care for me,' he went on. 'I'm sure he did, but business always dominated his life. In the eighties he was a very successful bicycle manufacturer in Philadelphia. But then he got the electrical bug and decided to diversify the business. He went on personally to invent new types of dynamos and generators far superior to the ones used by the other big companies. So they went for him, sued him for patent infringement, even though his designs were completely original. *They* sued *him*! The irony of it! It should have been the other way round. They drove him into financial ruin by forcing him to spend all his money, and more, trying to defend his patents. They simply dragged him through the courts until those carpetbagger lawyers had bled him dry. Being much richer and bigger companies, they could afford to wipe out the competition that way. American Capitalism at work!'

'So what happened to your father?'

'He died two years ago. The doctors said it was a heart attack, but I think his competitors just broke his will to live.'

'I'm sorry.'

Joe continued, 'My father had made me a nominal director of his company - not foreseeing the problems this would cause me - so I got landed with his debts. I still owe his creditors thousands of dollars but I'm determined to pay them off rather than declare bankruptcy so I can re-start my father's business in time. The factories still exist, even if the workforce has all been paid off. But I couldn't get another bank loan to keep going; my father's creditors and business rivals have seen to that – they want to get their hands on the lot. I took the job with Pinkerton simply to make ends meet initially, but then this chance – the opportunity to come to Europe and search for Miss Winthrop - came up. This one assignment could pay off all my debts in one fell swoop, if I can succeed. Miss Winthrop's grandfather was an old friend of my father's and he has effectively promised to pay off my creditors if I bring her safely home. Then I could get the factories and other assets back from the administrators.'

'So...you aim to follow in your father's footsteps. I too have that motivation. Whatever we do, it seems we are always unconsciously seeking our fathers' approval.'

Joe stood up by the still glowing fire. 'I can't tell you how much I want to triumph over my father's competitors. My father had other brilliant ideas, you know, other inventions that aren't public knowledge yet. But I need money and time to develop those ideas. I'm talking about radio communication, Albert - and not only short-range stuff. Have you heard that the Italian, Marconi, has recently sent signals right across the Atlantic?'

Albert grunted. 'Yes, of course I heard. I'm not so impractical, such an ivory-towered thinker, that I don't keep up with the practical advances of technology. Although I still don't fully understand how Marconi managed his trick - light travelling in straight lines should end up in outer space, not following the curve of the Earth's atmosphere.'

Joe seized upon that. 'My father was convinced that there must be some layer in the upper atmosphere that has electrical properties and will deflect electro-magnetic waves.'

Einstein was thoughtful. 'Yes, I had been thinking something similar myself.'

'But my father was looking beyond simply sending bleeps through space. He'd even thought up ways of perhaps encoding and sending sounds directly through the ether. Imagine sending direct speech between continents, almost instantaneously.' Einstein looked at him sharply and Joe smiled, understanding. 'Ah, of course, I forgot – your private obsession. According to you, there's no such thing as the luminiferous ether, is there? But nevertheless it still carries radio waves, Albert. And one day, we might even be able to hear music sent through the air on electro-magnetic waves, mark my words. Who knows, maybe even transmit moving images...?'

'I think you're letting your imagination get carried away now, Joseph. But you always had inventive ideas...' Albert changed the subject with brutal suddenness. 'If you don't want to go to the police about this woman's murder, what are you planning to do, may I ask?'

Joe sniffed. 'Get out of Bern, I suppose.'

'Aren't you concerned about getting justice for this dead woman? To at least direct the police in the direction of the likely murderer, Herr Blumenfeld?'

'Would you be shocked if I said I wasn't? Fraülein Langevin was probably a murderess herself, so my concern for her is not great, I'm afraid. And I don't have time to get embroiled in a long police investigation, even if I can prove my innocence in the end. I came to Europe to find Eleanor Winthrop and I can't do that from inside a police cell in Bern.'

Albert looked apologetic. 'Perhaps you may not be able to avoid it...'

'What do you mean by that?'

'I didn't find your bowler hat when I found you. Yet you were certainly wearing one when you fell from the bridge.'

'Yes, I must have lost it in the water...' Suddenly it occurred to Joe what Einstein was saying. 'It's got my name inside,' he remembered dismally.

'Then let's hope the police don't find it, or - if they do – pray they don't realise the connection.'

Joe thought for a second. 'And I still have the problem of how to get out of Bern. The police will presumably be watching the *Hauptbahnhof*.'

'Assuming you do manage to leave Bern undetected, what will you do then? Return to Paris and try and find the man, Gaspard, who has some connection with your missing heiress?'

'If all else fails, that's what I'll do. But first it's worth trying Zurich.' Joe reached over and picked up the Gideon's Bible he'd taken from the Hotel *Landhaus*. It was now ruined irrevocably by its exposure to the glacial water of the River Aare but the folded pamphlet inside, clearly made of sterner socialist print, was still readable enough. 'Monique Langevin came here to Switzerland for a reason, and it seems she might have been considering attending this meeting in Zurich on Friday...'

Albert took the pamphlet and looked wryly at the four matching holes created on the folded version by Herr Blumenfeld's knife.

'Eleanor always wanted to visit this country,' Joe explained. 'I have a strong feeling that she's right here in Switzerland, perhaps in Zurich.'

'That sounds to me more like wishful thinking than sound detective work,' Einstein commented, with gentle mockery.

CHAPTER 7

Thursday 13th March 1902

Joe Appeldoorn spent the whole of Wednesday laying low in Albert Einstein's one-room apartment, immediately above the noisy café in G*erechtigkeitgasse (*whose surprisingly boisterous late-night activities had kept him awake until nearly midnight on Tuesday night.)

Albert had lent him a cutthroat razor to shave with and made a space for him on the floor to sleep, so Joe had felt no need to venture too far – only as far, in fact, as the communal bathroom and WC on the top floor of the building. Perhaps the caution had been unnecessary, though. There'd been no sign of the Bern police frantically searching the *Altstadt,* house by house, for their chief suspect in the murder of the Frenchwoman at the Hotel *Landhaus* – this *was* liberal Switzerland after all, not Kaiser Wilhelm's militaristic German Empire.

Yet in truth Joe did feel like a fugitive, even though he knew he was entirely innocent, and had even come very close to becoming a victim himself. He had maintained his adamant stance to Albert that he wasn't going to go voluntarily to the police, no matter how liberal and understanding they were. Let the Swiss police find the real murderer of Monique Langevin by themselves, if they could; he wanted nothing to do with the investigation, and certainly nothing more to do with the murderous Herr Blumenfeld – assuming he was the guilty party...

Joe spent most of that Wednesday sitting at the window, watching the pretty girls of Bern parading in their spring finery in the street below, or, when he became bored with that, browsing through Albert's books and papers. In desperation to occupy his mind, he had even tried reading Albert's draft papers on Statistical Mechanics in which he was attempting to prove the Second Law of Thermodynamics. It occurred to Joe halfway through, though, that the theory looked rather familiar – in fact much like an already published work he'd seen on the same subject last year by a little-known American professor, Josiah Willard Gibbs. When Albert asked him what he thought of the paper, Joe didn't have the heart to tell him that he might have been pre-empted. He just hoped that Albert's thesis project, applying statistical techniques to find a new way of calculating Avogadro's Number, might be more original...

Joe also studied the local morning newspaper in as much detail as Albert's paper on thermodynamics. Despite the lack of any visual evidence of it that Joe could see from his window, it seemed that the police *were* combing the Old Town – looking in particular for a young Swiss man from Zurich called Ernst Bergmann, identified by an employee of the Hotel *Landhaus*, one Elsa Grommer.

Joe was pleased that his accent (and his suit, for that matter) had passed muster and not given him away as an American interloper. But the description of young Ernst was indeed embarrassingly close to his own: *190 centimetres tall, dark-haired, muscular build, blue eyes...*

Well! So that young chambermaid, Elsa, had even had time to notice his exact height and the colour of his eyes. (She did have beautiful cornflower-coloured eyes of her own, Joe now remembered slightly wistfully, realising that the chances of him forming a closer friendship with that young lady were gone forever.) It certainly boded badly for him if the police caught him now and paraded him in front of the attentive Fräulein Grommer, who obviously had the makings of a fine detective herself...

*

Joe had decided that there was no point in prolonging the discomfort and embarrassment of his confinement here in Bern for too long. He knew he would have to leave the security of this apartment and the genial company of Albert sometime soon, and risk trying to leave Bern by train. Albert had given no indication of it, yet Joe did feel very much an embarrassment to his friend, so was anxious not to test his hospitality too much. And an early departure was better, he told himself – particularly as he wanted to get to Zurich for that political meeting on Friday. That remained the one tenuous link he still had to the late unlamented Monique Langevin...*and perhaps also to Eleanor Winthrop*...

When Joe told him of his intention to leave on the Thursday evening train to Zurich, Albert made no protest or comment, and even agreed to go to the *Hauptbahnhof* and make a reservation and buy a first-class ticket for him.

On Thursday afternoon at four, Joe was finally ready to leave the protection of Einstein's apartment. As he was putting on his jacket – now newly pressed and cleaned, thanks to the attentions of Albert's kindly neighbour, Frau Goppert - a thought suddenly occurred to him. 'Isn't it your birthday tomorrow, Albert?'

Albert smiled. 'You have a good memory, Joseph. Yes, I reach the grand old age of twenty-three tomorrow. Time, the magician, is weaving her spell over me, as always. You know, I often think there is nothing quite as mysterious as time – it is such a commonplace concept, yet so little understood in reality.'

Joe grimaced. 'I'm sorry I can't stay and celebrate your birthday with you. We could have got drunk just like old times.'

'No matter, I have other friends here in Bern to celebrate it with. Conrad Habicht lives here now. Did you meet him in Zurich? And Michelangelo too – you certainly *did* know him.'

'Besso is in Bern too? You never said,' Joe chided his friend gently. 'I'm sorry to miss him.'

'I'll tell him you were here, and send him your regards.'

'Don't mention my troubles, though,' Joe warned.

Einstein coughed dryly. 'I won't, of course.'

'I'd better go now, even though the train doesn't leave until six. I still have to reclaim my bags from the left luggage counter at the *Hauptbahnhof*. And there may be problems with that...*if the police are watching the station...*' Joe left the rest of his worries unsaid.

'If you do manage to get on the train to Zurich, will you attend this political meeting you mentioned?'

Joe retrieved the pamphlet in question from the pile of other papers and books on the table, and looked at it again. 'It's the only possible clue I have at the moment to finding Eleanor, so I certainly will, even though political meetings are hardly to my taste.'

Albert smiled faintly. 'No, you were never very political, were you, Joseph?'

A long uncomfortable silence followed, broken finally by Albert. 'I believe I have even heard of this man, Ulyanov, who is speaking. One of the new generation of Russian émigré dissidents.'

Joe sighed. 'Then I hope he knows some dirty jokes at least, otherwise it sounds like a *long* evening.'

Albert smiled again broadly. 'You always were a good friend, Joseph. We should never have lost touch, even if there was an ocean between us.'

Joe turned to go, and then remembered something else he'd meant to say, a thought from his student days. 'Albert, I've been meaning to ask you. Did you ever solve that riddle you were always going on about when we were students together? A real conundrum that you used to plague Weber with in his lectures - *What would I see if I could fly at the speed of light alongside a ray of light?* You claimed that, according to Maxwell's laws, you should see a stationary electric and magnetic field. And yet such a thing doesn't apparently exist. I remember that question used to drive Weber crazy because he clearly didn't have an answer for it. Did you ever solve that paradox, and work out what really does happen when you reach the speed of light?'

Albert sighed ruefully. 'No, not yet. But perhaps I will one day. After all, if nothing else, I shall have lots of time for thinking, as a Patent Officer Third Class.'

'You mean *Second* Class, surely?'

Albert gave a great booming laugh. 'Yes, *Second Class* – absolutely! A Second Class civil servant – that shall be the height of my ambition from now on.'

They shook hands. 'Shall I come with you to the station?' Albert asked. 'Will that help or hinder you?'

Joe declined the offer. 'It's not necessary. I don't want to get you involved any further than you are. You've done enough for me already.'

'I am leaving Bern again in a few days, myself - returning to Schaffhausen to bring back some more of my personal possessions,' Albert said.

Joe looked around the quiet devastation of the apartment. 'Your landlady will be *so* pleased to hear that,' he commented with a grin.

Albert grinned back before handing Joe a slip of paper. 'If you're anywhere near Schaffhausen in the next week or so, you can contact me there if you need any help with anything. Alibis, character references, that sort of thing...' he added dryly.

Joe pocketed the slip of paper and was about to put the pamphlet about the meeting in Zurich also in his inside pocket when he had another thought. He turned the pamphlet over, and studied the word scrawled there. 'Albert, can you read this word?' he asked.

Albert looked puzzled. 'Let me see. It's certainly Russian. I think it says "*Narodniki*", doesn't it? But I can't say I've ever heard that word before, to my knowledge.'

'No, me neither...'

*

Joe was uneasy as he walked through the *Altstadt*. All along *Marktgasse,* and then *Spitalgasse,* he felt as if he was going to feel a heavy hand on his shoulder any moment, and then a bluff request from a stern-faced officer to accompany him to the nearest police station. But he was doing his best to look unconcerned, standing up to his full height, and even deliberately browsing in shop windows on the way. Finally, with great relief, though, he saw that he had reached *Bahnhofplatz* and the main railway station, the *Hauptbahnhof.*

It was then that he saw the scale of his problem. The square and the forecourt of the station were crawling with uniformed policemen, some even armed. It was an odd anomaly, perhaps because of their difficult history, that the peace-loving and amiable Swiss should be so enamoured of firearms.

Joe waited behind a tall stone pillar near the entrance while he decided what to do. Even more people were milling about on the concourse inside the station so, paradoxically, he thought he might be less exposed inside the station than outside. But Joe could also see from his vantage point that uniformed police were closely scrutinising the identity of everyone boarding departing trains.

First things first, though - he still had to retrieve his bags from the left luggage, before he could even begin to think about how to get past the uniformed policemen checking tickets and identities. He reminded himself that he had his English-made Webley-Fosbery automatic revolver inside one of his bags, a weapon which he had smuggled into Switzerland illegally. If the police were searching luggage too, then his goose was well and truly cooked.

Joe wondered what John Kautsky would say if the man he'd entrusted with the relatively straightforward task of finding a runaway girl in Europe should end up being arrested in Switzerland for murder and possession of an illegal weapon...

Joe could almost hear Kautsky's full range of rich and expressive expletives, if such a thing happened: *He's got himself arrested where, for Christ's sake? In Switzerland!* The home of cuckoo clocks and cheese...! *How the hell has he managed that...?*

Joe thought he'd much rather be shot here as a fugitive on Bern Station by Swiss police than undergo that kind of ignominy...

But perhaps it wouldn't come to that. His passport too was inside his bag, he reminded himself, and that remained his ace card. There was just a chance that the police wouldn't have the imagination to equate an American citizen called Appeldoorn with the mysterious Ernst Bergmann, despite their amazing physical similarity...

He was debating if the time was now right to try a casual approach to the left luggage office, when a deliberate cough behind him made him jump involuntarily.

'Miss Cordingly! How nice to see you again,' he said instinctively. *And your awful teeth, and dreadful frizzy hair*, he felt like adding. Apart from Blumenfeld, this was about the last person that Joe wanted to see at this moment, but he did his best to be polite.

She smiled slightly in response, but Joe could see her glancing curiously in the direction of the policemen on the concourse. *Was this woman dogging his steps deliberately,* he wondered. It seemed an unlikely coincidence for her to pop up again here at this most inopportune time.

'Where are you travelling to, Mr Appeldoorn?'

Joe tried to relax the tetanus-like rictus that gripped his face muscles and jaw, but decided not to lie. 'I'm taking the evening train to Zurich.'

'I too am going to Zurich. Perhaps we can board together. What carriage are you in?'

'H. Compartment seven.'

'That's my compartment too. We seem fated to travel together, Mr Appeldoorn. I believe that Orientals would call this "Kismet".'

Only if "Kismet" means "lousy luck", thought Joe dispiritedly. But then he quickly revised that opinion. Perhaps the company of a woman would be a good cover for him, despite the unpalatable prospect of having to engage this plain Englishwoman in conversation for several hours. The police were looking for a Swiss man on his own, after all, not an American in the company of an Englishwoman. And those teeth and that hair would probably deter even the sternest policeman from spending too much time questioning her...

'I'd be honoured to board with you, Miss Cordingly,' he said quickly, 'if you'll just give me a minute to reclaim my baggage from the left luggage.'

He calmed his nerves and walked confidently across the concourse to the left luggage counter. No one paid him the slightest attention, as far as he could tell. The young woman behind the desk, a girl with blonde plaits and physical proportions to have made Wagner supremely happy, made cow eyes at him as she tried her halting English on her sole customer. But in less than a minute he was back on the main concourse with his bags and heading for the staircase down to the platforms in company with Miss Cordingly and her porter.

Even in his present worried state it occurred to Joe again that Miss Cordingly would not be a bad-looking girl but for those protruding incisors and that wild red hair. He remembered the illicit glimpse he'd had in the Hotel *Landhaus* of a surprisingly shapely figure and bottom. But a quick glance showed her looking remarkably well-padded behind today.

'Is something wrong, Mr Appeldoorn? What *are* you looking at, may I ask?' she snapped at him.

Joe raised his eyes guiltily. 'Err...nothing, Miss Cordingly. I thought I'd dropped my ticket, that's all, but here it is.'

'Come along then,' she ordered peremptorily, like a kindergarten teacher to her pupils. 'There's a considerable queue at the barrier.'

They waited in line at the main gate leading down to the platforms. Miss Cordingly seemed to sense his nervousness and to be determined to make him feel worse. '*Now* I understand the reason for all the police, Mr Appeldoorn. It must be to do with that shocking murder that took place two days ago in the Hotel *Landhaus*. One doesn't expect such things to happen in a peaceful city like Bern, does one? I was actually staying in the *Landhaus* at the time, in fact right next door to where it happened. It appears that the woman who was murdered – a young Frenchwoman – arrived on the same train from Paris as us...'

Joe was beginning to wish something extremely heavy would drop on Miss Cordingly from a great height as she continued turning the screw. '...I saw and heard nothing myself though. Even so, I was questioned for hours, and had to make a statement to the police, before I was allowed to return to the hotel. And then of course I demanded to be moved to a different room – imagining sleeping next door to the place where something dreadful like that happened...'

They'd reached the barrier at the top of the platform stairs by now.

Miss Cordingly seemed suddenly to notice Joe's conspicuous lack of headgear; he hadn't yet had time to buy a replacement for his lost bowler. 'No hat, Mr Appeldoorn?' she inquired curiously.

'Err...no. I must have mislaid it.' Joe suddenly had a sinking feeling in the pit of his stomach, a welling up of incipient panic. There'd been no mention of his own name in the newspaper accounts of the crime, but suppose the Bern police had already found his bowler hat in the river and put two and two together? Perhaps they were simply waiting for a man called Appeldoorn to turn up at the railway station and then collar him...

But it was too late to turn back now...

The suave young policeman at the gate had cropped blond hair and was almost as tall as Joe. He took Joe's offered ticket and his passport, and examined them both with narrowed ice-blue eyes.

'You are an American citizen, sir?' he asked in good English.

'I am.'

'Do you speak German at all, sir?' the policeman continued politely, studying Joe's face intently.

'No, I don't.' Joe heard Miss Cordingly behind him draw in a sharp intake of breath – on that station concourse it sounded loud enough to disturb the pigeons in the roof. *How could he have been so stupid?* It was all over - she had heard him speaking German on the train from Paris! Joe waited for her to denounce him to the young policeman in her penetrating Surrey accent.

But she said nothing, even though she seemed acutely uncomfortable about something - as if she now realised she was travelling with a possible murderer, yet considered it bad manners to give him away.

They passed through the gate, Miss Cordingly herself being allowed through by the policeman with no more than a cursory glance at her papers. They walked down the stairs to the platform with the porter pushing their combined luggage on the ramp beside them; Joe doing his best not to let out a sigh of relief. Still Miss Cordingly made no comment on his clear lie to the policeman.

On the gas-lit platform the gleaming train was already waiting for departure, ablaze with electric light from end to end. The latent power under the metal hood of that vast rumbling black locomotive was almost a tangible thing, betrayed by the slow hiss of steam from valves, which drifted in strands over the polished cream and maroon paintwork of the carriages. The last traces of sunset were just being washed out of the western sky by the approaching night as Joe and Miss Cordingly finally boarded.

They found their first-class compartment and arranged for their bags to be stowed. Joe settled back into the deep marshmallow-like upholstery and finally relaxed. It seemed surprisingly that he and Miss Cordingly had the entire compartment to themselves...

*

'Have you ever seen real Red Indians, Mr Appeldoorn?'

'Only in a Wild West show.' Miss Cordingly seemed determined to talk but Joe had done his best to discourage her so far with monosyllabic answers.

They had already left the city of Bern far behind, and only the merest outline of the wintry hills and mountains of the *Mittelland* could be discerned through the encroaching blackness outside. 'A pity,' Charlotte said. 'They look such noble savages. So muscular and yet so smooth of skin, apparently without any body hair at all.'

Joe looked at her in surprise at the turn of this conversation. Yet Miss Cordingly's expression remained impersonal.

'You said you were from Philadelphia, I believe, Mr Appeldoorn. What kind of city is that?'

'It's where the United States was created, Miss Cordingly. The Declaration of Independence was signed there; the first Continental Congress was held there too. And Ben Franklin came from Philadelphia. What more do you need to know about it?'

'I think I already knew that much about Philadelphia, Mr Appeldoorn,' she replied tartly. 'I was hoping to hear some rather more personal insights into your homeland and home town.'

'Then you must also have heard that, because of its strong Quaker connection, Philadelphia is known as the City of Brotherly Love.'

Miss Cordingly raised her eyebrows. 'And what about the place of women there? Is it also a city of sisterly love, I wonder?'

Joe smiled wryly. 'Well, you've exposed my ignorance there, Miss Cordingly. I guess you would have to ask the women of Philadelphia that question.'

'Then tell me about American fashions at least. What do American women wear these days?'

'Pretty much the same as here in Europe, but for a quarter of the price,' Joe said flippantly.

Miss Cordingly gave him a frustrated look and then tried another tack. 'American music is completely different from ours, Mr Appeldoorn. You can't deny that at least. I've heard of Ragtime music; we have nothing like that here. And then there are the infamous American dances – people say they are very immodest.'

'We just know how to enjoy ourselves, that's all, Miss Cordingly.'

'For an American, you seem to know remarkably little about your own country, Mr Appeldoorn,' Charlotte said coolly. 'Do you know as little about your own profession, electrical engineering, as you do about your own country? Have you heard of Mr Westinghouse and Mr Tesla, for instance?'

'What are you trying to say, Miss Cordingly? Do you think me an impostor?'

'Of course not.' Miss Cordingly seemed less than apologetic, though, studying him with unblinking concentration from her side of the compartment.

Something in her stance annoyed Joe so much that he finally responded. 'I will tell you something about America, and New York in particular, if you like, Miss Cordingly. Something momentous has been happening there over the last twenty years, and is still happening. Its Anglo-Saxon monopoly is disappearing. America is becoming a true melting pot of many cultures: after the Irish have come Italians, Poles, Greeks, Russian Jews. From every corner of Europe over the last twenty years they have come through the immigration centre on Ellis Island. Now when they sail in, they pass Bartholdy's statue, the gift from France, in New York harbour. *Liberty Enlightening the World.* Perhaps that's what America is now: a beacon of hope in a tired world.'

'The huddled masses yearning to be free?'

It sounded to Joe as if she was sneering slightly. 'Something like that,' he agreed coldly.

'Would you like a soapbox to stand on, perhaps?' she asked, but then looked down at her feet. 'I'm sorry. That was rude of me.' She was quiet for almost a minute, then said, 'You don't like me very much, do you, Mr Appeldoorn?'

'No, that's true. I don't.'

She laughed heartily at that, a pleasant sound. 'Well, that's honest at least. One of the things I do admire about Americans is their straight-talking, and you have finally proved your nationality beyond all doubt.'

Joe didn't know what to say to that so took a cheroot from a pack. 'Would you like one?' he offered.

'No, thank you. What on earth kind of woman do you think I am?' She seemed more amused, though, than truly offended by the offer.

A good question, he thought. What kind of woman did he think she was? Joe was no longer so sure in his opinions of the seemingly straight-laced and conventional Miss Charlotte Cordingly...

'My apologies. I thought I'd seen you indulging in one of these.'

'Where and when was this?'

Joe detected some suspicion in her eyes now. 'Sorry, I must be confusing you with another lady,' he said quickly.

Outside, the last trace of light had disappeared, and even the horizon could no longer be distinguished from the sky.

Miss Cordingly looked up sharply and finally delivered the devastating question Joe had been expecting. 'So, Mr Appeldoorn, why was it that you told that policeman in Bern station that you don't speak German?'

Joe had been wondering when she would bring it up, so had an answer ready by now. 'Oh, I lie to policemen all the time, Miss Cordingly. No, seriously...he looked far too young and earnest. He would have held me up with lots more questions if he'd known I speak German.'

Charlotte looked at Joe. 'I think he was no younger than you, yourself, Mr Appeldoorn. And perhaps he was right to be earnest. That woman in the Hotel *Landhaus* was horribly murdered, after all.' Her eyes held him in a firm gaze. '*In fact, they say her throat was cut from ear to ear...*"

CHAPTER 8

Friday March 14th 1902

So far, the meeting of the Social Democratic Federation of Zurich had been just as dull as Joe Appeldoorn had been expecting – even *more* mind-numbingly tedious than he'd anticipated, if anything. The main speaker of the evening, however, Herr Vladimir Ilyich Ulyanov, had not yet got to his feet, so there was still a small chance that he might turn out to be moderately more interesting than his earnest colleagues and acolytes.

Joe sat in a secluded corner at the back of the gloomy meeting hall. The meeting was surprisingly well attended – a hundred people or more crowded into the hard pews. All these people were here apparently in search of sweeping social change rather than spiritual fulfilment, yet the similarities to a religious mood were plain to see. They did seem almost like an evangelical congregation: the same earnest expressions, the same affectation of humility before the Almighty – Karl Marx being the Almighty in this case. Even the meeting hall felt like a Spartan church: panelled wood, Gothic windows, stained glass, lofty interior.

The hall was located in *Ramistrasse* within a stone's throw of the *Eidgenössische Polytechnische Schule*, Zurich's Polytechnic, and Joe's *alma mater*. If he strained his neck to see out of the window, he could even catch a glimpse of the roof of the Neo-Renaissance building designed and built by Gottfried Semper in 1835, a building close to his heart.

The three years Joe had spent at the Poly had been the happiest of his life. The company of friends, like Albert Einstein and Marcel Grossmann; the intellectual stimulation of new ideas (Professor Weber notwithstanding); a beautiful location on a wooded hill above the exquisite city of Zurich and its blue lake. The terrace in front of the campus had wonderful views over the city and the surrounding mountains, and the local girls were the prettiest in all Switzerland. *What more could a young man have wanted?* It was, to paraphrase Voltaire, the best of all possible worlds. You didn't even need to climb the steep hill on foot when coming back from the Central district; a new funicular tram system, the *Polybahn,* had recently been built, and ran all the way down to Central, a large square on the east side of the *Bahnhofbrücke...*

*

Joe had found himself a room in a small family-owned hotel on *Limmatquai* within a few minutes of arriving in Zurich last night, and then spent the day wandering through his old haunts. On his first full day back in this city he knew so well, though, he had felt unexpectedly melancholy, perhaps affected by a bittersweet echo of his student days, which now seemed so long ago. His life had been less complex then, and certainly more fulfilling than at present.

The city looked exactly the same, yet he experienced an inevitable feeling of disappointment when he realised that so many of his friends from student days had now moved on to other places. The usual diaspora of young people after college, scattering to every corner of the world to live out their lives...

In this slightly wistful mood of reflection, he had wandered along *Limmatquai,* the attractive riverside boulevard that followed the East side of the River Limmat, from *Bellevueplatz* in the south to *Bahnhofbrücke* in the north. In his subdued state, he would even have been pleased to run into the egregious Miss Cordingly again, but she too seemed to have dissolved into the ether, like all his other acquaintances in this city. When their train had arrived at Zurich Station last night at eight-thirty, she had appeared almost in a fever to get as far away from him as possible. The last he had seen of her, she'd been practically sprinting down the platform with her porter. She did move remarkably well for a plump girl, though, he'd noted with surprise...

*

And so to this meeting, which was rounding off a surprisingly gloomy day – surprising because he had expected Zurich to re-invigorate him rather than the reverse.

He glanced around the room yet again. They truly were a severe-looking audience; Joe's only entertainment in the time he'd been here had been to try and classify them by degrees of awfulness. The Russian political exiles were actually the least offensive – they at least had *some* excuse for the way they were - followed by the more pious home-grown variety of socialist, the Swiss. These were mostly intense young men and women, with equally long solemn faces and equally lank hair. The dour German Marxists were easy to recognise, while there was a surprising number of foppish-looking Englishmen, bristling with talk of the class struggle back home. (Nobody, it seemed, despised themselves more than the English middle classes.)

Among none of these friends of the workers, though, Joe guessed, was there anything approaching a real blister, never mind a calloused hand, induced by hard manual work. But there was certainly a brooding sense of martyrdom in the air.

Joe wondered again why he had come here tonight. Yet he knew the answer to his own unspoken question: he was simply clutching at straws, of course. He'd lost his only direct link to Eleanor with the death of Monique Langevin, and, so far, he had not the faintest idea why she'd been killed, or whether it had anything to do with Eleanor's disappearance at all. And Herr Blumenfeld? *Who was he? What was his part in all this?* He had looked such an innocuous man, yet turned out to be a murderous thug...

Yet Joe had finally received *some* good news late this afternoon. When he'd gone to the Central Telegraph Office in Zurich to collect any telegrams waiting for him, he found a message that revived his flagging spirits and gave him fresh impetus for his assignment. He had simply been expecting to receive some angry missive by now from John Kautsky on his lack of progress (which he duly did find); but he also discovered, more unexpectedly, that he'd received one telegram directly from Eleanor's grandfather, James "D for Dangerous" Winthrop.

It transpired that, three days ago, a woman identifying herself as Eleanor Winthrop had wired the American Express office in Paris for ten thousand dollars more to be transferred from there to a Swiss Bank account in *Zurich*...

In her telegram she had used the code she had agreed beforehand with her bankers in Paris to identify herself. But the gentlemen of American Express, although convinced they were dealing with the real Miss Winthrop, had nevertheless wired her grandfather in Pittsburgh for permission to send the money. The permission was duly given because Grandfather Winthrop reasoned that this message *had* to have come from Eleanor, even though she might be acting under duress. James Winthrop informed Joe in his telegram of the number of the bank account to which the money had been sent, a secret numbered account held with a well-known Swiss bank on *Bahnhofstrasse* in Zurich. This was exciting news – Joe felt his instincts had been vindicated. Eleanor *was* somewhere near Zurich after all! He longed to tell doubting Albert – *"wishful thinking" indeed...*

Yet, ominously, Joe could tell from the telegram that Eleanor's grandfather clearly thought that he must already be close to finding her. Even given the cryptic content of James Winthrop's telegram, Joe could detect a note of anticipatory congratulation in those few brief words. Presumably he'd come to this conclusion because he knew from John Kautsky that Joe had already somehow found his own way to Zurich; but this kind of unrealistic optimism was the last thing that Joe wanted to hear. Although he might well be close geographically to Eleanor, Joe knew that, in real terms, he was as far off finding her as ever.

Even the name of the bank and the number of the account that "Eleanor" had requested to send the ten thousand dollars to would be of little direct help to Joe; Swiss bankers were the most secretive in the world and the manager or his minions were highly unlikely to be forthcoming about the real identity of the holder of that particular bank account.

But at least the news was *something* positive and, immediately afterwards, Joe had dashed off a letter to René Sardou in Paris telling him the situation, and asking if he could join him in Switzerland as soon as possible. In the meantime, while he waited in Zurich for reinforcements, Joe had hoped that by coming to this meeting tonight he might discover a further Zurich connection to help him trace the elusive Miss Winthrop...

*

Herr Ulyanov finally got to his feet after a rousing introduction from the chairman on the dais – a man with the face and mannerisms of a nervous polecat. Ulyanov was a younger man than Joe had expected from the build-up – in his early thirties, he guessed, quite slim and dapper, with a trimmed beard and moustache, but already completely bald on top and looking far more like a successful Swiss banker than a Russian revolutionary.

He did turn out to be a better speaker than the supporting cast, delivering his talk about the parlous state of Russian society in good, clear German - yet also at interminable length.

It only became moderately interesting for Joe when Ulyanov got on to some personal details of his own life story. He was born, he said, at Simbirsk on the Middle Volga, the son of a school inspector. When he was sixteen, his elder brother had been hanged for complicity in a plot to assassinate the Tsar. But that story had simply been an invention of the Tsar's secret police, made up in order to punish the whole Ulyanov family for their political beliefs…

He thundered on, '…Yet they couldn't stop my indomitable will to persevere. I graduated in law as an external student at St Petersburg University, while living under restrictions in Samara two thousand kilometres away. It was then that I began to study Marx…' - a ripple almost of applause went through the audience at the mention of that magical name - '…to find some way out of my country's political dilemma. I could see the situation in Russia was intolerable for the mass of people, but that I could do little about it there. So I left – regretfully - to stay in Germany and plan the salvation of my people from there. Now I write and issue pamphlets, and promote the future of post-Marxian socialism through my newspaper *Iskra* – The Spark. Recently I also became leader of the newly formed militant wing of the Russian Social Democrats abroad, while I bide my time to return. But that time is coming ever closer, comrades. Eventually I *will* return to the Motherland, when the situation is right, to support the resistance of Russian workers against the tyrant...'

Eyes were shining in the earnest young faces all around him yet Joe had to fight to stifle another yawn. Why was it, he wondered, that Germans have a "Fatherland", while Russians have a "Mother Russia"? Perhaps one nation has an Oedipus complex, while the other has an Electra complex...?

A young woman with dark intense eyes sitting near Joe was apparently not impressed with Herr Ulyanov either, and whispered to her companion in what sounded like a Polish accent, 'Is this what you dragged me all this way for? These damned Russians think they invented the socialist struggle, Karl. This man is just another Russian nationalist – a new Tsar – not a real socialist.'

Her companion – perhaps her husband - placated her. 'Yes, Rosa, I believe you're right. One day in Europe they will hear *your* voice – the true voice of the proletariat - above all these clamouring Russians.'

Joe was mentally agreeing with the Polish woman's opinion of Ulyanov when the sound of a chair leg scraping along the parquet flooring attracted his eyes to the front row of the auditorium, immediately in front of the raised dais. It was then that he realised with a shock that the man at the end of that row was none other than his murderous friend from Bern - *Herr Karl Jurgen Blumenfeld...*

*

Considering the political views that Blumenfeld had espoused to Joe in that café in Bern (while stuffing his mouth full of Black Forest cake) this meeting hall seemed like an odd place for him to be looking so much at home.

Yet Blumenfeld *did* look at home, enthusiastically applauding the tiresome Herr Ulyanov, as the Russian finally sat down. Joe did his best to crane his neck to keep an eye on Blumenfeld, but that also made him vulnerable to discovery, of course, should Blumenfeld decide to turn his head around suddenly. (*That* would be an interesting moment, at least, to liven up the evening, Joe thought.)

But he had to risk it – and was glad that he did, because he spotted Blumenfeld exchange a whisper with the woman sitting next to him.

Was she another closet political radical, Joe wondered, who simply happened to be sitting next to Blumenfeld? Or was there something more to it than that?

Joe suspected the latter; the young woman at Blumenfeld's side hardly had the look of a natural revolutionary about her. From what he could see of her when she stood up briefly to adjust her seat, she was both young and rather sophisticated-looking. Her hair was ash-blonde although a hat and veil hid much of her face. She had a tiny corseted waist and an extravagant bosom, and since she was the only woman in this audience with attributes anything remotely like that, they were hard to miss. She was dressed far too well for a revolutionary too, in a velveteen dress with a high collar and fur trim. (The deep red colour of her dress seemed in fact to be her sole concession to the political complexion of the meeting.) A string of pearls decorated her slender white neck. Joe had to wonder how she'd even been allowed to cross the threshold of this meeting looking as disgustingly bourgeois as that...

It was 10 p.m. by now and the meeting was clearly at an end; a babble of voices erupted, exactly like the release of tension in a school assembly at the end of a long speech by the school governors.

Joe desperately tried to burrow lower in his seat as he saw Blumenfeld get to his feet and take the arm of his blonde companion. Joe had to cover his face quickly with a pamphlet and let them pass, but then found himself blocked by the sudden press of people trying to leave the meeting at the same time.

By the time he did manage to get through the doorway and out into the gas-lit thoroughfare of *Ramistrasse,* neither Blumenfeld nor the blonde were anywhere to be seen...

*

Joe was still cursing viciously to himself when he caught sight of a gleam of platinum hair under a streetlight.

He muttered a sigh of relief - the woman was still here, at least, but clearly waiting on her own, a little apart from the rest of the people spilling out of the meeting hall. Joe guessed she was being met by someone, and a four-wheeler cab did indeed arrive within a minute, clip-clopping up the hill and pulling to a halt on the kerbside near her, as if pre-arranged. The woman climbed in the back unaided and the driver immediately urged his ancient horse to a leisurely walk back down the hill towards the centre of town.

No other cabs were in sight and, even if there had been, there was also a growing queue of people competing for one, as yet more socialists and Marxists filed out of the hall. So Joe made a rapid decision - he'd lost Blumenfeld already and would have to give up on him for the time being. He simply couldn't afford to lose the woman as well, though, so he took off at a brisk trot behind the rapidly disappearing four-wheeler. Fortunately the horse pulling the cab seemed destined soon for the glue factory because Joe found that he could keep up with it quite easily.

He did attract attention from the people he passed, though - particularly from a couple of bold and pretty girls who waved gaily to him as if he was a marathon runner in training for the next Olympics in St. Louis, but then rather spoilt that by yelling some saucy and suggestive remarks after him.

He ran the length of the hill down *Ramistrasse,* and crossed to the west side of the River Limmat at *Quaibrücke,* near where the river flowed north out of the *Zurichsee.*

Still the four-wheeler continued on along *General Guisan Quai*, the road that followed the northern edge of the *Zurichsee*. Joe knew *exactly* where he was; he was as familiar with these clean and tidy streets as he was with his own neighbourhood in downtown Philadelphia. He was glad that he was in good condition; in his thick worsted suit he was hardly dressed for running, and even in the cold of a Zurich March evening, had begun to sweat profusely. The cab crossed *Bahnhofstrasse*, and headed on towards the *Industrie Quartier* and Zurich West, the western suburbs.

At the southern edge of the city, where the suburbs had thinned to an occasional dwelling only, the four-wheeler finally reached the entrance gate to a grand house. This building overlooked the midnight black water of the *Zurichsee* on one side, while being discreetly concealed from prying eyes on the street side by high wrought iron railings and dense laurel shrubbery. Joe, only thirty metres behind the cab by now, stopped and caught his breath after his four-kilometre run, before sauntering casually closer to the scene.

The gate was opened for the cab after a rapid exchange between the gatekeeper and the lady inside – she seemed to be well known here. The driver prodded the worn-out horse up the short cobbled drive where it stopped wearily in front of the softly lit portico, steam rising in clouds from its back. (Joe had to sympathise with the ancient horse; he could almost feel a similar amount of steam coming off his own body.) The blonde stepped daintily out of the carriage, paid off the driver, then walked up the entrance steps where she rang a bell and was admitted with alacrity.

Before the cab returned down the drive and the main gate was slammed shut again, Joe had a brief opportunity to study the house. It was built in the Renaissance style but not that old in reality, rather a nineteenth-century architect's homage to the past. The walls were of decorated limestone, cut in large blocks, and were three-storeys high with ten substantial windows per floor. The windows reduced in size with each floor in geometric progression so clearly the architect had been an aspirant mathematician as well as a student of the Renaissance. Below the overhanging roof of red tiles, a row of international flags fluttered from flagpoles projecting from the walls. The sound of waltz music escaped from a window somewhere and filtered through the laurel hedges.

The building could have been a foreign embassy or the home of a wealthy Swiss banker. Yet it was neither of those; it was in fact, as Joe had recognised immediately from his knowledge of this area, a notorious brothel called *Le Royale*...

Not that Joe had ever been inside to personally witness its excesses and reputed decadence; it was rumoured to cost a small fortune in Swiss francs for an evening of gaming, drinking and restrained (or perhaps even unrestrained) debauchery and, as a student in Zurich, he'd been neither of a suitable age, nor with the means, to be able to enjoy it. (His father, although wealthy at the time, had deliberately not indulged him with overgenerous amounts of money - perhaps he'd heard of the many temptations that existed in Zurich for a young man.) Even money was not guaranteed to gain access to *Le Royale* however - this, the most select brothel in Zurich, was strictly reserved for the cream of society only. Certainly no riff-raff could get past the door anyway; the clients, so Joe had heard, were reputed to range from English aristocrats to Persian princes to Oriental potentates.

One student from the Zurich Polytechnic, an eccentric youth called Rudi Gessler, had once accepted a bet to try and gain entry, and, dressed in a pantomime Ali Baba fancy dress outfit, had managed to get past the guards at the door while purporting to be an Indian prince. But his disguise hadn't fooled anyone for long; within a few minutes he'd found himself being unceremoniously kicked out of the front door, with two black eyes for real to match the burnt cork stain on his face. Yet Rudi, as he'd confessed later that same night to Joe, had thought the cost of a few bruises more than worth the experience. 'I thought I'd ascended to heaven when I saw what was inside. Such women as mortal man can usually only dream of, Joseph. Helen of Troy, Aphrodite, Diana the huntress, Scheherazade...I saw them all tonight...My word, you should have seen the breasts on Aphrodite...'

Joe ruefully examined the jacket and sleeves of his plain worsted suit with its short English jacket, and saw that he was hardly dressed tonight for an audience with Helen of Troy or Scheherazade. While these clothes were neutral enough to gain him entry to the meeting of the revolutionaries in *Ramistrasse* without raising any eyebrows, they were unlikely to get him past the eagle-eyed guardians of this pleasure palace.

Joe approached the man on the gate nevertheless; an individual with a lantern jaw and Neanderthal brow who clearly countenanced no nonsense from the hoi polloi.

The man looked Joe up and down, metaphorically weighing up the cut of his clothes and the likely size of his wallet.

'May I go in?' Joe asked politely.

'No, *mein herr*, not dressed like that. Evening dress only. And in any case, only by personal invitation.'

It was what Joe had expected, but was annoying nonetheless. 'Then could you tell me, at least, who was that fair-haired lady I just saw arrive here?'

The Neanderthal sniffed. 'Forget it, *Junge*. That lady is well outside your league.'

'How about a hundred marks to let me in?'

'I'd be pleased to take your hundred marks, but it still won't get you in, sonny.' The Neanderthal glowered balefully.

'Suppose I won't take "no" for an answer? Suppose I stand here in the entrance until you do let me in.'

'Then I will just have to move you on by force, *mein herr.*' The giant managed to get a world of contempt into what was normally a polite form of address. He took Joe roughly by the collar, and they began to scuffle, as Joe struggled to get free of him.

'What's going on here?' An elegant figure in evening dress appeared at the small side gate, a young man with shining hair and perfectly trimmed moustache. The man looked at Joe for a moment, then said with a laugh, 'So, Joseph, you want to come in, is that it? I'm surprised, though, that *you*, of all people, have become a debaucher.'

Joe recognised him in return - an old friend and former student of the Polytechnic, Erwin Winteler, who, judging from his splendid attire at least, had gone up considerably in the world.

'I might say the same about you, Erwin.'

'What on earth are you doing here? I thought you'd quit civilization and gone home to America.'

'I did, but I'm back on vacation. So I thought I would see what this place was like inside – after all, I'd heard so much gossip about it as a student.'

Winteler laughed. 'Well, let me tell you, Joseph, the reality is much better than our fevered immature imaginations could ever have dreamed of.'

Joe smiled in response; he and Winteler had never been exactly close friends but had still got on well enough to enjoy occasional evenings of drinking and carousing together. Joe remembered that he had liked Winteler's slightly dark sense of humour and sometime surreal dress sense.

'So how can *you* afford this place?' Joe asked him curiously. Winteler, the seventh son of a Church pastor, had been as poor as a beggar all through college, always cadging from his friends for this or that. Now, though, Winteler no longer resembled that Bohemian scruff but looked every inch the wealthy gentleman, decked out in impeccable evening dress finery complete with white weskit and tie.

Winteler flicked a speck of dust from his perfectly pressed tail coat. 'Oh, I am not a customer, Joseph. I manage the gaming rooms here; the mathematical skills I learned at the Poly were finally of some use to me.'

The gatekeeper was still threatening to return and take a swing at Joe, but Winteler calmed him. 'It's all right, Ernst. I shall deal with this gentleman.'

'Oh, a gentleman, is he?' The massive Ernst said with a sneer, refusing to admit defeat quite that easily.

Joe had been surprised – perhaps even slightly shocked – to learn that Winteler, a graduate of physics and mathematics, even if a poor one, had been reduced to working in a place like *Le Royale*. It seemed ironic that the first of his fellow students he should run into in Zurich should be here of all places. Winteler himself seemed oblivious, though, to the surprise in Joe's voice, or the implied criticism at his choice of career. He raised a debonair eyebrow as the giant Ernst butted into his conversation yet again.

'He was asking about Ma'mselle Flammarion,' Ernst complained suspiciously.

Winteler raised an amused eyebrow. 'Were you indeed, Joseph? Then your taste in women has improved considerably since college. I seem to remember that, as a student, you were rather enamoured of Fat Heidi in the bursar's office at the Polytechnic.'

'She was a very sweet girl,' protested Joe. 'And she wasn't fat, just pleasingly plump.'

Winteler guffawed. 'Joseph, that girl was addicted to *Apfelstrüdel*. She is still working at the Poly, you know, and you had a very lucky escape there, my friend. You should see Heidi now! They've had to enlarge the door of her office specially, just so that she can get through it. If she keeps getting any bigger, they will soon have to lift her in through the window with a hoist...'

Joe didn't know if Winteler was simply pulling his leg or not with this unlikely tale, but decided to get back to the matter in hand. 'Tell me about Ma'mselle Flammarion. Does she work here?'

'She does indeed. Her name is Cecile – and she is a heavenly creature, I grant you. But you may be overreaching yourself if you want to come in here and meet her. That lady is a personal friend of kings and emperors. I do not jest.'

And is she also a personal friend of murderers and revolutionaries? Joe wondered.

Winteler frowned. 'I am almost tempted to let you in, Joseph, just to see how you might get on with the lady. But I simply can't let you come in dressed like a bank clerk. It's more than my life is worth; Madame Malet would have my head.'

'Who is she?'

Winteler coughed dryly. 'She is the manager and part owner of this discerning establishment. She personally vets all the ladies who work here, *and* all the gentleman clients.'

'Then can you at least find out for me where Cecile Flammarion lives? Not here on the premises surely?'

'No, this is not that sort of establishment, Joseph.' Winteler seemed to debate with himself for a moment. 'But you can ask Cecile that question, yourself, if you like. Let's call it a favour for an old friend, and for all the flagons of beer you bought me over the years. If you *really* want to see how the decadent half of society lives, then come back tomorrow evening. Full evening dress, though, and, I warn you, you will also have to pass Madame Malet's inquisitive eye before you will be allowed to...how can I say...make use of the facilities of *Le Royale*...'

CHAPTER 9

Saturday March 15th 1902

The interior of *Le Royale* was something of a disappointment to Joseph Appeldoorn on first inspection. He felt slightly cheated, after the extravagant build-up given to the place by his friend, Erwin Winteler.

It was certainly luxurious enough — Erwin had not exaggerated that at least - yet at first glance he could see little sign of debauchery, Saturnalia, orgies in development, or even much in the way of merry-making. The atmosphere of the ground floor was polite, restrained and gentlemanly, not so very different from a traditional gaming club, apart from the presence of so much female beauty at hand, anyway.

Joe had spent most of the day hiring suitable evening dress — tailcoat and trousers, white weskit and tie - for his visit to this the most famous brothel in Zurich, and perhaps even in all of Switzerland. Unusually for him he'd even taken a lot of trouble over his accessories too — taking time to choose from an enormous range of shirt stiff-fronts and rolled collars, and following the tailor's intricate advice about the latest treble knot for the tie.

He'd arrived by four-wheeler and this time - with a gilt-edged card signed by Erwin Winteler - had been dispatched through by the keepers on the gate without trouble. Ernst, the Neanderthal, had failed even to recognise him in his new finery. Even Joe, who was only moderately interested in fashion as a rule, had been quietly satisfied with the way he looked tonight. He had filled his pockets with as much cash as he could carry; for the first time in his European excursion, he might need to spend Mr James Winthrop's money with profligate abandon.

Joe was by no means sure of what he planned to do tonight, apart from trying to engage the beautiful Cecile in conversation, and then investigating the nature of her relationship with Herr Blumenfeld. *Yet what if Blumenfeld himself turned up tonight?* Joe wondered. But he preferred to put off that disquieting thought for the present: he would face that eventuality if and when it happened...

It was entirely possible, of course, that Blumenfeld and Mlle Flammarion had nothing at all to do with Eleanor Winthrop's disappearance from Paris, but there was also a chance at least that they were deeply involved. The link from Eleanor to Cecile, via Monique Langevin and Blumenfeld, was a tenuous one at best, yet it could be real enough. Blumenfeld's presence at last night's meeting might suggest that he was more anarchist and socialist than the German nationalist he had purported to be in Bern. And Eleanor was the extremely wealthy heiress of an American capitalist dynasty...so could it be that she had become the target for a kidnapping plot by revolutionary extremists...?

*

The ground floor of *Le Royale* consisted of gaming rooms, a music salon, and an outside stone-flagged terrace and garden overlooking the *Zurichsee*. With a chill wind blowing off the lake, though, the terrace was mostly deserted, while the gaming rooms – clearly the most popular attraction - were packed with patrons and their enchanting escorts. It was ten at night but the place was still clearly just warming up. Chandeliers glittered, electric light illuminating elegant silk dresses and fresh white bosoms, the green baize of the gaming tables, the deep plush velvet of the window-seats and ottomans, the brocade of the curtains. Champagne flowed in an endless stream from the bottles of attentive waitresses in decorative uniforms of white lace and green taffeta.

The customers were mostly middle-aged and elderly men - ugly, scrofulous or overweight individuals on the whole, with bulging waistlines and thinning grey hair – and no doubt counting many leaders of European industry, bankers, lawyers, and politicians among their number. But one or two young bloods also frequented the place so Joe didn't feel too out-of-place by virtue of his youth. Fortunately he didn't come across anyone that he recognised, so didn't have to explain his presence in this house of debauchery to any former Zurich acquaintances.

Joe moved to the music room where the floor had been cleared for a cabaret – a waltz display by a seductive line of couples. The girls were dressed in extravagant eighteenth-century hooped damask skirts that looked very elegant and proper until Joe realised they had no backs to them at all. But they and their "boy" partners, twirling in carefully choreographed time, cleverly contrived to mostly conceal their naked bottoms from the leering gaze of the gathered male audience. Even the "boys", dressed in top hats and tight trousers, were clearly girls; no boy alive could ever have managed to look as alluring and shapely as that, Joe thought.

Joe was looking at one familiar-looking girl in the line-up in particular and wondering whether she might in fact be Cecile, when Erwin Winteler appeared from nowhere at his side, and fingered the lapel of Joe's tailcoat. 'Very nice, Joseph. As handsome a young gentleman as I ever saw in here. Even I am envious of those broad shoulders and slim hips. By the way, Madame has given you her seal of approval.'

Joe looked around in bemusement. 'Where? When? I didn't see her.'

Winteler smiled smugly. 'Don't worry. Her beady eyes saw *you* on arrival all right, and I'm glad to say you passed muster. Otherwise you would have been out on your ear already.'

Joe studied again the face of the girl he'd noticed in the waltz line-up, who smiled sweetly back at him in response. 'So where is Cecile?'

Winteler tut-tutted. 'Ach, nein, *mein Freund*. I'm not making things that easy for you. You find her yourself, and earn her confidence. It is a house rule that the girls are not allowed to approach the guests but must wait for the gentleman to make the first move. And Cecile does not agree to escort just any client. She is one of the stars of this little firmament and you must pay proper court to her if you want to win her...*gratitude*. Still, looking the way you do tonight, you stand a very good chance. Compared with the other things on offer here, I mean...' Winteler glanced dryly at a passing octogenarian with a face like a wizened leprechaun. 'She may even get knocked down in the rush to meet you.'

'So where do I start?'

'Just mingle. I'll give you a tip, though, Joseph. The higher you go in this building, the more interesting it gets.'

*

After approaching the dancer in the music room he'd thought he recognised, Joe discovered regretfully that she was not Cecile after all. Nor was Mlle Flammarion any of the other girls in the dancing ensemble; it seemed that she was now of too elevated a status to take part any longer in the dancing demonstrations. So Joe reluctantly disentangled himself from his beautiful dancer friend and went back to the main gaming room, content for the moment to take his time in finding Cecile. He had been tempted to take Winteler into his confidence concerning the more serious reason why he needed to talk to Cecile Flammarion, yet decided against it in the end. To be frank, the new, sleeker, more cynical Erwin Winteler was not someone Joe thought he could particularly afford to trust.

In the gaming rooms, every conceivable game was available for the gentlemen guests - roulette, *rouge et noir, chemin de fer,* dice, baccarat. The visitors seemed apparently quite resigned to losing their money as fast as possible under the encouraging gaze of their pulchritudinous escorts, and fatalistically accepted the loss of yet another vast stake with the merest shrug of their sometime doddering heads, and the reward of a saucy smile from their pert companions. German and French were the commonest languages spoken by the girls and their clients but Joe also heard English,

Italian and, once, something he couldn't recognise at all but might have been Hungarian.

Joe didn't feel like getting embroiled in a gambling session, though, and preferred instead to concentrate his attentions on the gamblers' paid companions.

These girls really were all extraordinary beauties - every last one. Rudi Gessler had not exaggerated that at all; there were girls here who could indeed double for Helen of Troy, Aphrodite or Scheherazade. They were also sumptuously well-dressed in evening gowns, with perhaps only the amount of powder and colour on their faces and the low cut of their gowns giving the game away slightly.

One or two of the more spectacular beauties here were even perhaps the equal in physical beauty of the Comtesse de Pourtales. Reminded of that lady, Joe wondered with regret if she was perhaps being bothered by the Paris Police over the mysterious and violent death of her manservant, Jacques. Yet with her likely friends and influence in Paris, Joe somehow doubted that.

Joe strolled around, studying each girl in turn, and receiving often dazzling smiles in response. Yet none looked exactly like Cecile Flammarion, so he decided he would have to take Winteler's clear tip at face value and try the higher floors of *Le Royale* to see what was on offer there.

*

Joe soon appreciated Winteler's advice - the second floor (what the English would call a first floor) was a completely different proposition from the first.

On this floor the mood was more bacchanalian. The girls, in particular, had loosened up both their costumes and their behaviour.

Here were girls dressed in all manner of titillating wear, as Greek nymphs in diaphanous chiffon robes, as Oriental dancers with bare midriffs, in trousers, in pantaloons, in tight riding breeches with a riding crop in their hands and a glitter in their eyes. There were petticoats, crinolines, ballet skirts, basques, camisoles, corsets and flesh-coloured tights, a cornucopia of lingerie and extravagant female bodies. It was quite diverting, and for a few minutes Joe allowed the purpose for his visit here to slip to the back of his mind as he wandered around in a daze of enjoyment. There wasn't much evidence of the search for women's equality here, no earnest suffragette faces. These girls seemed content with their lot in life - to sit on quivering old knees, to stroke white-haired chins and fondle paunches. Or, more likely perhaps, they were simply accomplished actresses who'd learned how to hide their real feelings...

Occasionally a girl, after a whispered exchange with her paramour, would lead her particular elderly suitor to the staircase to ascend even higher up this temple of delight. The real action, apparently, took place on the third floor in private rooms and chambers.

Joe, overwhelmed by the beauty on all sides, was no longer so sure that he would even be able to recognise Cecile Flammarion amongst all these painted and extravagant sorceresses. On the positive side, Blumenfeld was thankfully not here though; Joe had no doubt he would still have recognised *him* without difficulty. By now, Joe had come to the conclusion that he was going to need someone's help to track down the elusive Cecile...

As if reading his thoughts, Joe suddenly found himself confronted by a girl who clearly didn't give two hoots for the "house rules". Before Joe knew what was happening, she had linked arms with his, and asked brightly, '*Etes-vous Français, M'sieur?*'

Joe couldn't get away now even if he wanted to; this girl had a grip like iron. '*Non, Ma'mselle, je suis Américain.*'

The girl seemed astounded by her luck. '*Un vrai Américain?*'

She appeared as likely a choice, though, as any of the other girls to try, so Joe didn't struggle too hard to escape and allowed himself to be led to a *chaise longue* in a quiet corner alcove.

'I'm pleased to meet you, M'sieur,' the girl said, as they sat down together. '*Je m'appelle Catherine. Et qu'est-ce que vous appelez-vous?...Oh, M'sieur Appeldoorn...Enchanté, M'sieur...*'

*

Joe soon realised from her accent that Catherine was not French, though. And that was confirmed when she told him – with seeing reluctance - that her last name was Walters. 'You're English, then,' he guessed.

Catherine smiled wryly and replied, still in French, 'Yes, I am, although I was hoping no one would realise it. I've worked so hard on my French accent. What gave me away?'

'More the way you look than your accent alone,' he responded diplomatically.

'Actually I already knew you were American before I spoke to you. I've had my eye on you ever since you came in.'

Joe glanced at her warily. 'Really? I don't remember seeing you downstairs at all.'

Catherine smiled enigmatically. 'I was one of the dancers in the music room.'

'You were? Boy or girl?'

'Oh, boy. I have the long legs for trousers and tights. When I played in Pantomime on the stage in London, I was always the Principal Boy. See...' She stretched out her limbs, which were undeniably long and shapely.

It gave Joe the opportunity to study her in frank detail, since she seemed to invite it. Catherine was about twenty or twenty-one, he judged. Dark-haired, with loose black glossy curls. Pretty and pert, of course, but perhaps not a classical beauty like many of the other girls here. Her mouth was painted in a red cupid bow; she had heavy rouge on her cheeks that rather spoilt her, Joe thought. She was not dressed as racily as most of the other girls on this floor, though, wearing a low-cut blouse and a flared skirt that stopped off at the knees. Her stockings were pink, held up with scarlet ribbons. As she stretched out her legs in front of her, Joe couldn't deny her attractiveness – he'd always had a soft spot for saucy girls in pink stockings.

'Since you're English, let's both speak our own language,' he suggested.

'All right. Yeah, why not? It makes a change to be able to relax and talk proper.' Her sudden change of voice was a shock to him, from a pleasant French accent to something much lower-class in English. Her accent sounded to him like an authentic London voice, although more working class than he was used to hearing. Not that he was an expert on English accents, but Catherine's vowels and dropped aitches did sound like those of the flower sellers he'd heard in Covent Garden on his visit to London two years ago. 'Are you from London?' he asked, to be polite.

'Yeah, East End, through and through. I'm a real cockney sparrer. I was born in the port area of Wapping – you can just about 'ear Bow Bells from there - but I grew up on the other side of the river in Rotherhithe.'

Joe knew enough to realise that those were two of the poorest and roughest slum areas in East London, so he had to wonder how a working class girl from there had managed to get to Switzerland and a place like *Le Royale*. 'So you were on the stage?'

'Yeah, music 'all dancer. But I can't sing or act, so that sort of limited my opportunities.' Joe wasn't sure whether she was being ironic or not with that last comment. She looked at him critically. 'You're not goin' to ask me 'ow I got 'ere, or wot's a nice girl like me doin' in a place like this, are yer?'

Joe had been about to ask something *exactly* like that, but quickly decided against it. 'Of course not!' he denied vigorously, before moving swiftly on to his real reason for being here tonight. 'Catherine, do you know a girl called Cecile who works here?'

Catherine made a pout. 'That's not a question I wanted to 'ear, either.'

'Do you know her?'

'I'm new 'ere,' she finally admitted. 'I don't know that many of the other girls by name yet.'

Joe sniffed suspiciously. 'How new are you?'

'A few days...' Catherine coughed in embarrassment, '...well, yesterday actually. They needed a new dancer for the waltz team so I was able to start immediately. It did feel a little like an animal auction – Madame checks your 'air and teeth as if she's looking for liver fluke.'

Joe muttered under his breath; this girl wasn't going to be of much help to him. Of all the girls here, he had to pick this one – although, now he recalled, actually it was *she* who had picked *him*...

'But I think I do know Cecile,' she offered with more eagerness - a little too much eagerness, he thought, as if she was trying to keep his interest. 'Blonde girl, very pretty. Could that be the one?'

Joe gave her the benefit of the doubt even though still suspicious of how suddenly her memory had improved. 'Have you seen her tonight?'

Catherine stretched out her legs again; it was clearly her favourite means of distracting his attention, and it worked all too well, Joe had to admit. 'I suppose she's with a gentleman hupstairs. Why do you want '*er* in particular, anyway? You don't even know 'er, do you? Aren't I good enough for yer? I can do more for yer than any French girl can.' She made an even more provocative pout with her painted cupid lips. 'Wouldn't yer like to go hupstairs where we can 'ave some privacy?'

Joe was tempted to agree; it seemed like the only way he was going to get within striking distance of Cecile on the third floor – assuming she *was* on the third floor somewhere. 'How much will that cost me?' he asked warily.

Catherine nodded in the direction of the far corner of the room where a number of boisterous men were sitting on a sofa, engaged in raucous conversation with an elderly woman. 'You 'ave to agree the fee with Madame Malet and pay 'er directly. I'm not allowed to negotiate. You are permitted to tip me for...*especially good*...service, though. But, perhaps, if you 'ave to ask the price, you can't really afford it.' Catherine gave him a coy look, clearly a challenge, but still seemed surprised when he readily accepted the idea.

They walked over to the far end of the room where Catherine bent over and whispered in Madame's ear. Madame Malet was a faded beauty in her sixties, rouged and powdered like a clown, and presiding over the men around her like a queen with her court of flunkeys.

Madame Malet eased her still substantial figure up from the sofa, her breasts threatening to explode from her low-cut dress as she strained herself to stand. She survived however, and pulled Joe aside to whisper a figure in his ear. He resisted the urge to drop his jaw in astonishment at the amount mentioned - it was *two month's* salary for him back in New York. Yet Joe reasoned that James Winthrop wouldn't mind spending this money if it really might lead to him finding his granddaughter.

But could he just be wasting Winthrop's money by going up to the third floor? Was there somewhere in this building even higher than the third floor, perhaps? Was it even possible that Eleanor Winthrop could be here in this very building, held in a secret room against her will? A brothel might be the perfect place to hide a young heiress, after all; Eleanor had been a good-looking girl at sixteen and wouldn't look at all out of place here among these disparate beauties.

Catherine was standing a little apart from Joe and Madame Malet while the deal was being agreed. The men on the sofa behind her were still in celebratory mood about something, blowing cigar smoke in Catherine's direction, together with the odd lewd comment. A bold military type among them - an Englishman, from his stiff little brush of a moustache and his awful French – went further than the others, though, lifting Catherine's short skirt and giving her bottom a thunderous eye-watering smack while licking his lips. 'And very nice too, Madame,' he complimented her sarcastically.

She turned on him in a fury and smacked him savagely across the face; despite the unpleasant look of the man, Joe had to give the Englishman a little begrudging credit for taking an impressive punch like without going backwards over the end of the sofa.

'Who's an uppity young whore, then?' the man complained peevishly, clutching his cheek.

Madame Malet was aghast and rushed over to the defence of her guest. Her rouged and sagging cheeks flared even redder with anger. 'Oh, my apologies, Colonel Blair,' she said in broken English. 'This girl is new. I will have her beaten and thrown out immediately.'

The colonel was magnanimous, though. 'No, Madame. It's not necessary,' he said stiffly.

'Oh, I insist.' But when the Englishman still declined to see her punished, Madame pushed Catherine forward roughly. 'At least say sorry, girl. This gentleman is a countryman of yours.'

Catherine seemed less than subservient, but she did mumble a begrudging sort of apology.

'I think you do deserve a good spanking, my girl,' the colonel said severely, touching his wounded cheek again.

The Madame intervened. 'On the 'ouse, Colonel Blair. Give 'er a good tanning.' She hesitated. 'But please no scarring of the cheeks – the girl must work after all...'

Joe finally butted in to rescue Catherine. 'Madame, this young lady is already promised to me,' he pointed out icily. 'I have agreed a price with you and I expect you to honour it.'

Catherine glanced at him but didn't look particularly grateful for his intervention.

The Madame wavered for a moment, but avarice won out. Joe suspected that he was paying considerably more than the usual rate. She eyed him up and down. 'Cash in advance, please, M'sieur.'

Joe paid up without a murmur and Catherine was allowed to go with a dismissive shrug of Madame's ancient head. She led him upstairs. 'Thank you. I don't even know your first name.'

'You should know that at least,' Joe agreed. 'It's Joseph.'

'Well, I'll call you "Joe"...it's a good East End name...' She smiled at him

– a genuine smile, Joe thought - and he felt a surge of real pleasure, '...because, Joe, you're young enough and pretty enough, that really I feel guilty to be costing yer so much sausage and mash...'

'Eh?' he asked, perplexed.

'Sorry, it's rhyming slang,' she explained. 'Sausage and mash...*cash*...'

*

In a private candlelit room on the third floor, Joe sat on a silk upholstered chaise longue, drinking champagne on ice, and wondering just how he intended to go about finding Cecile Flammarion in the rabbit warren of rooms that apparently existed on this level of *Le Royale*. He regarded without enthusiasm the erotic *Karma Sutra* pictures on the wall opposite, with portrayals of sex in quite utterly impossible positions. In his present preoccupied state, they did nothing to arouse him at all.

Catherine reclined on the green silk chaise beside him, apparently relaxed, and not at all put out by his apparent lack of interest in her, now that they were alone. 'Go on, tell me more about yerself,' she urged yet again, sipping from a glass.

'Nothing much to tell,' Joe said absently.

She put her glass down and moved closer. Then she placed her arms around his neck and kissed him tentatively on the lips.

He kissed her in return but only half-heartedly at best.

Her eyes widened. 'I'm not borin' you, Joe, am I?' she complained. 'Do yer want somethin' different? I could dress up as a boy again, if that's what yer prefer...'

Joe's thoughts were still elsewhere entirely. 'No, that's not what I want, Catherine. I'm sorry. I just need to clear my head a little and take a walk outside in the corridor.'

'There's a potty under the centre table,' she said pointedly.

'That's not what I want either, Catherine.' Joe excused himself. 'I'll be back soon, so please don't go away. Five minutes at most, I promise.'

'Where are yer going? It's not allowed for yer to wander around up 'ere alone.'

'I'm sure Madame would make an exception for me.' Joe didn't wait for an argument and stepped outside. The dimly lit red corridor was not a simple straight one, though, but seemed to have as many branches and turns as a maze. He took a few steps, then looked back. It would be easy to get lost in this maze and not be able to find his way back to Catherine again...

He noted the number 15 on Catherine's door and then went a little way down each corridor in turn, trying to familiarise himself with the layout of the rooms.

Then he set off properly down what looked like the main corridor. He tried every door on each side but all were either locked or empty.

So he reluctantly made his way back to Room 15 again and then followed the first side corridor. He tried the first door and eased it open expecting to find an empty room yet again. But instead, to his embarrassment, he discovered two voluptuous white beauties pummelling with birch twigs the shrivelled buttocks of an elderly naked man stretched out on a bed like a wire coat hanger. All three were so engrossed in their task that Joe was able to withdraw discreetly and close the door without anyone noticing.

In the second room he came to, a languid oriental beauty in a sarong was contorting herself into remarkable shapes in front of a bearded fat man who looked exactly like the King of England. This girl saw him, though, and her eyes widened briefly before Joe breathed a silent apology and retreated into the corridor again.

Joe moved on hurriedly. The third door was locked, *and* the fourth. But in the fifth room he struck gold: the beautiful Cecile without a doubt, naked from the waist up and with her hands bound, bare back riding a portly man who Joe recognised from the Paris newspapers as being the current French Minister of the Interior. Joe was certain it was her, as she squeaked in alarm at the sight of him. He muttered another rapid apology before closing the door again.

Although Joe was elated to find her, this did not seem like the best time for a private *tête-à-tête* with Mlle Flammarion...

This was harder than Joe had possibly imagined. And what would he say to Cecile if he did manage to have a private conversation with her? *Have you and Herr Blumenfeld kidnapped an American heiress by any chance? Would you like to tell me where you are holding her...?*

If Eleanor really was here, imprisoned in this building somewhere, then Joe realised he would need a close ally who understood the layout of this place, to have any chance of finding her.

Pensively he made his way his way back to Room 15 and Catherine. She was still sitting in the same forlorn pose on the chaise, her face bemused.

And then something timeless happened to Joe Appeldoorn... something to do with the way the girl on the chaise looked at this particular moment, the candlelight reflected on her bare shoulders, the way she held her head to one side, the depth of momentary sadness in her eyes.

Joe felt his senses uplifted by this common girl - by the sight and sound of her - such a welling up of tenderness for her that it deprived him of the power of speech for a moment...

'Why are yer lookin' at me like that? What's wrong?' she asked, and even her voice seemed heightened with a new sense of mystery and tension.

'Nothing.' His voice sounded hoarse and unfamiliar – Joe Appeldoorn had never felt like this about anyone in his entire life and had no idea how to respond...

'Just who are yer, Mr Appeldoorn? *Wot* are yer?' she wanted to know. '*You* 'aven't come 'ere tonight for a girl at all, 'ave yer?'

He fought to re-establish his self-control. 'That's *exactly* what I came here looking for. I'm a detective, Catherine, and I'm trying to find a missing woman.'

Catherine's eyes seemed huge in the half-light. 'Who?'

'A girl called Eleanor.'

'I thought you wanted Cecile. Now it's someone called Eleanor. You really should make up yer mind, Mr Appeldoorn...' Catherine stirred resentfully. 'Do yer want to make love to me or not?' she asked coldly.

Oh, if only she knew what powerful and uncontrollable desires she was stirring in his mind...

But he realised it might wreck his newly formulated plan entirely if he did make love to her, so he kept his voice deliberately cool and detached. 'I'm sorely tempted, but this is work. I need your help. I'll pay you well for any information you can find, Catherine. I want you to keep your eyes and ears open for any talk among the girls about an American woman who might be being held here. Her name is Eleanor Winthrop. She is twenty-one years old, with very white skin and titian hair. Last seen in Paris three months ago.'

'You think she's bein' kept 'ere against 'er will?' Catherine didn't seem ready to ridicule such a notion completely.

'It's possible. Cecile may know the truth. That's why I wanted to meet her tonight. But I'm afraid she's a bit tied up right now...'

'You found Cecile, then, on your travels?'

'In a manner of speaking,' Joe said uneasily.

Catherine thought for a moment, and then seemed to decide. 'Tell me where you're stayin', Mr Appeldoorn - I assume you are in a 'otel somewhere near 'ere. And I'll ask all the girls discreetly and let yer know personally if anyone 'ere has seen or 'eard of such a woman. Is that enough for yer?'

'Thank you. You won't regret it.' He pressed two hundred francs on her immediately. 'There'll be a lot more money, if you can find out anything useful for me.'

Catherine looked uncomfortable, but pocketed the money anyway. 'So what shall we do now?' Her mood seemed as deflated as someone who had just received a brutal and insensitive rejection from a lover.

She really had a touchingly sweet face, he thought, despite the over-rouged cheeks. Joe sat down beside her, and, for all his fine resolve, couldn't resist her any longer. He leaned over to kiss her gently, completely entranced by her and this moment.

But she didn't respond, pulling her head away sharply - and Joe could hardly blame her, considering the cool and casual way he'd treated her earlier tonight.

'You'd better go, Mr Appeldoorn,' she said bleakly. 'I promise I'll see what I can find out for yer...'

CHAPTER 10

Sunday March 16th March 1902

Joe spent Sunday morning revisiting more of his old haunts in and around the city of Zurich. He even went so far as to find his former lodgings and was reunited with the aged Frau Wiedler, his erstwhile landlady, who insisted on cooking him lunch for old time's sake. So it was early afternoon before Joe was able to escape from Frau Wiedler's fulsome hospitality and stroll back along *Limmatquai*, the attractive riverside boulevard on the east side of the Limmat, to his temporary residence, the Hotel *Zurichsee*. This, despite its substantial-sounding name, was only a modest family-run hotel of twenty rooms or so.

Deep in thought, he took the stairs to his room on the fourth floor and closed the door behind him. The room was dim, the thick brocade curtains drawn tightly shut against the bright sun from the west, except for one wafer-thin beam of sunlight at the edge of the window. Joe didn't remember closing the drapes like that but assumed the maid must have left them that way.

Joe took off his short Norfolk jacket, *then jumped suddenly when something cold and metallic touched the back of his neck...*

His heart pounding, he heard a woman's voice behind him say quietly but balefully, in cultured English, 'Be very careful, Mr Appeldoorn. I can see you are unarmed so do *exactly* as I say. Place your hands on top of your head, then walk over to the armchair beside the bed, turn very slowly and sit down facing me. Move your hands anywhere else, and I *promise* I shall kill you! Please believe what I say; I don't indulge in idle threats. This weapon in my hand is a new Browning automatic pistol - British technology at its finest. It would blow a hole in your head the size of a doorknob, and that would be a pity because it is such a handsome head.'

Heart still thudding, Joe did as he was told – sat in the armchair with his hands on his head – and looked at her for the first time. She'd moved back and was standing in the shadows in the corner of the room. The woman was dressed in a long woollen skirt, blouse and chocolate-brown cloak, the hood of the cloak half-concealing her hair and face.

'In case you're wondering whether I would still hit you from here, the answer is yes. I am an excellent shot. The hole in your head might be a *little* smaller because of the distance but that wouldn't be much consolation to you, I'm afraid.'

He didn't recognise her at all, but tried to keep the fear out of his voice. 'Who are you? How did you get in here?'

She moved forward again from the shadows. He noticed something familiar about the way she moved - something he couldn't quite put his finger on.

'Never mind how I got in here. *Have you ever seen real Red Indians, Mr Appeldoorn...?*' the woman said with sudden bizarre irrelevance, and in a quite different voice.

Joe struggled to comprehend for a moment. It couldn't be...*it couldn't be*... 'Miss Cordingly!'

She stepped forward into the thin shaft of sunlight at the edge of the curtains and pushed her hood back to reveal her face. Yet she still seemed nothing like the Miss Cordingly he knew.

Joe didn't try to conceal his amazement. 'So what happened to your nice teeth? And your beautiful hair?'

"Miss Cordingly" shrugged, stepped back into the shadows yet again, and then spoke in another, entirely different, voice. 'Do you recognise this too?...*Yeah, I'm East End through and through - a real cockney sparrer...*'

For a moment Joe thought he was going mad...

Catherine...!

Last night this woman had totally entranced him in some mysterious way, stealing into his soul by some sort of feminine magic. He had barely recognised what was happening until it was too late to resist. He'd gone home from *Le Royale* unable to think of anything else but her. And now...*and now!*...she was holding a gun to his head. Worse than that, though, the girl who'd seduced his senses so completely didn't even exist...

He recovered his poise. 'Well, well. Sweet young Catherine and the educated Miss Cordingly, one and the same person. Who would have thought it? I take my hat off to you, Miss - *whatever your name is*. Perhaps you really were on the stage to pull off such different roles so convincingly.'

Joe was still bewildered despite his casual tone. Miss Cordingly and Catherine Walters – *how could they possibly be the same woman?* And neither resembled this purposeful-looking young woman standing in the shadows in front of him. Joe tried desperately to remember the details of his conversations with both women - he still couldn't quite grasp their merging into one single entity.

The woman's voice was completely different from either of her *alter egos* – "steely" was the only word for it. He would have sworn that he had never seen those eyes before either. Midnight blue, and so striking. She seemed three inches taller than Catherine and thirty pounds lighter than Charlotte. And her features, he could also swear, didn't seem to resemble either woman. And was this short glossy black hair her real hair? It bore no similarity either to the frizzy red of Charlotte, or the dark curls of Catherine.

The woman's eyes glittered dangerously. 'Everywhere I go in this last week, Mr Appeldoorn, *you* seem to turn up like the proverbial bad penny.'

'I could say the same thing about you...'

'Shut up! *I* will ask the questions, Mr Appeldoorn, if that *is* your real name. And I warn you to tell me the truth. Lie to me just once and I shall certainly shoot you. Is that perfectly clear?'

Joe could feel the fear building in him like an ebb tide sucking through his body, threatening to overwhelm him...

'I said – *is that clear?*' the woman repeated with almost a snarl.

Joe forced himself to respond with a sullen nod of acquiescence.

'Did you kill Ma'mselle Langevin?'

Joe was shocked – *how much did this woman know...?* 'No, of course not.'

'But you followed her to Switzerland from Paris. Don't lie! – I know you did. I saw you following her to the Gare de Lyon last Monday.'

'As I told you last night – or "Catherine" anyway -' this was making his mind reel, Joe thought – 'I am looking for an American woman called Eleanor Winthrop. Ma'mselle Langevin worked for her in Paris and I believed she was involved in Eleanor's disappearance.'

'So *you* say, but I'm really not sure I believe you.' She came closer again, keeping the Browning pistol pointed at the centre of his forehead. 'You see, *I* am looking for someone too. A man called *Johan Plesch*. Does that name mean anything to you, "*Mr* Appeldoorn"? No? Well, let me enlighten you, then. Plesch kills people for a fee. He is without doubt the most dangerous man in Europe, a man of many identities. No one knows what he really looks like. I do know for a fact however that he was involved in the assassination of King Umberto of Italy two years ago. More to the point he was also the mastermind behind the murder of your own President, William McKinley, in Buffalo, New York, last September. Where were *you* last September, *Mr* Appeldoorn?'

Joe *had* been in upstate New York that month, but wasn't prepared to admit to it with this woman in such an apparently volatile state of mind. 'I wasn't in Buffalo, you can be sure of that -' he quickly changed the subject - '...I suppose it was no coincidence that you were on the same train as me, leaving Bern on Thursday evening?'

"Miss Cordingly" shrugged. 'Hardly. I knew Plesch would have to leave

Bern for Zurich within a few days so I had the railway station watched. And, lo and behold, *you* showed up, looking nervous and lying relentlessly to policemen. It certainly wasn't difficult to obtain a seat in your compartment at short notice; even Swiss railway clerks are susceptible to bribery, *Herr Plesch*.'

Joe could feel his heart still hammering uncontrollably against his ribs. 'I am not Plesch.'

The woman gave him a cold unwavering stare. 'On the train, you did almost manage to convince me that you weren't Plesch. But when you turned up at *Le Royale* last night, I realised you *had* to be...'

'I am *not* Plesch!' Joe repeated hoarsely. 'You really think this man Plesch could make himself look like me?'

The woman was unimpressed by Joe's argument. 'I told you – no one knows what Plesch really looks like. But one thing we do know is that he can change his appearance in remarkable ways.'

'*He* can,' Joe interjected bitterly.

'I *know* that you are Johan Plesch!' the woman insisted. 'Ma'mselle Langevin was a known associate of yours, and you killed her to silence her.'

Joe felt an increasing desperation as this woman, with relentless but demented logic, built up her seemingly watertight case against him. 'I told you! My name is Joseph Appeldoorn. If Ma'mselle Langevin were my associate, why would I need to follow her at all?'

'Perhaps you'd been planning to kill her for some time...'

'I work for the Pinkerton Agency in New York! Please don't do this! You're making a terrible mistake.' Joe tried frantically to think how he could prove the truth to her. 'Look! In my suitcase there, you'll find my business cards...'

'Anyone can print business cards!' she hissed.

'There are also telegrams in there – from my boss, John Kautsky, in New York, and from Eleanor's grandfather, James Winthrop. Surely you've heard of him? He's one of the richest men in America...'

For the first time, a look of doubt crossed the woman's face. She went across to the suitcase.

'There, in the folder on top,' Joe pointed. 'Read them.'

The woman picked up some of the telegrams and glanced through them, while still keeping the gun trained on Joe the whole time. Finally she shrugged. 'These could just be forgeries. Or perhaps you really are the hapless American you claim to be. But even if you are, I simply can't afford to take that chance and let you go. My instincts still tell me I should kill you. If I'm wrong about this, then I apologise in advance...'

Joe could sense she really was going to kill him; this was no mere game of bluff designed merely to frighten him into talking...

He saw her finger tighten on the trigger; his throat felt so dry that he could barely get out a last panicked plea for his life. 'Wait!' he croaked. 'Kill me, and the real Plesch will still be alive and at liberty. But I can help you find him...'

'How?' The woman was implacable.

Joe felt exhausted, his breathing uncoordinated and his head spinning, but a plausible idea had finally occurred to him despite his predicament. Perhaps Blumenfeld and this Plesch were one and the same man? – that would explain everything! 'I think I might have seen Plesch,' he babbled. 'I can identify him for you.'

She stared at him contemptuously, as if disappointed at this craven attempt to save his life by denying his true identity. 'How would you recognise Plesch, "*Mr* Appeldoorn"? You *claim* not to know anything about him,' she demanded cynically.

'I don't know anything about Plesch as such.' Even to himself Joe thought his hoarse voice sounded like the rasp of a guilty man's. 'But I do know the man who really killed Ma'mselle Langevin. And he knows me.'

The woman sniffed suspiciously. 'Then - if that *is* true - I'm afraid you're unlikely to live very long, Mr Appeldoorn. You see, I too was on the Zurich train last Monday in order to follow Ma'mselle Langevin. And I went to her sleeper compartment in the middle of the night, where I overpowered her eventually... after she'd first done her best to cut my throat.'

'Snap,' Joe said facetiously.

"Miss Cordingly" studiously ignored the comment. '...But I was magnanimous and didn't just offer her the chance to live in return for betraying her master to me, but even a thousand pounds in gold.'

'And she accepted such a generous offer?' Joe commented with bitter sarcasm.

"Miss Cordingly" was apparently immune to irony today, though. 'Yes, Ma'mselle Langevin did decide to cooperate with me...but more because of the gold, I suspect, than anything else,' she added. 'She told me she was on her way to meet Plesch for a new assignment in Zurich, but she didn't yet know where and when. Their previous mission in Paris had been cancelled because their designated victim had suddenly left the city. Ma'mselle Langevin had taken a job there as a maid with the Comtesse de Pourtales, the mistress of the planned victim...*Ah, I can see that name means something to you!*' the woman said triumphantly. 'Ma'mselle Langevin's job was to get close to the lady in question, obtain compromising photographs of her and the gentleman together, and prepare the way for Plesch to then murder them both. The wish was to create a great scandal – to make it look as if the man had murdered his mistress and then taken his own life. Actually it was *my* doing that the planned victim left Paris early, although I didn't tell Ma'mselle Langevin that.' Joe could hear no note of pride in the woman's voice at that statement, even though, if true, it seemed she had foiled a plot and saved two lives. While he, with his meddling, seemed only to have cost a man his life – the unlucky Jacques...

The woman continued. 'Ma'mselle Langevin and I arranged a second meeting in the Hotel *Landhaus* in Bern. There I would give her the thousand pounds in gold, and in return she would give me information about where and when she would keep her next appointment with Plesch in Zurich. She was going to collect a message from Plesch at one of their regular contact points – a certain shoe shop in Bern...'

Joe couldn't stop himself from nodding involuntarily as he realised where Monique must have picked up that notice about the meeting of the Social Democratic Federation of Zurich...

"Miss Cordingly" gave him a studied look. 'But, of course, you know all this already; *you* killed Ma'mselle Langevin before I could get the money and deliver it to her in the hotel...'

Joe had been beginning to think that he had persuaded this woman of his innocence, yet she seemed as unremitting as ever. 'I told you! I am *not* Plesch! Please believe me, for God's sake! I was following Ma'mselle Langevin for an entirely different reason. I told you the truth in *Le Royale* last night. I am a detective looking for a missing woman called Eleanor Winthrop. Ma'mselle Monique Langevin was the paid companion to Eleanor and disappeared from Paris at the same time as her in December. Monique Langevin was my key to finding Eleanor so I would hardly kill her, would I? And if I *am* Plesch, why on earth would I have come to *Le Royale* last night with a story like that?'

The woman still didn't seem persuaded by his argument and remained stubbornly suspicious – yet there was a subdued note in her voice for the first time that Joe found slightly encouraging. 'If what you're saying is really true, then I'm afraid you were following the *wrong* Langevin sister. Did you not know that Ma'mselle Monique Langevin had a twin sister? The woman who was murdered in Bern was *Martine* Langevin. I think perhaps you should have been concentrating your attentions on her sister, Monique.'

Joe was dumfounded. *Could there really be two of those wildcats?* 'You mean *Monique* Langevin is still alive?'

The woman finally lowered her pistol with a sigh. 'Presumably. You don't usually die of old age at twenty-three, after all.' She breathed out with grim resignation. 'I think perhaps you really are who you claim to be. Nobody can pretend to act quite this stupidly – *not even Johan Plesch...*'

*

'Can I put my hands down now?' Joe asked, feeling like a drowning man who'd just been pulled from the ocean and was still gasping for breath on the shore, unable to quite believe he was still alive. When she indicated reluctantly that he could, he continued, with a long exhalation of breath, 'So what's your real name? I can't go on calling you "Miss Cordingly" or

"Catherine".'

'Then call me Amelia.' The woman now seemed ready to trust Joe – to a point anyway. She had even relaxed her guard sufficiently to take a seat, although one well away from Joe's armchair by the bed. She also maintained a wary look on her face and a steely grip on the Browning so Joe could see he wasn't entirely out of the woods with this frightening woman just yet.

'And your last name?' he went on.

'In my business, we don't use last names.'

'I am not *in* your business. So you can tell me, Miss…'

Her eyes suggested amused derision. 'It's Peachy, if you really must know.'

'Miss *Peachy*…?'Joe said disbelievingly. Perhaps it was the association of ideas with that unusual name, but Joe suddenly recalled that intimate, through-the-keyhole view he'd had of "Miss Cordingly" in her underwear in the Hotel *Landhaus* in Bern. The woman did certainly have a bottom like a peach, to match her surname, and seemed to know it too from the way she had been admiring herself. Surely a woman given to admiring her own backside in a mirror couldn't be quite as tough as she made herself out to be, could she? The disrespectfulness of that thought pleased Joe more than somewhat, and he nearly made the mistake of smiling at her as he repeated, 'Miss *Peachy*…? How appropriate…'

She regarded him coldly. 'What do you mean by that?'

He struggled to recover. 'Err…it's an American expression. "Peachy" means "swell" – good.'

Her eyes were still cold. 'Then you're far from peachy, Mr Appeldoorn.'

Joe averted his eyes from hers and tried to recover from his slip. '*Miss Amelia Peachy?* That can't be your real name, surely…'

She shrugged, her expression still icy. 'Who knows any more? But it's as good as any other. And you will need to call me something as I've decided we are going to be working together, Mr Appeldoorn.'

Joe had a feeling he was on the back foot in this conversation again, even if no longer scared out of his wits. 'Whom do *you* work for, may I ask?'

'I work for the British government…'

'You're a spy – a secret agent? You certainly don't look like one.'

'Oh? And what do spies look like, Mr Appeldoorn?' she asked derisively.

Joe conceded that. 'Yes, a fair point, I suppose.'

'I work specifically for the Foreign Office in Whitehall, Mr Appeldoorn. I collect information and take action against anti-British elements. A source – a South African man - had warned us secretly in December that an important Englishman would shortly be assassinated. The chosen assassin was believed to be the infamous Herr Plesch. I had been tracking Plesch for two years before that, trying to eliminate him, but so far without success. So I was given the task of foiling this new crime and hopefully catching Plesch at the same time.'

Joe made a wry face – the dour Miss Cordingly a British agent. Who could believe that? '*Eliminate*?' he said, querying the word she'd used. 'That's an interesting way of putting it...' He had a sudden insight. 'This important prospective victim you mentioned is not the Duke of Lancaster, by any chance, is he?'

Amelia gave him an odd look in return. 'Among his other titles, he is known as that. But how did you know?'

'I did discover that Ma'mselle Langevin was acting as a liaison between this gentleman and the Comtesse de Pourtales. I of course thought she was Monique at the time, though, not Martine...' Joe was silent for a moment at his own stupidity. The concierge in the Rue Lamarck had even told René that Monique was one of *two* sisters, although she hadn't specifically mentioned twins. But when Ma'mselle Langevin had come to his apartment to kill him last Sunday evening, she'd *told* him her real name was Martine, and he'd been too stupid to find out why. Her attempt to kill him had seemed like an overreaction, if all she was involved in was a bit of extortion from a rich American girl. But it made more sense now, if Martine was in the political assassination business and had mistaken him for a government agent on her trail. Presumably that was also the reason Blumenfeld had tried to kill him...

Amelia was becoming suspicious of him again. 'You really know far too much for such a supposedly innocent fool.'

Joe was resentful: *she*, after all, hadn't done any better than him against Mlle Langevin and Herr Plesch, had she? – well, not much better, anyway. 'I may know even more than you think,' he said, slightly boastfully, wanting to impress her. 'Why did you get a job at *Le Royale*? Did you have information from your source that a second attempt would be made on the duke's life there?'

Amelia shook her head. 'I knew Plesch was going to Zurich, and I simply guessed that *Le Royale* was the most likely place where he would try again.'

Joe smiled grimly. 'Well, Amelia, your judgement seems to have been vindicated. Perhaps you need to have a good long talk with your colleague at *Le Royale*, Ma'mselle Cecile Flammarion.'

'Why would I want to do that?'

'Because I have a feeling she might have taken over Martine's new assignment with Plesch. I saw her on Friday evening, here in Zurich, meeting a man called Blumenfeld. This man was on the same train from Paris as Ma'mselle Langevin – Martine Langevin - and you and I. After Ma'mselle Langevin was killed in Bern, Blumenfeld tried to skewer me too. That's why I think there is a good chance *he* is the person who killed Martine. In other words, he and your mysterious Plesch could be one and the same man.'

'You don't know that for sure, though, do you?'

'Of course I can't be sure.' Joe was becoming more irritated by this woman now than frightened.

Amelia studied him with hooded eyes for a moment before admitting, slightly begrudgingly, 'It would make sense, though. If Plesch had learned of Martine's betrayal in some way, then it seems logical he would silence her. But how could he have found out?'

'Perhaps he overheard you and Martine plotting to betray him?'

'Perhaps, but I don't think so, otherwise I don't believe *I* would still be alive now. More likely he was on the same train from Paris as her, without her knowledge, and spotted you following her. So he decided to dissolve the partnership permanently.'

Joe felt a sudden chill through his bones as he considered the likelihood of that suggestion. 'And what about Cecile?' he countered uneasily.

'It does also make sense that Plesch would need another accomplice to replace Martine. And perhaps Cecile would be a suitable choice. I asked the other girls about her after you left last night. It seems that, although she is French, her mother is South African. It can't be a coincidence...'

Joe let out a long sigh of exasperation. He'd got it all wrong. Martine Langevin, Blumenfeld/Plesch, Cecile Flammarion – none of them probably had anything to do with Eleanor Winthrop at all...

He was precisely nowhere, and had been chasing all over Europe in entirely the wrong direction.

Yet - *a puzzle* - it did seem that Eleanor was in Switzerland judging from her recent request for money to be sent to an account in a Zurich bank...

'All right,' Joe said, becoming assertive again. 'I've told you what I know about Blumenfeld. He could be your Herr Plesch. So, Miss Peachy, I suggest you go and find him. He's here in Zurich somewhere, and he will no doubt appear at *Le Royale* in due course. Presumably Plesch, in some guise or other, is planning to kill the duke if he is foolish enough to turn up at *Le Royale*. Now let me get back to my more mundane job of finding *Monique* Langevin and my American heiress. What do you say if you go your own way from now on, and I go mine? Is that agreeable to you?'

Amelia's nostrils flared and Joe thought for a moment that she was entertaining serious thoughts of shooting him again. 'It's *not* all right, Mr Appeldoorn. The "Duke of Lancaster", as you call him, is indeed in Switzerland right now. He will certainly visit *Le Royale* - he always does have a regular assignation there – and I doubt that he can be persuaded to give up that pleasure without better evidence of a plot against him than we've presently got. But Plesch can disguise himself as a gentleman client, *any client*. And I am the only one on the inside at *Le Royale* who can stop him. If you're really as innocent as you claim, then you will help me.'

'How can I help you? And more to the point, what the Hell do I care about the Duke of Lancaster?'

She raised her Browning pistol again threateningly. 'If you don't help me, I shall give your name to the police in Bern as the murderer of Martine Langevin.'

Joe was incensed. Without thinking, he reached beneath the bed and pulled out his own concealed Webley, which he cocked and pointed at her. 'Checkmate, I think, Miss Peachy.'

She laughed sourly and lowered the Browning. 'You really think a gun like that will keep you alive, Mr Appeldoorn. Let me tell you, it won't. You have to help me find Plesch and kill him, otherwise your own life is as good as over. Plesch doesn't like loose ends, and *you* are the loose end to end all loose ends.'

'Brilliantly put.' Joe had to admit sourly that her analysis of the situation was probably correct, though, as he lowered his gun again. He'd seen Blumenfeld in action; that man was not a person to leave someone alive who could identify him.

Amelia tried to be more encouraging. 'Consider this, Mr Appeldoorn. Plesch is a direct link to Martine, and perhaps therefore also to finding her sister Monique and your heiress. If you help me, perhaps *I* can help *you* in due course...'

Joe remained stubborn in his refusal to get involved, though. 'But I have complete faith in you, Miss Peachy. I think you'll be more than a match for Plesch, all by your sweet self.'

'No, I won't. The truth is he knows what I look like, but I have never seen him.'

'But he doesn't know Miss Cordingly or Catherine Walters, does he?'

'Not as far as I know. But I still need your help inside *Le Royale*. You claim you could recognise Plesch. And as a customer at *Le Royale*, you have a freedom of movement denied to me. Don't you see? Together we could get this man and solve both our problems.' She cast him a doubtful look. 'You do know who the Duke of Lancaster really is, don't you, Mr Appeldoorn? It's a *nom de guerre* only, an alias. There is no such title in reality as the Duke of Lancaster...'

'Then who is your mystery man, Miss Peachy?'

Amelia was solemn. 'He is Edward the Seventh, King of England, Scotland and Ireland...Emperor of India...undisputed head of the greatest empire on Earth...'

Joe was dumfounded for a moment. 'Then, Miss Peachy, I suggest you'd better hurry and catch Plesch as soon as possible.'

'Why?'

Joe remembered the man he'd seen in the room with the contorted sylph-like Oriental beauty. 'Because I think, Miss Peachy, that the King was already at *Le Royale* last night...'

CHAPTER 11

Sunday March 16th 1902

Another evening in Paradise.

Yet the mood of *Le Royale* was subtly different on this Sunday evening from the previous night. Or perhaps it was simply Joseph Appeldoorn's own mood that had darkened, and with it, his perceptions of this place...

Last night he'd been entertaining the slight optimistic hope that a meeting with Cecile Flammarion might soon lead him directly to the missing Eleanor; while the problem of Blumenfeld had only been a peripheral one: that of trying to avoid him should he turn up here. But tonight, thoughts of Eleanor were far removed from his mind; tonight was all about trying to catch Blumenfeld who was now revealed to be a much more dangerous adversary than even his behaviour in Bern might have suggested...

Such reflections did serve to concentrate the mind at least, Joe thought, as he circulated through the gaming rooms on the lowest floor of *Le Royale*.

Winteler spotted him almost immediately. 'Oh no, Joseph. Two nights in a row? You haven't been seduced by the glamorous ladies of this place too, have you? Well, I can hardly blame you...' – he shook his head in mock sadness – '...but a fine, upstanding, all-American boy like you...shame on you...' Erwin went off, laughing to himself. Joe was glad that someone at least was getting a little cynical amusement from the evening...

Joe soon felt compelled by something that felt uncomfortably like voyeurism to wander into the music room and watch tonight's cabaret. The floor had again been cleared for a waltz display by the same seductive line of couples as the previous night, but the outfits had changed at least. Tonight the girls were dressed in columbine outfits - again with completely bare bottoms, though – while their "boy" partners were white-faced Pierrots. The Pierrots twirled their columbines in carefully choreographed time and as on the evening before, still cleverly managed to conceal all but an occasional tantalising glimpse of their partners' naked derrieres from the lascivious gaze of the assembled male spectators. Somehow the prurient overtones of the performance were still outweighed by the sheer charm and panache of its execution – in Joe's mind anyway.

Joe saw the same beautiful girl as last night – the one he had mistaken for Cecile – but this time his attention was mostly concentrated on the "boys", the Pierrots. And one "boy" in particular...

He spotted her at once, even in white face make-up, because this was Catherine again. And, ridiculously, he felt his heart race because he was, in a sense, still strongly attracted to "Catherine". What a fool he was! How René would mock his stupidity, if he knew. He had fallen for a chimera, a figment of another woman's imagination.

He stood watching, absolutely entranced by her – the same woman who had scared the wits out of him this afternoon; but she made not the slightest sign of recognition towards him in return. A true professional to the end, he realised morosely. Or had he simply dreamed this afternoon's encounter with her after all?

*

Tonight, after the show, Joe did not linger long in the gaming rooms but soon made his way to the second floor to make his assignation with "Catherine", as agreed.

He was not armed with a firearm, although he would have dearly liked to be. There'd been simply no way of getting his massive Webley past the eagle-eyed Ernst on the door without the bulge in his tail coat being all too noticeable. But he did have an eight-inch knife taped to his right calf that he could reach within a second's notice. He knew he was putting his own life on the line tonight; Blumenfeld/Plesch had the advantage that he was, reputedly, a master of disguise and could be almost anybody here within reason, while he himself was patently exposed. Perhaps that was the intent of Miss Peachy's plan – *he* was to be the live bait, the tethered goat, to draw out the assassin without risking the neck of her own philandering monarch.

This afternoon he'd still taken some persuasion to come here tonight in these circumstances.

'Since you claim to work for the British government,' he'd asked Miss Peachy petulantly, 'why can't you simply advise the King, or his aides, to give *Le Royale* a miss on the royal itinerary through Switzerland this time? That's what you did in Paris, wasn't it, to warn him of the danger at the Comtesse de Pourtales' home? Anyway, a monarch must also have an entourage of aide-de-camps and detectives to protect him - kings don't travel around alone, even when engaged in hanky-panky, do they? Why do I need to risk *my* neck?'

But Amelia had been blunt in her reply. 'Your neck is already half in the noose if Blumenfeld knows you're still alive, Mr Appeldoorn. So you are saving your own life by doing this. And, in any event, it's impossible for me to give a direct warning; the King is travelling incognito in Switzerland with only a butler and a single detective as companions. They simply wouldn't believe me even if I managed to find them and warn them in time.'

'Then inform them through your official channels in London,' Joe had riposted.

She shook her head impatiently. 'My name, and my connections to the Foreign Office, are known to only a handful of people in Whitehall - in fact, only *two* government officials in London knew of my true identity and my mission in search of Johan Plesch. And since I believe the King is already in Zurich, there simply isn't enough time to try and contact these two men and get a warning to him through official channels, as I did in Paris...'

So Joe had been forced to concede that she was probably right, and had eventually agreed to help her. In the end, he had done it almost willingly, for the chance to see his "Catherine" come to life again. He had to wait for her to appear, though – presumably she was changing from her Pierrot costume.

Despite himself, his heart raced at the thought of her. How strange that he should find the one *alter ego* of this woman so appealing, and the other frankly intimidating. He was still quite unable to think of them as one woman; he wondered who she would be tonight – would she be Catherine, or simply Miss Peachy in disguise? In his heart he knew he wanted "Catherine" to be the real essence of this woman, and the hard and practical Miss Peachy to be the illusion...

He watched the debauchery and carousing going around him with a detached mind. The tall girl who favoured tight white riding breeches and a riding crop as her mode of seduction tried to catch his eye. But Joe was keeping watch more for Cecile and any man with her who might vaguely resemble Herr Blumenfeld. The man did indeed have an anonymous kind of face – Joe found it difficult to picture that face or remember its salient features. He'd certainly been clean-shaven. But did he have a large nose or a small one? A dimpled chin or a flat one? He couldn't say.

But the eyes – yes, there'd been something odd about the man's eyes. A strange yellow-amber colour like the glow in a cathode ray tube.

He was going to attract a few odd comments, though, if he spent the night here staring into men's eyes, looking for an amber glow...

In order to try and secure his help voluntarily, Miss Peachy had finally deigned this afternoon to tell him what she knew of the background of the Langevin sisters, Martine and Monique. It did reflect a life rather different from the home life of the late dear queen...

*

Joe had suppressed his excitement when Amelia had asked casually, 'Have you ever heard of the *Narodniki*, Mr Appeldoorn?'

'No, I don't believe so,' he lied, with barely a flicker of his eyes.

'Thirty years ago that was the name of a secret revolutionary student movement in Russia. The *Narodniki* derived their name from the activities of their first student members, something they called *hozhdenie v narod* - meaning literally "going to the people". These student idealists went out from universities disguised as peasants to try to convert villagers to socialism.' Amelia shook her head vaguely. 'But socialism has always appealed far more to middle-class intellectuals and the urban working class than the peasantry, particularly in Russia. The *Narodniki* found that their ideas were simply too complicated for the ungrateful peasants to comprehend, so the movement was stillborn - an abject failure. One of the young student leaders of this movement was a man called Vasily Melikov. The Tsar was one of the few people not to realise that the *Narodniki* were a joke rather than a serious political threat, so Vasily was duly arrested by the Tsar's secret police and tortured...' Amelia frowned as her thoughts seemed to wander for a moment, '...which of course turned him into a martyr of sorts and rescued his political credibility. Vasily escaped eventually from exile in Siberia and fled to Paris in eighteen seventy-five with his beautiful sister, Olga Melikova. In Paris, Vasily met and fell in love with Sylvie Langevin, the daughter of the Mayor of Rouen. They had twin daughters born in 'seventy-eight, regrettably out of wedlock, but Sylvie died of typhus shortly afterwards. When the twins were still only a year old, their father, Vasily, was murdered in Paris by Tsarist agents, and the girls were orphaned. They were subsequently brought up by their Russian maiden aunt after they had been rejected by their bourgeois grandfather, who apparently refused to take them into his house. So perhaps their uncompromising attitude to the world was formed very early on.'

'What happened to their Aunt Olga?'

Amelia shrugged. 'I don't know. The file I read on the Langevin sisters didn't say. She died too, probably.'

'And then?'

'The girls grew up both intelligent and rebellious. The sisters were close as children; each hated the political order and establishment represented by her grandfather – for understandable reasons perhaps. They both became nihilists, but eventually they had a falling out of their own. According to the British file on them, Martine is – or was – the crazier, more violent of the pair. Monique, by contrast, is the more naïve and idealistic type of revolutionary. As far as I know, unlike her sister, Martine, she's not actually wanted by the police for any crime so far, if that's any consolation to you in your search for Miss Winthrop.'

'So where does Plesch come into the story? He doesn't sound like a political idealist.'

'He's not and never was. But then we know so little about him, to be honest. Probably born in Linz in Austria; his father may have been a Customs official. We don't know how or when he started his murderous career, but he has killed at least ten notable people to our knowledge. We do believe that Martine Langevin met Plesch about three years ago and, somehow or other, fell under the thrall of the man. He is apparently renowned for his ability to mesmerise susceptible women...'

'That would preclude you, Miss Peachy, I suppose.'

She regarded him coolly. 'It would, Mr Appeldoorn.'

'What else do you know about Plesch?'

'As I say, nothing at all about his personal appearance. He is the ultimate assassin, though. Since he took Martine under his wing, she too has become an accomplished and remorseless assassin.'

'And the other sister, Monique? What is the last sighting that British Intelligence had of her?'

'Paris, two years ago. Since then, she has completely disappeared from view. As I said, she is more a political revolutionary and idealist than violent anarchist. That's not to say that she might not be involved in the disappearance of your Miss Winthrop, though.' Amelia frowned unexpectedly. 'Is this woman your sweetheart, Mr Appeldoorn? Is that the reason such an ill-equipped person as you was sent to Europe to find her? Is it a personal mission of yours rather than a purely professional one?'

She really did know how to wound his feelings, but Joe replied smartly in kind, 'If I'm so inept, Miss Peachy, why is it that *you* need my help so badly?'

But she only smiled thinly in response, clearly not wanting to lose her sacrificial tethered goat for the evening...

'Your American heiress could be in big trouble, though, if Monique really has her claws in her, filling her head with politics. Maybe she has even turned your rich and, no doubt, spoilt American girl into a fire-spitting revolutionary like herself...'

*

Madame Malet had recognised him from the last evening and came over to congratulate him on his good sense in returning again so soon.

'One of my girls has clearly won your affections, M'sieur,' she simpered as she tried to remember which girl. 'Who did you escort last night? Ah yes, the new English girl. An interesting choice...'

Joe had to agree privately with that.

Madame Malet was dressed even more bizarrely and provocatively than the previous night - a tight-laced bodice of green silk and a skirt that was stretched taut over her massive buttocks like the planking on a water barrel. Her breasts had been forced up by the bodice into huge mountains of white flesh, a trembling mass that resembled an imminent avalanche about to descend on the green valley below.

'Is Mam'selle Catherine here tonight?' he asked.

'Yes, she is. And I'm sure I can make her available.' This was said with the relieved air of someone anxious to get rid of a troublesome relative. Yet Madame Malet, despite the clear sounds of the cash register ringing in her ears, seemed nervous and ill at ease. Was the King of England already on the premises, Joe wondered? Could that be the reason for her discomfort?

Joe spotted the English colonel who had given "Catherine" that hefty smack last night (and received an even better one in return) – clearly here was someone else who couldn't bear to stay away from *Le Royale*. What was his name again? - Blair! – that was it. He was circulating the room admiring the girls and their semi-naked lacy finery, a definite gleam in his feverish eye.

And then "Catherine" herself appeared, dressed in a pink corset and flesh-coloured tights that showed every contour of her body. It was an eye-catching ensemble even in this room full of mouth-watering female delight. Even Colonel Blair couldn't take his eyes off her as she glided across the room. But she sidestepped adroitly away from him as he seemed about to intercept her, and, with a look of distaste in his direction, joined Joe and Madame Malet instead. Joe was dazzled by the change in her looks and personality; this woman truly was a born Sarah Bernhardt. Her skin glowed; she seemed more voluptuous. It was frankly impossible to believe that she and the relentless Miss Peachy could be one and the same person.

She was definitely putting on a *tour de force* of her acting art tonight, but also trying to impress and seduce simply with the way she looked. And Joe, without any justification at all, had the absurd conviction that she had dressed like this to entrance him in particular...

And it was working...he was seduced by her physical presence as completely as on the previous night, even knowing she was a complete fake. Perhaps that knowledge even heightened the attraction, knowing that inside the pink silk and gauze of that seductive costume was the practical and resourceful Amelia Peachy.

She was completely in character. 'I'm glad you came back, tonight, M'sieur,' she said in French. But it was Catherine's voice entirely – no trace of Miss Amelia Peachy.

Madame Malet beamed her approval. 'My dear, you look enchanting tonight. Does she not, M'sieur?'

"Catherine" accepted the accolade with a graceful bow.

'I'd be honoured if I could escort you again tonight, Ma'mselle,' Joe said, not to be outdone in the gallantry stakes. The deal was soon made again with Madame for three hours of her time.

'Perhaps we can give you a concession rate next time,' Madame Malet suggested with a smirk. 'It is allowed to try the other girls, you know. Gretchen the huntress, Juanita, our Terpsichorean delight, Magda, the graceful horsewoman...' She indicated the girl in the white riding breeches who was still fingering her riding crop in a distracted manner.

'Perhaps another time,' Joe responded politely.

Catherine smiled faintly. 'Shall we go up to our private salon on the third floor, M'sieur?'

As he climbed the stairs behind her, Joe had a lot of time to admire the perfection of "Catherine's" figure. But his admiration for her enticing figure and her revealing outfit was offset by his concern that she was clearly unarmed tonight. In that skin-tight outfit, there was certainly no place that Miss Peachy could be concealing her Browning pistol, that much was certain...

*

Even in private she stayed mostly in character, even if she had dispensed with the East London working class accent.

By now Joe thought he was beginning to understand the truth about Amelia Peachy. It may well have been the truth that playing these roles maintained her anonymity in a dangerous business, yet it was clear she also enjoyed submerging her own identity and taking on new ones. She didn't simply act the part of Miss Cordingly or Catherine; she *became* them, she inhabited every fragment of their imagined lives. That was why Miss Cordingly and Catherine Walters had seemed so real; in a sense, they *were* real.

The illusion was so complete, it was as if he was talking with Catherine for the first time since he took his leave of her in this same room last night. Except that now they were talking of rather different things...

She poured Joe a glass of champagne, sitting beside him on the same chaise longue as last night and playing the same part without a hint of embarrassment or self-consciousness, even though her "audience" was now in on the act and knew this was a performance. The candlelight picked out the white satin sheen of her skin, the shadows under her eyes, the delicate bone structure of her face. Her toenails were pink – he hadn't noticed that detail before, nor the slight enticing indentations of her vertebrae along the nape of her slender neck.

'Do you know for certain if the King – sorry – the Duke of Lancaster – is here tonight?' he asked her finally.

'He arrived half an hour ago, and has already been escorted from a private entrance at the back to one of the rooms on this floor, where he is no doubt being entertained by his lady for the evening.'

'He must have his detective guard with him, surely.'

'His detective is in the building, but he usually waits below with Madame's kitchen staff. The King does not like having his every movement watched.'

'I can't blame him for that. So how many rooms are there like this one?'

'Sixteen, I believe. And I haven't been able to find out which one the King is using tonight. However the rooms are usually locked from the inside – for obvious reasons...' - "Catherine" coughed and looked at him wryly '- ...particularly after a man was seen prowling these corridors last night and entering rooms he shouldn't have...'

Joe tactfully avoided her eye.

'Therefore the King should be in no danger for the present,' she continued, 'provided he's with a trustworthy girl. The real risk will come when he leaves the security of his private room and is escorted back down to the secret exit. If I were Plesch, that's where I would strike – on the stairs or in the garden...'

'Who is the King with tonight? Not Cecile, I hope?'

'No, I'd be far more worried if he was. But from what I've learned, it seems he has asked for the company of Jacqueline Samedi, his current favourite - the same lady you claim you saw with him last night. She is a Eurasian from the city of Saigon in Indo-China.'

'Is he safe with her?'

'That rather depends what you mean by "safe"...' she said with a faint smile. It seemed that in the guise of "Catherine", she could be gently ironic in a way that the real Amelia Peachy could probably never be, Joe thought.

'...She is reputed to be capable of incredible bodily contortions so he may suffer a slipped disc or hernia if he attempts to keep up with her.' "Catherine" even laughed at her own little joke. 'But if you're right about Cecile working with Plesch, then better the King develops a hernia caused by a surfeit of Miss Samedi, than a large bullet wound caused by a Mauser.'

'Does the King ever ask for the company of more than one girl at a time?'

'Oh frequently, if you believe the gossip – but not tonight, apparently.' "Catherine" fell silent for a moment, then moved closer and almost snuggled up to him - Joe was taken too much by surprise to say anything at this slightly surreal turn of events. 'That woman, Madame Malet, will check up on us, so we have to look the part,' she whispered as explanation for her intimate behaviour. 'I'm sure there are peepholes in the walls in each of these rooms, and I suspect her beady eye may be trained on us very soon. Her name really should be Madame *Malaise,* not Malet.'

'Is this not mortifying for you - playing the part of Catherine?' Joe was losing his sense of detachment with her so close.

'Not when I know that I am in control,' she said, staring into his eyes. She really was an alarming girl in so many ways, Joe thought, but also undoubtedly an entrancing one.

'Perhaps, if Madame Malet is watching, I should do this to convince her of my ardour.' Deciding to teach her a lesson, Joe bent down and kissed her fiercely on the lips, and when she didn't object, persisted in that pleasurable activity for quite a long time.

Finally he released her and she responded dryly, if breathlessly, 'I believe the prodigious use of the *tongue* was a little more realism than strictly necessary to convince Madame Malet of your devotion, Mr Appeldoorn.' For the first time Joe heard Amelia Peachy's true voice make an entrance, even though slightly out of breath.

He settled back on the chaise, quietly satisfied that he had outmanoeuvred her for once. 'So, have you a plan? Or do we just wait for events to unfold?'

She sat up straight again. 'Yes, I have a plan. It's now ten fifteen. The King is unlikely to leave his private room before midnight – and in all probability, it will be even later than that. Therefore we have time to try and identify Plesch, if he is here in the public rooms. I want you to go back downstairs and study all the gentlemen guests carefully.'

She obviously wanted to push her tethered goat out into the jungle clearing where the tiger could see it more easily. Did she really not care for him at all...?

'Don't study the hair of the person,' she advised. 'Wigs are almost perfect and are hard to detect. Ignore the build too - it is easy to change the shape of the body with padding. Look instead at his height, although be aware he could be wearing lifts in his shoes to make himself look taller. Look also at hands and jaw lines – those are difficult to disguise – and they might jog your memory of Blumenfeld. But above all, be aware of an individual's reaction to you. A blink of the eye, a frown, any suggestion of surprise – that's what gives people away.'

'And what will you be doing, Miss Peachy?' Joe asked her stonily, the illusion finally broken.

'Planning the next stage of this operation. Also, see if you can find out who is with Cecile tonight – that may be the best indicator to Plesch's identity.' She smiled slightly, a ghost of a smile in the candlelight. 'He may be with his co-conspirator, as I am with mine...'

*

Worryingly, the first person Joe saw when he descended to the floor below was the Eurasian woman, Jacqueline Samedi. And she clearly recognised him in return from their embarrassing encounter the night before, giving him a secret complaisant smile from behind the back of the man she was talking to in sibilant French. Her escort was a young, fair-haired dandy, who was nearly as tall as Joe. Surely that person can't possibly be Blumenfeld? he thought.

Mlle Samedi was wearing a green silk cheongsam, slit nearly to her waist where it overlapped her immensely long raven hair. She had a waist so slender Joe thought he could have spanned it with his two hands. It was certainly a worry seeing her here because *she* was supposed to be the girl enjoying a private *soirée* with the "Duke of Lancaster". And if she wasn't, then who was…?

Joe decided not to rush straight back upstairs with this troubling news, though, but first try instead to fulfil the major part of the task Miss Peachy had set him. He found himself a glass of wine and moved around the room. Only six other guests were on this floor, most in conversation with one or other of the girls.

Magda, the graceful horsewoman, in her skin-tight white riding breeches, was in the company of a bald, middle-aged Prussian officer in full dress uniform. His hand was stroking her long thigh to apparently soothing effect on both sides. The height of the man was about right, Joe decided, and the build. Could Blumenfeld have transformed himself by shaving off all his hair since Tuesday? A major sacrifice if Blumenfeld/Plesch was a vain man in any way. And the duelling scars on the officer's cheeks too looked genuine enough, and old.

Juanita, the Terpsichorean performer, in a white tutu, her long legs encased in silk, was smiling dreamily into the eyes of a Swiss banker type – corpulent, of middle height, moustachioed. Blumenfeld had been clean-shaven, Joe reminded himself, but fake facial hair could of course hide a lot.

Gretchen the huntress, in a diaphanous chiffon robe reminiscent of a frieze from the Temple of Artemis, was remonstrating slightly with an over-enthusiastic Italian. But the man had to be at least eighty; surely no disguise could represent old age quite as authentically as that?

Even Colonel Blair had found himself a partner, Joe saw – a glacial Nordic goddess with hair the colour of ripening wheat and eyes as blue as lavender flowers. She was three inches taller than the Englishman and looked a girl well capable of defending herself against his roving hands.

Two other men – a dark-skinned individual, perhaps a Turkish pasha despite his Western suit, and another, clearly a middle-aged German Jew – seemed equally unlikely contenders to be Blumenfeld in disguise. None of the men had demonstrated any sign of recognition towards him, not even Colonel Blair.

A hand touched Joe's arm as softly as gossamer and he found himself gazing into the almond cat's eyes of Jacqueline Samedi. She really had an extraordinary face, he decided – almost a child's face on that splendid woman's body.

'May I join you?' she asked politely. 'I thought I saw you earlier with the new English girl.'

'Yes, you did. I'm just taking a break from her.'

'Then take it with me. Can I get you some more champagne?'

He refused her offer in a distracted way because he was still concerned why she wasn't with the "Duke of Lancaster" as Miss Peachy expected.

How could he phrase a difficult question? 'Actually, I don't wish to be ungallant, but I was looking for Cecile,' he told her.

The woman laughed, her voice like the tinkle of oriental music. 'Then I'm afraid you will be unlucky tonight, M'sieur. Cecile is in demand. She is with an important guest, an English milord, the Duke of Lancaster.'

Joe's smile became a little forced after that bombshell, a sudden dryness in his mouth. As soon as he decently could, he excused himself to Mlle Samedi and rushed straight back upstairs to Room 15 to break the bad news to "Catherine"...

CHAPTER 12

Sunday March 16th 1902

Joe could see Amelia was deeply disturbed by this turn of events. She was definitely the formidable Miss Peachy again now - Joe had for the present given up entirely thinking of her as "Catherine".

'The King is with Cecile?' she asked, frowning. 'Are you sure? Do you know in which room?'

Joe had to admit that he'd forgotten to ask Jacqueline Samedi that vital piece of information. 'But she seemed sure of her facts.'

Amelia paced the room like an athlete preparing for a difficult race. 'Then I've been misled and this changes the complexion of things. I may have miscalculated,' she admitted, although she still made it sound almost as if it was *his* fault. 'If Cecile really is an associate of Plesch, he may be able to make his attack while the King is still in his private salon. Did you see anyone on the floor below who could possibly be Plesch?'

'No.' Joe held out the palms of his hands helplessly. 'He could be any of them, or none of them. I didn't observe anyone who even vaguely resembled Blumenfeld, but then you say he's a master of disguise and I have simply no idea what's possible.'

Amelia coughed impatiently. 'But then, I can't be absolutely sure that Blumenfeld and Plesch really are the same man, can I? I only have *your* word for that. Perhaps Blumenfeld is entirely an invention of yours, Mr Appeldoorn, made up on the spur of the moment to save your own wretched skin.'

'I told you the truth, *Miss* Peachy,' Joe said coldly, beginning to wonder how he could ever have entertained any feelings for this woman - in *any* of her guises.

She avoided his eye and frowned. 'I'm sorry. That was rude of me. But it's possible that Plesch has other associates of whom we know nothing.

Blumenfeld could be one of those.'

Joe was only partly mollified by her apology. 'Perhaps. But I still believe Blumenfeld must be your friend, Plesch. There can't be two individuals that deadly. Perhaps Plesch is not here tonight, after all,' Joe added hopefully. 'Could he have given up his assignment completely because of the authorities closing in on him?'

Amelia was dismissive of the idea. 'I think not. Plesch *never* gives up, no matter what he thinks the odds are. He is here in this building, without a doubt. I *know* it...I can feel it in my blood. *This* is the night. He will kill the King tonight unless I can prevent it.'

'Don't you mean unless *we* can prevent it?'

'Don't tempt me, Mr Appeldoorn! There is no "we"! You haven't been any assistance to me so far!' She was utterly business-like again, the same woman who had broken into his hotel room this afternoon and treated him with such casual contempt. Her sombre mood contrasted bizarrely with her appearance, though, as she strode back and forth in her pink corset and flesh-coloured tights. Despite the rapid cooling-off of his feelings towards her, she was still an arousing sight, and for a moment Joe allowed himself to be aroused...

'And just *what* do you think you are looking at, Mr Appeldoorn?' she simmered.

'Err...nothing, Miss Peachy.' Joe was at a loss to know how to deal with this completely unpredictable woman; a few minutes ago she had snuggled up to him and allowed him to kiss her passionately and improperly. Yesterday evening she had even apparently been prepared to dress up like a boy to amuse him. And now she was behaving as imperiously as Miss Cordingly at her very worst...

She halted in mid-flow, her mind apparently decided. 'I will have to go and try and find the King's room, and then make sure that Plesch – or anyone else for that matter - doesn't get anywhere near it.'

Joe looked at her stonily. 'You're going to stand guard outside in the corridor dressed like that, Miss Peachy? Where are you going to hide your pistol in that outfit?'

She glared at him for a moment, but then Joe saw a suggestion of a smile. 'You may have a point. What am I going to do? Think, Amelia, think!'

She looked at him pointedly, eyeing up his own perfectly tailored evening suit. 'If only I could find some male attire and disguise myself as a guest...'

'Oh no,' he muttered. 'Anything but that. These clothes wouldn't fit you anyway,' he argued desperately. 'And frankly I would rather take on Plesch myself unarmed than lose my own clothes to you. Where is your Browning pistol, by the way? You *do* have it, don't you?'

She nodded reluctantly and produced it as if from nowhere, like a dove from a conjurer's sleeve. 'I smuggled it up to this room earlier today.' She looked sheepish. 'As you say, it would be quite difficult to conceal it in this particular outfit…'

Joe had a better idea. 'You go and find the right room for me, and then *I* will stand guard over it and deal with Herr Plesch,' he suggested quickly. 'I have a personal score to settle with that man, if he really is Blumenfeld.'

'I don't doubt your courage, but he will kill you without a second thought; you are simply no match for him, Mr Appeldoorn,' Amelia said bleakly. 'Anyway, guarding the room like that won't help catch Plesch. There is no place in these corridors to guard the outside of a room without being observed yourself, and a man on his own will stand out even more than a lady in tights. Normally men are only allowed on the third floor when they are with one of the girls. Madame Malet does not like stray visitors wandering around on their own up here; only she has the complete run of this place.'

As she said this, Joe noticed with interest that her eyes seemed suddenly to light up from inside. He realised with some trepidation that she had apparently just thought of another plan entirely.

Amelia soon confirmed that. 'I have just had an excellent idea, Mr Appeldoorn…' she said triumphantly. 'But I must leave you alone for a few minutes, if that is all right…?'

Joe studied her face with concern as he wondered just what sort of madcap plan she might have come up with this time…

*

After she had been gone for ten minutes, Joe tried the door and discovered to his annoyance that the witch had locked him in…

His initial response to his imprisonment was anger that she didn't apparently trust him in her newly thought-out plan to save the King's life. But then he started to feel a more complacent reaction as another possible interpretation of her action came to him. Perhaps it was not a question of her not trusting him; could it be that she simply wanted to protect him from harm by keeping him locked up in here? And if that were true then…

She cared for him. That was it! Impossible as it seemed, Miss Peachy cared about his welfare…

Perhaps there was more of the entrancing Catherine in her than he'd dared hope…

But then a grimmer thought intruded. She hadn't said what she was going to do, or what her newly thought-out plan entailed, but there was a possibility that she was seriously thinking of taking on Plesch all by herself.

He couldn't allow it…even someone as formidable as Amelia would need help to deal with an evil and dangerous man like Plesch. Yet what could he do to prevent it? He checked the lock on the door but it was a complex type unfamiliar to him, and one certainly impossible to pick quickly with the meagre tools he had available.

The minutes ticked by at leaden pace as he paced the room in a fever of apprehension. When half an hour had come and gone, he tried banging vigorously on the door to attract the attention of anyone passing in the corridor outside. But no one responded. Probably no one could even hear him; these rooms were very well soundproofed for obvious reasons of privacy, otherwise the squeals of passion and delight regularly issuing from the third floor of this building might have disturbed the swans and the other more sedate residents on the shores of the *Zurichsee*.

By midnight, when Amelia has been gone for an hour and still showed no sign of returning, Joe finally decided in his desperation to try the leaded window...

The glass had a central hinged panel that could be opened outwards to let in the fresh easterly breeze from the lake. The room was located at the rear of the building and the window looked out over a formal French garden, with box hedges arranged in intricate swirling patterns, and decorated with mysterious topiary figures and statuary. Beyond the garden, moonlight silvered the tranquil water of the *Zurichsee*, while the gaslights of *Limmatquai* showed as a distant line of phosphorescence on the far side of the lake.

Below the window was a sheer fifty-foot drop onto flagstones. If he fell, Joe knew he would either kill himself or, at the very least, break both of his legs. Neither prospect was frankly appealing.

Yet Joe saw that there was a narrow horizontal ledge of sorts that followed the bottom line of the windows, an architectural feature in the limestone walls, no more, to add a shadow line to the building façade. It certainly had not been intended for any human being to ever walk along; in fact it seemed too narrow and sloping even for pigeons to make much use of it.

Joe Appeldoorn had done some amateur rock climbing in the recent past, although admittedly never in evening dress and patent leather shoes. Yet he was suddenly determined to attempt this as a way of escape, even though his instincts and training told him it was suicidal folly. But driven on by the thought of "Catherine" lying in a pool of her own blood, a bullet hole through that beautiful brow, he made the fateful decision and climbed through the window panel.

Outside, he found he could just about balance with his toes on the ledge, if he pressed his face uncomfortably flat against the limestone. The problem was he could hardly move without losing that balance and tipping over backwards, and there was not the remotest feature in the limestone at fingertip level – not a bump or indentation or hairline crack – for him to get any purchase on.

He saw the vague shapes of couples walking in the garden below and knew he couldn't just stand here, waiting to be seen. He would have to try and make a move.

Looking along the wall, he did find a little encouragement in his suicidal venture: near the corner of the building a statuesque Cedar of Lebanon spread its immense branches close to the limestone walls, and Joe thought it might just be possible to reach one of those branches from the ledge and climb down to garden level. And - an even more tempting sight - there was also a sturdy flagpole projecting horizontally from the wall between the last two windows on this side with a Swiss flag fluttering patriotically from its end, which might offer him a chance of climbing higher and perhaps reaching the roof. And surely there would be some means of getting down from the roof – a fire escape or something similar...?

Yet the fifty feet and four windows between his window and the corner of the building seemed an infinity to Joe, as daunting as traversing the north face of the Eiger. The sloping ledge was slippery with moss and slime after the damp Swiss winter, and it was so dark on the ledge that Joe couldn't even see his own feet beneath him but had to rely on sense and instinct alone.

Yet, despite the fear churning his innards, he did finally risk a tentative step sideways, like an ungainly crab. He only managed to move a few inches but this modest success did encourage him enough to try a second step. With each further minuscule step he seemed certain to topple back onto the flagstones far below; but somehow he found he could make progress, if at excruciating slowness.

He reached the first window and was able to take a breather, with something - the window frame - to clamp his fingers on to and relieve the terrible strain of balancing on his toe muscles. The curtains were drawn, though, and the hinged windowpane closed, so he couldn't get into the room without breaking the glass, which would inevitably attract the attention of everyone in the building and surroundings.

Reluctantly he carried on to the next window, another five minutes of purgatory. This one, when he reached it, did at least reward him with an interesting sight: a girl, who looked like Magda the horsewoman, but now divested of her riding breeches, and a man whom Joe instantly recognised again, even in this unfamiliar situation, as the French Minister of the Interior. Magda was currently whipping the bare buttocks of her French political guest, with apparently manic enjoyment on both sides.

The third window, the second last one before the corner of the building, was almost more difficult to pass than the previous one without lingering: inside, a naked black beauty, almost as splendidly built as Corazon, was having swirls of whipped cream applied to various parts of her anatomy by the Turkish pasha Joe had seen downstairs.

Perhaps it was the thought of Corazon popping into his mind that disturbed his concentration, but at that same moment Joe felt his right foot sliding on the moss. He toppled outwards, and as he fell, made a despairing grab at the nearby flagpole projecting from the wall. The pole was at least six feet away from him but slightly lower than his flailing fingers so he was just able to get a slight grip on the round wood section with his hands.

His body promptly arced through one hundred and eighty degrees around the axis of the flagpole but, unable to maintain his fragile grip, he found himself flying off at the other end of his trajectory like a trapeze artist, his feet landing hard but fortuitously in the next window recess. The window panel was thankfully open, he saw in that brief instant, and he was able to lunge and gain a handhold on the wooden frame before his feet slid out of the recess again. His lungs heaving, and his hand trembling with the strain, he collected his breath before hoisting himself up with his other arm. Then, with one more major effort, he opened the window to its full extent and squeezed through like a cork in a wine bottle, finally landing in an ungainly heap on the floor of the room.

Fortunately an *empty* room...

He lay on the thick carpet, winded and gasping. Getting his breath back he wondered bleakly if he had risked his neck for nothing. *It would be just his luck if this room were also locked...*

The room was furnished in similar luxury to the one he had recently shared with Miss Peachy. It had a chaise longue with green striped silk upholstery - almost identical to the one in which Joe remembered – slightly wistfully – that he had first appreciated the beauty of his "Catherine". Regency candlesticks and intaglio-engraved champagne glasses stood in readiness on a "Boulle" centre table. An Italian cabinet-on-stand occupied one side of the room. The pictures on the walls were less erotic than the Karma Sutra ones in Room 15, Art Nouveau designs of women with flowing hair in stylised medieval garments.

Joe was vaguely wondering who the artist might be, when he heard someone coming along the corridor and had only a moment to conceal himself in an alcove behind a red brocade curtain, before the door was abruptly pushed open.

*

A girlish voice giggled. And then an elderly man's voice answered her, gruffly and impatiently.

Joe risked a peek through the curtains of the alcove, and sucked in his breath in astonishment when he saw who the new arrivals were. *Mlle Cecile Flammarion and Edward VII, the King of England...*

Joe resisted the urge to be impressed at finding himself alone in a room with royalty – or almost alone anyway. Joe Appeldoorn had nothing against this monarch in particular, but his own republican leanings, together with those knocked forcibly into him as a child by his father, had long made him detest the very idea of kingship, and, more particularly, the fawning and knee-scraping of courtiers and subjects that it always seemed to entail.

Yet at least you had to admire this king's taste in women, if nothing else, judging by the beauty of the Comtesse de Pourtales, and of the present immediate recipient of his attentions, Cecile Flammarion.

Through the slit in the curtains, Joe saw the King lock the door behind him. 'No more interruptions, *ma jolie,*' he said in excruciating French. His French was perhaps as bad as René Sardou's English - Joe would rather have enjoyed hearing a conversation between these two gentlemen. Certainly their earthy enjoyment of women seemed to be on a similar par...

The King-Emperor was built on the substantial side, short, rotund, with a thick grey beard but not a lot of hair on top of his head. The candlelight shone on his gleaming bald patch as he faced Cecile and whispered endearments into her shell-like ear. He was wearing a short dark blue jacket with silk facings, complemented with a black bow tie and black trousers – this was the new type of "dinner jacket" that Joe had read that the King had pioneered.

Joe tried to breathe quietly, yet every inhalation and exhalation seemed so loud that he thought they must hear him when he was as close as this, and separated only by a curtain.

Joe had a sudden terrible thought. What if she doesn't wait for Plesch/Blumenfeld? What if the plan is simply that she herself kills him? *Could the assassin be Cecile herself?*

He prepared himself to act if such an eventuality looked likely. Yet his instincts about women told him not; she might be a conspirator of sorts but she didn't have the face of a girl who could kill a man in cold blood. Stripped down to her essentials, wearing a gauzy silk negligee and apparently little else, she scarcely had room to hide an offensive weapon anyway – not even a nail file.

So perhaps the King was safe for the moment, Joe tried to tell himself....

The King sat down on the chaise longue, licked his lips emphatically and then pulled Cecile onto his lap. She stroked his beard in return with seeming affection. 'Oh, Bertie, you are so strong!' she said in delightfully broken English. 'And I believe you've grown even more 'andsome.'

'What? Since yesterday?' the King asked dryly.

'I meant since you were 'ere last year, Bertie,' she chided him gently.

'My dear late mama never did like the French, do you know? Dashed uncivil of her, I always said. *Je crois que vous autres Françaises avez les derrières les plus délicieuses du monde.*' He lifted her robe and gave her bottom a gentle squeeze.

Cecile seemed distracted by his roving hands. 'Oh, Bertie, you are too kind.'

Joe wondered what to do. He had been in embarrassing situations before, but nothing like this – the thought of having to listen to the laboured coupling of the King of England with a French girl young enough to be his granddaughter was more than he could stomach. He would have to reveal himself before things went too far. Tell the King about the plot on his life, and expose the unpleasant truth to him that the beautiful blonde minx with him was implicated in it up to her gorgeous neck.

Would the King believe him? Or would he simply be thrown out? Regardless, the ruction it would cause might be enough for Plesch to abandon his plan of assassination.

For a brief moment Joe wondered about Miss Peachy's reaction if he proved to be the King's saviour. *Gratitude?* Unlikely, given her past record. *Annoyance at being side-lined?* Yes, far more likely. Tonight was perhaps more to do with Miss Peachy triumphing over Plesch than preserving the life of her monarch, he suspected. It was Plesch's scalp she seemed to want above all.

Cecile stood up and smoothed down her near transparent robe. 'You're a naughty boy, Bertie. Just let me fix my hair a little.'

'Why? I'm only going to mess it up for you again, my dear.'

Cecile backed away from him and circled the luxurious room. But standing with her back to the door, Joe saw her covertly and adeptly turning the key with her hands concealed behind her.

Then she floated back to the chaise where she leant down and planted a kiss on the King's corpulent cheek. 'My dear Bertie, I wonder what your country will do without you?'

'What do you mean by that, Madame?' The King-Emperor was obviously puzzled by the remark.

Suddenly the door opened and someone - a man – entered without speaking. Joe couldn't see his face, though, because Cecile was standing in his line of sight through the gap in the curtains.

Then the man moved forward slightly and Joe realised who it was: the Englishman, Colonel Blair. Yet he moved differently now, panther-like, his eyes glittering in a mask-like face. Strange-coloured eyes...

Joe didn't know why he hadn't seen it before. The face of Blumenfeld seemed to materialise from the ether...

The King was sitting on the chaise longue looking perplexed. *'Que faites-vous ici, M'sieur?'* He tried again in English. 'What is the meaning of this, my good sir? I locked that door, so how did you get in? Answer me, sir? Why, I shall complain to Madame Malet over this unforgivable intrusion.'

Colonel Blair reached casually for his inside pocket. He seemed quite clearly Blumenfeld now, even the voice. Joe wondered how he had missed it before, yet his characterisation of the perpetually inebriated English colonel had been perfect. 'This is in the nature of unfinished business, your majesty.'

The King's face was growing red with anger, not yet fear.

Surprisingly to everyone, though, including Blumenfeld apparently, the door opened abruptly yet again, and this time Madame Malet appeared in the room, her rouged and puffy face concerned, her immense white breasts still threatening to burst forth from her tight green bodice.

'Excuse me, your 'ighness, but did someone call my name?' She then seemed to spot the colonel whom she regarded with puzzlement. 'Forgive me, Colonel, but why are you in zis room, may I ask?'

'Yes,' the King spluttered. 'Why indeed? It's like bloody St Pancras station at rush hour in here. You, sir, out! This minute!'

Colonel Blair – Blumenfeld – snorted in disgust and proceeded to pull a gun from a concealed holster - a Mauser pistol - which he pointed at the astonished King. Cecile shrank back into a corner of the room, apparently fearful now of the invidious consequences of her own actions.

Joe didn't hesitate any longer but yanked the curtains aside and propelled himself across the room, a suicidal leap at the armed man.

He hit Blumenfeld solidly with a grinding football tackle that would have destroyed most men's resistance in one go. The Mauser did fall from his grasp at least, but Blumenfeld was still full of fight as they collapsed together in a heap, gouging and punching each other, while Joe tried with his right hand to gain hold of the knife strapped to his thigh and slit this devil's throat.

And perhaps he would have done just that if the King had not got up from the chaise and tried to intervene in the mêlée, ending up falling clumsily over both of them.

Joe gave up any hope of reaching the knife with the vast bulk of King Edward VII of Great Britain, Ireland and half the rest of the world, pinning his right arm to the carpet. So he fought Blumenfeld desperately with his left hand as he tried to gain possession of the Mauser. But just when it seemed within his reach, the King compounded his earlier sin by managing to accidentally kick the Mauser further across the carpet to within reach of Blumenfeld's grasping hand...

Blumenfeld was incredibly fast, and agile. He managed somehow to roll free, then reached the gun and stood up with it in his hand in one flowing movement while Joe was still struggling to release himself from the King's floundering embrace. The "Colonel" took deliberate aim at the King on the floor as Joe finally freed and flung his body at Blumenfeld's legs.

As he did, Joe heard a woman's voice command, 'Get down, Mr Appeldoorn!' Madame Malet had a gun of her own, a small Browning automatic...

And she fired it in a disconcertingly professional manner, as far as Joe could tell in that split second blur when time momentarily stood still.

The three things happened almost simultaneously: Blumenfeld's gun going off perhaps a split second before Madame Malet's shot, which was followed almost instantly by Joe's crunching impact with Blumenfeld's legs. Blumenfeld toppled and the Mauser flew high and wide this time, spinning through the air and, quite by chance, out the window.

Joe tried to throttle Blumenfeld on the ground but the man was clearly unhurt and was slippery to the end. It was like trying to hold on to water; no matter what he did, the man somehow evaded his flailing arms, and his frantic attempts to grab his windpipe.

In a second Blumenfeld had both regained his feet and managed to grab Cecile, whom he now held, with a knife to her throat. Joe had no doubt he would slit her pretty neck open, if pressed, confederate or not. The King still lay sprawled, open-mouthed, on the floor, but refusing to cower for his life. Joe stood up slowly and held up his hands to Blumenfeld in mock surrender, and the man smiled humourlessly in response, before propelling Cecile viciously in Joe's direction with his right boot.

Blumenfeld once again displayed his remarkable agility, diving through the door and out into the corridor, before Joe could recover and stop him.

Joe was still about to pursue him, though, when he turned and saw Madame Malet lying on the floor, holding a bloodied hand to her side.

He bent down to her. Madame Malet whispered in Joe's ear almost inaudibly as she swooned.

'Please get me out of here, Mr Appeldoorn...'

CHAPTER 13

Monday March 17th 1902

In his room in the Hotel *Zurichsee,* Joe Appeldoorn stood at the balcony window, looking out over the thoroughfare of *Limmatquai*, and the panorama of the city of Zurich.

The sun was just settling low over the verdant western hills beyond the steeples and rooftops of the *Altstadt*. From this vantage point Joe could see a picturesque view of the whole of the Old Town, laid out in architectural splendour on the far bank of the Limmat, its medieval heart dominated by the *Fraumünster* and St Peters *Kirche*. The riverside boulevard below was busy with traffic, and formed an entertaining panorama of its own: the riding-carriages and landaus of Zurich's banking elite, their occupants as grand and extravagant in their gestures as royalty; horse-drawn trams, bicycles, two-wheeler cabs and horse traps for the more modest citizens of this metropolis – and even the occasional clatter of a motor car for the more technologically-minded modern citizen. Gentlemen strolled on the quayside in padded tweed suits and capes, and in every imaginable sort of headgear: homburgs, green Tyrolean hats with feathers, bowlers and Panamas. Ladies promenaded with parasols to protect themselves from the afternoon glare from the lake, yet wearing tightly moulded dresses designed clearly to show off every curve of their bodies, and even occasional glimpses of a shapely ankle. In this new century, the younger women of Zurich, as elsewhere, were becoming much more eclectic and adventurous in their dress, casting aside convention and wearing fashions that sometimes scandalised their elders who mourned the loss of the stately crinoline and bustle...

Joe turned away from these reflections on twentieth-century fashion to look at the even more natural female figure lying on his own bed. She was wearing his dressing gown and - he scarcely needed reminding - nothing else...'

'How are you feeling, Miss Peachy? Are you absolutely sure you don't need a real doctor?'

'No, you are an excellent physician, Mr Appeldoorn. A qualified doctor could not have done better. Where did you learn those skills?' Her face, washed clean of powder and paint, was like a young girl's, even if deathly pale. Her dark hair, still damp from her recent ablutions, was nearly as short as a boy's, yet there was nothing remotely boyish about her. It was hard to recognise any trace of Catherine or Miss Cordingly in that girl's face, Joe thought. Somehow she even contrived to look quite different from the formidable Miss Peachy who had threatened his life in this same room barely more than twenty four hours ago. Joe was still unsure how close this woman had come to killing him then, when she believed he might be Plesch.

Their relationship certainly had moved on apace since then, yet it was still odd that he didn't hold that frightening experience against her rather more than he did...

'All Pinkerton operatives have to learn basic medical skills,' he explained, 'and particularly how to deal with gunshot wounds. And I do more than most: I brought surgical instruments, dressings, antiseptics and even morphine with me to Europe. This is a violent age we live in, after all...' Even as he said it, he realised how foolish this platitude must sound to *her*, of all people. 'But I only stitched, dressed and disinfected your wound, Miss Peachy, nothing more. Please don't exaggerate my medical abilities. You were very lucky, though.'

The bullet had nicked the side of her abdomen and sliced a shallow, but long and painful, wound through her skin. A few inches to the left and the shot would have ripped through her abdomen proper.

She would have been as good as dead, and it would have been his fault...

'Yes, I was extremely lucky, but I am still grateful for your prompt help. And thank you, too, for letting me stay here in your room, and for taking your bed. Where did *you* finally sleep last night, may I ask? Or was it morning, by then?'

'It was, but I managed to get myself another room on the floor below where I could catch up on my sleep.' Joe didn't elaborate for the moment on the fanciful tales about a sister he had had to invent for Herr and Frau Gessler, the owners of the hotel, to explain the presence of a sick young woman in his room. 'I shall sleep down there until you are recovered enough to leave.'

'Then you're a gentleman, Mr Appeldoorn. But it was an unnecessary piece of gallantry on your part. I have shared rooms with gentlemen before.'

Joe wondered if she was deliberately trying to test him, or even provoke his dislike, by telling him such a thing. Was she worried about him perhaps forming some unintended attachment for her, and therefore attempting, with such a remark, to distance herself from any possibility of his regard? Yet he had no doubt she was speaking the literal truth, and it did undeniably hurt him. Although he couldn't say exactly why, since his feelings for this woman now were so complex and confused that even he couldn't have explained his own heart to her...

Joe kept his tone neutral in response, though - no hint of censure or moral outrage, or even any indication of his hurt feelings. 'I thought you would appreciate being on your own at this time, Miss Peachy. That's all...'

*

He'd brought her in a cab to his hotel room in the early hours, not knowing where else to take her. Being a small family-owned hotel, he had been given a key to the main door, and at one-thirty in the morning, there'd been no one around to witness his arrival carrying his bloodied female cargo. He'd simply bluffed his way out of *Le Royale,* carrying "Madame Malet" in his arms before anyone had the wit to argue. Fortunately he hadn't run into his friend, Erwin Winteler, on the way down from the third floor, who was the one person who would have questioned why Joe Appeldoorn of all people should have been carrying the wounded Madame Malet to safety. In the confusion and panic after the incident on the third floor, Joe hadn't seen what had happened to the King or Cecile, but he presumed that the King at least had been escorted safely from the premises to more secure lodgings. The sovereign's own detective guard now hopefully realised that their lord and master had been under real threat last night, and would therefore be performing their duties with a great deal more diligence over the next few days. Because of the security scare, it seemed highly unlikely that Plesch could, or would, be able to mount another attempt on the King's life - in Switzerland, at least.

Even in her considerable pain last night, Amelia had been adamant that she didn't want to go to a doctor or to a hospital for treatment. And Joe had to admit that it would have caused some considerable controversy if he'd brought her to a doctor's surgery dressed like that, padded and painted and still wearing one of Madame Malet's wigs. But at the time he'd been in a torment of indecision over what to do for the best, since he really had thought her wounds could be life-threatening.

It had been such a relief when he'd cut away the padding and silk of her bodice and found, despite the copious amounts of blood, a relatively innocuous wound...

He'd undressed her completely, and she had borne that indignity without protest or complaint. Yet even caught up in the intricacies of stitching her wound, he had been momentarily diverted by the sight of that wondrously athletic body. In her acute pain – before he gave her a little morphine - the muscles and tendons in her long tapering legs and taut waist were tensed to their fullest, yet her musculature didn't detract from her femininity in any way. Her skin was gloriously perfect, and while stitching it, he felt the onus of his responsibility – it would be sacrilegious to leave an ugly scar on that satin exterior. Hopefully – because of the time and the care he had taken, and because of Miss Peachy's stoic resistance to pain – he believed he had done a first-rate job...

*

'I didn't ask you last night,' he said. 'What did you do with the real Madame Malet?'

Amelia eased herself up into a sitting position, a guilty expression on her face. 'I'm afraid I trussed her and her maid up in a wardrobe in a room on the third floor. I'm sure one of her girls has found her by now, though. After all, you should be able to smell that scent she uses from the other side of Lake Zurich...' She coughed wryly. 'I suppose this will be a slight setback in my career as a courtesan at *Le Royale*, but I shall just have to work hard to get back in her good graces in due course.'

This was stated in such a straight-faced manner that Joe had to wonder for a moment if she was really being serious. But he detected a reassuring gleam of humour in those blue eyes that told him she was mocking him – *or was it perhaps herself she was gently mocking?* This woman truly was an enigma to him, but one that was exerting a growing attraction for all sorts of reasons - from the occasionally sentimental to the downright lustful. And while Joe had not yet formed the same level of affection for the indomitable British agent Miss Peachy that he had for the sweet and sometime playfully erotic "Catherine", even the formidable character of Amelia was improving steadily in his regard...

Joe said, slightly uncomfortably, 'I'm sorry. I got in your way last night. You would have killed Plesch and fulfilled your mission if I hadn't interfered. Instead he got clean away.'

'It wasn't your fault. I should have paid far more attention to "Colonel Blair".'

Joe was intrigued. 'Why? How could you have known? I talked to the man in a café in Bern for nearly an hour, and even I didn't recognise him as "Colonel Blair".'

'Because when he smacked my...' she hesitated, '...when he smacked me in *Le Royale*, the night before last, it should have instantly alerted me to him.'

Joe was still puzzled. 'You think that smack was part of some deep plan, and not just Herr Plesch giving in to his baser instincts?'

Amelia shook her head vigorously. 'His baser instincts are to do with killing people, Mr Appeldoorn, not smacking bottoms.' She snorted with anger. 'Of course it was deliberate! He would have found out beforehand from Cecile if any new girls were working in *Le Royale* and, always sensitive to the possibility of such a person being a government agent, would have tested them, as he did me. And he must have been particularly suspicious of me after he saw you and me together. And I – unforgivably – reacted exactly the way an agent would. Instead of simpering and smiling at his boldness, I hit him back. I may as well have worn a sign advertising my true profession. And he made the most of that knowledge, I'm sure.'

'How?'

'By feeding me false information, of course. Every one of the girls at *Le Royale* I asked discreetly about the "Duke of Lancaster" told me that his companion last night was to be Ma'mselle Samedi. I'm sure this rumour was spread deliberately by Cecile, at Herr Plesch's instigation.'

Joe whistled softly. 'Then you have to admire the man's attention to detail.'

Amelia nodded solemnly. 'Oh yes, he is the best. The most devious, the most accomplished, the most dangerous assassin in the world.'

'Yet you would still have ended his career last night but for my interfering. I'm sorry.'

Her head jerked up, and her eyes made forthright contact with his. 'No, you were very brave, Mr Appeldoorn. And I'm sure you did save the life of the King by your prompt action in jumping out from that alcove. In the end it was my own inept shooting that allowed Plesch to escape summary justice.'

Joe had never heard Miss Peachy so complimentary towards him.

'In fact *I'm* the one who really should apologise to you when I have been so abysmally stupid and incompetent. I have insulted your professional abilities as a detective several times in our brief acquaintance, yet last night you proved me wrong. Somehow you managed to escape from room fifteen...'

'Yes, why did you lock me in?' Joe interrupted.

'I asked for your help last night simply in order to try and identify Plesch beforehand. But when it seemed you couldn't recognise the man, I thought it would be safer for you, Mr Appeldoorn, to be out of the way. It wasn't malicious; I never intended that you would personally have to help me deal with Plesch.'

His heart sang at the admission: perhaps she did really care for him...

He even felt emboldened to move forward and sit down on the edge of the bed. Amelia didn't seem put-out by this encroachment on her space, but did seem puzzled by something. 'How *did* you manage to escape from room fifteen, Mr Appeldoorn? And, moreover, how did you find out which room the King was to use for his assignation with Ma'mselle Flammarion, and manage to secrete yourself in there, in the brief time you had? I am still baffled...as well as impressed.'

Joe tried to look modest. 'Trade secret, I'm afraid. That would be telling.' Nothing, he decided, was ever going to wrest the truth from his lips...

*

'So what will you do now?' he asked. 'When you're fit to travel again, I mean. I'm not trying to rid myself of you.'

Amelia made a tired gesture with her arm. 'I could hardly blame you if you were. But when I am ready, I shall resume my unfinished mission, of course. I will get Herr Plesch in time; I promise you that, Mr Appeldoorn.'

Joe was taken aback for a moment. 'What a single-minded woman you are! You have just saved your sovereign's life,' he reminded her. 'Isn't that enough kudos for you with your government employers? Can't you resume a more normal secret agent life now?'

Amelia smiled faintly. 'No, I hardly think so. I would have earned five thousand pounds for the head of Herr Plesch because His Majesty's Government has many reasons for wanting to repay this man for his crimes. For saving the King's life, though, I get precisely *nothing*. Not even any kudos, official or unofficial...'

Joe couldn't hide his annoyance. 'You're doing all this simply for money? You sound quite as mercenary as Plesch sometimes...and you have the same strange chameleon-like quality, I might add. Have you ever thought how much like him you really are, Miss Peachy? Perhaps you and he deserve each other.'

She tried to remain impassive, but Joe could see from the struggle in her face that he had touched a raw nerve with that accusation – perhaps because she could recognise some truth in it. But she nevertheless defended herself robustly, anger bringing some colour back to her face. 'And your search for Miss Winthrop – are you not also expecting a reward if you succeed in finding her, Mr Appeldoorn?'

'Yes, of course. I hope to earn *twenty-five* thousand if I restore Eleanor unharmed to her family. But that is a personal reward from her grandfather, not a bounty.'

Amelia looked impressed for a moment, despite the red spots of anger in her cheeks. 'Twenty-five thousand *pounds*?'

Joe felt slightly deflated. 'No, of course not. Dollars. But it's still a lot of money.'

'Yes, in fact it's about the same as my five thousand pounds for catching Plesch, isn't it?' Amelia declared with quiet triumph in her voice.

'But it's quite different,' Joe protested.

'*How* is it different?'

'I don't have to kill anyone for it. And you're a *woman*...' And he wanted to add, *a woman I could care about...*

'You think it's morally wrong to kill a man like Plesch, Mr Appeldoorn? You can hardly say that without risking the charge of hypocrisy. You seemed quite prepared to kill him yourself last night, as I recall.'

He wanted to say, '*Yes, for you, I would have done it...*'

'So is your moral outrage about being paid to destroy a man like Plesch simply because I am a woman? It seems you would not be similarly outraged if I were a man doing this job. I wonder why that is.'

Joe didn't know how to respond to that so resorted to his usual tactic when losing an argument with a woman: he quickly changed the subject. In a more subdued voice, he said, 'I have to compliment you on your guise of Madame Malet – that was extraordinary: you had her mannerisms perfectly. And it was a clever choice, too, because it gave you the virtual run of the third floor of *Le Royale*.'

Amelia seemed flattered by his compliment, if reluctant to accept it. 'Oh, paint, powder, a little cotton wool inside the cheeks to pad the face. I was an actress after all, and I played far more difficult roles than Madame Malet in my short career. I used one of her own wigs, and her own cosmetics. Her voice is quite easy to mimic, and, in the dim lighting on the third floor, it was relatively easy to fool people.'

'But it can't just have been padding. Madame Malet has an enormous bosom, which she displays mostly uncovered, while yours is more...more...modestly...err..'

'Yes, Mr Appeldoorn?' she inquired innocently. 'Go on.'

'May I ask? How *did* you make your bosom look so...so...' Joe was floundering but was still determined to know how this particular miracle had been achieved.

'So *large*? Is that what you mean?' she continued, even more innocently.

He nodded, reluctant to put his foot back in his mouth.

'Trade secret, I'm afraid,' she said primly. 'That would be telling...'

*

In the morning he returned with an English breakfast tray of coffee, marmalade and toast, scrambled egg and bacon.

She seemed almost fully recovered after twelve hours' sleep and she allowed him meekly to move aside the dressing gown to examine the wound.

'It's healing nicely. Perhaps you won't even have much of a scar,' he commented, not without a little pride at his own medical skill.

He could see her salivating at the sight of the hot food, so he took pity on her eventually and placed the tray in front of her.

Just as she was about to tuck lustily into the scrambled egg, he said, 'Do you mind if I stay here while you eat? No? Well, the least you can do in return for the food is to tell me something about yourself...'

*

Surprisingly, to Joe's mind anyway, Amelia *was* willing to tell him something about her past life. And like the Langevin sisters' lives, it too was a life completely different from the home life of the late dear queen.

Joe had been surprised enough that she would be willing to talk about her own life at all, but he was soon taken aback even more by her complete frankness. But perhaps this was because, for once, she was not able to dissemble and hide behind a mask of powder or paint, or a costume. Dressed only in his plain dressing gown, reclining on his bed, and still in some physical discomfort, she no longer had the energy to play a part but had to be herself entirely.

Yet Joe could not help but harbour some suspicions too about her frank revelations. Perhaps this was a deliberate ploy on her part to either test his potential loyalty, or to discourage any growing affection that he might be feeling for her. If the latter was the intention, though, it had the opposite effect on him to that planned.

How had she got into such an extraordinary line of work, he wanted to know. She must have had an exceptional upbringing, surely?

She smiled as she finished her toast and drained the last of her coffee. 'Hardly,' she said. 'My name really is Amelia Peachy, and I was born in Elstead, Surrey. Twenty-six years ago today, in fact. You see, I am hiding nothing from you any more, Mr Appeldoorn.'

'Then many happy returns. Considering the dangerous life you lead, you are quite fortunate to have achieved that milestone,' Joe observed tritely, still wondering, though, if she was being entirely truthful about her age. Twenty-six was about the right age for Miss Cordingly, but five or six years too old for Catherine. Yet Joe could see, with her still girlish face, how she could easily carry off such deceptions of age. He imagined that it must be much easier for a youthful-looking actress to make her face look older, than vice-versa.

'I would like to tell you that I had a deprived childhood and an evil stepfather who beat me,' she went on, 'in order to explain the bizarre way my life has evolved. But it's not true. My parents were both kind and understanding people, if undemonstrative in their affections. My father was a doctor, my mother a piano teacher. But they both died of cholera within a few weeks of each other when I was ten, and so I was sent to live with a maiden aunt in Cobham. You see, Charlotte is much closer to the real me than Catherine.'

Joe grinned ruefully. 'You have no idea how depressed I am to hear that.'

She laughed at that, a girlish response that sounded a little like Catherine's laugh.

'I'm afraid I just became bored with life with my Aunt Georgina. So at sixteen, I rebelled. When a touring Italian circus came to Guildford, I fell promptly in love with an Italian circus performer twice my age called Luigi Belzoni, and ran off with him.'

'You ran away with the circus?' Joe couldn't quite keep a straight face.

'Yes, that's precisely what I did,' she said without a hint of embarrassment. 'For three years I travelled all over Europe, performing with Luigi as an acrobat and tightrope walker. He taught me much. I found I had a talent for dangerous tricks, as well as for looking good in spangles and tights. I learned several languages too during this interesting time – French, Italian, German – even a little Russian.'

'And what happened to spoil this interesting life?'

She shrugged, glossing over a tragedy. 'Luigi was killed in Vienna while attempting a difficult trick on the trapeze. He broke his neck in the fall so The Flying Belzonis were no more. Afterwards I didn't have the heart to go on with a circus career so I returned to England where I decided that being an actress might be more fitting. I have a natural talent for mimicry and perhaps even metamorphosis. I did play in musical theatre and pantomime, as I told you; that was no idle boast about my career as a Principal Boy. And I did also briefly take a turn on the music hall stage as a male impersonator in the style of Vesta Tilley. Yet my legs were not matched by my singing or dancing talent so I gradually moved on to serious theatre, particularly Shakespeare. I *loved* playing Shakespeare, but not the roles you might expect: Rosalind or Juliet or Viola. No, I preferred to play one of the witches in *Macbeth,* the Nurse in *Romeo and Juliet,* Regan or Goneril in *King Lear,* or Mistress Quickly in *Henry the Fourth*.' Amelia smiled. 'It seemed I always liked to submerge my own identity beneath padding and paint and powder. I've no idea why.'

'It has come in useful in your later career, though,' Joe interrupted dryly.

'Ah, yes. I can see you want to know how an acrobat and actress graduated to become a spy and government agent. Well, I'm sorry to reveal my feet of clay yet again, but it was the doing of yet another man in my life, a person called John Ballantyne...'

'And how did he achieve that?' Joe prompted her.

Amelia seemed reluctant to go on for a moment, but finally relented. 'I met John during my time in the theatre. He came regularly to see me perform for several months, and I got used to seeing him in the audience. Then he began calling at my theatre dressing room after performances, deluging me with flowers and attention. I was flattered by his interest, of course; he *was* the second son of an earl.' Her eyes stared straight into his, unashamed, daring him to look disapproving. 'We eventually became lovers. At the time I was playing a courtesan in a play, a working girl from the East End who becomes the mistress of the King.'

And that must have been where the character of Catherine was born, Joe decided...

'One night John persuaded me to play a trick on a young bachelor friend of his, a German banker called Meidinger, who had, so John claimed, a predilection for common street girls. I had to pick up this Herr Meidinger on the street by pretending to be a prostitute, and to gain admittance to his own home in Kensington. Then I was to steal from him the key to his safe...'

'You believed all this?' Joe asked incredulously.

'I'm afraid I did,' Amelia admitted, now finally shamefaced at her naivety. 'And you've guessed it. Meidinger was no friend of John's, only a casual acquaintance at best. Actually he was no banker either, but a naval attaché with the German Embassy. And the safe for which I obtained the key contained the draft of a secret military treaty between Germany and a certain Balkan state.'

'So Ballantyne worked for the Foreign Office, did he?'

'Yes, he eventually told me the truth...and I immediately fell out of love with him. But he still came back regularly to see me at the theatre afterwards and finally offered me the chance to train as a government agent.'

'What was wrong with simply being an actress? Not dangerous enough for you?'

'Exactly. I needed to feel the thrill of something like the high wire again, and this profession gave me the opportunity to do that as well as serve my country. I was an accomplished actress after all; I spoke four languages; I was intelligent and beautiful...' She smiled faintly. 'I am not being immodest, Mr Appeldoorn. I am simply repeating the compliments that were paid to me to induce me to join the British Secret Service. Eventually I was recruited to the intelligence group within the Foreign Office itself. Initially I was used in London, while still working as an actress, to make assignations with Russian and German Embassy staff.'

Joe was even more amazed at her frankness. 'Should you really be telling me all this?'

'No, I certainly shouldn't. Although I'm not sure what you could do with the information if you did wish to profit from it. Be warned: you wouldn't live long enough to enjoy it if you ever did betray my confidence, Mr Appeldoorn.'

Joe sucked in his breath in astonishment at the matter-of-factness in her voice, yet he was convinced that she meant every word she said. This woman had the ability both to enchant him, and to frighten the life out of him, an interesting combination. It was at moments like this that he could almost feel some slight sympathy for Herr Plesch with this implacable enemy pursuing him relentlessly. 'It's a pity the stage lost such an actress as you, Miss Peachy,' he said finally, and rather tamely. 'You quite put Sarah Bernhardt, Lillie Langtry, Ellen Terry and Mrs Patrick Campbell in the shade.'

Amelia's face relaxed a little. 'I certainly don't mind comparisons with three of those august ladies, Mr Appeldoorn. But Lillie Langtry cannot act to save her life. Her career relied entirely on *other* attributes than her ability to act.'

Joe didn't know *what* to say to that.

*

On Wednesday morning Joe fetched Amelia's trunks of possessions from the room she had rented in a *pension* near the *Hauptbahnhof*. He was nervous, though, as he returned through the cobbled streets in his hired two-wheeler; Plesch was still alive and could very well still be in Zurich, plotting revenge on those who had upset his plans.

Joe had scoured the Swiss newspapers for any report of the incident at *Le Royale*, but clearly such places did not exist as far as the press was concerned. Joe couldn't even find any information to suggest that King Edward VII of Great Britain, Ireland and the Empire was even in Switzerland at the moment. He wondered how the European Press would have reported it if the King had indeed been found dead in a notorious Zurich brothel, his body riddled with Mauser bullets.

He had the trunks delivered to his former room on the top floor of the Hotel *Zurichsee*, and an hour later returned there to talk with Amelia as she had requested. She was up and dressed for the first time in three days, seated at a dressing table, her hair newly washed and shining.

'No sign of Herr Plesch on the streets?' she asked, tongue-in-cheek.

'Given the circumstances, I think it's highly unlikely he would stay in Zurich, don't you?'

'Perhaps,' she agreed cautiously, regarding herself in the mirror with a critical eye. 'I felt well enough to get up and dress myself, Mr Appeldoorn, as you can see – those pills you gave me last night are surprisingly effective in easing pain. What are they?'

'Don't worry; they're nothing addictive. Merely a new analgesic developed by the Bayer Laboratories in Germany. They call it aspirin, I believe – I take a supply with me everywhere now, just in case.'

She nodded. 'Then I shall have to do the same from now on.'

'You look like you're making plans to leave, Miss Peachy. Where are you intending to go from here, may I ask?'

She stood up, still moving slightly gingerly, and went to the window. 'First, to Germany, to report to my head of section on what happened here. Then hopefully I shall try to pick up the trail of Plesch again.'

Joe shook his head with a wry smile. 'You're incorrigible, Miss Peachy.'

She hesitated, stumbling over her words a little as if nervous. 'Why don't you...err...come with me, Mr Appeldoorn? And help me find Plesch, I mean... Otherwise, be warned, he *will* come looking for you. I don't say this to frighten you or persuade you – it's the simple truth. Before, you were simply a loose end who could possibly identify him. Now, you are the person who foiled his attempt on the life of the King. He will never forget that slight, I'm afraid. So come with me and help me find him first...'

Joe stood looking at her, his mind in turmoil. In truth, he was sorely tempted to do exactly that - to walk away from the life he knew, to give up everything he cherished, in order to stay with this woman. But his voice seemed to have a mind of its own today. He heard his own bleak pronouncement as if someone else was forcing him to say these words. 'I can't, Miss Peachy. I have made a personal commitment to her grandfather to find Eleanor Winthrop, so that must remain my first priority. So it is Monique Langevin that I need to go in search of, not Herr Plesch, even though that 'gentleman" may well be a threat to me in the future, as you say.' He studied her face in a deliberately critical manner. 'As I recall, you promised that if I helped you at *Le Royale*, then you would help me in return find Monique.'

'And so I will,' she assured him, 'but only after I complete my job of catching Plesch. I'm afraid that I cannot be distracted from my own primary task until it is finally accomplished.' Amelia turned her head to the window, clearly still suffering with the continuing pain in her side, despite the aspirin. She looked very fetching, though, with the morning sunlight on her pale face, and with the slender lines of her figure outlined against the view of distant blue-grey hills. A fresh wind scoured the surface of the Zurichsee, bringing with it the spring scent of pines. A violinist in the street below was playing an atmospheric piece of Brahms, the music accompanied by the deeper rumble of a horse-drawn tram. Soon that latter evocative sound would be heard no more in Zurich: the horse-drawn trams on *Limmatquai* would shortly be replaced by electric ones; already the overhead cables were being fixed all over the city to announce this brave new world. *A new century indeed.* What other marvels and changes would it bring? Joe wondered, torn between a melancholy regret for what was being lost, and excited anticipation of the wonders to come.

Amelia regarded him with eyes as blue and striking as the waters of the lake behind her, before unexpectedly taking his hand and gripping it tight. What she said next surprised him even more than the intimate way she held his hand. 'We work well together, Mr Appeldoorn. Come with me and be my partner...my partner in crime, so to speak.'

Joe was too astonished to respond for a moment. It was the nearest thing he'd ever had to a proposal from a woman. And from such a woman as this, a vast compliment indeed...

So was it perverse obstinacy that made him turn her down when every fibre of his body was screaming *yes*? *Or was it simply fear of the unknown – fear of leaping into the void?*

'I can't, Miss Peachy. I simply can't...'

*

On Thursday morning he escorted her by cab, with her bags, to the

Hauptbahnhof. As they reached the platform where the train for Munich was standing ready to leave, with a slow exhalation of steam leaking expectantly from the locomotive, he turned to look at her.

She was Miss Cordingly again in every respect: frizzy red hair, wire-frame eyeglasses, prominent teeth and well-padded figure. Joe didn't know what she'd done to her natural complexion to achieve that roughened red look to her skin – It must have taken her hours, using all her mysterious arts with powder and paint, to achieve that convincing effect. Even knowing her thoroughness and dedication to her acting art by now, it still amazed him that she was prepared to conceal her natural beauty in this deceiving way, transforming the look of her face and her body entirely to play this plain young woman.

At least she was moving freely, though, with no hint of her injury, even though he knew the wound was far from fully healed yet.

'Remember to go to a doctor and get those stitches taken out within a week, Miss Cordingly,' he advised her. In this realistic guise, he found bizarrely that he did almost think of her as that plain young English teacher again rather than as the exotic woman of the world that she truly was.

She nodded dutifully, fully in character as Miss Cordingly. 'I will, Mr Appeldoorn.'

He studied her face; she had even coloured her eyebrows somehow to match the red hair. 'Why are you travelling as Miss Cordingly?' he asked her finally, unable to play the game of pretence completely.

'In the interests of self-preservation, Mr Appeldoorn. Anyway...' she smiled faintly and showed her awful teeth, 'Charlotte is the nearest persona to my true self, and almost like a sister to me. And I can travel in this guise without fear of being molested, or even of anyone noting my presence. I think Miss Cordingly is not a likely subject for anyone's lust, or even close attention, do you?'

Joe smiled uncomfortably. 'Don't be too sure of that any more. I believe I find Miss Cordingly a very arousing young beauty now.'

She appeared flustered for almost the first time in their entire acquaintanceship. Joe wondered how "Miss Cordingly" would react if he now decided to give her a lustful French kiss in full view of a hundred assorted railway passengers.

'You are beginning to arouse me too, Mr Appeldoorn,' she admitted, slightly breathlessly, 'so I had better go while I still have the resolve to leave you.'

Joe felt a great wave of longing for this woman surge through him, just like that first night in *Le Royale* when he'd fallen for her so completely in her guise as Catherine. But he controlled himself with an effort and kept his voice neutral. 'And where are you going exactly, Miss Cordingly? All the way to Munich?'

'No, I am meeting my chief at Lake Constance.'

'Well, I hope *he* recognises you at least. Why are you meeting there, of all places?'

'I'm afraid I can't tell you that. And you need have no fear – I will not be meeting Sir Charles in this guise.' She smiled again, toothily - slightly nervously. 'Goodbye, Mr Appeldoorn. I do hope you find your American heiress eventually, but it will be much better for you if you do not go in search of Monique Langevin first in order to accomplish that. Monique may not be the equal of her sister in her depth of evil but she is certainly her late sister's match when it comes to violence and unpredictability. You should listen to my opinion on this matter: after all, *I* certainly should know all there is to know about dangerous women...' she added mischievously.

He helped her on board the railway carriage, and carried her bags to her compartment, to the annoyance of an elderly porter standing by hoping for a tip. Then he returned to the platform as the train made ready to leave with a slow welling up of noise and vibrant steam power from the locomotive.

Almost in a mood of dejection, he waited on the platform as her train carriage finally jerked into motion. As he watched her slowly disappearing from his life, probably forever, he felt almost compelled for a moment to run after the train and leap on board again. But he resisted the urge in the end, determined not to look foolish.

He was just about to turn away with a heavy heart when, with a flutter of fresh excitement, he saw her poke her head out of the open window of her moving carriage, and heard her call back to him. 'I shall be at the Hotel Adler in Friedrichshafen for the next week or so, Mr Appeldoorn, *if you need to find me...*'

CHAPTER 14

Friday March 21st 1902

Four kilometres west and downstream from the town of Schaffhausen, the waters of the River Rhine tumble off a mighty cataract a hundred and fifty metres wide to form the *Rheinfall,* the largest waterfall in Europe.

Joe Appeldoorn climbed down the final few feet of a steep forested track and found himself standing on a bare shelf of limestone rock overlooking the tumbling white water of the Rhine, a perfect natural platform for viewing the grandeur of this mightiest of European waterfalls.

For some reason, Joe had never been to see this wondrous natural spectacle at Neuhausen during his three years as a student in Switzerland, and it did now seem an odd omission given the undeniable majesty of the scene. The falls were not that high - perhaps twenty five metres – yet even so, with their immense width and perfect setting between forested banks and steep cliffs, the vertical curtain of foaming water did form an awe-inspiring display of nature's power.

After seeing Miss Peachy off at Zurich *Hauptbahnhof* yesterday, Joe had wandered up in melancholy mood from the Old Town to the Polytechnic campus, mostly for old time's sake. There, on the student notice board in the familiar Physics department, he had found an unequivocal message left for him by Albert Einstein, dated two days ago, asking him to come to Schaffhausen as soon as possible. The message had gone on even more encouragingly, "*...I have discovered some useful information that might help in the search for a certain missing person.*"

The pretty town of Schaffhausen was only fifty kilometres north of Zurich so Joe had naturally packed his bags and taken the next train, arriving late in the evening. He had thought it too late to go calling immediately on his friend but did leave a note at the modest schoolteacher's house where Einstein apparently lodged in Schaffhausen to say that he would call again in the morning.

It had been a surprise, then, when Albert had appeared at his hotel at seven o'clock this morning without further bidding, having checked all the few likely hostelries in town where Joe might have elected to stay. But, for all the unusual display of initiative and energy on his part, and despite the even more unusual feat of early rising, Albert had been less than forthcoming immediately about what "useful information", if any, he might possess. He had instead suggested a morning hike to see the *Rheinfall* and, despite the unlikely source of the proposal, Joe had known better than to argue, and had joined his old friend, if not exactly with enthusiasm, at least with patient resignation.

This vantage point they'd trekked to was located on the north side and just upstream of the falls, and Joe stood watching the swirls of rainbow-tinted spray lift and turn in the morning wind while he waited for Albert to finally scramble down the steep path through the trees to join him.

Joe allowed Albert plenty of time to get his breath back before he finally pressed him – Einstein had always been a shockingly unfit boy with an almost pathological dislike of physical exercise. So Joe reasoned there had to be a good reason for a strenuous walk like this so early on a fine March morning. 'So, Albert, we've reached the falls, and they are a stupendous sight, I agree. But are you going to tell me finally why you've dragged me all the way here?'

Albert was still blowing hard, his tweed trousers and high-laced boots caked liberally with mud. 'I see you're still a bit of a sadist, Joseph. Why don't you let me enjoy the view a bit more, first?' he complained amiably. 'See that castle over on the other bank – that's the famous *Schloss Laufen.*'

Joe looked beyond the falls to the snow-covered hills on the south bank cloaked in dense forest of pine and larch, and to the fine turreted Renaissance castle overlooking the river. From the walls of the castle, steps led down to a stone terrace and man-made viewing platform, providing similar views of the falls to the natural platform on which they were standing. Joe was captivated by the beauty of it all for a moment: the low emerald hills in front, the steeper blueish slopes behind fading into a line of distant white peaks, the gloss whiteness of their flanks stippled with sunlight and blue-purple shadows. Those mountains of the Western Alps had to be fifty kilometres away, yet seemed, as ever, close enough to touch. He watched as an eagle – or a lammergeier perhaps – soared above the river at an immense altitude and turned languidly south with a beat of its majestic wings towards the distant peaks.

Albert seemed to understand what Joe was thinking. 'It would take us days on foot to reach that mountaintop, Joseph...'

'It would take *you* months, Albert...' Joe butted in dryly.

Albert ignored the interruption and sailed serenely on, '...but that bird will be there in...*in*...' he smiled his most childlike and endearing smile, '...why he's almost there already.'

Joe enjoyed the thought too, holding a companionable silence with his friend for a full minute or more.

Albert finally broke the silence. 'I take it that you haven't found your missing heiress yet, Joseph?' he suggested wryly.

'No, not yet.'

'And the murdered woman in Bern? What news of her?'

Joe was reluctant to talk about it but felt compelled in the end to answer the question, when this man had done so much to help him in Bern. 'I did attend that political meeting in Zurich and it did help me track down her murderer to that city. I do know the man's true identity now – his name isn't really Blumenfeld - but unfortunately he got away.' Joe turned to look Albert in the eye. 'But neither he, nor the murdered woman, is really my concern. I am *not* a policeman, Albert; I'm not being paid to do their job for them. I got myself involved quite accidentally in this unpleasant affair, and now I plan to extricate myself and resume my search for Eleanor Winthrop.'

It wasn't true, of course. Joe hadn't "extricated" himself completely from the affairs of the last ten days, and probably never would now. In fact, in the last twenty-four hours, he had found it impossible to put the thought of Amelia Peachy completely out of his head, nor even perhaps the shadowy figure of Johan Plesch...

*

Last night "Catherine" had come to his bed in the dead of night, stealing into his room like a ghost. She sat on the side of his bed and smiled down at him, leaning her head forward and parting her sweet lips to kiss him. She was wearing the costume from *Le Royale* - the pink corset and flesh-coloured silk tights – because she knew how much he liked her that way, complaisant and tempting. And all he wanted was for her to stay that way forever, not to change. But she *did* change; every time he tried to touch her, another layer of her came away in his hand like a sinister Russian doll...

At five in the morning in his hotel room in Schaffhausen he'd woken to find himself bathed in a cold sweat, his heart aching with longing for her...

*

Over breakfast this morning he'd read again through a selection of local and international newspapers. But there was still no mention of the incident at *Le Royale* five days ago, nor any reference to the King of England's presence in the country. Joe was beginning to wonder now if he had dreamed that whole bizarre episode.

Before leaving Zurich, Joe had been tempted to try and find Cecile Flammarion, and had even located the apartment of Erwin Winteler and spoken to his old friend to see what he might know about her. But it seemed, according to a puzzled Winteler, that Cecile had simply disappeared. No one had seen her since the strange affair on Sunday night when Madame Malet had apparently been hurt in an argument with an angry customer. And Joe, seeing the question forming on Winteler's face of why *he* apparently had been the person seen carrying Madame Malet down the stairs that night, rapidly made his excuses and almost ran away down the street.

No! *Finding Johan Plesch had nothing to do with him any more...*

He was here in Europe, spending James Winthrop's and the Pinkerton Agency's money, for *one* reason only. And that reason, he reminded himself forcibly, was simply to find Eleanor Winthrop. And now Albert's cryptic message had offered him some slight hope of resuming his search for her...

*

They sat on the very edge of the rock, feet dangling over the precipice, the refreshing spray of water in their faces. The roar from the falls was phenomenal but Joe felt re-invigorated by the overwhelming noise, by the iridescent air, the spring warmth.

Drops of spray had collected on Albert's black moustache, and on his curling hair, giving him a slightly mournful look. Yet Joe sensed a genuine sadness about Albert's mood today, despite the usual banter. Perhaps it was simply the natural melancholy of being separated from his beloved Mileva, yet Joe wondered if there might not be something deeper to it than that. Joe reflected on the fact that this river flowed west, then north, from here into Baden and the Black Forest in Germany...

Germany... The land of Albert's birth, but not a place he'd ever felt comfortable with. Joe had always wanted to ask Albert just what it was about Germany that he detested and feared so much, but he'd never been able to bring himself to probe that deeply into his friend's sometime troubled psyche.

'You brought me here to give me some useful information,' Joe finally reminded him gently.

Albert nodded. '*Ja*, I did. The word you mentioned to me in Bern, the one written on the back of that political meeting notice: *Narodniki*. Have you found out what that means yet?'

Joe tried to hide his disappointment. Had he come fifty kilometres, and then undertaken a hard morning's hike, just to hear what he already knew? 'Yes, I know now. They were apparently a Russian student revolutionary movement of the 'seventies. A not very successful one, from what I heard.'

Albert was disappointed too. 'Ah, you discovered that for yourself already.' He smiled. 'Perhaps you are a real detective now after all, Joseph.'

'Is that all the information you've got? Or is there something more?' Joe asked hopefully.

'Yes, there is more. I told you that I came back to Schaffhausen this week to pack up my remaining belongings and take them back to Bern. But I also wanted to visit an old friend, Jost Kleiner. He's a teacher here in the high school where I taught this winter. Or he used to be, anyway...'

'*Used* to be?'

'I'm afraid he fell rather passionately for one of his former girl pupils. It has caused a great scandal in the town. I can't blame him in a way; Greta is a beautiful creature, but still only seventeen so it's hardly appropriate behaviour for a teacher. I must admit the business has surprised me. Jost always seemed to me such a conventional and deeply intellectual man, quite immune to the temptations of the flesh. And now his wife has thrown him out of their family home and he is living in a wretched hut in the woods on the edge of the town. Yet he seems not to mind any hardship, disgrace or ostracism in order to stay with this girl. I admire his resolve to be with her; she simply took possession of his soul. It always amazes me how a human being who has conformed to the social norms for so many years with such rigid authority may suddenly reach a tempting fork in the tracks and decide to take it, forgetting the inculcated habits of a lifetime.' Albert smiled wistfully. 'Perhaps it's one of the most endearing things about humans that we are so unpredictable in the end.'

Joe had listened to this vignette in silence, wondering if Amelia Peachy had practised a similar trick on him – creeping into his soul and forcing him to take a radically different course in life from now on. Perhaps he had after all made the right decision in not going with her to Germany...

Albert cleared his throat and wiped some of the spray from his eyes. 'To get back to the important point, Jost is very knowledgeable about many things, so when I visited him in his little hut this week, I happened to ask him about the *Narodniki*. For some reason that word had stuck in my head, which is unusual for me. And Jost *had* heard of such a group and knew all about their history. But more than that, he'd actually met some of them...'

'*Met* some?' Joe turned his head expectantly. 'Recently, you mean?'

'Yes, indeed. Jost told me of a group of rather mysterious women who live near Schaffhausen and who style themselves the "Daughters of the *Narodniki*." They apparently live a rather ascetic life style, cloistered in a medieval *Schloss*.'

'Where exactly?' Joe asked.

'Up there.' Albert pointed up the wooded hillside above them, to the sloping roof of a distant gothic-looking tower that peered above the spruce trees. 'I thought these ladies might interest you, Joseph...'

*

That afternoon Joe took a closer look at the *Schloss Narodniki* as he had inevitably begun to think of it – although its real name was apparently the *Schloss Bielenberg*.

After their visit to the falls in the morning, he and Albert had taken a forest path part of the way back to Schaffhausen, climbing away from the river, to the rustic hut in a woodland clearing where Jost Kleiner, the disgraced former schoolteacher, now resided with his child lover.

Joe had discreetly chosen to stay outside while Albert had gone in to see his friend. On the basis of the discussion they had inside, Kleiner had agreed to join them this afternoon on their further walk through the forest, while revealing to Albert's American friend what he knew of the "Daughters of the *Narodniki*".

Jost Kleiner turned out to be an archetypal Swiss schoolteacher: forty years old and bone thin, but with a dry manner, a scholarly stoop to his thin shoulders, and a sag to his belly. Joe hadn't expected that he would want to bring his girl, Greta, with him, but it seemed they couldn't bear to be apart even for a few hours, because she did duly appear.

Joe had been curious, though, to see this siren who had destroyed a man's reputation, marriage and career. She was an exceptionally pretty girl, it was true - fair-skinned with golden braided hair, and wearing a colourful dirndl - yet it still took an effort of will to imagine how such a girl could have turned a man's head so completely. That was until she reappeared from the hut ready for the hike, when her attractions became clearer. Wearing a tight pair of man's breeches and knee length walking boots, Greta's spectacular anatomy was revealed in unexpected and glorious detail. Even Albert had gulped at the sight of her. She and her greying schoolteacher did make an unlikely couple, as she strode up the forest track, helping him along, as she would her infirm grandfather.

Joe and the rest of this strangely mismatched party climbed higher through the woods until they reached a curving mountain road. From there they progressed faster until, after one final turn, the *Schloss Bielenberg* appeared out of a wall of white mist.

It certainly had a dramatic setting, Joe had to admit, located on a spur of hillside above the road with steep bluffs behind and a backdrop of silver firs. And a definite look of the Gothic in the uncompromising architecture, Joe decided, its soaring stone walls merging with the natural marl and limestone rock of the cliffs behind, a mass of yellow ochre against an ice-blue sky. This was a fortified castle on a grand scale: massive masonry; narrow windows, parsimonious with the amount of light they would let in; a series of stepped roofs surrounding a central courtyard. At the back of the *Schloss,* a higher square tower rose above the general level of the roofs, from which fluttered a Swiss flag.

Though really it should be a Russian flag by rights, Joe reminded himself. These Russian émigrés, whoever they were, had certainly found themselves a romantic place of exile. They might be socialist revolutionaries, but there had to be somebody of affluence and power behind an establishment like this...

'So what do you know about this group, *mein herr*?' Joe asked Kleiner. 'Do they have a recognised leader? How long have they been here? Who pays for it all?'

Kleiner reluctantly turned his gaze from the statuesque Greta for a moment. 'The leader is a middle-aged woman – a foreigner, not a Swiss. I met her once in Schaffhausen when she came to me because she needed some legal documents translated from German into Russian. They were concerned with various legal bequests from people. I am a fluent Russian speaker having taught in St Petersburg as a young man...' Kleiner said it matter-of-factly, without any hint of pride. 'The lady gave her name to me as Marina Borisovna Rschevskaya. She has to be Russian of course with such a name, although her French was perfect. I only saw Madame Rschevskaya that one time; a younger, very pretty Frenchwoman, Marie Weyland, came the second time, to collect the translated documents and to pay me for my work.'

Marina Borisovna Rschevskaya... Joe reflected on that name for a moment, while resolving to find out a little more about the background of this apparently mysterious Russian émigré.

'So how long has this group lived in the *Schloss*?' he went on.

'Over ten years, I think. But we know little about them in Schaffhausen. They apparently rent the *Schloss* from an impoverished aristocratic Swiss family who fell on hard times. But we never see any of the group in town, apart from occasional visits by some of the younger women.'

'Do they dress in proletarian style?'

Kleiner laughed. 'Hardly. They appear extremely bourgeois in their habits. Certainly Madame Rschevskaya was well-dressed in silk and ermine when she came to my door.'

Joe wondered again who could be paying for such a strange institution. Could it be that they managed to attract rich recruits to fund their cause? Like Eleanor perhaps? It seemed unlikely, though, that such a level-headed girl as Eleanor Winthrop could be persuaded of her own free will to become a recruit to the Russian revolutionary cause. She'd certainly not been the most politically naive girl Joe had ever come across – in fact her main political conviction, as he recalled, had been a unerring belief in the untrustworthiness and corruptibility of all politicians. In that respect, at least, she had been very much like himself...

*

After Jost and his Lorelei had returned down the track to their rustic idyll in the woods, Joe and Albert retraced their steps to the *Rheinfall,* intending to follow the same track back to Schaffhausen as they had taken this morning.

Joe and Albert had done this for other reasons than the chance to see the falls again, though; the truth was that Jost and his Greta had been so absorbed in each other that it almost made it uncomfortable for anyone else to be with them. Wouldn't such passion burn itself out quickly? Joe wondered, the routine and prosaic nature of life wearing down their love in time to boredom and disillusion with each other...

Joe and Albert reached the slab of limestone rock overlooking the falls, and took the opportunity to rest there again.

'I'm sorry I can't help you further, Joseph,' Albert said glumly, staring at the water. 'I have found the detective business quite a stimulating diversion but, regrettably, I must return to Bern tomorrow. I have important things to do.'

Albert still seemed a little melancholy so Joe wondered if it were money problems that were troubling him. 'No news yet on the job with the Patent Office?' he asked solicitously.

Albert shook his massive head. 'No, but I'm sure Marcel is doing his best to get my appointment confirmed. The wheels of Swiss bureaucracy turn slowly, after all.'

'But you are still optimistic about the future, aren't you?'

'Oh yes, about the job, certainly.'

Joe finally plucked up the courage to ask him what was wrong.

Albert didn't answer for a long time, and Joe wasn't sure if he had heard the question above the roar of the foaming cataract. But then, finally, he said in a tiny voice, 'I didn't tell you before but I became a father in January, Joseph. A girl.'

Joe kept the astonishment out of his voice. 'A baby girl, Albert. That's wonderful. Mileva is the mother, I assume?'

Albert looked at him wryly. 'Yes, of course. She gave birth in her hometown in the province of Hungary.'

'Then the time it takes to get your job confirmed doesn't matter, does it, Albert? You can marry Mileva when you are established in Bern, and bring your daughter back there in time.'

A tear trickled down Albert's cheek. 'No, Joseph, I can't. It *is* too late. Mileva and I have already given up our little Lieserl forever...'

CHAPTER 15

Saturday March 22nd 1902

René Sardou looked remarkably fresh and rested even after his long overnight journey from Paris, Joe Appeldoorn thought. In fact, his French visitor seemed in rather better condition than he felt this morning.

Joe had stayed up until the early hours drinking and talking with Albert in his lodgings on the edge of Schaffhausen, doing his best to cheer his friend up about the melancholy state of his life, before he returned to Bern. But Joe had paid the price for his concern for his old student friend: this morning his mouth felt as if it had a coating of fur, and his head was throbbing with steam hammer regularity.

It was late morning and Joe was sitting with René drinking coffee on the terrace in front of a café in Fronwagplatz, a square in the centre of the ancient town of Schaffhausen. If Joe had been a tourist with a clear head he might even have enjoyed this picturesque medieval town and its cobbled streets lined with Gothic, Renaissance, and Baroque buildings. Schaffhausen had not always been as peaceful and sleepy as it was now, though; during the Reformation it had apparently been a violent breeding ground of Protestant dissent – as evidenced by the impressive sixteenth-century circular keep, the Munot, set on a hill to the east of the town.

But on this sunny spring morning in March, neither Joe nor René were in any mood for beautiful buildings or the threads of ancient history; they were far more concerned with the present.

Even though suffering from his unforgiving hangover, Joe had nevertheless travelled back to Zurich first thing this morning to meet René off the overnight train from Paris, as they'd agreed by telegram a few days earlier. Then Joe had taken him immediately on to Schaffhausen, something René was still complaining peevishly about, when he had been hoping to see a little of the glamorous ladies of Zurich.

'Why *have* you dragged me here from Paris, Joseph? Corazon is missing you, by the way,' René leered. 'She sends her love.'

'And *how* did she send it?' Joe asked dryly.

'Like this.' Rene aimed a grotesque pouting kiss in Joe's direction. 'In fact she was missing you so much that in a fit of absentmindedness she even let me into her dressing room the night before last. What a feast for a man's eyes that was! Since her costumes are so flimsy, I thought I would know exactly what she would look like naked. But I was wrong...' René nudged Joe's arm, '...women always have something to surprise you with, don't they? I think I dreamed about that glorious honey-coloured ass of Corazon's all the way from Paris to here...but now I'm here, I don't know why I bothered coming. I know the streets and the low life of Paris, Joseph. I shall be no use to you at all in this cardboard toy town of a country.' Then he nodded with a jaundiced Gallic eye at the bank across the way, a beautiful Rococo building decorated with frescoed facades and graceful oriel windows. 'See what I mean: that looks like a toy bank, not a real one. This place really is the back edge of beyond, my friend.'

'There is always the scenery to admire, René.'

René's eyes did suddenly light up with interest as he turned his head to watch a young Swiss lady stroll past. She *was* a distracting sight: a grey dress of brocade, a red silk coat drawn tightly to a tiny waist, fir trim at her collar, a silly confection of a hat in red silk and primrose, pouting cupid lips, spectacular flashing eyes. 'Yes, perhaps it will not be so bad here after all,' René murmured.

'Not that kind of scenery!' Joe growled. 'I need your attention to the matter in hand.'

René studied the enchanting gait of the retreating figure. 'Ah, q*uel dommage.*'

In truth, Joe rather agreed with René that the Frenchman was only going to be of limited help to him here when he knew nothing about the country, and, even more, because they were in a German-speaking Canton. René's German was perhaps even worse than his English, and Joe had called for his help more because he missed the man's earthy company than for any better reason.

A lot of unexpected things had happened in the twelve days since René had seen Joe off at the Gare de Lyon in Paris, and Joe had filled him in during the morning with the things he needed to know relating to the search for Eleanor Winthrop. This didn't include however any reference to Miss Peachy, or to attempts to assassinate the King of England in a Zurich brothel. Those were pieces of information that Joe definitely *didn't want* broadcast all over Paris on René's return to the French capital.

René's eyes twitched as Joe told him again what had happened in Bern. 'So you thought Monique Langevin had been murdered in her hotel room in Bern, yet it turned out in fact to be her twin sister? *And Monique,*' he lapsed into English, '*that other dangerous piece of pussy...is still alive?*'

'I believe so, yes.'

René was still bemused – or was it *amused* - by the revelation that he and Joe had been following the wrong woman in Paris, and then all the way to Switzerland. 'So what are we doing here in this glorious metropolis of Shithausen?'

'It's *Schaff*hausen, René,' Joe explained patiently, for about the tenth time today.

'Whatever...Have you got another lead to Monique, then?'

Joe pointed west of the town towards the line of green forested hills where the sloping roof of a tall tower was just visible above the trees. 'Perhaps I have. You see that chateau? I am going there this afternoon to try and talk with a lady called Marina Borisovna Rschevskaya.'

René was unmoved. 'Why, may I ask?'

'Because I think there's a possibility that Eleanor Winthrop may be in that chateau...'

*

The late afternoon sun streamed through the tall window of the *Schloss Bielenberg* library where Joe had been granted an audience with Madame Rschevskaya.

An "audience" did seem like the appropriate word because Marina Borisovna Rschevskaya was a distinguished-looking lady of aristocratic, if not royal, bearing. She was still an exquisitely beautiful woman, even though apparently in her fifties. Her white lace blouse and grey velveteen skirt revealed a still youthful-looking figure and a pair of dainty ankles. Her feet in patent leather shoes were as tiny as the bound feet of Chinese concubines.

She seemed on the face of it an unlikely revolutionary; Joe thought she seemed much more a natural part of the hedonistic world of St Petersburg society, a glimpse of the imported neo-classical style of Peter the Great's capital.

'Do you know Russia at all, M'sieur Appeldoorn?' she said, after Joe had asked her how long she had lived away from her homeland. Her French was, as Jost Kleiner had suggested, absolutely perfect with no trace of an Eastern European accent.

'No, not at all.'

She sighed. 'Tsar Nicholas the Second, Tsar of all Russia, rules a deeply troubled country. We remain always on the verge of revolution, it seems, but never quite able to take that full irrevocable step. But this particular hapless, uxorious Tsar has created a deeper cultural split than even most of our previous despotic rulers managed. There is a virtual ravine of hatred and mistrust now between the mass of people - the rural poor, conscious of their Russian identity - and the ruling House of Romanov, contaminated as they are by foreign influence, and crippled by the actions of his obsessive wife. This Tsar has an obstinacy born of weakness, and he is leading my country to inevitable disaster.'

'And you and other Russian exiles are trying to prevent that?'

'Of course. But it is difficult. The nobility and the thoughtless rich sense that their privileged existence is sliding towards disaster, but seem determined to lose themselves in parties and debauchery. Drinking up their old wine cellars, eating smoked sturgeon and caviar – even the taking of cocaine is now fashionable among St Petersburg's elite.'

'It doesn't sound promising,' Joe commented.

A sloe-eyed languid young beauty, who had been introduced to Joe as Mlle Marie Weyland, sat in the corner of the room, taking note of the conversation and eyeing Joe occasionally. She nodded regularly in agreement with the vehemence of her patron's opinions. With her porcelain white skin, Mona Lisa eyes and black silk dress, she seemed an even less likely revolutionary than Madame Rschevskaya.

'Is this decadence among the rich the reason why you became a dissident, Madame?' Joe asked the older woman.

'No, I became a dissident many years ago, after my parents were killed by the Tsar's secret police. But no one can be happy with the present state of governance in Russia, not even the wealthy oligarchs and the aristocracy. They will sink too, with the rest of Russia, if it all goes up in flames.'

Joe nodded. 'Perhaps you were a member of the original *Narodniki*, if I understand the name of your movement now.'

'Ah, you understand the meaning of the term *Hozhdenie v narod?* That was exactly what we did: we went to the rural poor, the peasants, and tried to teach them about their socialist rights. Yes, I admit I was one of those idealistic young students of thirty years ago, and I certainly don't apologise for it - we stood for peaceful change, not violent revolution. If we had succeeded, then Russia would not be in the parlous state she is in now. But our language was perhaps a little too complicated for the peasantry to follow, even though our motives were noble, and so the movement was a glorious failure in the end.'

'Is that when you were forced to flee the country?'

'Yes, in 'seventy-five, I believe.' She smiled graciously. 'I suppose that seems an impossibly long time ago to a young man like yourself, M'sieur Appeldoorn. The political situation in Russia has only got worse, since then. In 'seventy-seven, when many *Narodniki* had been arrested, murdered or had simply fled like me, the successors to our movement, the much more violent Populists, organised a campaign of terror called "*Land and Liberty*" which carried out a number of assassinations. A few years later they too were superseded by even more violent organisations such as the "*People's*

Will", which was responsible for the murder of Tsar Alexander the Second in 'eighty-one. Unfortunately these violent dissident movements have left little or no opportunity in Russia for more moderate political opposition to the Tsar, such as my own. There is a terror war going on now between the Tsar's secret police and the "People's Will", which has divided our country completely. I simply hope that we will be able to find a saner way to bring justice to our country than with all this bloodletting.'

She almost sounded sincere – even likeable - to Joe, who had been expecting to find this woman to be some sort of a crank. But she seemed disconcertingly sane and normal, and certainly not the type of person who might have been guilty of abducting an American heiress to gain control over her wealth.

Madame Rschevskaya went on. 'In recent years, Russian exiles abroad have organised themselves into political parties to press for change at home, but everything is still too fragmented to be effective. The Populists abroad, for example, have just formed the "Social Revolutionaries Party" - they want to appeal to the support of the peasants. While other groups, like Ulyanov's Social Democratic movement, the so-called "Bolsheviks", look only to the industrial workers and care nothing for the rural peasantry.'

'I went to a talk by M'sieur Ulyanov in Zurich last week,' Joe interjected.

'You did? What did you think of him? I believe he now uses the sobriquet "Lenin". How these people love a romantic *nom de guerre!* Personally I think he is a rogue. Both his movement, and the Populists, still believe in violent revolution to overthrow the Tsar, and their views seem to be prevailing: in March last year rioters prompted by Lenin's supporters set Russian cities alight. Anger with the status quo is growing again among the common people, but such violence will simply begat more violence and will only lead to a new kind of dictatorship in the end, not to true freedom for the Russian people. So I and my organisation, the "Daughters of the *Narodniki*", have chosen not to join the Populists or the Bolsheviks, but instead to press for peaceful change in our own way.'

'Who pays for your movement?' Joe tried slipping in an awkward question but Madame Rschevskaya took it in her stride without a falter.

'We have generous supporters, including some of your fellow countrymen, M'sieur Appeldoorn. I was rather hoping that's why you were here today, but perhaps I am being presumptuous.' She paused for breath. 'Your own country is so much more fortunate than mine, M'sieur. I have visited New York. The restlessness and brashness of the New World is extraordinary, isn't it? It's so noisy there, I found. A dance hall for every three houses. Everything catching up and overtaking the rest of the world. You have theatres and concert halls in New York but, to be frank, your nation does not seem to have a drop of artistic blood in it, except what it borrows. Yet it is a kingdom of incredible adventure. You go out in the evening and don't quite believe your eyes. I didn't know where to look, walking the streets of New York. A sea of light, everything on the move, shimmering, restless, boundless energy. I saw the future and I cannot tell you, M'sieur Appeldoorn, *how much I hated it...*'

She had almost made Joe feel homesick, until that last cutting remark. 'Did you ever know a man called Vasily Melikov or his sister, Olga Melikova, perhaps, Madame? They were student members of the same movement in Russia as you.'

Her eyes flickered almost imperceptibly. 'There were many young students. I'm sorry but I don't recall all their names.' That was the first hint of evasion in her manner and Joe could see he had taken her slightly by surprise with those names...

*

Joe had hired an impressive four-wheeler carriage to take him from Schaffhausen to the *Schloss* this afternoon. And the journey, through pine and spruce woods dappled with sunshine, with the light glinting on the river far below and the steady clop of the dainty Swiss horse, had been a pleasure, but for the slight nervousness he'd felt at the reception he might receive. But he needn't have worried: he had gained entry to the *Schloss Bielenberg* with remarkable ease, even welcome. Madame Rschevskaya had personally come to meet him only minutes after his carriage arrived in the main courtyard. She'd been extremely courteous throughout, as she'd showed him around the castle - and extraordinarily patient too in not pressing him about the purpose of his visit. Although the reason for that had perhaps become clearer, in that she seemed to think he might be a potential convert or donor to her cause.

The *Schloss* was a Gothic marvel of architecture and art treasures, Joe had observed, even more substantial seen from the inside than from the outside view he'd had of it yesterday...

*

Joe decided to take the bull by the horns, even though he'd almost abandoned his theory that Eleanor might really be here, given the behaviour and measured language of this woman. 'Madame Rschevskaya, you have been polite enough to see me today and not to question the reasons for my visit. But now, regrettably, I must be blunt. If I am wrong in what I suggest, then please forgive me. I came here today because I have information that a young American woman, Eleanor Winthrop, may be being held here.'

'*Held?* That is a very emotive word, M'sieur Appeldoorn. That suggests coercion and threat.' Madame Rschevskaya straightened her back perceptibly. '*No one* is held here against their will.'

Joe conceded his lack of tact. But his heart was racing, and for one simple reason - *because she hadn't denied that Eleanor was here...*

'I'm sorry, Madame. Then perhaps Miss Winthrop is your guest,' he suggested.

Madame Rschevskaya made a stately if reluctant inclination of her head. 'She is, M'sieur.'

Joe's heart was really racing now, and conjoined now with almost a surge of pleasure. *He'd done it!* He was going to be able to justify John Kautsky's, and James Winthrop's, faith in him. 'I am an old friend of Eleanor's, so perhaps I can see her?'

Madame Rschevskaya's blue eyes had glazed over a little, like a grey fog rolling in from the sea. 'Regrettably not. Eleanor is a little under the weather today, and our doctor has advised no visitors for the next few days. But, you may rest assured, she is perfectly able to leave when she wishes. I believe, though, she has no desire to leave for the present.' A touch of steel entered Madame's voice. 'I regret that I can't give you any more of my time, M'sieur.'

'Perhaps I could come back tomorrow and check if Eleanor is well enough by then to see me,' Joe said in a harsher tone.

'Again, I regret not, M'sieur. Aleksandr Gregorivich will see you out.' Madame Rschevskaya swept out of the room accompanied by her faithful amanuensis, Mlle Weyland, who did at least bow in Joe's direction before withdrawing with a ghostly smile.

Joe had not seen this Aleksandr Gregorivich on arrival, but the man turned out to be a six foot eight leviathan Cossack, a creature apparently from hell, with granite face and yellow eyes. He was even bigger than Jacques, the Comtesse de Pourtales's late manservant. *Where did these refined ladies find such grotesque and oversized guardians?* Joe wondered moodily.

*

At least he now knew roughly where Eleanor was, but it obviously wasn't going to be quite as easy as he'd hoped to obtain her release.

This group might call themselves the Daughters of the *Narodniki* but apart from the few winsome ladies he'd seen, including Marina Borisovna Rschevskaya and Marie Weyland, the *Schloss Bielenberg* appeared to be mostly occupied by rather tough-looking men. In fact, it seemed fortified heavily enough to resist an armed attack, with a large contingent of burly men in support wearing Cossack shirts, baggy pants and leather boots - almost a military uniform.

Joe knew he could go to the police of course, but there remained a considerable risk with that step of finding himself under arrest - or at least having to answer a lot of awkward questions - if the local Schaffhausen police had a good description of the man wanted for the murder of Martine Langevin in Bern only eleven days ago. *Or an even worse possibility*: that the Bern police had found his bowler hat by now in the River Aare and were anxious to talk to a man called Joseph Appeldoorn about the events at the Hotel *Landhaus* on March 11th.

And perhaps Eleanor really was in the *Schloss Bielenberg* entirely of her own volition; he would look embarrassingly stupid if he brought the local police along and that turned out to be the case...

Joe crossed the courtyard on the way out to his carriage, his grim Russian companion towering several inches above him. As he went through the main gate, Joe glanced back at what looked like a series of small windows in the high tower behind him.

The Princess in the Tower perhaps? Could that be where Eleanor was being held? – if indeed she *was* being held. Yet it seemed too obvious, too pedestrian a choice of prison for a woman as sophisticated and intelligent as Marina Borisovna Rschevskaya.

Yet was it his imagination? Did he just see a hand flutter a handkerchief, or something larger in white, in one of those high windows...?

CHAPTER 16

Sunday afternoon March 23rd 1902

'Are you absolutely sure about this?' René Sardou asked nervously, as he surveyed the view from the cliff top.

Joe Appeldoorn smiled grimly in return. 'I would love there to be some other way, René. But there are two of us, and an army of them. Well, ten to fifteen men anyway. We can't simply knock on the front door again and ask them to send Miss Winthrop out. I don't think they would take us seriously, do you?' he finished sarcastically.

The wind was rising, tossing the heads of the fir trees on the steep slope behind them. Below them a vertical cliff face of Jura limestone fell away into deep shadows, while the vast bulk of the *Schloss Bielenberg* loomed large against the darkening southern sky.

René frowned and tried another bit of English improvisation, his brow wrinkling with the effort. *'But you don't even know in which cubby 'ole in zis Bastille your Yankee belle 'ides 'erself, do you?'*

'Eh? Speak French, René, will you please?' Joe demanded gruffly.

'You are going to kill yourself if you try this insanity, Joseph. Go to the Swiss *flics*,' advised René earnestly. 'After all, you have strong suspicions Miss Winthrop is being held against her will.'

'Suspicions, yes. Evidence, no.' Joe had not shared with René the fact that he wished to avoid the Swiss police, given that they were presumably still looking for someone matching his description for the murder of Martine Langevin. Perhaps they might also have heard by now of a shooting at an infamous brothel in Zurich in which a similar looking mysterious man might have been involved, although privately Joe doubted if that incident had ever been reported to the police. Brothels, and royal households, did not wash their dirty linen in public as a rule, and things would have been quickly hushed up, if there had been any inadvertent report of the shooting to the local Prefect of Police.

But no, he still did not want to go calling voluntarily on the Swiss police for help, when that help might blow up in his face...

It was near sunset and only a few minutes of daylight remained for him to attempt a covert entry into the *Schloss Bielenberg*. Even this far away from the *Rheinfall*, a distance of three or four kilometres at least, he could distinctly hear the sound of the falls, a distant muted version of that continual cascading roar. Perhaps the sound carried here so well because on this exposed wintry hillside they were three to four hundred metres above the level of the falls. Beyond the Rhine valley itself, the sky was blood-red and streaked with fire; it seemed like an unfortunate portent of unpleasant things to come.

This vertical cliff on which they were standing rose sheer behind the *Schloss Bielenberg*, with rugged fir-covered slopes beyond. It had been a steep if undemanding climb up here from the nearby road where Joe and René had left their carriage and driver, but perhaps worth the effort. During his visit to the Schloss yesterday, Joe had seen the slight possibility of making use of the proximity of the cliff to the back of the tall tower to gain unseen entry to the building. At one point the meandering cliff face of fossil marl and limestone came within no more than a few metres of the high square tower, as far as Joe had been able to tell from his view from inside the library.

It was still a daunting prospect, though. Because of the topography of the cliff he could see no way of gaining direct access to the top of the cliff at the point where the back wall of the tower came closest. To reach that point meant therefore he would first have to traverse fifty metres of sheer vertical limestone cliff. And even if he managed to make it across to the wall of the tower, there was no point in going down, since the lower part of the tower was a blank masonry wall without a window or even a discharge pipe to penetrate its relentless solidity. Instead, he would have to go *upwards* and there was the rub: a vertical climb of twenty-five metres up the smooth back wall of the tower to reach a series of small windows just beneath the sloping darker tiled roof.

Now that he was here, the chance of reaching those tiny windows did seem suicidally small. His recent experience of climbing a building – at the rear of *Le Royale* – had proved how much more difficult climbing a bare dressed stone wall was than a rough rock face – at least without the aid of special equipment. The vertical twenty-five metres up the wall of that vertiginous tower appeared more like ten times that height from here. But then he thought of James Winthrop's persuasive reward: it did after all represent roughly a *thousand* dollars for every metre of the climb.

And that *was* a considerable incentive when viewed that way.

Joe took out his Webley-Fosbery automatic revolver, and checked it thoroughly, before replacing it carefully in the makeshift holster under his jersey.

René watched this performance with clouded eyes. 'Are you expecting trouble? Ma'mselle Langevin and her knife, for example.'

'*That* Ma'mselle Langevin is dead, René,' Joe reminded him. 'But her sister, if she's here, may have equally bad social manners for all I know. Anyway, you didn't see the size of the Cossack who looks after the security of this place, did you? Or the army of private militia that Madame Rschevskaya also keeps on the premises? So I may well need this gun if I want to get Eleanor out of there tonight.'

'What do I do if you fall, Joe?' was René's practical question.

Joe looked at the vertical drop onto jagged rocks. 'Easy, René. If I fall, there won't be enough of me left to scrape off the rocks down there.' He slapped René's shoulder and tried to smile. 'If it happens, then go to the police and tell them everything – and make damned sure it's in French! And when you do get back to Paris, you and Corazon drink a toast to me in the *Café Américain*.'

René's eyes glistened with emotion for a moment and Joe had a queasy feeling he was about to be given a Gallic kiss on both cheeks. 'I'll do better than that. If you kill yourself tonight, Joseph, I promise that when I return to Paris I'll give Corazon a *special* night of pleasure she'll never forget, all in honour of you,' René offered hopefully.

'Oh, *merci beaucoup*, René. I'm truly touched. And whoever said that self-sacrifice for a friend was a thing of the past,' Joe said dryly.

René somehow missed the irony in Joe's voice and gripped his hand in gratitude. 'If you do make it to the tower, will you come back the same way?'

Joe gave him an even more caustic look. 'You mean, climb down that tower and back across this cliff with Eleanor draped over my shoulder.' He coughed derisively. 'I hardly think so, René. No, If I find her, I'm going out through the front gate. That's really what I need the Webley for. You just make damned sure you're there with the carriage when I come through that door.'

*

He lowered himself down by rope from the cliff top and began his perilous and slow traverse across the cliff. This time he had a clear advantage, though, compared to his improvised climb on the outside of *Le Royale* - he had the right climbing equipment: rock hammer and pitons, ropes and a grapple, an axe, proper boots fitted with crampons.

The surface of the limestone was hard and dry after the recent fine weather and he found it took his hammered-in pitons with ease, as well as providing good foot- and handholds. He was aware of René's face, with the russet sunset light on it, watching his slow progress across the cliff face from above with morbid fascination.

Joe was breathing hard by now with the effort, and even more with the rush of nervous tension – René's careless talk about falling had undeniably spooked him a little and caused a niggling thread of uncertainty and self-doubt to unravel in his brain about the wisdom of attempting such a dangerous climb. And the dark void beneath his feet, filling now with deepening violet shadows and swirls of mist, seemed to grow ever deeper and more threatening.

As if to confirm his doubts, he came to a particularly difficult section of the cliff face where the limestone structure was crumbling and soft, full of fossils of extinct marine creatures. But he carried on, after a glance back at the reassuring line of rope he'd left behind him, belayed to a couple of strong cleats hammered into the harder limestone.

The weak face of weathered marine limestone was too soft to provide support for pitons so Joe was forced to climb this section unaided, using only whatever fragile finger- and toeholds he could find to keep making infinitely slow progress. It seemed an endless and painstakingly tortuous climb but finally the quality of the limestone began to improve again, and Joe began to think he had passed the worst.

Joe was just about to fix a new piton in the rock and re-secure his ropes when he felt something brush across his cheek, almost like the soft touch of a woman's hand. His heart thudding even faster, he turned his head just as something black reared out of the dusky gloom and tried to stab him in the eye.

In his fright Joe lashed out blindly at this devilish apparition but the creature – a huge black crow with red eyes, he saw now – again launched an attack with a baleful flap of its wings, its massive beak aiming to peck his eyes out. Joe hit out at it again with his axe; he meant only to frighten it off, but somehow the pick end of the axe took the bird cleanly in the chest, and it expired downwards with a malevolent hiss and an explosion of black feathers. It seemed to take forever to hit the bottom of the cliff far, far below.

Joe wondered morosely if he would now be fated like Coleridge's *Ancient Mariner* to wander the earth forever with the corpse of a bird on his conscience. But that damned bird had surely asked for it, hadn't it...?

Joe was just hammering in a fresh piton into the lime rock to secure himself when, for apparently no reason, the slight ledge on which his right foot rested gave way without a warning and he found himself sliding away into the void to follow the corpse of his crow victim. He couldn't hold back a scream of anguish as his belay rope jerked him to a halt, dangling over the void...

*

The pain was excruciating; the rope and tight harness cutting deep into his flesh. Joe looked up and saw René far above him and off to the left, his head bobbing up and down in almost comic perplexity at this turn of events, which seemed almost to confirm an unsuspected prescient side to his nature. Joe could tell from the tremulous feel of the rope that the jerk of his weight had loosened up the cleats supporting the rope and they were about to pop out and release him to his death...

As the belay cleats above him finally gave up the ghost and pinged out of the rock above one by one, Joe nearly panicked completely, knowing he had only a few seconds to save himself from an awful death. But summoning up some inner resolve from deep within himself to steady his trembling hands, he just managed to find a tenuous finger- and foothold on the soft weathered rock and release his climbing harness with frantic fingers, before the ropes and cleats flew past him and landed in the shadows far below.

Joe was stranded now on this crumbling cliff face, without the protection of a safety rope or axe, which he'd dropped, and with only his (limited) climbing skill, plus a hammer and a few pitons, to get him out of this precarious mess. He forced himself to get his wildly beating heart under some sort of control again, and began to climb once more – diagonally this time – across and upwards, to try and attain his original destination point opposite the back of the tower. He attempted to switch off his mind and simply respond to the feel of the rock as he'd been taught by a grizzled old Italian climber in the *Bernese Oberland* – Paolo had claimed that climbing could be almost a spiritual experience of self-discovery if done properly.

Joe tried to remember what Paolo had taught him about the rhythm of climbing. *Breathe...transfer a handhold...take the strain in the fingers...feel the sinuous strength in your body....stretch out a leg...grip the rock...feel its texture like the surface of a living beast...breathe again...become one with the mountain...*

*

Somehow he made it – the most difficult climb of his life, and, by the end, in near darkness. Once he got back up to the right level again, the limestone improved in quality sufficiently to take his pitons, and he made the last twenty metres in a relatively short time. Joe was not a conventionally religious man yet his deliverance from that treacherous cliff face did seem almost like an act of divine providence when he'd thought he was a dead man for certain.

He glanced back at René who was now only a distant blurred face in the gloom, and gave him a casual thumbs-up as if everything had gone perfectly to plan. Even René would know enough about climbing to know that such a claim was horse feathers though...

Then a new problem presented itself to Joe: he now realised the gap to the tower was more like four metres than the one-to-two metres he'd optimistically imagined when starting out on this mad scheme. These medieval Swiss architects clearly weren't so stupid or short-sighted, after all. It was true there was a slight ledge in the cliff face here from which he could conceivably launch himself across the void, but he could see nothing on the wall to gain a hold. The limestone was cut into smooth unweathered blocks with almost invisible mortarless joints between them.

But then, higher up the smooth face of the wall, barely visible in the dusky half-light, Joe spotted something that might possibly be his salvation: a raised stone feature, a small pilaster, projecting from the masonry. He still had a short length of rope and his grapple hooked over his shoulder - could he reach that pilaster with these aids if he balanced himself precariously on this narrow ledge on the cliff face?

Joe had come this far and didn't relish the thought of having to give up – or even worse, having to retrace his terrifying journey back across that damned cliff. So he tied the free end of the rope around his waist and got into position, teetering on this narrow projection of rock as he tried swinging his grapple into the air. He couldn't resist a whoop of satisfaction when he succeeded with his second throw. He took up the slack of the rope and gingerly tested it against his weight by tugging strongly. It seemed adequate to do the job so, without further deliberation about the appalling risk, he simply launched himself across the gap.

Hanging by the rope, he quickly secured himself in place by hammering two of his last pitons into the wall, before beginning the dizzying climb upwards. The impact of his rock hammer on the pitons seemed as loud as a pile driver; he imagined that any occupants of the tower must be thinking that they were under assault from diabolical forces. Yet he had no alternative but to do it this way, and simply hope that everyone in the castle might be completely deaf.

Joe hadn't done any real climbing since leaving Switzerland two years before, but the eye and hand coordination he'd learned then from his old Italian climbing mentor, Paulo, was still standing him in good stead. And even with no pitons left, he found - because of the extra purchase provided by the crampons on his boots, and by the fact that the joints in the masonry were wider and deeper than he'd first thought - that this actually was a much easier proposition than his bungling escapade on the outside of the third floor of *Le Royale* a week ago.

He discovered in fact that he could make surprisingly rapid progress. From his higher vantage point, he could now even see the sun again, just setting over the rim of the distant western mountains. He looked up hopefully as the tower roof and the line of high windows drew tantalisingly within reach. But would any of those damned windows be open...?

Yet it turned out, when he did finally get within stretching distance, that they weren't really windows at all, merely small holes or embrasures let into the stonework to allow some natural light and ventilation into the roof space. They weren't more than eighteen inches square, barely large enough for a man of his size to squeeze through.

Joe divested himself of as much of his remaining equipment as he could, storing the rope, grapple and hammer in the next opening to the one he intended to try. Even so he nearly got stuck halfway through, which would have been an ignominious end to his adventure, to spend the night with his backside sticking out of this tower until someone spotted him in the morning. It was perhaps the thought of that disgrace that persuaded him to make a superhuman effort and eventually to pop through the opening, like releasing a blockage in a pipe.

*

There was unfortunately no sign of any princess in this particular tower.

In fact, at this level of the tower there wasn't even a floor for a princess (had there been one) to stand on. Whatever Joe thought he'd seen fluttering from the window of the tower yesterday certainly hadn't been Eleanor waving a handkerchief, or perhaps a pair of her silk drawers, to attract his attention, as he'd rather been hoping. Nobody had been up here for years. Here were only dusty roof trusses and beams; inside it looked like a bell tower or campanile without the bell.

Joe took off his unwieldy crampons, which were only an impediment now, and recovered all his other climbing equipment from the embrasure in the wall, storing it safely out of sight on one of the ancient oak beams. Regrettably, despite the money he'd expended on it today, he would have to leave it all behind. He balanced on a beam and, straining his eyes in the dim light, could make out what seemed to be a solid floor a few metres below. He lowered himself from the beam and dropped onto the hard oak planking. It was only a disused storage space, though, thick with centuries of dust, and with only one exit: a musty dark void, down which a staircase fixed to the outer walls descended mysteriously.

Joe waited and listened for several minutes; then, having heard nothing much, took the creaking helical wooden staircase down. The *Schloss* was really a series of interlocked fortified Gothic buildings arranged around a courtyard, all more or less of similar height. This tall, disused square tower, standing at the back of the complex of buildings, was the one element that was substantially higher than the rest.

Joe followed three turns of the helical stairs until he reached what looked like a main floor level that might connect to other parts of the *Schloss*. A window in the wall at this level confirmed that he was now below the general roof level of the main buildings grouped around the courtyard. He found a door that held the promise of giving access to the rest of the castle, but it was locked. Yet the lock was child's play to pick open, even though stiff with age, and Joe soon found himself in a long gallery with a whole series of doors on each side.

The gallery had oil lamps at intervals along its length but they weren't lit yet so it was difficult to see much among the twilight shadows. Outside, the sun had now disappeared completely behind the serrated edge of the distant mountains so only a ghostly half-light issued through the narrow windows. Joe investigated in each direction, his feet echoing on the waxed parquet floor. The fittings in the gallery were Spartan, the walls of plain stone with recessed alcoves and hard benches at intervals. Occasional gloomy landscape paintings, scenes of mists and stags on wild expanses of moorland, added a little sombre decoration. He found staircases at each end of the gallery presumably connecting with the lower levels of the *Schloss*.

Joe had been hoping to find Eleanor in the tower and, now it had transpired she wasn't there, he was in a quandary. He wondered where to begin searching yet these rooms adjoining the gallery seemed as good a place as any, because it was the location most remote from the main entrance gate and the rooms accessible to casual visitors.

Then Joe's heart thudded as he heard someone coming up the staircase at one end of the gallery...

Joe quickly stepped back into the shadows of an alcove, and listened as he heard footsteps approaching, high heels clicking on the polished wood. It sounded like a woman on her own, and this was confirmed when he saw her pass. Even in the dim light, he recognised the face of Marie Weyland, as she stopped to light one of the wall lamps. Her white skin gleamed like porcelain in the sudden brightness of the flame.

Joe took out his Webley-Fosbery automatic revolver and stole up behind her. In one flowing motion he put his hand over her mouth to silence her, and pressed the massive gun to her temple.

He felt the racing of her heart, and a nerve jumped visibly in her neck, yet she didn't panic. He let her turn to face him, motioning her not to scream, which she certainly didn't seem about to do. She was a cool customer, all right, fixing her Mona Lisa eyes on his with confidence. This woman might even be able to teach Miss Peachy a thing or two about implacable calm in the face of danger, Joe reflected...

Her sloe-eyed beauty was even more evident at such close proximity than it had been in the library yesterday. 'M'sieur Appeldoorn. What a pleasure to see you again...*and* so soon. But a rather surprising visiting card.' She pushed the barrel of the Webley away with contempt in her voice.

Joe reluctantly let the gun drop and put it back under his jersey. This was obviously going to take tact on his part rather than brute force. 'Ma'mselle, I've come to see Miss Eleanor Winthrop. *Ou est-elle?* I want you to take me to her.'

Her eyes widened in mock alarm. 'Are you trying to abduct her, sir?'

'Don't play games with me, Ma'mselle. Just show me where Miss Winthrop is being kept.'

She shrugged prettily. 'Why? You won't be able to leave with her. Madame Rschevskaya has told us expressly that Miss Winthrop must remain a guest of ours for a little longer. Therefore I can't allow her to go.'

'Really? Well, it would of course be regrettable to go against Madame's wishes in this matter, but they are not perhaps my primary concern, Ma'mselle.'

'Perhaps not,' Marie agreed, but then smiled seductively. 'Yet M'sieur Yezhov - Aleksandr Gregorivich - has also been told not to allow Miss Winthrop to leave, and he may perhaps be more of a concern to you.'

Joe decided to put any thoughts of the giant Cossack to the back of his mind for the moment; the giant guard was obviously going to be a more worrying potential obstacle to leaving this place than merely going against Madame Rschevskaya's wishes, but Joe would consider that problem when he came to it. 'That is not your problem, Ma'mselle,' Joe said with mock confidence. 'All I need from you is to show me the room where Miss Eleanor is being held.'

She studied him for a moment with amused derision written on her face, then apparently reached a decision of some sort. 'All right. I can at least take you to meet Miss Winthrop, although I'm sure she'll tell you she doesn't wish to leave yet either. She will not want to leave her *lover...*' - she pretended to sigh heavily - *'...la première amour de sa vie.'*

Marie then took off along the gallery with surprising speed, and Joe had almost to run after her to keep up. Marie even seemed anxious now to have him meet Eleanor again, which surprised him greatly. This wasn't how Joe had expected things to go; he knew he was rapidly losing control of this situation, being led about like a bull with a ring through his nose by this supercilious slip of a girl. Could she be telling the truth, though? Was Eleanor staying here voluntarily to be with the man she'd apparently run off with from Paris? *What was his name again*? Gaspard...that was it...*Paul Gaspard*...

A short flight of stairs led up from the end of the gallery into a smaller wing of the *Schloss*. Marie knocked at the first door on the right, then opened it and stood aside to let Joe pass.

Joe was wary. 'No, after you, Ma'mselle.'

Marie shrugged and entered the room. Joe followed her into what was clearly a lady's bedroom. Simple rather than grand - a plain eiderdown quilt on the bed, rustic Swiss furniture, Alpine scenes on the walls. A dressing table by the window was a veritable clutter of creams and skin potions.

A door led to an adjacent bathroom. If this was Eleanor's prison cell, then it was a comfortable one at least, Joe had to admit – perhaps it could even be considered a luxurious prison since it seemed to have its own private bathroom attached. The view from the window of forested hills and distant snow-capped peaks was probably quite spectacular in the daytime too.

Yet there seemed to be no one at home until Joe heard a soft humming from behind the bathroom door. A Stephen Foster song - *The Old Folks at Home* - that he recognised all too well; Eleanor had always been singing it softly to herself back home in Connecticut. '...*Way down upon the Swanee River...*'

Joe motioned Marie threateningly to wait by the bed, as he walked over to the bathroom. He was just about to knock politely on the bathroom door when it suddenly opened from the other side.

For a moment Joe was confronted by the face and figure of Miss Eleanor Winthrop – an almost *déshabillé* Miss Winthrop, clad only in a transparent chemise, who stared back at him for a moment, before shrieking in alarm...

*

It took five minutes for Miss Winthrop to recover from this outrageous intrusion on her privacy. 'Please accept my apologies, Miss Winthrop,' Joe repeated yet again, while Marie looked on in interest. 'But it has taken me some considerable effort to find you. Your family is very worried about you.'

Miss Winthrop had by now covered herself in a voluminous dressing gown that encased almost every part of her body except her face. That visible part of her skin was still glowing pink, though, partly from her bath, and partly from her acute embarrassment. Her fine auburn hair was wet and slicked back from her high forehead in a particularly fetching way. Joe had to fight hard to put from his mind the thought of the spectacularly more intimate view he'd had of Miss Winthrop a few moments before.

'I don't know what you mean, sir. I have been sending my grandfather regular letters ever since I came here.'

'Well, he hasn't been receiving them, Miss Winthrop.'

She looked puzzled. 'Is there perhaps a postal strike?'

Marie almost snorted with laughter, but Joe silenced her with an angry finger.

It was then that Eleanor belatedly recognised him. 'Why you are...let me see...Mr Appeldoorn, are you not? Mr *Joseph* Appeldoorn...?'

'Ah, you do remember me, Miss Winthrop. Then that will save on explanations.'

The five years since their last meeting had turned Eleanor from a pretty girl into something of a society beauty, Joe saw. Her face had thinned, revealing high cheekbones and a delicate neck, while her thick glossy hair was still the same glorious colour. And that bosom that had held so much promise, and over which he had fantasised so much, had more than lived up to expectations; she was now a very statuesque young woman indeed.

Joe began wondering how he would keep René from molesting her, if he did succeed in getting her out of the *Schloss Bielenberg* tonight...'

'Your grandfather sent me to Europe to find you. I've come to take you home, Miss Winthrop, if you wish it. Are you in good health? Can you leave immediately?'

Marie continued to sit on the bed, watching balefully, her cat's eyes glowing with some dangerous inner fire.

Eleanor glanced at her, seemingly scared of her presence. 'Will Madame Rschevskaya allow me to go?' she asked doubtfully. 'This institution has rather rigid rules.'

'Well let's be rude and not ask her permission, shall we?' Joe said testily. 'I assume you have no wish to stay,' he went on pointedly, looking across at Marie Weyland for some sign of whether she'd been telling the truth or not.

'I...I...I'm not sure. I promised Paul I would stay here until he came back. I am engaged to be married to Mr Paul Gaspard,' she explained to Joe, 'although I've seen so little of him recently.'

'How long has he been gone?'

'Oh, he has been and gone several times during my stay here, but always returned in the end. He left again just a few days ago.'

'Miss Winthrop, we don't have time for long deliberations! If you want to leave with me, you have to decide quickly,' Joe said impatiently. 'It's now or never. Do you want to stay here or not? Do you enjoy living here in the *Schloss Bielenberg*?'

Eleanor hesitated. 'No, hardly that. It has become tedious in the extreme since Paul left.'

'Who persuaded you to come here? Was it Monique Langevin?' Joe asked her.

'No, it wasn't Monique's doing. I came here with Paul. He said this was a wonderful place, and full of interesting thinkers I should meet. Monique did visit here later, though, from time to time, also at Paul's invitation.'

Marie shook her head in amusement. 'I suppose you also believe the tail wags the dog, Miss Winthrop,' she commented tartly to Eleanor in perfect English.

Miss Winthrop almost blushed in confusion.

Marie laughed unpleasantly. 'You really are an incredibly naïve and stupid girl, aren't you, Eleanor?'

Eleanor refused to be cowed. 'I don't know what you mean. You are a very rude and disagreeable person, though, Ma'mselle. I've always thought so.' She turned to Joe, her chin lifting. 'Yes, I do want to go with you, Mr Appeldoorn.'

Marie gave them both a stony look. 'I'm afraid neither of you will be allowed to leave until Madame gives her permission.'

'You're forgetting I have a gun, Ma'mselle,' Joe said balefully.

She laughed again. 'No, I am not, M'sieur. But that will not get you past

Aleksandr Gregorivich...

*

Joe waited in the corridor with Marie while Eleanor dressed. She surprised him by taking no more than three minutes, when he had been expecting thirty. That rather reassured him that she did really want to leave.

'Have you got everything important, Miss Winthrop?' Joe asked her.

Eleanor blanched and put her hand to her forehead. '*Madame has my passport* – for safekeeping, she said.'

'It doesn't matter,' Joe reassured her. 'We'll get you another one from the American consul in Bern.'

Marie made no attempt to stop or dissuade them further but cheerfully led the way down a staircase to courtyard level.

There appeared to be no one about at all. 'Where is everyone?' Joe demanded suspiciously.

Marie was still quietly amused. 'Madame is away in Zurich tonight but will return tomorrow. Most of the girls are in their rooms or at meetings. The servants are celebrating somebody's birthday in the kitchens, I believe. They usually get very drunk by late in the evening, although it's still only seven-thirty so they may still have some way to go before they are completely incapacitated.'

It all sounded rather hopeful, but Joe could hardly believe Marie was telling him the whole truth.

They reached a door leading to the courtyard – Joe could feel the draught through it of cold night air. He opened the door slightly and peered through the gap. The courtyard too seemed deserted, although the entrance gate was closed, unlike yesterday.

'How do we get out, Mr Appeldoorn?' Eleanor seemed to think Joe must have worked this out already.

Marie yawned ostentatiously. 'The main gate is not locked, M'sieur.'

It seemed far too easy, but Joe decided he had to risk it. He stepped out into the cold spring air and stared up at the stars. Capella and the familiar Pleiades winked back at him from the night sky; they seemed like reassuring old friends guiding him home.

Joe moved tentatively towards the gate.

It *was* too easy...

As Joe approached the gate, a giant figure stepped out from the shadows to bar his way. A grotesque figure from hell...*Aleksandr Gregorivich Yezhov.*

Eleanor and Marie had followed Joe into the courtyard. Marie said dryly to Yezhov, '*M'selle Winthrop et M'sieur Appeldoorn veulent partir. Voulez-vous ouvrir la porte,* Aleksandr Gregorivich?'

Yezhov smiled, took off his coat, and spat into his hands. 'I think not, Ma'mselle' he said in a voice like a gravedigger's.

*

Joe took in the massive build of the man as he approached, and considered using his Webley on him. But what would he do if the man refused to yield to the threat of his gun? The giant Cossack appeared to be unarmed; it would be murder if he shot him...

Was there another way? He weighed the man up: forty or fifty pounds heavier than himself, five inches taller. The man looked experienced with his fists but he was at least fifty and must therefore be a little slow and ponderous. Joe had boxed in college, and felt a sudden urge to take this man on and wipe that supercilious smirk off Marie Weyland's porcelain face.

He was too encumbered in his thick jersey and shirt to fight, though, so he began calmly stripping off in preparation.

Eleanor gasped when she realised what he intended. 'This is insanity, Mr Appeldoorn, or foolish male bravado. He will kill you! I will go back to my room.'

'You will *not*, Miss Winthrop!' Joe barked at her, and she came to attention like a recalcitrant child under the lash of his tongue. 'You will stand there and be quiet until I've dealt with this man. Is that quite clear?'

Her half-hearted protests tailed away as Joe took his shirt off and exposed his well-developed pectorals to the cool evening air.

Even Marie was looking on in interest now. 'Don't you want to get your blood all over that fine snowy shirt, M'sieur Appeldoorn?' she sneered.

'No, Ma'mselle. I don't wish to get all Monsieur Yezhov's blood over it...'

*

Eleanor Winthrop's private diary, entry for March 23rd 1902...

...I confess that I had no idea that young Joseph Appeldoorn would ever turn into such an inspiring man. He seemed such an insipid and immature boy as I recalled him from our brief acquaintance in Hartford five years ago. He did seem abnormally preoccupied then with my bosom as I remember. I felt quite embarrassed by this unhealthy side to his nature, even though I am no prude, as I'm sure all my friends will testify. And he was such a clumsy boy too, as if he hadn't yet become accustomed to his huge size (which perhaps he hadn't, it now occurs to me.) I couldn't help laughing, rude though it was, when he managed somehow to spill an enormous bowl of fruit punch all over himself on the night of the county ball...even though he had looked moderately handsome up to that point, dressed as an English redcoat.

But the intervening years have certainly improved him both mentally and physically. He is an imposingly manly figure now, a true Ajax or Achilles. I admit with perfect honesty (to my diary at least) to a hot flush in my loins when he revealed his magnificent chest. Such perfection of the male form – it actually made my knees go weak.

Yet the Russian, Mr Yezhov, was even bigger than Mr Appeldoorn, towering over him in a frightening way. My heart raced as they approached each other, this seemed a true battle of Titans.

I have to acknowledge my excitement at the prospect of this intriguing physical contest. I had never seen bare-knuckle fighting before, and these men were fighting over me - which of course greatly intensified my interest in the outcome...

I noticed everything in fine detail as the fight got underway - the dewy perspiration on Mr Appeldoorn's skin, his lightning reflexes, his grace and power. Mostly, though, I noticed his surprising lack of fear when faced with such a daunting and frightening opponent...

They fought for what seemed like hours (although strangely, according to my watch, it was actually only nine minutes and fifteen seconds.)

Both were soon bloodied by the fierce interchange of blows, their muscular bodies glistening in the starlight. That slut, Mademoiselle Marie Weyland, was almost in a frenzy of excitement by this point, but in her case it was highly inappropriate, of course. I'm not even sure which of the gentlemen she was supporting, though I suspect she too was rooting secretly for Mr Appeldoorn by the end.

Yezhov finally caught Mr Appeldoorn with a ferocious (if lucky) punch that would have felled any normal man. And my champion did indeed falter and shake his head woozily, but it may just have been a clever deceit on his part. A confident Yezhov then closed in for the kill, sure that he had his man beaten. What Mr Appeldoorn did next surprised even me — in response to that awful blow, he seemed somehow to twist his body into a tight coil of steel, then to suddenly unleash with his fist the mightiest punch I think I have ever seen in my life. Yezhov's eyes almost revolved in his head under the severity of the blow, and he slowly toppled to the ground like some great felled oak.

I rushed over to my champion, but all he said, with perfect modesty, was, 'Are you quite ready to leave now, Miss Winthrop?'

At that moment, I felt so proud to be an American. Our boys can still show these darned Europeans a thing or two, when it matters...

CHAPTER 17

Tuesday 25th March 1902

'Good morning, Mr Appeldoorn.'

Sitting on the sunny terrace in front of the Hotel *Rheinfels*, Joe heard the cheery greeting behind him, and turned his head to see Eleanor Winthrop bearing down on him from the entrance steps.

Eleanor studied the unblemished blue sky and the soft green meadow landscape by the river with approval. 'A beautiful warm spring morning, is it not?'

That it certainly was, Joe agreed, and Miss Winthrop too looked suitably fresh-faced and full of the joys of spring, as she stood in front of the decorative painted façade of this small chalet-type hotel. Joe had considered leaving directly for Zurich and Paris on Sunday night, immediately after he and Eleanor had walked out of the gates of the *Schloss Bielenberg*. But in his slightly bruised condition, he decided he couldn't face the prospect at once, while Eleanor also seemed in too tired and emotional a state to embark on a long journey just yet. Besides which, she didn't have a passport, and that would take time to arrange. So Joe had seen no alternative but staying locally for a few days until both of them were better able to face starting the long trip home.

Joe had brought her to this relaxing location late on Sunday night, thinking it better than taking her to one of the larger but more noticeable hotels in Schaffhausen.

Joe had placed her in the adjacent room to his own to keep her under his close stewardship. Having found her, he certainly wasn't going to lose her again easily. And despite a certain relaxation in his mood in the last twenty-four hours, he was still anxious to get her back to Paris as soon as he feasibly could, and then on a ship home to New York.

He'd made a good choice of temporary home, though, he decided. The hotel was set in a rural location outside the town of Schaffhausen, with fragrant pine and spruce woods all around, and a lush emerald green meadow in front falling away to the banks of the Rhine. The Hotel *Rheinfels* - a three-storey, timbered, square-plan chalet built in the Baroque style – certainly had an old-fashioned rustic Swiss charm that made it the ideal place for him and Miss Winthrop to recuperate. The steep roof, projecting at eaves and gables, handsomely enclosed the whole building almost down to ground level as protection against winter snow. Pretty balconies ran along the front at two levels, each decorated with elaborately carved railings.

Eleanor, in her newly bought white cotton dress and with her Titian hair worn up to an immense height and tied with cream ribbons, made a striking image, posed in front of the picture postcard perfection of the hotel.

Yet it did seem like a slightly unnatural pose, Joe decided, as if she was deliberately looking to be admired. Which was a perplexing thing for Miss Winthrop to do, since in Hartford she had seemed such an uncomplicated girl with no such affectations at all. In some ways Eleanor had become a more attentive and agreeable person than then, but also a little unpredictable in her moods. In particular he found the way she looked at him now sometimes quite disconcerting, as if she was examining every pore in his skin, or hair on his head, for defects. With a cut over one eye and massive bruising of his right cheek, he was carrying more defects than usual, it was true, so perhaps it was merely natural concern on her part.

He tried to tell himself that her attentiveness to him was probably only a temporary and natural aberration brought on by her unfortunate experiences in Europe, and soon she would revert to the rather cool and aloof Connecticut girl he'd encountered five years before.

'You wouldn't care to join me in a walk along the river, would you?' Eleanor asked circumspectly. 'If you're feeling well enough, I mean.'

Joe had nothing else to do. 'Yes, of course, Miss Winthrop. I'd be pleased to. I'm feeling perfectly well so please don't trouble yourself any more about my condition. The doctor who checked me yesterday said I have no serious injuries, only superficial ones at worst. I've had much worse playing college football.'

Eleanor smiled shyly. 'I had no idea you could be so ferocious, Mr Appeldoorn.'

'No, neither had I,' Joe agreed amiably...

*

They followed a track through the woods that criss-crossed on delicate wooden bridges over a foaming stream that tumbled over mossy rocks down to the Rhine. The stream flow was heavy, but not yet in full spring spate. The distant peaks of the Jura Mountains were still encrusted with snow, although the lower slopes and valleys were now largely free of ice and turning a thousand spring shades of green after the last few days of warm sunshine.

Eleanor seemed to take a constant delight in the scenes of nature around her. The banks along the stream were bright with primulas, marsh marigold and cuckoo flower. 'Look, Mr Appeldoorn,' she said excitedly, 'a swallow - that's the first I've seen this year. Summer is coming.'

Joe smiled. 'I believe that was a swift, Miss Winthrop, not a swallow.'

She raised her chin defiantly. 'It was a swallow.'

'Swift.'

'Swallow!' Clearly in playful mood, like a small girl, Eleanor leaned down and liberally daubed her hands with soft black mud from the riverbank. Then she held her dirty palms close to his face, laughing. 'Now what do you say?'

Joe hesitated, before smiling again. 'Well, perhaps it *was* a swallow after all.'

Eleanor beamed happily. 'There, I thought you would see the error of your ways.'

'I'm sorry, my dear, but, actually, I believe that *was* a swift,' a deeper voice interrupted, '...although it is remarkably early in the year. They don't usually arrive here from Africa until the middle of April.'

Joe and Eleanor turned simultaneously to see a man watching their childish antics from higher up the riverbank, with a benign smile on his face.

Joe recognised the middle-aged man immediately, another guest at the hotel – a Scotsman, judging from his accent. The hotel staff all addressed him deferentially as "Sir Arthur" so clearly he was a regular visitor here, as well as a big tipper. Joe had talked to him briefly at dinner last night without learning too much about him – apart from the fact that the man was grey-haired, plump, and did have an unhealthy looking mud-brown complexion, as if he had been in the tropics recently. According to Heidi, the pretty waitress who served breakfast in the *Rheinfels,* the reason for that was because "Sir Arthur" had recently returned from a tour of duty as a doctor with the British Army in South Africa.

'Good morning.' The Scotsman doffed his hat. 'Mr Appeldoorn, isn't it? I don't believe I had the honour of meeting your wife last night, sir.'

Joe was about to correct the man's mistaken assumption, but Eleanor clung intimately to Joe's arm – getting mud all over his coat sleeve in the process - and smiled engagingly as she introduced herself. 'My name is Eleanor, Sir Arthur,' she said with a slight bow to the Scotsman.

'Ah, you know me, then, Madame. You have a charming young wife, Mr Appeldoorn,' the Scotsman complimented him.

Eleanor still made no attempt to correct the man's mistake so Joe too decided to let it pass.

Joe and Eleanor made small talk with Sir Arthur for a few minutes more before the Scotsman excused himself and, doffing his deerstalker hat, proceeded on his way.

Eleanor went down to the water's edge again to clean her hands in the stream. 'Imagine meeting *him* here,' she said mysteriously, as she re-joined Joe on the track.

Joe didn't know what she was talking about, but Eleanor did seem in a fey mood today so he let that pass too...

*

They walked on. 'Has M'sieur Sardou returned to Paris already?' she asked casually, although Joe thought he detected a slight note of apprehension in her voice for the first time today.

'Yes. I saw him off at Schaffhausen station at seven this morning. There seemed no good reason for him to stay on, now that we have found you.'

Eleanor seemed relieved by the news; Joe wondered uneasily just what sort of improper advances René might have been making to her yesterday. With such a lavish figure, Eleanor was always going to be a natural target for René's earthy expression of his admiration for women. He had been sitting up front with the carriage driver when a bloodied Joe had finally appeared through the gate of *Schloss Bielenberg* on Sunday night, with Eleanor in tow. Yet, even preoccupied with the injuries he'd sustained in the fight, Joe had been uncomfortably aware that René had been making eyes and slightly familiar gestures at her all the way back to Schaffhausen.

Joe had decided in the circumstances that it would be better to pack René off to Paris this morning, while he and Eleanor would follow on in a couple of days.

Yet Joe could see now that might have been a mistake because it would inevitably throw him and Eleanor even more together over the next few days. And he could no longer deny to himself his worrying suspicions about her behaviour towards him, because Eleanor did seem to regard him with something that he could only interpret as extreme admiration.

It was natural, of course, that she should have some gratitude towards the man who had liberated her from the grip of the "Daughters of the *Narodniki*". But the way she sometimes looked at him now was unsettling, and suggested that a different level of attachment than mere gratitude was forming in her mind. And she was still in theory engaged to this man, Gaspard, he reminded himself, yet that seemed to have slipped completely to the back of her mind for the moment.

Miss Eleanor Winthrop was an attractive, even beautiful, girl, but Joe Appeldoorn found this attention she was paying him an uncomfortable compliment. Not so long ago, perhaps, he would have welcomed it openly, even enthusiastically. Yet now another woman loomed constantly in Joe's thoughts and he couldn't shake himself free of his obsession with the enigmatic Miss Amelia Peachy. Something about Miss Peachy had aroused Joe Appeldoorn's feelings in a way no other woman ever had. "Remarkable" was the only word for her.

And for all her youthful beauty, "remarkable" was not a word that Joe would have used to describe Miss Eleanor Winthrop, apart perhaps from her extreme wealth. Joe couldn't deny that the thought of her wealth had crossed his mind briefly now that he could see that Eleanor apparently felt something for him. Joe had plenty of ambitions to be rich himself, but simply marrying into wealth had always seemed an underhand and disreputable way of achieving it, unless he really loved the girl in question. And Joe seriously doubted whether Eleanor's amorous feelings for him would be permanent ones anyway, once she was reintroduced to the routines and confines of her life in America.

Yet it was still going to be a tricky task to remain aloof from her, while travelling all the way to America by train and boat, especially if she was going to indulge herself with these intimate gazes into his eyes at every opportunity...

*

'Tell me about Monique Langevin, and how you got involved with her,' he said, as they continued walking through the woods.

Eleanor stumbled on a rock and took his arm again. Joe wasn't sure if she had done so deliberately or not, but she did keep hold of it for quite a long time, while he found he could hardly disentangle himself from her without appearing rude. And, to be honest, the touch of her hand on his arm wasn't too disagreeable a sensation, he confessed to himself.

Finally she did let go of his arm, though, looking a little shamefaced. 'I really don't want to talk about her, Mr Appeldoorn. I admit I was taken in by her, and no one likes to admit their gullibility, do they? She had good personal and professional references, which I had no reason to doubt. She was charming, well-spoken and educated. And she introduced me to a whole world I had certainly never encountered before, of European art and music and theatre. I suppose I was ripe for the picking. You will have to excuse my lack of sophistication, *Joseph*.' Eleanor paused significantly. This was the first time she had addressed him as anything other than "Mr Appeldoorn"; even in Hartford she hadn't ever called him "Joseph".

Joe wondered what he should call her now in return; it would be ridiculous for him to go on calling her "Miss Winthrop", though, if she was prepared to use his first name.

'I loved everything Monique showed me, especially the art – the Impressionism of Monet and Pissarro, the Primitivism of Gaugin and van Gogh – even the work of the "Fauvists", like Matisse. She also read to me some of the new French Literature and introduced me to the ballet. She even gave me a fascinating book to read called *The Science of Dreams* by a certain Austrian doctor called Freud. You wouldn't believe the things this man says in his book.' Eleanor turned to him with a knowing gleam in her expression. 'It was eye opening, reading things like that which I'd never heard of before,' she went on. 'For all my family's wealth, Joseph, I had led a relatively sheltered life.'

Joe smiled grimly. 'Your family were foolish to allow you to go to Europe, unsupervised and unchaperoned.'

'I was over twenty-one, and in control of my own destiny. I was planning to take my personal maid Ruthie as my companion, but she was sadly taken ill with a recurrence of her childhood tuberculosis and had to go into a sanatorium. I wanted to stay in America and help Ruthie recover, but Ruthie herself wouldn't hear of it, and insisted I should go, regardless of her condition. So in the end I took Ruthie's advice, and decided to go alone and hire a companion when I got to Paris. I can't blame anyone but myself for what happened. Hopefully I've learned a useful lesson.'

'It was Monique who introduced you to Paul Gaspard, I assume,' Joe suggested.

'Yes. We met him - accidentally, I thought - during the interval in a performance of *La Dame Aux Camélias*. Monique said he was a gifted writer – I think that may even be true. He is certainly very good-looking.' Eleanor studied Joe's face for a moment as if she was seeking comparisons with Gaspard's. 'He too taught me new things, in art and science, in politics and history. Things I'd never understood before - about the iniquity of poverty, and the unfair distribution of wealth and opportunity among the classes of European society. It was Paul who persuaded me to visit Switzerland with him, although it was only meant to be for a few days. I wrote regularly to my grandfather and Paul always diligently took my letters for posting. I trusted him and he betrayed me; clearly he never sent them. I should perhaps have wondered why I never received any letters in return but my grandfather has always been a reluctant correspondent. I really had no idea my leaving Paris was regarded as a deep mystery, or that my family in America were concerned for my safety.'

'Well, I'm afraid they were.' Joe was too discreet to go on and ask her whether she and Paul Gaspard had become lovers in Switzerland; it seemed to go without saying.

Yet it was also clear that Eleanor was now disenchanted with Gaspard and with the politics he preached. 'To be honest, I grew a little bored with Paul's sermonising. I appreciate the unfairness of life as much as any one, but is redistributing wealth evenly to everyone, regardless of ability, really a solution? I think not; it would create a society where talent and hard work would almost be frowned upon. And these people, for all their proselytising zeal about changing the world, seemed to lead a very comfortable material existence themselves. Madame Rschevskaya struck me eventually as a hypocrite, going on and on about the poor peasants in Mother Russia and yet living like a countess. I did willingly give her money at first – thousands of dollars – and I promised her even more. It was foolish, I know now, but I simply wanted to help her cause. It was not until these last few days, though, that I realised I was a virtual prisoner. They never actually harmed me but it was made clear, when I suggested it was time I returned to Paris, that I must first sign a piece of paper saying I had been there voluntarily and that all my gifts to them were unsolicited - I imagine to deter the chances of any future legal action on my part. I refused to sign at first. But I was wavering until you came and rescued me...'

Joe shifted uncomfortably under her gaze. 'Please don't thank me again. Your grandfather is paying me and the Pinkerton Agency very well to find you...' He hesitated but finally said her name, '...Eleanor,' and saw a pink flush of pleasure rise in her cheeks. 'I'm only doing a job, that's all,' he added with deliberate roughness.

Eleanor sighed. 'I suppose this whole enterprise of Madame Rschevskaya's is just a worthless confidence trick. Monique Langevin clearly uses her work as a paid companion to ensnare silly young women like me to donate to their coffers...'

'You're being too hard on yourself, Eleanor,' Joe suggested.

'Am I?' she said derisively. 'But things weren't all sweetness and light between Monique and Madame Rschevskaya,' she went on. 'I did hear them rowing ferociously sometimes. The last time was only a few days ago and the argument seemed to have been provoked by the visit of a man to the castle, who came apparently to see Monique.' Eleanor paused. 'And Monique left *Schloss Bielenberg* with the man shortly afterwards.'

'What kind of man was he?'

Eleanor shrugged. 'German, I think. Under forty. Nondescript to look at. I could hardly give you a description of him, except that his eyes were a strange yellowish colour.'

Despite the warmth of the spring sun, Joe felt a shiver ripple his skin. It had to be Plesch... But what was he doing at the Schloss Bielenberg with Monique Langevin when, only a week or so before, he'd been murdering her sister in Bern?

'When exactly was this?' he demanded brusquely.

Eleanor thought for a second, clearly disturbed by the change in his tone. 'Last Wednesday, I believe.'

That was six days ago, and only three days after Plesch had been at *Le Royale* trying to murder the King of England...

Joe didn't know what to make of this sinister development.

The path left the comparative gloom of the woods and emerged into a sunlit meadow. The distant Rhine sparkled with diamond glints, leaves rustled, the meadow grass swayed and shifted in the soft wind, sinuous ripples of movement spreading through the long strands. Yet, despite the sun, Joe's mood became darker as he struggled to think.

Eleanor asked him diffidently, 'What will you do when you return to America, Joseph? My family and I owe you a great deal.'

'I've told you already: I'm being well paid for finding you, Eleanor.' Joe was determined to emphasise the mercenary nature of his arrangement. 'I guess, when I do go back, that I shall resume working for Pinkertons in New York.'

'But surely you have more ambitions than to remain a Pinkerton's operative all your life. A man of your education. You told me yesterday that you studied at the Polytechnic in Zurich, one of the best colleges in Europe.'

'I did, and perhaps I can make use of that education someday. I would like to restart my father's electrical engineering business in time, if I can find the sort of partners I could trust.'

Eleanor smiled tentatively. 'I'm sure my grandfather could help you. He practically owns the Pittsburgh steel industry, after all.'

A long silence ensued, while Joe uneasily contemplated a possible future under the thumb of Eleanor's domineering grandfather. 'Don't you want to see Gaspard again before you return to America?' Joe asked her. 'To confront him and finally clear the air.'

Eleanor looked embarrassed. 'No, I don't think I do. It was a mistake, a foolish infatuation, that's all. I'm allowed one mistake, aren't I, Joseph?' After a second she went on, 'I feel as if I've been hypnotised these least months and have only just woken up again. Perhaps I was almost in a state like sleep. Sleep and the state of consciousness are very different, you know. Freud, that Austrian doctor I told you about, believes that sleep is never just a continuation of our life when we are awake, but that something much deeper is going on. To him dreams express the frustrations and resentments of our waking hours, and are a means of satisfying our...*desires*.' She gazed into his eyes as she put a strong emphasis on the word "desires". 'Sometimes our wishes are socially unacceptable and so are suppressed by day. Do you want to hear what I dreamt last night, Joseph? I think it might have been about you...'

*

Late in the afternoon, Joe was lying dozing on his bed in the Hotel *Rheinfels,* when two men swept into the room. His heart pounding, he was bundled up into a sitting position.

He cursed his own stupidity for not taking more precautions; he should have known that Madame Rschevskaya wouldn't give up so easily. The men were certainly two of her staff from the *Schloss Bielenberg* but, thankfully at least, Aleksandr Yezhov was not one of them,

Marina Borisovna Rschevskaya entered the room, like a queen to her court.

Joe was pulled roughly to his feet, then Madame Rschevskaya ordered her men to withdraw. 'Let us talk in a civilised way, M'sieur Appeldoorn, shall we?'

'About what?'

Madame Rschevskaya cleared her throat peremptorily. 'You can keep Miss Winthrop; I have not come here to take her back. She is a silly girl anyway, and of no further use to my cause.' She pulled what looked like an American passport out of her bag and tossed it contemptuously on the bed. 'There! Her passport – proof of my good intentions.'

Joe pursed his lips in disapproval. 'Aren't you worried she will press kidnapping charges against you, Madame?'

'She came to the *Schloss Bielenberg* of her own accord, M'sieur Appeldoorn. She gave us money quite voluntarily.'

'But you prevented her from leaving. That's extortion and false imprisonment.'

'Nonsense, M'sieur Appeldoorn.' Madame Rschevskaya smiled languidly. 'Or, at the very least, impossible to prove. And the local Prefect of Police is a personal friend of mine.'

Joe relaxed his face. 'All right, then just let us go. I don't believe Miss Winthrop has any desire to expose her indiscretions and poor judgement to public ridicule anyway.'

Madame Rschevskaya turned and looked out of the window at the distant Rhine. 'But in return for my consideration in letting you go freely, I need a favour from you, M'sieur Appeldoorn.'

Joe was outraged. '*You* need a favour? *From me?*'

'Do not call it a favour, then. Let us say I am offering you the chance to make a great deal of money.'

'By doing what?' Joe demanded suspiciously.

Madame Rschevskaya's voice faltered a little. 'Monique has left me – forever, she said. And somehow she has persuaded Paul Gaspard and his sister, Hélène, to go too. Although perhaps it is understandable with Paul at least; Monique and he were ardent lovers...'

Joe was quite willing to believe that but thought that fact should best be kept from Eleanor; the poor girl had suffered enough humiliation as it was. 'Where have they gone?' he asked.

'I don't know for sure, or what they plan to do. That's why I have come to you for help. Monique has been turning more and more radical recently in her political beliefs, much as her sister did before her. I was already worried that history might be repeating itself.'

'Why has Monique chosen to leave you at this particular time?' Joe demanded, interested despite himself.

Madame Rschevskaya looked confused. 'I'm not sure. But a man came to the *Schloss* last week, who seems to have some unsettling influence over her. I believe he persuaded her to leave with him. This man told Monique that her sister, Martine, had been murdered by British government agents. Do you know if this is true, by any chance, M'sieur Appeldoorn?'

Joe nodded. 'I do know Martine is dead. I saw her myself...'

The woman went white and her beautiful face seemed to crumple instantly into old age.

Joe gave her a few seconds to recover her poise. 'You are Olga Melikova, the aunt of Martine and Monique, aren't you?' he guessed, although the suspicion had been in his mind for some time.

The woman stiffened. 'Olga *Borisovna* Melikova. How strange to hear that name again, after all these years.'

'Why did you change it, Madame?'

She sighed. 'To stay alive, M'sieur Appeldoorn - as simple as that. Tsarist agents had killed my brother, Vasily, and I was next on their list. For ten tears I lived a quiet life in a rural French village, bringing up Vasily's twin daughters.'

'So why did you go back to politics?'

'For Russia's sake, of course. Everything I told you three days ago is true. Someone has to try and change Russia for the better without the constant threat of violence.'

'So you have been here plotting to spread your quiet revolution in Russia ever since. But it must be difficult to maintain revolutionary fervour in such an agreeable place as Switzerland, especially when there are so many other more vocal and violent revolutionary movements to appeal to dissident Russians. Perhaps you are in danger of becoming just another money-making organisation like the Capitalist enterprises you purport to despise so much.'

Olga Borisovna flushed. 'Easy for an American to say, M'sieur Appeldoorn. When did you ever have to struggle for anything?'

Joe decided to leave the talk of politics. 'What is it you want me to do?' he asked bluntly.

'I have already lost Martine; I don't want to lose Monique in the same way too. Find her for me, and persuade her to return.'

Joe's mind was racing. 'Do you know that Martine became a mercenary political assassin and an associate of a man called Johan Plesch? I think they had a falling out, and *he* was the person who killed your precious niece. Not the British at all.'

Olga Borisovna turned white again. 'I...I...*suspected* something of the sort, but I didn't know for certain. But could Plesch be the man Monique has now gone away with?'

'I'm afraid he almost certainly is.'

Olga Borisovna became frantic. 'Then find her for me, M'sieur Appeldoorn! Bring her back before she does something irrevocable. I will pay you – the thirty thousand dollars that Miss Winthrop has given me. You have certain talents that make you the most suitable person for this job. You know Monique by sight, and you are obviously an accomplished detective. And you can clearly take care of yourself - Aleksandr Gregorivich is still nursing the injuries sustained in his fight with you. That I have never seen in thirty years.'

'We all have our day, Madame, and grow old. But I am not sure I can help you. My main interest is only in seeing Miss Winthrop safely home to America.' Despite his words, though, Joe was sorely tempted by the amount of money involved to take on this improbable assignment.

'You *have* to help, M'sieur Appeldoorn. Monique and Paul were in dangerous mood these last few days, perhaps even suicidal. I think they could be planning some momentous crime, especially if this man, Plesch, is now motivating them with dangerous ideas. Monique was always more of an idealist than her sister, but idealism can so easily be perverted by evil men. Monique was more a rival of Martine's than a truly loving sister but she might still do almost anything against the people she believed murdered her sister – *the English*...'

Joe stared at her for a moment as a deepening suspicion grew in his mind. 'Do you not have any idea where Monique and Plesch and the others might have gone?'

Olga Borisovna nodded almost imperceptibly. 'Perhaps. Another of my girls – Marie – overhead a snatch of conversation between Paul and Monique before they left. A place was mentioned in that conversation.'

'What place?'

'Friedrichshafen in Germany. On Lake Constance.'

Joe felt a quiver of alarm as he remembered that was where Miss Peachy had gone from Zurich. It surely couldn't be a complete coincidence...

CHAPTER 18

Wednesday March 26th 1902

Strolling along the scenic northern lakeshore of the *Bodensee* - or Lake Constance, as the English preferred to call it - Joe Appeldoorn thought he and his companion must have looked a reassuringly normal couple to anyone observing them. Nobody seeing them could have possibly guessed the true nature of their conversation, or their relationship.

She was still in the guise of Miss Charlotte Cordingly – padded figure, wire-frame glasses, buckteeth and all - and completely in character, talking effortlessly like the irritating Charlotte. And Joe simply couldn't take his eyes off her.

She hadn't been at all pleased to see him in the lobby of the Hotel Adler in Friedrichshafen, though. Perhaps she'd even been angry when Joe had called out her name across the lobby and everyone's head had turned to study their slightly tense and embarrassed encounter. But he had been so ridiculously happy to see her, even made up like that, that he'd simply forgotten the serious reason why she was probably here, or the fact that her life was almost certainly in real danger. At least he had remembered to call her "Miss *Cordingly*"...

It was only six days since he had seen her off in Zurich *Hauptbahnhof* - less than a week – and yet his heart had leapt when he saw her, as if this was an old sweetheart he hadn't seen in years. This woman really had bewitched him, just as the wood nymph Greta had enchanted her Swiss schoolteacher, Jost Kleiner.

But, even knowing how foolish he was being didn't detract from his pleasure in seeing her.

'I'm sorry I surprised you like that in the hotel,' he apologised, wondering uneasily if he might have betrayed her disguise to someone watching.

"Miss Cordingly" smiled primly. 'It's all right, Mr Appeldoorn. I was a little taken aback to see you, that's all.' They had walked west along the lakeside out of the town of Friedrichshafen, and were now more or less alone on a woodland path close to the edge of the water. This beautiful tranquil lake, set in the foothills of the Alps, was the source of the majestic Rhine, which formed, a few kilometres downstream, the mighty *Rheinfall* at Neuhausen.

Joe could see that she was still moving a little stiffly from her gunshot wound of ten days before. 'Have you had a doctor look at that wound, and remove my stitches yet?' he asked her sternly.

She frowned in best school ma'am fashion. 'No, not yet, Mr Appeldoorn. Don't nag, please, otherwise I might regret you showing up here so unexpectedly. I will get the stitches taken out soon, I promise.'

'You'd better. Or I'll do it myself,' he promised balefully.

She patted his hand unexpectedly. 'Perhaps you *should* do it, Mr Appeldoorn; I might then enjoy the experience a little more than I would otherwise.'

It was the most forward thing she'd ever said to him – dressed as Charlotte anyway – and he blinked in surprise.

She studied the bruises on his face. 'So you found your American heiress, I take it, from what you said earlier.'

'I did.' Joe was still recovering from the thought that Miss Peachy might have been missing him just as much as he'd been missing her.

Amelia frowned. 'From the bruises on your face, you clearly didn't have things all your own way, though.'

'No, I had to do a bit of real detective work to find her, and then use some strong-arm tactics to actually expedite her freedom. But it was child's play compared to the things you get up to, Miss Cordingly.'

He still felt compelled to call her "Miss Cordingly", even though they were to all intents and purposes alone. How strange was that...? Yet the thought of making love to her in the guise of Miss Cordingly now held a certain erotic fascination for Joe Appeldoorn, if the truth was told.

She almost smiled at the veiled compliment in his words. 'So, congratulations are in order. Imagine! You'll soon become the proud possessor of twenty-five thousand dollars. You're a very rich man.'

Joe shook his head wryly. 'I'm afraid not. All of it will go to paying off my creditors.'

Amelia wrinkled her brow. 'Which creditors are they?'

Joe told her briefly the story of his father's venture into the electrical equipment business, and how his competitors had manoeuvred him through endless litigation over patents into near bankruptcy. 'My father had thought he was doing me a big favour by naming me as a director of his company, but, on his death, it made me liable for all his debts.'

'Why didn't you just declare yourself bankrupt?'

Joe smiled. 'Obstinacy, I suppose, mixed with the right amount of stupidity. I still have this silly dream about perhaps reviving the business in time. That's the main reason why I don't want to be a declared bankrupt.'

Amelia took his arm, and steered him towards a bench on a slight rise with a view of the lake. There they sat down to admire the scenery. The weather was still unusually warm for the time of the year, as it had been for the last few days - more like early May than March. Primulas, campions, and blue gentians were flowering in the damp slopes by the lakeside; bejewelled kingfishers darted above a small tributary stream as it splashed over mossy rocks on its way towards the lake.

Joe had been forced to bring Eleanor with him from Schaffhausen to Friedrichshafen this morning, and find rooms for both of them in the Adler. It was only a journey of fifty kilometres or so by train, but this lake formed the North-eastern boundary of Switzerland and they were now in German territory. Eleanor was resting in her room this afternoon. Joe had advised her to stay there out of sight, but hadn't revealed to her why he had come to Germany.

'So where exactly did you find your Miss Winthrop?' Amelia asked.

'I found her being held in a castle called the *Schloss Bielenberg* near Schaffhausen – not very far from here actually. It was as I thought. Monique Langevin had been working as her companion and language teacher in Paris, and introduced her to a man called Paul Gaspard who seduced her, both with his handsome face, and his romantic brand of socialist politics...'

'You're jesting, of course.'

'I wish I was. Monique and Paul managed to persuade Eleanor to travel to Switzerland where she has been the guest ever since of Monique's aunt, a lady called Olga Melikova. But then you know all about her. It was *you* who informed me of her existence.'

Amelia raised her eyebrows. 'Olga Melikova is still alive?'

'Yes, although she now uses the name Marina Borisovna Rschevskaya, and heads a rather odd organisation called the Daughters of the *Narodniki*. I think honestly she is trying to re-live her glorious youth in Russia as a student radical, but she seems a little old-fashioned and out of her depth in the bloody cauldron that is present day Russian politics. I'm sure the other Russian émigré groups – socialist or anarchist or whatever – probably don't take her very seriously at all.'

'Unfortunately your Miss Winthrop did, though?'

'Yes, and to the tune of thirty thousand dollars.'

Amelia smiled wryly. 'I think I want to cry.'

'Oh, but don't shed tears just yet, Miss Cordingly. Olga Melikova is sportingly giving me the chance to win that money for myself...'

'And who do you have to kill to earn it?' Amelia asked sarcastically.

'No one. All I have to do is wrest Monique Langevin from the company of a rather invidious individual and restore her to her aunt's loving care.'

'And who is this invidious individual?'

'His name, unfortunately, is Johan Plesch...'

*

The blue of the lake was an extraordinary sight in the late afternoon sun, Joe thought, the vibrancy of the colour accentuated by the white sails of a dozen boats. The *Bodensee,* seventy-five kilometres long by fifteen wide, was a significant stretch of water, and one of the most beautiful places Joe Appeldoorn had ever seen. Beyond the deep azure blue of the water, forested hills rose in hazy violet folds and silhouettes, with the snow-capped Alps forming a distant tantalising backdrop – like a glimpse from earth of the outskirts of heaven.

Around the lake, in the scattering of small towns on its shore - Meersburg, Lindau, Wasserburg - Baroque churches and palaces peeped above trees just turning spring green, while white, half-framed houses decorated the forested hillsides. Fifteen kilometres away on the other side of the lake, the light was so clear that Joe could even make out the roof of the famous Romanesque cathedral at Konstanz.

Amelia had taken his surprise announcement about Plesch in her stride, and, in a few minutes, had learned everything that Joe knew about this possible unholy alliance between Plesch, Monique Langevin, and perhaps also Paul and Hélène Gaspard. Not that Joe had much, if any, direct evidence for a plot, yet it seemed terrifyingly plausible.

Joe concluded with the meagre details he had wormed out of Olga Melikova about her niece's impromptu departure from the *Schloss Bielenberg.* 'I came to warn you that Monique and Plesch may be planning some sort of criminal outrage here on Lake Constance. You did advise me that Monique Langevin had the potential to be just as crazy as her late sister, and maybe she's about to prove it. And Plesch must have convinced her that it was the evil English who killed her innocent twin sister.'

Amelia was clearly worried, although trying to hide it. '*This* evil Englishwoman certainly would have killed Martine, if I'd thought it necessary.' She turned her eyes to his. 'And are you seriously tempted to try and earn this money promised by Olga Melikova?'

'No, I'm not. Persuading Monique Langevin back to the course of truth and light, and extricating her from Johan Plesch's loving care, appear to me considerably more difficult than threading a camel through the eye of the proverbial needle. I told you; I came here only to warn you what might be about to happen.'

Amelia said nothing for a few seconds.

Joe had a sudden flash of intuition. 'Why did *you* come to Lake

Constance? Something big is going on here, isn't it? Something that might attract a bunch of crazy anarchists and conspirators?'

'It's not your business any more, Joseph,' Amelia warned him. 'I suggest you stay out of it. Thank you for coming to warn me of your suspicions, and I promise I'll take them into account. Now you have done your duty, you can leave and take the gullible Miss Winthrop back to America where you can both live happily ever after.'

Joe was stung by the casual nature of her dismissal. 'Eleanor means nothing personal to me,' he objected.

Amelia gave him a wry look. 'Well, give it time. Now I really must be going, Joseph.'

'Stop treating me like this, Amelia. I came to help, and I think you need all the assistance you can get.' Joe glared at her. 'When the King left Paris nearly three weeks ago, his ultimate destination wasn't really his favourite brothel in Zurich, was it? I bet that was just an entertaining diversion on the way to wherever he was really going.'

Amelia gave him a knowing look but no answer.

'The King is here in Friedrichshafen, isn't he?'

Amelia finally nodded. 'Yes. But it's even worse than you think...'

*

They walked back towards town as the sun began to set.

'There is a secret meeting being held over the next few days at Friedrichshafen, between two of the most powerful men in Europe,' Amelia admitted.

'Who? Not the King *and* the Kaiser.'

Amelia confirmed that with a grimace. 'Even I can't gain admittance to this secret meeting, although we know Plesch remains a real threat to the proceedings.'

'Why can't you get in? You work for the British Foreign Office, don't you?'

Amelia twisted her face. 'Because Sir Charles Gorman, my distinguished boss, head of the Foreign Office Intelligence section, has decided to take direct charge of security for the King's safety during this meeting. He has told me that my help is no longer needed here since I had the stupidity to allow Plesch to escape in Zurich. He blames me personally for that; I am – not to put too fine a point on it - in a state of obloquy.'

Joe was angry on her behalf. 'Then your boss sounds a very stupid and insensitive man. Doesn't he know how close you came to getting yourself killed, saving the worthless life of your adulterous monarch?'

Amelia smiled. 'I suppose Americans are allowed to say such things, but I would be flung in the Tower of London if I said anything similar.' She paused. 'Sir Charles doesn't know all the details of the incident in *Le Royale*, but I doubt it would change his opinion if he did know all that happened there. It would probably confirm his opinion of me if he knew what a hash I made of it.'

Joe frowned as a thought occurred to him. 'Yet you're still here in Friedrichshafen after a week. You're here *illegally*, Miss Peachy, aren't you?' he said abrasively. 'This guise of Miss Cordingly isn't just to fool Plesch if he is about, but also Sir Charles and your own colleagues. Your boss thinks he's sent you packing back to England, and yet you've remained here, working behind his back. Don't you trust Sir Charles to keep the King alive?'

'I am merely keeping my ear to the ground, as you Americans would say,' Amelia said with quiet dignity. 'I have hired local people to keep me informed of anything unusual going on around the *Bodensee*, spending my own money. I was worried about Plesch before, but after what you've just told me, I am *doubly* worried now.'

Another thought occurred to Joe as they were walking. 'Why are the King and the Kaiser meeting here of all places? It's a bit out of the way. Why not Berlin or London?'

'Because the Kaiser wants to show off to his English relative the fruits of German science and technology...'

Joe wasn't listening to her, though, as he stopped dead in his tracks at the astonishing sight before him. Just rising above the trees was a colossal shape that slowly drifted upwards into view over the lake, casting a massive silvery reflection in the water.

This was truly a stupendous creation; Joe felt stunned at this vision from the future, this huge, metal, cigar-shaped, monstrous flying machine. It seemed like something from the pages of Jules Verne, rather than reality.

Joe's voice sounded like a croak. 'What on earth is that?' he gasped, even though he thought he knew the answer.

Amelia smiled grimly. 'That is the LZ1 Zeppelin. *That* is the piece of German technology the Kaiser wants to show off so much to his English uncle...'

*

Joe had read reports of these Zeppelins, of course, but had seen no photographs since the German builders of these machines had chosen to keep the details as secret as possible. Yet he had just imagined that they would be some modest improvement over conventional balloons; he'd certainly had no real comprehension until this moment of the scale of this vast machine, the first true airship, built by Count Ferdinand von Zeppelin....

For a few minutes he forgot everything else, as his engineering brain took over, and he wanted to know every technical detail of the LZ1's performance.

Amelia proved to be extremely knowledgeable about the technical specification of the machine, which made Joe cock an eye at her in suspicion. How did she know so much about this machine? – was it the result perhaps of a previous spying mission of hers in Germany?

He realised with slight depression that he knew virtually nothing of this woman's past life as a spy, and all the murky affairs and double dealings she must have been involved in. Yet it still didn't detract from his admiration for her in the slightest...

'Zeppelin's airship first flew two years ago,' Amelia explained. 'Your own country must take some of the blame – or credit – for Germany having this awesome new technology at its disposal. Count von Zeppelin first flew in an observation balloon while serving with your Union Army in the American Civil War forty years ago. But he apparently long dreamed of producing a fully steerable rigid balloon, which might one day turn into an ocean liner of the skies, carrying passengers and freight all over the world. It took him more than ten years of effort to produce the LZ1, because of the number of technical problems that had to be overcome to make a rigid hull of this size possible. But, as you see...' - she watched the majestic progress of the airship as it moved over the lake towards Konstanz – '...he seems to have succeeded. The LZ1 has a wire-braced aluminium hull, covered in cotton cloth, with sixteen hydrogen gas cells to give it lift, and two sixteen-horsepower engines, which give it a top speed of twenty kilometres per hour.'

'What happens if the wind is blowing at twenty-one kilometres an hour?' Joe asked dryly.

'Then it would probably be better to steer in the same direction as the wind is blowing, wouldn't it?' Amelia frowned at him. 'I wouldn't mock it, though, Joseph; the technology will only get better, the hull design stronger and the engines more powerful. And then who knows what these machines might achieve in the end...'

'Bombing cities from the air, perhaps?' Joe interrupted.

'I know it sounds far-fetched, like something from Mr Wells' pen, but we British do consider that a serious possibility and a future risk to our national security,' Amelia commented soberly.

Joe came back to earth from his reverie about the future of air travel. 'So what else haven't you told me yet about this meeting between the crowned heads of Europe on Friday?'

Amelia looked evasive for a moment, but then answered. 'You know everything else so I suppose you may as well know this too. Another special visitor is arriving secretly for this conference two days from now. He is coming by special train from St Petersburg.'

'Who?' Joe asked, fearing the worst. 'Not the Ts...'

His worries were confirmed as Amelia bit her lip like a little girl. 'Yes, I'm afraid it is indeed Nicholas the Second, Tsar of all Russia, who is coming to see his English and German relatives in Friedrichshafen on Friday...'

CHAPTER 19

Thursday March 27th 1902

Joe Appeldoorn hadn't been able to find Amelia since the evening before; she had disappeared soon after they had arrived back at the Hotel Adler, and there'd been no sign of her anywhere in the hotel since then. He'd left a note for her at the desk, of course, but had heard nothing in response.

Perhaps it was simply that she didn't need his help any more, yet it was worrying...

After breakfast, a concerned Joe walked up to the reception desk in the foyer of the hotel, and rapped impatiently on the counter.

'I wonder if you could tell me if Miss Cordingly has already gone out this morning?' he asked the startled hotel receptionist in English. 'I am an acquaintance of hers,' he added hopefully, doing his best to sound English.

'That would be the English lady in Room thirty-one...?' The young and rather effeminate man behind the polished mahogany desk made a face, as if to add, *the one with* s*uch revolting teeth and hair, don't you think?* 'Her key is here so she must be out, sir. But to be frank, I have not seen her since yesterday.' The German desk clerk spoke English in an extravagant way, quite unlike the understated accent of Swiss hotel staff.

'She *is* still staying here, I presume,' Joe continued worriedly. 'She hasn't checked out, has she?' Could she have just walked out of his life without a word of farewell, even after he came here especially to warn her? He wouldn't put it past her, somehow.

The man behind the desk smoothed down the temple of his glossy black hair, before consulting the hotel register in front of him. 'Oh no, sir, her room is still booked for several more days.'

Joe didn't know whether this was good news or not. He was deeply troubled on Amelia's behalf – he sensed she was heading irrevocably for some disastrous final encounter with Plesch, and perhaps with Monique

Langevin also, and he felt powerless to help her in the face of this impending Armageddon.

He had belatedly wired John Kautsky in New York, and Eleanor's grandfather, James, yesterday with the news of his success in finding Eleanor. A wire had come back to the telegraph office in Friedrichshafen within three hours – even though it was early in the morning in New York - instructing him to bring her straight back to America on the next available boat. So he had been fully intending to leave today for Zurich with Eleanor, before moving on to Paris within another day or so. But now, not being able to speak to Amelia and tell her of his plans to leave, he was pitched again into uncertainty.

He stood in the lobby, his mind in turmoil, wondering what to do. He tried to tell himself that he already gone out of his way to warn Amelia Peachy – *more than out of his way* – and now he should give up on her and resume his own more conventional life. But that was easier said than done.

'Are *you* leaving us today, sir?' the receptionist asked, sizing Joe up with his eyes. 'You did say yesterday that you might be.'

Something in the man's irritating voice decided Joe instantly: another day or so here surely wouldn't matter to John Kautsky or James Winthrop. 'No, please extend my reservation for another two days – Joseph Appeldoorn, Room twenty-four - and also that of Miss Eleanor Winthrop in twenty-five.'

Joe turned away and saw Eleanor coming down the main stairs to the lobby, a thoughtful smile on her face.

Joe smiled back at her uneasily, knowing he was getting into dangerously deep waters with Miss Winthrop now.

They had dined last night at a restaurant overlooking the lake. With moonlight on the water, the smell of lavender in her hair, and a lot of that wonderfully white bosom on show to admire, Joe had been hard pressed to remain business-like in the face of such provocation to his senses. He'd tried to be professional and reticent throughout, but it seemed that everything he said, no matter how brusque or charmless, just dug him in deeper with her. She hung on his every serious word as if he was expounding the Wisdom of Solomon, and she responded to any lighter remark from him as if he was being as witty as Oscar Wilde in his heyday.

If he wasn't careful over the next few weeks, as he escorted her personally all the way by train and ocean liner back to the arms of her family, he might find himself "Mr Eleanor Winthrop" before he even managed to get her halfway back.

But, looking at her fresh-faced beauty, would that really be such a bad thing? What was the matter with him? He should be fighting for the attention of this girl, not treating her like a bad dose of Influenza to be avoided.

Yet Amelia beckoned even in his sleep. Last night he had dreamed again about *her*, not Eleanor. This time he'd seen her hanging from a great height over an improbable precipice, and he'd tried desperately to save her, his fingers groping frantically for hers. Yet he couldn't hold on to her and he saw her slide away into the formless void, falling silently, looking back up at him with a note of entreaty in her face, but no fear...

He had considered asking Eleanor, from her knowledge of Doctor Freud's book, what a dream like this about falling might mean. But he dismissed the notion on seeing the sweet look on Eleanor's face this morning; the connotation of that dream seemed understandable enough, anyway.

'Good morning, Joseph. What another wonderful day,' she said, gazing out of the front entrance of the hotel at the azure blue of the sky and the calm tranquillity of the lake. 'Have you booked our rail tickets to Zurich and Paris yet?' she asked circumspectly.

'No, I haven't,' he admitted. 'I think we can afford to stay here until Saturday before starting our journey. We do have a long way to go, and I'm still a little sore and bruised.'

She half-smiled again, more to herself than anyone else. 'Well, I can understand why you want to stay here for a few more days. It was a lovely idea to bring me here, Joseph. This really is an enchanting spot; I had no idea Germany was so beautiful. So...what shall we do today?' she asked brightly.

'I need to do a few things on my own, first, Eleanor.' Last night, at dinner, Joe had tried going back to calling her "Miss Winthrop" – a desperate rearguard action – but he had soon been forced, after finishing a bottle of *Spätburgunder* wine with her, to finally renounce that hopeless measure.

Eleanor accepted his words without question and, with an innocent smile, said, 'Then I'll look around the town and perhaps buy myself some more new clothes. This place really is *bliss*.'

With misgivings Joe watched her leave with a cheerful parting wave in his direction. He had the feeling now that, even if he admitted to being a homicidal maniac, Eleanor would simply smile complacently back at him and say, '*Well, no one's perfect, Joseph...*'

*

A minute later, Joe himself went through the hotel front entrance, and turned left straight into the main street.

Friedrichshafen was a pretty enough little German town, but with nothing much to distinguish it from a dozen other similar medieval Swiss towns Joe had seen in the last weeks: long cobbled streets, old Baroque and Renaissance houses converted into shops, painted-facades above, lots of red-tiled roofs. Joe was just reflecting on where to begin looking for

Amelia in this place of quiet and quirky charm, and also, more prosaically, reflecting on the state of his badly scuffed and worn shoes, when he looked up from contemplation of the cracked leather and suddenly saw Monique Langevin approaching him...

And worse still, she was only a few feet away, and walking purposefully along the sidewalk towards him as if about to accost him directly...

Joe was aware only of the woman who had recently tried to slit his throat in Paris bearing down directly on him, and almost panicked, not knowing where to turn to avoid this harpy. He froze in his tracks as her face loomed ever larger, his eyes drawn for some reason to the mole on her cheek.

But Monique looked straight through him, without a flicker of recognition, and brushed right past him.

Joe breathed out slowly, letting out a long release of tension...

Of course *this* Langevin sister didn't know him from Adam, did she? Why should she? But it was disconcerting nevertheless to see this woman apparently restored to life, the same face he'd last seen in a Bern hotel, lolled back in that bath of blood, her skin so white and waxy against the violent red of the bathwater...

Except that Monique's mole was indeed on her *right* cheek, unlike her sister's, and also much higher up, nearer her eye. Joe made a mental apology to the concierge of Eleanor's apartment block in the Rue de la Boétie in Paris. The Widow Signoret had been right after all in her description of Monique, even down to the location of that mole.

The resemblance between two sisters was natural, of course, seeing that they were identical twins. Yet Monique wasn't dressed in the high fashion way that her sister had been dressed in Paris and Bern, Joe noted, but was instead attired more modestly in a common maid's uniform. Was this a disguise, or was she perhaps back doing the same sort of job as she had with the Comtesse de Pourtales in Paris? *Was she still up to her old tricks?* But no! This was a *different* woman, he reminded himself irritably. It had been her sister Martine*,* who had worked for the comtesse, not Monique. And the uniform Monique was wearing today did in fact look more like a hotel chambermaid's uniform than a more stylish personal maid's dress.

This was all very confusing, but Joe put aside such thoughts for the moment as he followed Monique down a side street towards the lakeshore and the bustling Friedrichshafen quayside.

It all seemed eerily reminiscent of him following the other Langevin sister through the streets of Bern a little over two weeks ago. So much had happened since then, but the wheel seemed to have turned full circle.

And, to heighten the parallel, Monique walked to a hotel, as her sister had that day - though not one perhaps as grand as the *Landhaus* in Bern, yet still probably the largest in Friedrichshafen. It was called the Hotel *Der*

Adelshof, and stood right on the lakeshore, four modern storeys forming a U-shaped plan around an ornamental garden of pine trees, rocks and decorative miniature waterfalls.

But there the similarity with Bern ended. Monique was certainly not dressed like any guest, and this was confirmed when Joe saw her enter through the staff entrance behind the kitchens. He followed closely on her heels as far as the door and heard a clatter of pans and cutlery from inside - the sound of frenzied cooking activity as lunch was being prepared. The delicious smells of *Wurst*, dumplings, and *Schwartenbraten* drifted out through the air vent in the wall.

Joe sat in the garden for nearly an hour and watched the kitchen entrance, waiting to see if Monique would reappear. But it seemed she really was working there full time; it was no trick. Once he tried pushing the kitchen door open for a peek and caught a glimpse of her working hard at a bench, peeling potatoes with determined concentration.

He decided that watching Monique further was hardly helping him – at least he would know where to find her again – so he retraced his steps back to his own hotel, the Adler.

Eleanor met him in the foyer, almost flinging herself up from her chair with excitement as soon as she saw him come though the entrance door. 'I saw Paul here in Friedrichshafen,' she exclaimed breathlessly. *'Paul Gaspard...!'*

*

Eleanor had seen Paul dressed in ordinary workman's clothes, walking down a side street, leading west out of town. His clothes were covered in sawdust, so that he looked nothing like the suave and dapper little Frenchman she knew so well.

'But I'm still sure it was him,' she protested, when Joe had tested her by suggesting she might have been mistaken.

Eleanor's curiosity about what Paul Gaspard was doing here, and dressed like that, had made her follow him surreptitiously nearly a kilometre out of town to a little lakeside hamlet of three or four houses. There she'd seen him go into a lumberyard, next to a carpenter's shop that apparently made coffins, trestle tables, and bits of rustic Wurttemberg furniture.

'He didn't see you, did he?' Joe had asked her worriedly.

'I don't think so. No, I'm sure of it. I kept religiously to the cover of the woods while I followed him.'

Joe took her hand. 'Come on, then. Show me where this place is...'

*

Eleanor dutifully led the way out of town, a pleasant walk mainly through sun-dappled woods along the edge of the lake, until they reached the hamlet she had described. There she pointed out the carpenter's. The shop was now closed, though, and the gate to the adjacent lumberyard – identified by a sign on the gate as belonging to *Wassermann und Sohn* - bolted.

'They were both open before,' Eleanor complained. 'I saw inside the yard from the cover of that cottage over there.'

'Did you see anyone else inside the yard, part from Paul? Any of the others from the *Schloss Bielenberg*? Paul's sister, Hélène, for example.'

'No, I didn't see her. What would *she* be doing working here in a lumberyard in Germany?' Eleanor was frankly puzzled now. 'In fact, what is Paul doing here? I don't understand this.'

'Did you see any other men in the yard?'

Eleanor puckered her pretty brow. 'Yes, two, I think.'

'Did you recognise either of him? Think, Eleanor!'

She looked hurt at the brusqueness in his voice. 'No, not really.'

'Could one of them have been the same man who came to the *Schloss Bielenberg* last week and left with Monique Langevin?'

Eleanor wrinkled her nose this time. 'It could have been; I can't be sure. I only saw that man for a few moments, remember.' She strained her memory. 'Yes, it *might* have been the same man...'

Joe's heart sank...*it could be Plesch, right here in Friedrichshafen*. And with Paul Gaspard and Monique Langevin also here, they had to be hatching something diabolical, just as he'd been fearing.

Faced with these confirmations of his worst fears, Joe didn't know what to do now.

Eventually, conscious of Eleanor's safety, he told her to go back to the Adler and stay in her room until he could join her.

'What is going on?' she asked him peevishly.

'I want to know what Paul Gaspard is getting up to here, that's all. Please go back to the hotel and wait for me.' In desperation to stop any more questions, he leaned his head down and kissed her. He had meant it to be no more than a brotherly peck on the cheek to encourage her to leave, but Joe suddenly found himself almost suffocated by her kisses in return as she embraced him. It was a full five minutes before he was finally able to extricate himself from the pressure of those wonderful lips and breasts and persuade her gently to return to Friedrichshafen. When she did, she seemed almost to float away as if on a cushion of air.

She really was a *very* sweet girl, Joe decided, feeling like a complete rat for some reason, as if he'd been leading the girl on deliberately, which he certainly hadn't. He knew now that he would have to nip this growing relationship with Eleanor in the bud somehow before it went any further. Still, he had more serious problems than that to solve first...

After Eleanor had disappeared from sight with a wave and a blown kiss, Joe tried to see inside the small lumberyard belonging to Herr Wassermann and his son. But although he began to hear plenty of noises from inside - robust banging and hammering and sawing, as if an afternoon shift of carpenters had just started work - he could see nothing at all. In desperation he even tried climbing a nearby cherry tree, just coming into pink flower, but soon abandoned that idea in the face of the blatant suspicion of two small boys in lederhosen, who stood watching him with stony implacability until he finally gave way and scrambled back down the tree again.

*

At three in the afternoon, Joe went back to the Hotel *Der Adelshof* and asked if they had a room - it seemed one possible way of keeping close tabs on Monique Langevin, at least. But it appeared to be a bad time to want to stay there: no rooms available at all.

'What? None at all? Are you sure?' Joe commented in surprise, when the pretty Bavarian girl behind the reception desk revealed this unexpected fact. For all its quiet charm, Friedrichshafen didn't look like a town that would be so full of tourists this early in the season.

The girl had blonde plaits piled up on top of her handsome head, and was trying not to smile and reveal the steel braces on her teeth. 'No, *Mein Herr*, we cannot take any new guests for the next few days even though the hotel is far from full. Most of the catering staff is required to serve at a big event tomorrow at the Zeppelin Works here in town. The event has been booked for many months...'

*

Joe waited outside Amelia's room on the third floor of the Adler for the whole of the rest of that afternoon and evening. He'd told Eleanor on his return to the Adler that he had a headache and needed to lie down in a darkened room. And she had kissed him on the brow and offered to sit holding a cold towel to his head all evening, but somehow he had managed to persuade her otherwise...

Joe suddenly woke up with a jerk, and realised he had fallen asleep on the carpet outside Amelia's room – the headache now a real one rather than fictitious. It had to be late from the stale way he felt, perhaps near midnight. Then he realised a figure was standing in the shadows in the corridor near him, regarding him with frank curiosity.

Perhaps she had even woken him up with a shake; he couldn't be sure in his drowsy state.

'What's wrong, Joseph?' she asked worriedly, stepping into the pool of illumination from a wall gaslight. She was dressed as herself again, the same Miss Peachy who had come to his room in Zurich and threatened to shoot him like a dog. But as he looked up at her, that now seemed a far-off and implausible event, and he had to repress the urge to put his arms around her and give her the kind of kiss Eleanor had recently given him.

She looked exhausted, though – dark shadows under her luminous eyes. He had seen that face in so many guises – Catherine, Miss Cordingly, even Madame Malet – and yet had never noticed one simple incontrovertible fact about it before. How unique and perfect that face really was...

He kept his voice light. 'Miss Peachy. How nice to see you again. I was wondering when you would finally turn up. Don't you *ever* sleep?'

She ignored the question. 'What are you doing here, Joseph? I thought you'd be on your way back to America by now.'

Joe finally got to his feet and ran a hand roughly through his hair. 'There's some kind of big reception taking place at the Zeppelin Works tomorrow, isn't there?'

Amelia nodded reluctantly. 'Yes, there is. I told you: the Kaiser wants to show off the new airship to his important visitors, so they are spending tomorrow afternoon at the Zeppelin works. But I am banned from attending.'

'I'm afraid Monique Langevin *is* planning to attend, though – banned or otherwise,' Joe said dryly.

Amelia didn't look too surprised at that troubling news. 'How do you know?'

'I know because she's working in the hotel, the *Der Adelshof*, that is doing the catering for this extravaganza.'

'Thank you for telling me.' Amelia seemed so tired herself that she could barely think, never mind move, almost swaying with fatigue.

Joe coughed. 'I'm afraid there is more. Paul Gaspard and probably Plesch are here in Friedrichshafen too. Today I think they've been working in a lumberyard belonging to a Herr Wassermann, to the west of the town.'

That information seemed to galvanise Amelia again. 'Doing what?'

'I really have no idea, but whatever it is, I suspect it means trouble.'

Amelia raised her drooping eyes to his. 'I agree with that judgement.'

A long enigmatic silence hung in the air as Joe waited expectantly. Finally Miss Peachy found her voice again and, in a much gentler tone, said something completely unexpected and out of character. 'You really liked me as Catherine, didn't you, Joseph?'

Joe felt as if his heart had stopped, so complete was the silence. 'Yes, I did like you as Catherine. Very much. It was a blow to me to discover she didn't really exist.'

'She does exist! She's still part of me, you know,' she claimed suddenly. 'Still inside here.' She took his hand tentatively and clasped it to her left breast.

Half an eternity more seemed to go by until she leaned her head softly against his chest, as if to a pillow. 'Do you want to stay with me tonight, Mr Appeldoorn?'

His voice sounded like the croak of a frog, but an exultant frog at least. 'Yes, I do, Miss Peachy...'

CHAPTER 20

Friday March 28th 1902

Aware somewhere in his subconscious that it was turning light, Joe Appeldoorn stirred and slowly returned from the arms of Somnus...or should it more properly be Morpheus? he wondered idly, still only half-awake at best. He had enjoyed a deep, dreamless sleep tonight as far as he knew, with none of the troubled dreams of recent nights. But then the object of his erotic fantasies had shared his bed with him throughout this night, and perhaps that was the reason for his serene and untroubled sleep.

He reached across to feel again the comfort of her body next to his, but found he was now alone in the bed. Yet that side of the sheet, and the pillow, was still warm with her scent and touch. She couldn't have gone very far, he thought complacently, guessing that she had just gone along to the bathroom at the end of the corridor.

Through the stirring drapes at the window, the sun was just rimming the mountains across the lake, gilding the mother-of-pearl water with fiery hues.

Last night, she had fallen asleep in his arms almost as soon as they'd lain on the bed, but it had still felt wonderful just being able to hold her to his chest, to caress that soft skin and feel its smooth texture, to run his fingers through her short glossy hair. He had always thought until now that a woman must have long flowing hair to be truly feminine, but Miss Peachy had disproved this old prejudice of his, as she had with so many of his other outdated notions of womanhood.

Before he'd finally fallen asleep himself, he'd spent his last few waking moments profitably, studying her face on the pillow. He was supremely touched by this woman's trust in him –allowing him this intimate glimpse into her private world. He suspected she didn't reveal herself like this to many people, if any. He felt – there was no other word for it – *privileged*...

Asleep, she really did have a beautiful child's face. Yet there were so many complex personalities concealed behind that exceptional face that it was hard to grasp her essence...

Now, the morning after, he dozed fitfully again in the dawn light, only to wake a few minutes later with a start, and a feeling of deep foreboding.

The feeling of foreboding turned out to be well justified. Time, ever mysterious as his friend Albert had often claimed, had deceived him; Joe realised he must have fallen asleep again for at least an hour, and the sun was now well above the mountains. He experienced a sudden rush of panic as he leapt out of bed, pausing only to find his clothes on the chair by the bed.

Amelia had gone! Gone to do whatever she could to stop Plesch, by herself...

'Oh, what a woman!' he cried out loud, encompassing both extreme nuances of meaning in the one exclamation – admiration *and* exasperation...

*

After washing quickly and getting a change of clothes in his own room, Joe went, at a trot, to Wassermann's lumberyard to the west of the town.

The place was apparently just opening for business, even though it was already past eight o'clock. A rumpled man in his fifties, dressed in a leather apron and blue serge overall, eyes still heavy with sleep, was yawning widely as Joe ran into the untidy yard. A plump woman, perhaps a youngish wife or a daughter, with a vast bosom like the stern of an ocean liner, peered through a window of the adjacent carpenter's shop, an eyebrow raised in question at this unexpected early visitor.

The place was a mess inside, far removed from the usual Germanic efficiency. Timber sections lay scattered about, together with clumps of unused nails, sawdust, pools of machine oil and mountains of wood shavings. Even the tools had been left in disarray: saws, mauls and hammers dropped anywhere as if whoever had done it had departed in a pressing hurry.

Joe buttonholed the yawning man. '*Mein Herr*, are you the owner of this place?'

The man nodded and introduced himself as Herr Wassermann. 'Yes, it's my business, as it was my father's before me, and his father's before that. But it's never been in such a fine mess as this before...this is certainly not *my* doing,' he denied vigorously. 'It'll take me hours to clean up after those *gentlemen*.'

'Are you talking about the men who were working here yesterday? They don't work for you normally, do they?'

The man ran a hairy paw through his tousled greying hair. 'Why do you want to know?'

'I need to find those men urgently.'

Joe could see from the man's suddenly shrewd expression that he would have to hand over a few Reischsmarks if he wanted any cooperation from him in this matter. But on receipt of a wad of notes handed over carelessly without accurate counting, Herr Wassermann's surly countenance turned almost as sunny as the day. '*Ja*, I did let them use my shop and my yard, and my timber, for the last two days. They paid me very well, but I would have charged them more if I had any idea what kind of mess they were going to leave behind. They've ruined some of my best tools too – just look at that blade saw! They said they needed to make themselves a long trestle table. For a wedding celebration.'

Joe was suspicious. 'Can't you just buy things like that ready-made?'

The man laughed. '*Ja*, I said precisely the same thing. But they wanted to make a special one for themselves to particular dimensions. I offered to do it for them – neither of them looked like expert carpenters to me - but they said "No, Herr Wassermann. You take the day off." So my wife and I went and did exactly that: travelled to see some relatives up the valley and had a picnic yesterday. But leisure all day isn't suitable for a young woman -' he nodded in the direction of the carpenter's shop next door – '...she was absolutely insatiable in bed last night,' he confided with a weary sigh. 'My own fault for marrying a woman twenty years younger than me. Actually I doubt there's another woman in the whole of Wurttemberg with a higher libido than my wife – she'd have the cassock off a pastor given half a chance...'

Joe interrupted impatiently. 'Describe the men who were here, Herr Wassermann. Just to make sure we're talking about the same men I'm interested in. How many were there?'

'Two only. One was a Frenchie in his twenties. Very good-looking boy. My wife wanted to stay behind on her own and bring him drinks all day. But she would have had his trousers off in ten minutes, if I'd allowed that.'

That was clearly Paul Gaspard, Joe thought. 'And the other?'

'About thirty-five and...' The man struggled to think of something else to say, his face bemused.

'That's it?' Joe muttered sarcastically. 'That's what I get for all my money.'

Wassermann looked a little chastened. 'To be honest, *Mein Herr*, yes. I'd give you a description if I could, but there was almost nothing worth noting about the man. He really was Herr Nobody.'

His wife had come into the yard by now, and she eyed Joe with a lascivious smile while puffing up her enormous bosom. 'He had strange eyes,' she said, offering an insight of her own. 'The colour of cat's pee.'

Herr Wasserman shooed his wife back to the shop. 'She really talks too much,' he explained tartly.

'No, that was a very useful observation by your wife, *Mein Herr*. She's an observant woman.'

'Then you wouldn't like to take her off my hands, would you?' the man muttered with savage sarcasm. 'I just can't keep up with her any more; she'll bury me before the year is out if she keeps up these demands.'

Joe smiled thinly, not taking the offer seriously. 'I think not, but thank you for the kind offer.' He was just turning to leave when he noticed something glinting on the sawdust-covered ground, something metallic. He picked it up and, with deep misgivings, recognised a spent cartridge case.

'What's that?' Herr Wassermann asked curiously.

Then Joe saw another cartridge case, *and* another. But also something worse, three gouge marks in the sawdust, the mark of a heavy tripod, with a large patch of machine oil in the middle.

He smelled the cartridge he had picked up; recognised the distinct tang of cordite. That and the distinctive marks scarred in the ground told him ominously where these cartridge cases might have come from.

Joe had seen similar marks to those a couple of years before – these earlier tripod marks in the ground had been at a demonstration in the Military Academy at West Point of a new kind of weapon…

A Maxim machine gun, the first fully automatic machine-gun in the world…

*

The helmsman urgently throttled back the controls of the steam launch *Plattenburg* at Joe's shouted command from the stern.

Eleanor lounged in a canvas chair on the stern deck beside him, as pretty as a picture by Jacques Joseph Tissot, dressed in a patterned grey gingham skirt and cream white lace blouse that showed off her impressive proportions. Only the large straw hat seemed a mistake on board the steam yacht, as she constantly had to struggle to hold it in place under the blustering northerly wind. Still, she managed to retain her sunny disposition even with this annoying provocation.

She really was an extremely sweet-natured girl, Joe told himself yet again, which was doubly astonishing considering the ordeal of her time in Europe, and also the vast wealth she possessed, something not usually noted for building a pleasant disposition of character.

She had been undeniably curious, though – if restrained in her questioning – about whether Joe had really had a confrontation yesterday with Paul Gaspard, and what her former French suitor might have had to say for himself. Or, for that matter, what he was doing working at carpentry in an isolated lumberyard on the outskirts of Friedrichshafen. Even Eleanor apparently realised something exceedingly strange was going on, but nevertheless didn't press Joe when he declined to explain…

After leaving the lumberyard this morning, Joe had gone directly to the Hotel *Der Adelshof* where he'd seen Monique working yesterday. But he'd discovered that what the receptionist with the plaits and the teeth braces had told him was the literal truth. Today the hotel was virtually closed and being operated by a skeleton staff for the benefits of a few long-term residents only. All the rest of the staff, including most of those who worked in the kitchen, had gone to serve at the important reception being held this afternoon at the Zeppelin works on the lakeshore to the east of the town.

So, although he'd suspected it was a forlorn hope, Joe had gone on from there in a horse cab to the main gates of the Zeppelin works, with the idea of seeing someone in authority and perhaps warning them. From the size of the crowds gathering inside, it was soon confirmed to Joe that there was an event of some importance going on today, even though most ordinary people in the town he'd spoken to seemed remarkably unaware of it. (And certainly, the presence of the three most important crowned heads of Europe in their small town - King Edward VII, Tsar Nicholas II, and even their own ruler, Kaiser Wilhelm II - was an honour completely unsuspected by most of the citizens of Friedrichshafen.)

As Joe had expected, though, he'd found at the gate that there was no chance of him gaining entry to this select party without an invitation. The security was as tight as one would expect in the circumstances: fearsome-looking uniformed soldiers marched in regimented rows just inside the barbed wire perimeter fence, while the steel gates were manned by armed Prussian military officers rigged out in pickle-helmeted and polished jackboot splendour.

Worse still, the officer on duty at the main gate – a bull-necked Prussian with a face like the young Bismarck - had refused to even listen to what Joe had to say. In desperation Joe had tried mentioning the name of Sir Charles Gorman, and had asked if he could see him; but that had only produced more blank looks and a swift barked order from a Prussian captain for him to remove himself at once.

So Joe had retraced his steps wearily to the Hotel Adler as he contemplated what to do next. He had just been making enquiries at the desk about where he could hire a boat to take him on the lake (from where he might at least get a good view of proceedings at the Zeppelin works) when he encountered Eleanor accidentally coming out of the ground floor restaurant. And when she'd found out about his planned afternoon excursion on the water, he'd simply had no alternative, without grossly offending her, to inviting her along...

*

According to the grizzled boat hands on the Friedrichshafen quayside, the *Plattenburg* was reputed to be the fastest steam yacht on the lake. Joe had managed to hire her and her crew for the afternoon at short notice, but only by offering a king's ransom. But she was a wonderful piece of German craftsmanship, he'd soon realised, even though her engine was actually a new British-made Parsons steam turbine that produced a high-pitched whine rather than the usual clanking throb.

And a fine sight she made on the water too, her superstructure gleaming white against the blue lake, her sharp, steep prow parting the surface effortlessly in a swirl of cream foam, with two neat rolling bow waves to right and left. Even Eleanor had been completely enchanted by the style and grace of this steam yacht, as Joe had ushered her on board. The brass lanterns on each side of the cabin swayed in time to her motion, the brasswork of the rail shone, the deck vibrated with the great metallic turbines spinning below.

At Joe's command, the helmsman now hove to, five hundred metres offshore, as close as the yacht could feasibly get to the Zeppelin works without arousing suspicion from the armed military guard there. The old helmsman of the *Plattenburg* was holding the brass wheel like a toy in his hands, clearly enjoying the feel of the polished metal beneath his ancient fingers. It occurred to Joe that a boat such as this, with its awesome turn of speed, would have been unheard of in this man's far-off youth, the improvement of technology moving at such a frenetic pace these days. Joe wondered what miracles he might hope to see by the time he was as old as this man – *should he live that long anyway...*

Joe studied the scene in the Zeppelin works through the high-powered Zeiss binoculars he'd bought in town today. These were also a fantastic piece of German technology, bringing the distant scene bounding close within his sight.

Yet the LZ1 airship, its immense aluminium hull gleaming phallus-like in the early afternoon sunlight, put all these other pieces of twentieth-century German technology entirely in the shade. Just her size alone inspired awe – she had to be sixty or seventy metres in length and six to eight metres deep. The airship stood on a floating apron slab in front of an immense steel hangar that projected far out into the water. This was probably the largest building in terms of volume that Joe had ever seen; even from five hundred metres away, the scale of it - and of the giant airship - dwarfed everything else around it.

The Zeppelin was clearly being readied for a test flight, presumably to impress the gathered dignitaries. A gang of men were stationed at the mooring lines. The airship was moving nervously in the blustery conditions, though, rather like a prize racehorse straining for the off in the *Grand Prix de l'Arc de Triomphe*. The size of the machine was impressive, but the absurd *lightness* of it was also evident in the tense struggles of the ground crew to control it and hold it down.

Perhaps machines like this really would be the future of travel and warfare, Joe thought, with deep misgivings. Maybe everyone would fly around the world one day; perhaps even wars would be waged in the air...

'What are you doing, Joseph?' Eleanor was smiling still, but clearly feeling a little neglected by his lack of attention to her, even though one of the crewmembers, a handsome boy of about seventeen, more than made up for Joe's inattentiveness by gawping at her unashamedly.

'I'm just looking at what's going on at the Zeppelin works, over there on the lakeshore.'

'What *is* happening over there? My word, that airship is so enormous! I had never imagined anything so big.' Eleanor had seemed oddly uninterested in this colossal flying machine, and all the related activity in the Zeppelin works, up to this point. 'Is there a ceremony of some sort going on, do you think?'

The ceremonial proceedings did indeed seem to have started, the sounds of German military brass band music drifting across the water. How Joe detested the sound of German martial music! How could the nation that had given the world Beethoven, Brahms and Mendelssohn also produce this awful "oompah-oompah" noise?

Through his binoculars, Joe could see coloured bunting and national flags fluttering in the stiff breeze. A row of dignitaries sat in a small temporary grandstand near a white marquee. And yes! Joe could make out the Royal Standard of Great Britain as well as the Union Jack, billowing next to the Imperial German flag. Then his heart sank as he recognised the Russian flag too...

It was true; the three great royal figures of Europe were all gathered here in this one place, the heads of the houses of Prussia, Saxe-Coburg and Romanov all seated in that one small grandstand.

In front of the nearby marquee, a long table had been laid out with what must be food and drink for the guests, to be served no doubt after the demonstration flight of the Zeppelin. Joe assumed that Monique Langevin and possibly Hélène Gaspard were there at the marquee table, working as part of the staff drafted in from the Hotel *Der Adelshof*. And perhaps Paul Gaspard and Plesch were also there somewhere, waiting in the wings for their chance.

Could they really be planning to murder the crowned heads of Europe in one fell swoop?

And what was Amelia doing about it? Knowing her, she would be doing *something* – at least warning her own chief of her suspicions anyway. Surely Sir Charles Gorman would listen to her now, even if she were in temporary disgrace over Plesch's near success in assassinating the King in Zurich.

Had Plesch put Monique and the Gaspards up to whatever was being planned today? Joe guessed that he must be the organising brain behind whatever they were intending to do – there had to be a Machiavellian schemer like Plesch involved to have concocted any sort of plan in the short time available.

But would Plesch be *personally* involved in it? This kind of direct action seemed somehow too risky and suicidal for a secretive professional like him. Not his style at all, if what Amelia had said about him was true. He worked deviously, in secret, and with a minimum of confederates as a rule. A man like Plesch would be more than happy to incite confederates to suicidal acts of violence, but would always make sure to have a way out for himself.

If Amelia was right, then Plesch's personal mission this time seemed to be only to kill the King, not the Kaiser and the Tsar too. Or did he simply not care any more after his humiliating failure in Zurich? Was he determined to kill the King now, no matter who else would die, or what the ramifications for European politics might be?

How were they actually going to do it, though? Joe racked his brain. *The table...the machine gun...*

Could that long table, loaded up with choice dishes and drinks, possibly be the one that Plesch and Gaspard had been working on in the lumberyard? Perhaps they'd only modified an existing trestle table and somehow managed to deliver it to the Zeppelin works for use in the festivities. But how could they get that machine gun past the guards on the gates and into a position where it could do damage?

And then the solution came to him. How could he have been so stupid? They must have concealed the machine gun *inside* the special table Plesch and Gaspard had been making. Perhaps it had a secret compartment that would open at just the right time.

Joe caught his breath as he imagined the imminent carnage. Back home they would call it a *turkey shoot...*

Joe shouted at the figure of Methuselah at the helm. 'Can you take me closer to the shore, *Mein Herr*?'

There was almost a flotilla of small boats with soldiers on board immediately blocking the way to the slipway and the floating apron slab of the Zeppelin works. But Joe had spotted a convenient place a little further along the lake where a wooded promontory protruded from the shore, from which it might be possible to break into the Zeppelin works, without being seen by the numerous guards.

Eleanor watched, first with surprise, then a deepening blush - and finally unabashed interest - as Joe kicked off his shoes, took off his jacket, and then stripped down to his undershirt and drawers.

When the *Plattenburg* came within two hundred metres of the wooded place on the shore, he turned apologetically to Eleanor. 'Sorry about this, but there's something I really have to do, Eleanor. I'll be back soon, so keep the boat waiting for me here.'

With that, he plunged cleanly into the water.

CHAPTER 21

Friday March 28th 1902

The swim was pure purgatory – exhausting work for his frozen muscles in the icy water. But Joe eventually reached the shore and clambered stealthily into the cover of the woods.

What should he do now? he wondered, his pulse racing despite his goose-pimpled skin and stiffening sinews. He'd swam ashore with no clear plan of what he intended to do apart from seeing better what was going on in the Zeppelin works. But now, shivering in the gusting wind on the exposed shore, even that limited aim seemed a preposterously ambitious one. In fact he was strongly tempted to swim straight back to the launch and give up this mad idea.

He glanced back at the *Plattenburg* to see Eleanor – if still looking completely perplexed by his odd behaviour - waving gaily at him. Joe waved back half-heartedly from his hiding place trying to indicate to her to desist from attracting attention, but Eleanor continued her affectionate hand waving so Joe gave up finally and ducked completely out of sight into the undergrowth.

Then he made his way between the dense ranks of pine trees, bent double to stay as invisible as possible, the pine needles underfoot murder on his bare soles. He was still shivering violently from the swim; the water had been even colder than he'd imagined - straight from the icy heart of an Alpine glacier.

He didn't have his Webley with him either, which was a problem; in his panicked hurry this afternoon to arrange the hire of the boat he had simply forgotten to go and fetch the weapon and bring it on board with him.

Some detective he was...!

So, in his unarmed state, what could he do to stop Plesch or Monique even if he managed to spot them? His appearance might bemuse them a little but would be unlikely to worry them otherwise.

He saw with alarm that his cotton drawers and undershirt had clearly not been intended to double as a swimming costume and that now, soaked through, they were virtually transparent. This was going to raise some interesting questions if he paraded himself like this in front of the crowned heads of Europe and the other VIPs – particularly the women among them.

But he put such thoughts to the back of his mind for the present – the first priority was to gain access to the Zeppelin grounds somehow to see what was going on.

A three-metre high barbed iron palisade fence still separated him from the Zeppelin factory site, which projected several metres out into the lake and had to be negotiated somehow. But after crawling through a spiky undergrowth of dwarf alder and pollarded willow covered in ivy, he saw a possible way around it, provided he was prepared to go back into the icy water again. Even the mere *thought* of that was hard to bear so Joe allowed himself no time for deliberation but simply sucked in his breath and plunged back into ice blue of the *Bodensee* yet again. The bottom of the lake shelved steeply and he found it was possible to dive to the bottom and pull himself along the serrated submerged rocks ten metres or more to get around the fence. Then, with extreme caution, he clambered on shore again into the shelter of a holly bush before any soldiers on the nearby boats spotted him.

Joe waited expectantly for the worst in the shelter of the holly bush. But no Prussian armed guards came screaming, with rifle butts ready to crush his skull. He breathed again – he was safely inside the Zeppelin factory premises now.

But where to go from here?

The brass band music was much louder now from this closer perspective, and even more irritating to Joe's musical ear. He could see much the same view that he'd witnessed from the boat, but now from a different angle and in more detail. He took in the elements of the scene again: the giant floating hangar and apron slab, and the Zeppelin itself, still not airborne; the white marquee; the small three-tier covered grandstand – the latter a temporary structure only but one splendidly decorated with brocade, tapestry and flags, as well as housing an elegantly attired ensemble of the great and good of Europe's ruling elite.

Even from a hundred metres, Joe could clearly make out the three central figures in the grandstand, all in dress uniforms, dripping with decoration, gold tassel and medals. The grey-bearded King seemed to be relaxed, and puffing on a cigar (though still looking considerably more formal and dignified than Joe had seen him in *Le Royale* twelve days ago.) The Tsar, a more dapper figure in white and gold, was not indulging in anything much that Joe could see – he might even have been dozing. The

Kaiser, bull-necked and red of face - glowing with national pride, perhaps, or possibly with anger at the delay in launching the Zeppelin - sat between his two close relatives. Both the Kaiser and the Tsar were, after all, nephews of the King; this was a family gathering indeed.

Of all the elements in this pageant, though, it was the long trestle table in front of the marquee, facing the assembled figures in the grandstand, which troubled Joe the most. He could see a dozen or more young women in maids' uniforms, waiting patiently behind the tables for their work to begin - the same uniform Joe had seen Monique Langevin wearing yesterday, the uniform of the serving maids of the Hotel *Der Adelshof.*

One of those girls *had* to be Monique Langevin, Joe thought; and perhaps Hélène Gaspard was there too, if she was as crazy a revolutionary as Monique. The "Daughters of the *Narodniki*" might finally be about to strike a violent blow for the proletariat of Europe, with Johan Plesch pulling the strings from off stage somewhere...

But where were Johan Plesch and Paul Gaspard? Legions of waiters and other minions were milling about near the long trestle table too, as well as an array of military figures in various colourful national uniforms. Plesch and Gaspard could be any of those people - Plesch particularly; he was, after all, a master of disguise. Joe remembered the inebriated English Colonel Blair, and the bourgeois Bavarian salesman, Herr Blumenfeld. There'd been no physical or behavioural similarity at all between those two gentlemen, it had seemed.

Joe tried not to imagine what a Maxim or a Vickers machine gun might do to those finely dressed people sitting in that grandstand, from a distance of twenty metres or less.

But how could he possibly prevent it? He was wet and practically naked, and frozen solid to boot - his hands and fingers like hardened lumps of white pork that he could scarcely feel, never mind flex. And there was a stretch of a hundred metres or so of open grass between him and the celebration area where even a blind man couldn't fail to notice him, if he dared to venture out into the open. He could hardly just walk casually across that vast expanse of grass, whistling "Dixie" and hope no one would notice him, and then start searching discreetly under the trestle table in front of the marquee to see if there might be a machine gun concealed within.

His attention transferred for a moment to the airship as the engines hummed into life. The size of the LZ1 was even more impressive from this close vantage point – truly staggering, it seemed to Joe – more like a soaring cathedral constructed in aluminium than a mechanical form of transport. Even in his feverish state of worry, Joe couldn't help but admire the men whose engineering minds had made this great leap of the human imagination a practical possibility. He could imagine that sleek cigar shape soaring upwards effortlessly into the sky forever - it seemed so futuristic and unearthly that it might even be capable of reaching into space...

The ground crew, kitted out in blue sailor uniforms like the *Kriegsmarine*, were now having even more difficulty controlling the airship, it seemed, working rapidly to fix extra tethering cables to the anchors in the ground. Perhaps the powerful gusting wind was upsetting the Kaiser's carefully thought-out plans to impress his relatives and national rivals. Maybe it would even make the test flight impossible today – a rather humiliating loss of face for the Kaiser, if the Germans had to admit that their new technology still had a long way to go to be of practical use. It was something that the Kaiser, and the Zeppelin's creators, would want to avoid at all costs.

The band music had stopped and an elderly man now mounted the central dais and began addressing the invited VIPs in the grandstand. Could this be the great Count Ferdinand von Zeppelin in person, Joe wondered, the man who had first flown in a balloon while serving with the Union Army in the American Civil War...

Joe was contemplating his next course of action when he saw with despair that he'd left it too late...

*

It started with a commotion at the long table when one of the maids suddenly seemed to go berserk, sweeping off the assembled food and crockery and glass in front of her.

Count von Zeppelin stopped in mid-sentence and turned his head around, yet seemed only mildly annoyed by the interruption, clearly thinking it was no more than a domestic accident. But then his annoyance changed, like everyone else's in the vicinity, to utter perplexity and a frisson of terror, as a section of the table seemed to split magically open to reveal a man crouched behind something sleek and black and evil-looking – *a machine gun...*!

Joe began to run across the grass, not caring if he was seen now; nobody, after all, would be looking in his direction any more...

Joe was labouring with the effort of getting his frozen muscles to work – a seven-year-old could probably have outpaced him in his present condition. One of the members of the Zeppelin ground crew seemed to have a similar idea to him, he saw, abandoning his station and running at top speed to presumably tackle the machine gunner. And this man – little more than a boy really from his size – was much closer to the table than Joe, and much faster.

The machine gunner hadn't fired yet, though; he seemed fortuitously to be having technical problems with the weapon. Something had jammed –a cartridge probably - giving Joe and the ground crew boy an extra chance to get there in time. The gunner was frantically trying to clear the jammed cartridge in the breech and seemed to have finally succeeded just as the boy launched himself athletically through the air and across the table, bowling over the machine gun and its gunner. Joe was still fifty metres away when this happened, but closing fast now as his muscles warmed.

The armed soldiers gathered by the grandstand were slower to respond than the boy from the ground crew, clearly not sure what to do, or even who the enemy was, but holding to their orders to protect the VIPs in their charge like typically unimaginative military men.

The boy and the machine gunner were both winded by the impact of their horrendous collision, but the boy seemed to have come off worse of the two and looked badly dazed. One of the *Der Adelshof* maids – it didn't look like Monique so Joe guessed it had to be Hélène Gaspard – then pulled a pistol of her own from under her uniform, and ran screaming towards the dignitaries in the grandstand as if she intended to shoot a few of them herself before she was taken by the soldiers.

Joe watched helplessly, still a few metres short of his destination, as the machine gunner recovered enough from his mauling to stand the gun up again on its tripod and get behind it. Joe could even see the man's finger tighten on the trigger. As Joe skidded to a halt close behind him, the machine gun finally erupted viciously into life. But the gunner clearly hadn't seen his own confederate running from the side, and the spray of bullets hit her in the back and sent her flying sideways like a grotesque mannequin. This elicited a collective gasp from the distraught guests in the grandstand who now panicked and dived belatedly for cover.

The machine gunner – Joe assumed it had to be Paul Gaspard - stopped firing and screamed his anguish to the heavens. *Had Paul Gaspard just killed his own sister, Hélène...?*

Joe recognized the maid who had swept the dishes off the table initially and started this mayhem; it was no surprise to him to find that it was Monique Langevin. But she seemed quite unfazed by the unexpected turn of events, or by the arrival in their midst of a mysterious semi-naked man from nowhere. Pulling a gun of her own, she motioned Joe to stand still.

The machine gunner was still sobbing uncontrollably so Monique hissed an order at him in French, 'Pull yourself together, Paul. Hélène is dead and there's nothing we can do about it! Fire the gun again. Make up for Hélène's sacrifice. Kill them all.'

The man laughed hysterically. 'I can't...it's jammed solid again.'

The soldiers had by now formed an armed wall around the guests in the grandstand, and were beginning finally to advance towards the machine gun and the four people still grouped around it. Everyone else had scattered or was lying prostrate on the ground.

Monique, ever resourceful, pulled the heroic ground crew boy to his feet - he was still badly dazed, it seemed - and pulled off his hat, revealing a rich head of glossy dark hair. Short hair, but still much too long for a boy's...

Joe's heart sank as he realised it was Amelia...

'Leave it, Paul. It's too late.' The pragmatic and unflappable Monique Langevin put a gun to Amelia's head and retreated backwards with her towards the airship. 'Don't shoot!' Monique called out to the advancing soldiers, 'or I'll kill this woman. Is that clear?' Paul Gaspard followed close behind her, stumbling blindly, eyes still streaming.

Joe tried to follow too, but Monique pointed her gun briefly at his forehead – '*Not you*!' - and he stopped dead in his tracks at the clear menace in her eyes.

Joe didn't know what else to do as Monique and her prisoner retreated towards the airship. Soldiers arrived alongside him and one prodded him with a pistol barrel.

'Not *me*, you oaf. Them!' Joe said in German, pointing to the departing Monique, who was still holding a gun to Amelia's head as she approached the gondola of the airship, and forced the ground crew to stand aside. 'That's who you want! They're kidnapping that woman!'

Where was Plesch? Joe wondered, his mind racing wildly. Watching all this from a safe vantage point somewhere close?

Yet something was completely wrong in all this...

Joe saw the ebullient King of England push his way forward through the protective ranks of Prussian soldiers to take a closer look at the table and the sinister-looking machine gun. He seemed unperturbed, if puzzled, by the strange happenings – and particularly by this semi-naked man standing in the middle of all this confusion. Joe wondered if the King had possibly recognised him as the man who had jumped out of that alcove in the third-floor room of *Le Royale*...

Joe was trying desperately to think - Plesch wouldn't rely on only the machine gun, would he? Assuming he was here, he would certainly have a Plan B: a means of creating a diversion and getting away if things went wrong.

Plesch *must* be here somewhere, Joe thought, turning to look at the airship again.

A Prussian major barked something in Joe's face, but his mind was too distracted to answer. Then the major hit him in the solar plexus with a fist like a ball of iron.

Joe hadn't been expecting the blow and fell back against the table top, part of which collapsed under his weight.

Then Joe, winded and dazed, and lying with his face buried in the wreckage of the table, saw something taped to one of the table legs. Sticks of something – explosive...*dynamite*! Joe felt a sudden rush of blood to the head as he thought of the power of Alfred Nobel's invention and heard the distinct ticking of a clock...

'Run! Get away! It's a bomb! Clear the area for God's sake!' Joe screamed, as he got rapidly to his feet, then grabbed the King by the lapels of his impressive uniform, steering his vast bulk away from the trestle table like a tug with a reluctant ocean liner.

Everyone else scattered too, in all directions, as Joe screamed again his blood-curdling warning.

They were perhaps thirty yards away from the table when the dynamite blew up with a force to knock a building over. The power of the explosion lifted Joe and the King completely off their feet; Joe felt himself blown through the air by the shock wave like a an autumn leaf, losing what was left of his undershirt in the process, before being dumped again painfully onto terra firma.

Dazed, and with his ears ringing with the force of the explosion, he came slowly to his senses again, and saw that the King was lying a few feet away from him on his side, but groaning and apparently not seriously hurt. Joe believed he had taken more of the blast himself, so had probably inadvertently protected the King-Emperor from the worst effects. Certainly Joe felt bruised and battered from his head to his toes, yet he had no time to rest on his laurels because he soon became aware that the Zeppelin was already lifting sedately off the ground...

With his attention naturally fully occupied elsewhere for the last few panic-stricken minutes, Joe hadn't seen what had happened when Monique and Gaspard had finally reached the airship with their hostage. Looking around now, Joe could see no sign of Amelia, so assumed that Monique must have taken her on board the gondola with them. The ground crew of the airship had all scattered by now - perhaps they had done so even before the explosion, because three or four of the ground crew lay dead on the ground beneath the departing airship.

Joe realised the truth now; Monique couldn't have shot all those ground crew by herself. *Plesch had to be in the gondola* too...

He must have got on board earlier while everyone's attention was on the trestle table and the hidden machine gun, and taken over control of the airship. Plesch and his confederates were probably now holding guns on any surviving members of the crew in the gondola, forcing them to do their bidding. Joe had no idea why they had taken Amelia with them, but if she was in that gondola with Plesch and Monique, then she was as good as dead, unless he could do something about it...

Joe didn't hesitate but urged his aching body into motion again, and ran towards the airship as fast as his heaving lungs would allow him. The tether cables were flapping about in the air as the Zeppelin rose higher. Joe aimed for the longest one, still slithering along the ground, and made a grab at it. It was an absurd notion – *did he imagine that he alone could hold the airship back?* But the truth was he did it instinctively without thinking, and before he knew what was happening, was literally yanked high into the air.

As the Zeppelin rose with extraordinary speed, Joe found himself dangling a hundred feet above the water...

*

Joe hung on for dear life, buffeted and twisted by the swirling wind, the breath being sucked out of his body, as the airship flew out over the Bodensee. Joe could see the whole length of the lake from up here: the towns of Konstanz, Meersburg, even Überlingen. Yet he felt exhilaration too mixed with the fear, this glorious exultant feeling of flying like a bird. It was an extraordinary sensation to soar free like this.

He could even see the steam yacht *Plattenburg* far below, and a white-clothed figure in the stern craning her neck and holding on to her straw hat to look up at this unusual sight. *Should he let go?* It seemed like the sanest option; he *might* just survive the fall.

But he was rising all the time and it was already too late for letting go: he was a hundred metres above the ground now, and falling from this height meant certain death. The only way to survive was by going up and getting into the gondola somehow...

Joe started to climb the twisted wire cable, which cruelly tore the skin on his hands. It might be relatively warm still down on the ground, but up here, tossed about by the wind, he felt frozen again. The run across the grass and the subsequent events had at least warmed up his body a little and unfrozen his muscles and sinews, yet his fingers, forearms and biceps still felt ready to burst under the immense strain as he inched himself up painfully, bit by bit. It was the highest twenty metres he had ever climbed, and the longest three minutes of his life.

But faced with a challenge where he couldn't afford to fail, he made it, somehow eventually reaching his target. The cable he'd climbed had fortuitously been attached to the back of the forward aluminium frame gondola, which housed the main control cabin of the airship. There he found a minuscule ledge on the back of the gondola where he could rest his shaking arms and aching muscles, and assess the situation.

The giant engines were luckily mounted at the rear of the airship and far removed from him, the two great propellers whirling in concerted harmony. The front gondola was a substantial construction, though, containing the ten-metre-long control cabin, which was laid out like the bridge of a ship, with a wheel and a battery of clock dials and scientific instruments. Joe could see that a ladder in the roof of the cabin gave entry to the main interior of the airship where presumably internal access walkways led aft between the gasbags.

Joe began to wonder where the airship might be headed. He guessed that Plesch was probably going to make the captain of this vessel land the airship somewhere far away on the other side of the lake, out of reach of chasing boats or carriages, where he could get a substantial head start on his pursuers. But there must be only a limited number of large enough flat areas around the lake where it would be possible to set down a machine as vast as this one – most of the lakeshore was certainly unsuitable for a landing site, being heavily wooded, or hilly, or both.

Joe raised his head above the solid back panel of the gondola to the rear window and risked a quick look inside. Fortunately the attention of all the five still living persons inside the cabin was entirely engaged with each other.

One surviving crewmember stood at the controls. Even though he was hatless, he conveyed an air of maturity and authority with his white beard, so looked likely to be the captain of this colossal machine, Joe thought. Some of the airship crew had obviously tried to put up some resistance to Plesch earlier: two of them already lay stretched out on the floor of the cabin with bullet holes through their foreheads and the blank look of surprised death in their eyes. A uniformed Prussian officer – a major or equivalent – had a revolver trained on the putative captain's head, but the man at the controls still managed to look spectacularly unperturbed by his perilous situation. That Prussian major *had* to be Plesch, Joe decided bemusedly, although he could recognize nothing of the English Colonel Blair or the German businessman Karl Blumenfeld in the man's appearance. How could the man transform his face like that? Perhaps he really was the Devil after all, Joe thought with a shiver of primeval fear. But his disguise as a Prussian officer would, of course, explain how he had managed to inveigle his way on board and take over the ship in the first place.

The three latecomers to the gondola were also there, of course, but in rather differing states of mind. Paul Gaspard, still weeping and white-faced, looked as if he was about to be sick. Monique Langevin, sterner of face and apparently still in full control of herself, told him to stop his childish wailing, then whipped him savagely across the face with the barrel of her pistol when he didn't comply at once.

Amelia stood in a corner, surprisingly subdued. Yet Joe sensed from his brief glimpse of her, and the way she turned her head in awe at the aerial view, that she was as calm and self-possessed as ever. In fact she seemed more diverted by the exhilaration of flying than by this bizarre human drama unfolding around her.

The wind still buffeted Joe fiercely on the outside of the gondola but he thought he was comparatively safe for the present, if entirely frozen. Certainly no one in the cabin – not even Amelia – seemed to suspect his presence, hanging by his fingertips to the back of the gondola. He could perhaps manage to stay here until the airship landed, yet Joe doubted if that was a sensible option even if his frozen fingers could maintain their hold that long. Amelia had to be surplus to Plesch's requirements; now that they'd managed to take off, Joe couldn't see why they wouldn't simply push her out of the door at the first opportunity. Unless she had something – information possibly – that Plesch might need to aid his escape...?

By listening carefully, Joe could just about make out the continuing conversation in the cabin, above the gusting of the wind and the steady whine of the propellers.

'What was that explosion on the ground?' Monique was asking Plesch suspiciously. 'That wasn't part of the plan, M'sieur.'

Plesch shrugged and replied in perfect French. 'I swear that it was nothing to do with me, Monique. The soldiers must have fired something to cause that explosion.'

Amelia smiled dangerously from her corner of the cabin. 'Even Monique is not naïve enough to believe your protestations of innocence any more, Herr Plesch,' she commented dryly, before looking at Monique directly. 'Your friend Plesch hatched this plan, but misled you about its true aim. His only aim was to kill the King, no one else. An important client is paying him a king's ransom for that service, and that service alone – *literally* a king's ransom in this case. Isn't that true, Johan? The South African gold of Oom Paul Kruger, looted from the Transvaal treasury as the former President of the Transvaal fled to Mozambique, is paying for your services. Only it seems you might have failed again; from what I saw below, the King has somehow survived against all the odds.' She turned her head and regarded the woman pityingly. 'But I'm sorry, Monique. You know nothing of all this, do you? You were merely the expendable tool to carry out this wicked deed for him. Once you had completed your task and murdered the King, it was time to dispense with your services, while providing a suitable smokescreen to allow Herr Plesch himself to escape. Despite the vast reward that he had been promised, Herr Plesch is not the kind of man who would be inclined to share any part of it with mere confederates and underlings. So Johan had kindly arranged a little surprise of his own for you, to round off an entertaining day – enough dynamite to send you and everyone else down there to kingdom come.'

'She's lying,' Plesch said icily. 'This is the British agent who killed your sister, Monique. Now you can get justice for Martine...'

Amelia was unnervingly calm. '*He's* the one who killed your sister, Monique. He slit her throat in a Bern hotel room while she was taking a bath.' She smiled faintly. 'Now whose handiwork does that really sound like?'

Monique was wavering in the face of this convincing argument, clearly not wanting to believe Amelia, but gradually seeing that there could be no other sensible explanation.

Amelia pressed on. 'Give up, Monique. Tell the captain to turn the ship around and go back to Friedrichshafen. Where can you go? When you land, Plesch will only kill you anyway, as he murdered your sister and the crew here...'

Plesch raised his gun to silence Amelia, the weapon a metallic gleam in the afternoon sunlight spilling into the cabin.

Amelia seemed untroubled. 'Captain, tell Herr Plesch that no one can use a gun in here, now that we are airborne. Not without the risk of thousands of cubic metres of hydrogen gas igniting right above our heads.'

'Frankly I'm not sure that I care any more, Miss Peachy.' Plesch raised the gun and pointed it balefully at her forehead. 'This is the best way...perhaps you and I should burn together...*it seems fitting somehow...*'

Joe didn't wait any longer to intervene and stop this madman, but slid the side door open savagely on its tracks and forced his way into the gondola. Plesch was completely startled for once by this unexpected interruption, and changed his target at the last moment, turning the barrel of the weapon on Joe instead. But Amelia blocked Plesch's arm with a scything blow of her own, and the two shots he managed to get off went wide somewhere. Amelia and Plesch tussled viciously for the gun, and he lost his grip on it. Joe saw it hit the floor with a sharp metallic clunk and slide harmlessly out of the gondola into the water far below. Although the shots had missed their intended target, one of them had shattered a pane of window glass, increasing the blustering power of the wind blowing through the cabin to gale force.

Yet Joe realised that the other stray shot had done even more damage as the Zeppelin captain clutched his chest in agony. A rosette of red erupted in his shirtfront and with a death rattle in his throat, the bearded captain fell forward violently against a bank of control levers.

Whatever the levers were for, one of them at least had to be something important, Joe realised, because the Zeppelin immediately began to nose-dive towards the surface of the lake, dropping like a stone, with all its positive buoyancy apparently gone. Everyone in the cabin, living and dead, was thrown violently about by the uncontrolled descent, and they all collapsed together in a heap at the front end of the gondola.

'I think that was the emergency release. We've just dumped a large part of our hydrogen gas,' Amelia yelled to Joe, hanging on to a strut despairingly as the stricken Zeppelin plunged earthwards.

The airship and the suspended gondola were standing close to vertical now. Plesch and Monique lay sprawled together at the front in an entwined heap, both apparently unconscious, or stunned into stupefaction by the force of the sudden descent. Paul Gaspard *was* still conscious but moaning to himself and no threat to anyone. The captain was clearly dead; the stray shot intended for Joe had probably gone straight through his heart.

Joe shouted to Amelia above the roar of the wind through the open door and the shattered window. 'Have you...any idea...how to fly...this damned thing?'

'Without gas, it doesn't...fly very well...Joseph. In fact... in this state...it's just...*a large brick*...' Amelia managed somehow to free herself and reach the wheel, which she then attempted to turn with her outstretched hand. She grimaced as she used all her strength on the wheel. 'I'm trying...to manoeuvre the nose...of the airship...at least back towards...the shore,' she explained to Joe when tried to come to her assistance. 'I really...don't want...to get...my feet...wet.' She glanced at his bare chest with a strained smile. 'At least...I ...got to see...your fine manly chest...one more time...before I die...Mr Appeldoorn...'

The airship *was* turning back to shore, Joe realised in amazement, but also spiralling wildly out of control as it fell to earth. But somehow, whether because of Amelia's desperate turning of the wheel or not, it began to come out of its steep inclination just as the trees on the shore loomed large below them.

'Hold tight...*like this*!' Amelia ordered, squatting on the cabin floor and putting her hands over her head, braced for impact.

The metal frame was torn viciously apart as the gondola ploughed into trees with savage ferocity. Joe felt something massive hit him with immense force and then explode, plunging him into the deepest, darkest abyss he'd ever known.

Strangely, though, he had no sense of falling...

CHAPTER 22

Saturday March 29th 1902

In his hospital room, Joe Appeldoorn re-emerged slowly from the depths of his private abyss. His head ached and his neck felt as if it were encased in an iron clamp. But he was alive – *gloriously alive...*

As his memory slowly returned, he vaguely remembered the aftermath of the Zeppelin crash as if in a dream. He had come to, suspended precariously in the bare branches of an oak tree, but not knowing at the time how or why he'd come to be there. Then the memory of those last few frantic moments in the gondola of the Zeppelin had come back to him with a rush. He'd felt a great relief as he finally heard rescuers clambering up the tree to reach him – a relief that the Zeppelin hadn't turned into a fireball on hitting the ground. The one thing Joe Appeldoorn had always been terrified of was burning to death in a fire...

In his semi-conscious state, he had been lowered from his refuge in the trees and taken on a stretcher to a nearby German army field hut. He recalled trying to ask the two men who carried him to look for Amelia too, but the words, although formed perfectly in his head, refused to come out of his mouth in any coherent fashion. A Prussian officer, a major with duelling scars on his cheeks and a notable lack of compassion, only stared at him on the stretcher belligerently as he tried to say something intelligible. Perhaps this was the very same man who had punched him earlier that day in the stomach without provocation, causing him to collapse on the makeshift trestle tables. Ironically that brutal act had, as it happened, probably saved *all* their lives, because Joe knew that he would never have realised otherwise that the table had been booby-trapped with explosives...

What seemed like an endless bumping journey in the back of a cart then followed, first across fallow fields and then across rutted tracks through woods. The ruts changed abruptly to the harder stone cobbles of a road as

Joe saw buildings emerging into his view, the outskirts of Friedrichshafen, he hoped. They turned up a side road to an imposing Neo-classical building on a green hillside. In his dazed state, it looked far too splendid at first to be anything as bleakly functional as a hospital, but that was what it turned out to be. They wheeled him along infinite corridors to a hospital room with two beds, decorated in surgical green. There a doctor examined him in silence, before a young nurse, with eyes like a frightened doe, gave him something for the headache he complained of.

Then the abyss swallowed him again...

Now he was fully awake for the first time in many hours, and feeling surprisingly well considering what he'd been through. He surveyed the hospital room around him, took in the antiseptic smells and the shine of the waxed floor. It was dark outside; he saw only his own reflection gazing back in perplexity from the black rectangle of the window. No lights were visible outside at all, no comfortable speckling of streetlights to show that he was still connected to the rest of the human race.

He wondered if it was still Friday. Time felt curiously disjointed, and his memory seemed to be playing tricks.

He worried most about Amelia. *What had happened to her?* And to Plesch and Monique Langevin, for that matter? Was he the only survivor of the Zeppelin crash? The thought of losing Miss Peachy now left him heartsick.

*

A man entered his sick room and looked down at him from what seemed a great height.

Joe swivelled his eyes upwards to inspect his visitor. The man was in his sixties, with thick snow-white hair and the pink skin of a cherub. He also wore a frock coat and spats, so clearly was a natural conservative, a man not in a hurry to move with the times. But he had a look of steel in his penetrating eyes.

'Who are you?' Joe croaked.

'My name is Sir Charles Gorman.'

Joe didn't like the sound of the man's voice at all, the authentic ring of the English Whitehall establishment, rich and plummy, and exuding the smug confidence of a race who quietly ran a quarter of the world with so little fuss.

'Where is Amelia?' Joe demanded, his voice stronger. 'Did she survive the crash?'

It seemed to take an eternity for the man to answer that simple question, or perhaps it was just his dread of the answer that made it seem so long. 'She did survive, Mr Appeldoorn.' Joe breathed a sigh of relief, his muscles collapsing under him with the release of so much tension. 'And she is unhurt,' Sir Charles went on, 'apart from minor scrapes and bruises.' He coughed dryly. 'That young woman has a *remarkable* talent for survival, as it happens. But I will certainly have words with her about her clear lack of discretion in this case. When I introduced myself to you a second ago, you clearly knew of me already - and that can only be because you'd heard my name from *her* lips.'

Joe didn't want to get Amelia any deeper into hot water so said nothing in response to that. He merely let his happiness at the thought of her being safe seep quietly through him.

'What time is it, Sir Charles?' he asked after a long pause.

The Englishman consulted the pocket watch hanging from his waistcoat. 'Four in the morning, Mr Appeldoorn. Saturday the twenty-ninth of March.'

Joe had been out of commission for the best part of twelve hours. 'That nurse must have given me something strong,' he suggested. 'Was that to keep me quiet until somebody worked out who I was?'

Sir Charles gave him a desiccated smile. 'No, not at all. Miss Peachy vouched for you as soon as she realised that you'd been brought to the hospital here. You were found at least a hundred yards from the crashed airship, which, you'll be pleased to hear, was not irrevocably damaged. How on earth did you get so far from the Zeppelin, I wonder?'

'Divine intervention, perhaps,' Joe suggested weakly, tongue-in-cheek.

'Perhaps so. Miss Peachy says that she, and the British Government, owes you a considerable debt of gratitude.'

Joe blinked in surprise. 'I wouldn't rate my contribution that highly, Sir Charles. But you should certainly be grateful to Miss Peachy; she has saved the life of her sovereign twice in the last two weeks, to my knowledge.'

'I think perhaps you're being unduly modest, Mr Appeldoorn. Miss Peachy seems quite convinced that without your help Plesch might well have succeeded in decapitating the royal houses of Europe yesterday.'

Joe accepted the accolade with a wry shrug. 'Ah, yes...Herr Plesch. And what happened to him?'

Sir Charles looked grave. 'I'm afraid neither Plesch nor Monique Langevin has yet been found. Their co-conspirator however, M'sieur Paul Gaspard, managed to impale himself on the branch of an oak tree.'

'Dead?'

'As a door nail!' was the clipped reply.

'Herr Plesch seems to have as remarkable a talent for survival as myself and Miss Peachy, wouldn't you say?'

'He does indeed,' Sir Charles conceded. 'By the way, a lady called Miss Eleanor Winthrop - a countrywoman of yours, I believe - has been making a great deal of fuss about you with the authorities in town. She swears that she saw you hanging from the Zeppelin yesterday as it crossed the lake. Then of course she saw it crash a few minutes later, as many other people did. I did speak to her late last night at the Hotel Adler and assured her that you are all right, although I told her nothing of what had happened.'

'Thank you.' Joe didn't know what else to say. Eleanor had clearly shown a lot more authority and determination than he'd thought her capable of.

Sir Charles cleared his throat uncomfortably. 'Could I ask you also to be circumspect in what you tell this young lady about yesterday's events, Mr Appeldoorn? We would much prefer to keep our embarrassing security lapse here in our private domain, if possible.'

Joe forced his weary brain to think. 'Yes, that's probably wise. But perhaps I can also help you make amends with your political masters for what nearly happened here yesterday.'

'How?' Sir Charles raised an aristocratic eyebrow.

'Perhaps I can find Plesch for you.'

'And how would you do that, Mr Appeldoorn?'

'First things first, Sir Charles. Can I see Miss Peachy?'

*

Two hours later, Amelia poked her nose tentatively around his door. She was still wearing the uniform of the Zeppelin ground crew.

'You really couldn't wait to dress up like a boy for me, could you, Miss Peachy?' Joe said lightly.

She walked across the room and kissed him affectionately on the cheek. She smelled dewy fresh, as if she had just bathed before visiting him. 'No, indeed I couldn't, Mr Appeldoorn.' She straightened up and turned slowly around. 'How do I look? But make the most of it; they're sending over some of my own clothes from the Hotel Adler soon so I shall reluctantly have to go back to being a girl.'

'And exactly which girl will you be today, Miss Peachy?' Joe asked dryly.

She smiled. 'Oh, just myself for the moment, Mr Appeldoorn.'

The sun had just risen over the green mountains across the lake and a dawn wind ruffled the opalescent surface of the water. In the first ray of sunlight, Joe could see no marks or injuries on her face, although her skin was pale beneath the damp hair. And she was moving a little stiffly as if in pain.

'This is the second dawn we've shared in a row, Miss Peachy. I'm getting used to it. Perhaps we should make a long-term habit of this.'

She made a slight face again, as if in discomfort.

'Are you hurt?' he asked her in alarm.

'It's nothing. I'm afraid I opened up that wound again, though, and spoiled your fine handiwork with the needle. The doctor who just re-stitched it was not nearly as nice and considerate as you, Mr Appeldoorn.' She leaned over him and kissed him again, this time on the lips. 'So where do you think Plesch has gone? Assuming he did survive the crash yesterday anyway. Sir Charles seems to think you might know; he would still dearly like to apprehend him.'

Joe sighed. 'Ah, and I thought you'd just come to see me for old time's sake.' He struggled to sit up. 'There is just a chance that Plesch and Monique don't know that *I* know about the Schloss Bielenberg. Don't you think that there is a possibility that Monique may go and hide with her aunt temporarily in Schaffhausen...?'

*

Outside, a fierce afternoon rainstorm battered the tall leaded windows of the library in the *Schloss Bielenberg* - almost the first real storm Joe had seen since leaving Paris nearly three weeks ago.

Joe had again been granted an audience with Madame Rschevskaya – or more properly, Madame Olga Borisovna Melikova, as he should call her now. She'd smiled obligingly in welcome as if the unpleasantness of their meeting at the Hotel *Rheinfels* had simply never happened. The hard edges had disappeared completely from her manner and she was restored once again to the graciously beautiful woman in a dress of dark blue silk, who was content to show off her youthful-looking figure and her dainty ankles for her visitors. Yet the undercurrent of this meeting was distinctly tenser and frostier than the last one in this room, even though she was still minding her impeccable Russian manners.

'Have you found Monique, M'sieur Appeldoorn?' she inquired politely.

Mlle Marie Weyland again sat in the corner of the room, taking note of the conversation as before, but even more interested perhaps in the enigmatic figure of Amelia Peachy. Amelia was taking little part in the meeting, though, apart from being introduced by Joe, and he could see that Mlle Weyland's curiosity about his companion had been piqued, as well as perhaps a certain natural jealousy about her too. Amelia did look stunning today – remarkable enough given what she'd been up to the day before - and Mlle Weyland seemed to be comparing her own porcelain white skin and Mona Lisa eyes with Miss Peachy's figure and face, and not particularly enjoying the comparison.

After much persuasion, Sir Charles Gorman had allowed Amelia to accompany Joe on his return to Switzerland to test his hypothesis about the whereabouts of Monique Langevin - and possibly Johan Plesch too. Joe had also brought Eleanor back to Schaffhausen with him - an Eleanor relieved to see him in one piece, if still a little distraught. Joe could hardly have left her in Germany after all, since he had no plans to go back immediately. But he had chosen to leave Eleanor safely behind at the Hotel *Rheinfels* this afternoon, certainly not wanting to bring her back to the *Schloss Bielenberg,* her effective prison for three months.

The rail journey this morning had finally introduced Eleanor and Miss Peachy to one another. Joe had not been sure if this was a wise thing or not, yet the practicalities of arranging their journey in a sensible manner made it unavoidable. Eleanor had clearly been disturbed at meeting Miss Peachy, though, and having her included, for some unexplained reason, in their travelling party back to Schaffhausen. Yet she retained her perfect New England manners throughout, talking politely to Amelia for the whole journey, even though understanding some deep and imponderable things had been going on between Joseph and this mysterious English lady...

In the library of the *Schloss Bielenberg* Joe confronted Olga Melikova with the truth. 'I think you're playing games with me, Madame. Monique is already here, isn't she?'

Olga Melikova tried to deny it. 'That is ridiculous, M'sieur Appeldoorn. I asked *you* to find her and bring her back to me. As if she would just come back here of her own accord.'

'Do not pretend, Madame, that you don't know what happened in Friedrichshafen yesterday. Your niece was involved in a conspiracy to murder many people. I can't do anything for her now, and neither can you.'

Joe could see the truth reflected in her eyes, and her desperate sorrow at knowing what her niece had become. It must be an unbearable burden for her, he thought.

'Is Plesch here too?' he demanded.

Madame Melikova's eyes betrayed her, straying to the window. Then Joe understood suddenly what was going on: she had simply been playing for time while an escape for Monique had been arranged.

Joe heard a sound in the courtyard below and ran to the window.

A motor car was just screeching through the gates – a futuristic-looking car with a gleaming metal superstructure.

Olga Melikova was distraught. 'Let her go, M'sieur Appeldoorn! I will give you everything I possess if you do. *Everything!*'

But Joe, with a wounded look at Madame Melikova, was already following Amelia down the stairs to the courtyard...

CHAPTER 23

Saturday March 29th 1902

Reaching the courtyard at a run, Amelia broke the bad news to him. 'I think I recognised that car: unfortunately it's a new type called a Mercedes.'

Joe shrugged wryly. 'Then there probably was no need for Madame Melikova to offer me all her worldly possessions to let Monique go, was there? We haven't got a chance of catching a machine like that in our humble horse-drawn two-wheeler.'

Amelia frowned. 'Yes, I read somewhere that a Mercedes can reputedly do over *fifty* miles per hour. That's an incredible speed, if true. And so you're probably right about us not having a chance of catching up with them, but at least we have to try, Joseph,' she implored him.

As they ran to the carriage, he asked her, 'Did you see Plesch with Monique in the car?'

Amelia nodded. 'There *was* a man driving. It has to be Plesch, doesn't it? Who else can it possibly be?'

Joe took the reins of the carriage, with Amelia joining him on the driver's seat, and set the horse off down the steep mountain road at a gallop.

Joe wondered where Plesch and Monique had managed to get hold of such a vehicle as this new Mercedes; he certainly hadn't seen it in the courtyard on arrival otherwise his guard would have been well and truly up. Like Amelia, he had also read fawning newspaper articles about this wondrous new automobile, but had never seen one for real yet. They said it was a completely revolutionary new design – a high-performance car by Daimler, the original one in the series apparently having been built especially for Emile Jellinek, Consul General of the Austrian-Hungarian Empire in Nice. As Joe recalled, Daimler had called his wonderful new creation after Jellinek's photogenic daughter, Mercedes. Joe tried to remember what the article had said about this wonder car, but the only thing he could remember for sure was that it was, as Amelia had pointed out, blindingly fast...

The car was already far out of sight, but this was the only road leading away from the *Schloss Bielenberg*, so Joe wasn't too worried about losing Monique and Plesch for the moment. Plus the car also left a reassuringly pungent trail of petrol and oil fumes in its wake, which made it easy to follow even in this continuing downpour.

'Why do you think Monique is still consorting with Plesch?' Joe asked Amelia, as he took a bend at frightening speed. He knew women could be illogical creatures when they chose, yet Monique's behaviour in staying with Plesch seemed to border on lunacy.

Amelia had to shout above the rattle of the carriage, and the wind streaming through her hair. 'Perhaps she's got no alternative but to stay with him for the moment.' Her eyes were positively gleaming with the thrill of the chase, Joe saw with slight dismay. Part of him wanted to say to her for the first time, *Let's give up, shall we? We can't catch them now...*

But whatever happened here, Amelia was clearly determined not to let Plesch escape her once again, and he found this a disturbing side to her: just this once he would have liked to see her a little less relentless, and a little more human...

'Why would she stick with him?' Joe wondered aloud, 'when she must know by now he's the man who killed her sister in that brutal way. *And* was quite willing to blow *her* up at the Zeppelin works too...'

Amelia looked across at him and smiled dangerously. 'Perhaps that evil side is part of his allure...'

*

They continued to follow the twisting road at breakneck speed down through the thick spruce forest. The wind wailed through the trees and the lowering sky thundered and flashed above their heads. The horse, a young black gelding, his eyes wild and his flanks foaming, was scared but ran gamely on, allowing himself to be pushed to his limit.

Then they rounded a bend and Joe brought the carriage screeching to a halt. The Mercedes stood by the road, apparently abandoned, a nearly spent plume of steam issuing tiredly from its bonnet. The radiator must have blown a gasket under Plesch's frantic efforts to escape so perhaps the horse still retained a slight edge for a little while longer over mankind's mighty new technology.

Plesch and Monique were now on foot, which should in theory make them easier to catch. However, it meant also that the fugitive pair no longer needed to stick to the road but could disappear into any of a dozen tracks that criss-crossed through the fern-covered woods that bordered the road. As the rain continued to fall in biblical torrents, a bedraggled Joe wondered which way to go from here. In the end he decided to follow the main road a little further, believing for no specific reason that Plesch and Monique would probably have done the same, especially if they had baggage with them.

'How do you know they haven't left the main road?' Amelia was curious, but apparently impressed at Joe's rapid decision to go on. 'Did you notice something?'

'Oh, yes! An old Red Indian taught me everything I know about tracking game through a forest. You get to have a second sense for the signs,' Joe said facetiously.

Amelia cocked a suspicious eye in his direction. 'Didn't you once tell me that the only Red Indian you'd ever seen was in a Wild West Show?'

'Well, that was the one,' Joe went on hurriedly.

'And where was this?' Amelia responded dryly.

'Err...in Atlantic City, New Jersey.'

'And does Atlantic City still have a large area of forest wilderness left?' she asked dangerously.

'Oh, the whole city is practically all still wilderness...'

By now, Joe was glad to see that they had come to a fork in the road, the main turning signposted to Schaffhausen, the other - little more than a widened forest track really – with no sign, but probably leading to the river and the *Rheinfall,* Joe guessed.

'So which way do your well-honed Indian tracking skills tell you we should go from here?' Amelia demanded breathlessly.

Joe grunted. 'My instincts tell me Plesch would make for Schaffhausen. That's the nearest railway station.'

'So let's try the other way, then,' Amelia suggested tartly.

Joe didn't like her judgement of his instincts much but took her advice anyway, following the steep forest track that led south, and which grew even steeper and more treacherous the further they went. Eventually they were forced to leave the carriage behind and go on foot themselves because of the narrowness and steepness of the path.

Soon they were slipping and sliding down the track rather than walking, as it turned into a minor waterfall of its own, water cascading down the hillside through the trees and the thick carpet of Royal Ferns above, washing down a thick soup of brown mud and silt after them.

Then Joe skidded to a halt as he found a recent footprint. 'It *must* be them!' he muttered, examining the print with what he hoped looked like professional expertise. 'No one is going to be hiking for pleasure on a day like this.' He glanced at Amelia. 'Have you got your Browning, Miss Peachy?'

She patted her skirt and smiled grimly. 'Of course. And have you got your Webley, Mr Appeldoorn?'

'I have indeed.'

'Then let's go on,' she proposed.

They carried on down the hill, scrambling through the thick ferny undergrowth of the forest, but Joe soon began to pull ahead of Amelia and realised something was wrong. He stopped and checked behind him.

Amelia clambered down the track after him, labouring a little. 'Sorry. I can't run properly in this skirt,' she complained peevishly.

Joe studied her face and realised there was more to it than that. Her cheeks and brow were spattered with mud, yet even so he could see clear signs of exhaustion in her face. But it was the way she was holding her abdomen and grimacing that worried him in particular. That was where she'd been wounded by Plesch, the same injury she'd re-opened in the Zeppelin crash. It seemed likely to Joe that her exertions today had opened that wound yet again...

'Go on ahead,' she ordered peremptorily. 'Don't wait for me. I'm going to take off this skirt.'

He didn't move, still uncertain of what to do for the best.

'I said, go, Joseph!' she repeated angrily. 'Get them before they escape again! I will be right behind you as soon as I take of this damned tight skirt!'

Joe shook his head in frustration, but succumbed to her bidding and ran off down the path at a reckless speed. He'd travelled a few hundred metres more down the hill before the track took a sharp turn and then became even steeper.

Before he realised what was happening, he found himself sliding on his back in a muddy stream of water down the last twenty metres of the path, eventually ending his journey dumped unceremoniously in a painful heap on a flat rocky platform above the crashing waters of the *Rheinfall*. Joe recognised the place at once - this was the very same natural viewing platform he'd hiked to with Albert eight days before.

Plesch and Monique stood patiently on the edge of the cliff, as if calmly awaiting his arrival. They were both dressed conservatively and looked like any bourgeois Swiss couple out for a Saturday woodland stroll who'd found themselves caught in an unexpected downpour. *Apart, that is, from the threatening pistols in their hands...*

Even in his bedraggled state, though, Plesch still managed to appear as formidable and unruffled as ever...

Joe felt desperately for his Webley, but it was gone, dropped somewhere during his slithering slide down the path.

Another man was standing here on the viewing platform too, Joe realised in surprise, a man equipped with easel and paints rather than a pistol, therefore presumably an accidental participant in this tense drama. Judging by his appearance and his artist's accoutrements, this was clearly a tourist who'd been planning to paint the falls from this majestic viewpoint today, although the unexpected spring downpour had no doubt put paid to that ambition for the moment. Even though he was not thinking at all lucidly at present, Joe did belatedly recognise the man as his recent fellow guest from the Hotel *Rheinfels* - the middle-aged Scotsman who had taken a shine to Eleanor Winthrop and who'd mistaken Eleanor and him for newly-weds. He'd chosen a bad time to come and paint the falls, though, Joe decided bleakly, even apart from the inclemency of the weather. These two criminals would kill him too, merely because he was here and had seen them...

Plesch shook his head in disbelief as he regarded Joe. 'You are a persistent man, Mr Appeldoorn, if somewhat predictable. And is Miss Peachy not joining us?' he asked sarcastically.

Joe tried to get to his feet but the fall had badly winded him and left him gasping for breath. 'No, she's not...here...'

'I don't wish to doubt your veracity, Mr Appeldoorn, but I can scarcely believe that she is not somewhere in the vicinity. I think we'll just wait here for her to join us, don't you?' He studied Joe's face with wry displeasure. 'I cannot understand you, Mr Appeldoorn, to be honest. At times in this business you have seemed quite astute; at others hopelessly adrift and foolish. Why did you follow me down this track? *Surely you could see that I was leading you into a trap?* Surely you must have understood that I would have to deal with you and Miss Peachy after that damned automobile broke down, so that I could elude further pursuit and take your carriage?' He tut-tutted at Joe's naivety. 'Really, I can't be blamed for this situation − you and Miss Peachy have brought this fate upon yourselves.'

In his desperation Joe tried to appeal directly to the woman by his side, who had remained silent and sullen-faced during this diatribe by her Svengali. 'Why are you still helping this man, Monique? I was the person who found your sister in Bern three weeks ago. Believe me, Herr Plesch really did cut her throat, despite what he might have said to you to the contrary...'

Monique stared blankly at him, her eyes empty circles of hate, as if devoid of all remaining feeling. But then, with a jerk of her hand, she suddenly turned her pistol on Plesch. 'Perhaps, after all, it is time to put you down, Johan, while I still have the chance.'

Plesch was quicker with his pistol, though, and shot her casually through the head in one amazingly swift and blood-chilling movement of his hand. Blood spurted from a neat hole in Monique's forehead, and the impact threw her backwards like a discarded rag doll. Despite his revulsion, Joe was dazzled by the man's speed of hand and eye − he did seem to possess an almost superhuman skill and resolve when it came to the business of killing.

Then Plesch looked down at the body regretfully for a moment before pushing it contemptuously over the cliff with the side of his foot. 'What a waste! Now look what you've made me do, Mr Appeldoorn!' he hissed angrily.

Sir Arthur – Joe remembered the tourist's name now - was aghast. 'My God, sir! What sort of devil are you?'

Plesch smiled amiably. 'I am no devil, sir. I am not even an evil man, merely a necessary technician.' He appealed to Joe. 'Tell him, Mr Appeldoorn. Tell this gentleman the truth - that I simply provide an essential service in a changing world: removing the unwanted members of our strange species, like Ma'mselle Langevin there. I see myself as equally necessary as the woodlice and the scavengers of this forest are to keep the life of the forest floor turning over. I perform the same function for human society – eliminating the unwanted, the weak and the dying, creating new opportunities for the strong and the living to prosper.'

Joe sneered at him. 'Woodlice, eh? You really do have an overly high opinion of yourself, do you not, Herr Plesch.'

Plesch flushed. 'I *would* like your high opinion, Mr Appeldoorn, as it happens. After all, despite your naivety, we are quite alike in some ways...*in fact it almost pains me to do this...*'

With that, Plesch calmly raised his Mauser and, aiming clearly for the heart, shot Joe twice, just as a screaming wildcat burst through the trees onto the rock platform at the edge of the cliff...

Amelia...!

Even Plesch was completely taken aback for a moment by the sight of this vengeful angel in corset and silk drawers. Freed of her encumbering skirt, she flew through the air at her hated adversary like a veritable harpy of death...

As her slender frame collided with her enemy's more massive body with sickening impact, Plesch's gun was fortuitously knocked from his grip. For a long moment they both lay in a heap on the flat rock, heavily winded, unable to move. Yet Miss Peachy wasn't to be denied and, even in her distressed state, was the first to recover. She kicked out at Plesch's body ferociously, trying to send him over the cliff to his death.

But Plesch soon recovered from his initial surprise too and, with the benefits of his superior size and strength, evaded her further efforts to force him over the edge of the precipice with contemptuous ease.

Joe tried to get to his feet to help her but nothing about his body seemed to be working properly any more – his legs felt like useless lumps of alien flesh tied to his body rather than his own limbs. Plesch had taken the advantage by now in the fight and, having got back to his feet, was forcing Amelia back to the edge, his hands clamped tightly around her throat. She fought like a demon to release herself from the relentless pressure of his fingers but was squeezed back ever closer to the edge of the vertical cliff face, and oblivion. Then, with one final push, Plesch released his hands suddenly, trying to unbalance her with trickery and send her spinning over the vertiginous drop. But Amelia, perhaps making use of all her old circus skills, somehow recovered her balance at the last minute and managed to roll free of Plesch right on the edge of the cliff, to emerge in a standing position again. Joe saw through his haze of pain that it was *Plesch* now who was off balance and tottering on the edge of the abyss, and felt a brief surge of exultation despite his agony. But – *as always* - Plesch had a sting in his tail and, as he went over the edge, he flung out a despairing hand and wrapped it around Amelia's leg, bringing her crashing again to the rock floor. Plesch ended up dangling over the void, held only by his sinewy right hand, which was locked vice-like around Amelia's slender ankle.

Amelia made a superhuman effort to shake off his deathly embrace – kicking out savagely with her feet and scrabbling desperately at the mossy rock with bleeding fingernails to try and save herself. But Plesch's weight finally told, and with a last despairing look of resignation in Joe's direction, she was sucked over the edge, entwined with Plesch in a strange dance of death as they plunged into the foaming maelstrom far below.

Sir Arthur, finally galvanised into life, rushed to the edge of the cliff and looked down. 'Oh, my God! Did you see that? My God!'

Joe couldn't feel his legs at all by now but his ribs were on fire. Yet despite the pain, he still managed to drag himself inch by inch to the edge. 'Can you see her? *Can you see her?*' he repeated desperately. 'Has she gone over the falls?' For some reason he couldn't hear his own voice any more, though. The world was pulsing in and out of focus, turning red, then faint, then increasingly black. The only sound Joe could now hear was a rushing in his head even louder than the falls.

'I can't...I can't see her...' Joe could just make out the man's words, echoing distantly in his head like a voice at the end of a long tunnel; nausea was coming in waves, engulfing him in a shroud. Joe Appeldoorn could feel that death had him by the throat, sucking the life force out of him.

He struggled to control the movement of his shaking right hand and felt gingerly for his side; his quivering fingers came away bloody and streaming with his own gore. His vision cleared momentarily for some unknown reason, and he turned his head slowly and looked behind him uncomprehendingly at the ugly trail of blood and slime he'd left on the mossy rocks.

The Scotsman finally noticed the sickening trail of blood that Joe had left behind him and bent down to examine Joe's wounds. 'Oh, my word, sir!' was all he could find to say, his face turning a nauseous white against the rainbow-tinted spray of the falls...

'

CHAPTER 24

Sunday March 30th 1902

Eleanor stirred in the darkened corridor of the hospital as she heard someone's footsteps on the waxed parquet flooring.

The middle-aged man approached her diffidently, and she tried to smile a greeting in return when she recognized him.

'You should go back to the hotel, my dear,' the man suggested gently. 'I have a carriage outside. Let me take you. There is nothing more you can do for him tonight.'

Eleanor nodded patiently. 'You're very kind, Sir Arthur, particularly after you've been through such an ordeal yourself. That was a terrible experience for you too yesterday, seeing three people die like that. You did wonderfully well in the circumstances to get Joseph to a hospital so promptly.'

Sir Arthur stared out of the window at the lights of Schaffhausen below. 'I was very fortunate, my dear, that's all. Luckily two other walkers chanced to visit that viewing site near the falls within a few minutes of the incident, and these very capable Swiss gentlemen were able to bring help and transport for Mr Appeldoorn, before he bled to death.'

Eleanor raised her head from the shadows. 'Who was this Miss Peachy who tried to save Joseph?' she asked Sir Arthur.

'Did you never meet her?' the Scotsman responded evasively.

'I met her only once for a few hours. We travelled together from Friedrichshafen to Schaffhausen yesterday morning. It seemed she had been working with Joseph on one of his investigations.'

The Scotsman made a kindly face. 'To be honest, my dear, I don't know who this Miss Peachy was either, or whether indeed that was her real name. But clearly she was a remarkable young woman. From the little a gentleman from the British Foreign Office called Sir Charles Gorman has told me, it seems she was an agent of the British government. It appears that she and your friend, Mr Appeldoorn, may have foiled an assassination attempt by a group of desperate anarchists on some very important people in Friedrichshafen on Friday.'

Eleanor gasped in surprise at this revelation. From what she had seen and heard from the steam yacht on Lake Constance on Friday – the explosion, the gunfire, the airship crash - she'd known, of course, that something extremely serious had happened there. But Joseph had been less than forthcoming afterwards about his own part in these strange proceedings. In particular he'd denied that he had been the man she'd seen dangling from the airship minutes before it crashed, even though she could have *sworn* it was him...

'The man who went over the falls with Miss Peachy – was he an anarchist?'

'Yes, so Sir Charles said. And a very dangerous and determined assassin too. He killed his own woman partner, the Ma'mselle Langevin you mentioned, with no more thought than I would swat a fly.' Sir Arthur frowned. 'I'm sorry, my dear. I'm upsetting you with such talk.'

Eleanor lifted her chin determinedly. 'I am not as sensitive a soul as that, Sir Arthur, I assure you. Nor am I a child. I know there are evil and scheming people in the world – but I simply had no idea that a woman like Monique Langevin could be such a person. How had this anarchist become involved with Monique? And why was Joseph searching for him? He came to Europe only to find me.'

Sir Arthur held up the palms of his hands in a helpless gesture. 'I don't know the details of the story, Miss Winthrop. I suggest you ask Mr Appeldoorn when he recovers.'

'You think he will recover?' She clutched eagerly at this flimsy straw he'd offered her.

'He's fighting for his life, even though his wounds are extremely grave. Yet it could have been much worse for him, but for Miss Peachy's intervention. I am sure that the man aimed for his heart but that Miss Peachy's sudden arrival distracted this evil individual at the last moment and upset his aim. Even so, the situation is not encouraging: Joseph lost a great deal of blood and suffered considerable damage to both his spleen and intestines. Unfortunately there is no way of giving him blood from anyone else to replace his own. This has been tried recently, but the technique – "blood transfusion" as it is called - seems to kill people more often that it saves them. Infection remains the real enemy for Joseph, though; despite all our advances in medical knowledge in the nineteenth century, we still have almost nothing useful in our pharmaceutical armoury to fight infections once they take hold.' Sir Arthur paused. 'But he's a strong-looking boy. With God's grace he might live. I have seen men with worse injuries survive.'

Eleanor tried to be hopeful. 'I'm praying for his recovery.'

Sir Arthur studied her face closely. 'I'm sorry I mistook you for his wife when we met last week, Miss Winthrop. Yet you looked so much like a couple of newly-weds, playing delightfully together in the woods. You seemed so wonderfully happy.'

Eleanor felt the tears pricking her eyes at the memory of that day – it was only five days ago...*five short days...*

'You love him, I think,' Sir Arthur suggested sagely. 'Surely I can't be mistaken in that point, at least.'

'I wasn't sure before. But yes, I am sure now,' Eleanor said firmly.

'And how does he feel about you?'

'If he recovers, I will find out, won't I?'

'Yes, my dear, you will.'

They began to walk along the corridor to the main exit of the hospital. As she traced her steps slowly, her heels clicking on the wooden floor, Eleanor said, 'It's so odd that you of all people should witness such an incident as that at the falls yesterday. Did not your own fictional hero die in just such a way?'

Sir Arthur smiled faintly. 'Yes, he did, but I haven't been able to bury him completely since he went over the Reichenbach Falls ten years ago. Readers are always pressing me to write new stories so I have been forced to seriously consider bringing him back from the dead. Yet it seems a little implausible to imagine anyone surviving such a fall as I described in *The Final Problem...*'

He pondered that remark as he remembered cradling that boy in his arms yesterday, trying to staunch the copious flow of blood from his abdomen. The young man had been drifting in and out of consciousness, but in his more lucid moments he'd seemed convinced that the young woman who'd fallen over the cliff simply could not be dead.

Sir Arthur had done his best to humour the boy even though it seemed highly unlikely to him that anyone could have survived such a fall, given the height of the cliff and the ferocity of the maelstrom on the foaming rocks below. But it was certainly not impossible, and perhaps that young man's blind faith in Miss Peachy's instinct for survival might not be entirely misplaced. *Who could say for sure?* Sir Arthur wondered. Stranger things that this had happened...

He thought back to what Miss Winthrop had said, and wondered if it was indeed time to bring back his most famous literary creation from his own watery grave. It was true that he'd been struggling to write anything meaningful and entertaining of late, so perhaps it was time to recognize the truth and give in to the inevitable. And if Sherlock could be made to rise from his waterfall grave, then why not this Miss Amelia Peachy too...

*

"Oom Paul" Kruger stood in the garden of his rented Swiss villa listening to the spring chorus of birdsong. Dawn was just breaking and the wrens, thrushes and blackbirds were in full glorious cadence. Once, that sweet sound would have lifted his spirits beyond measure. But today he seemed to be gripped by a darkness of mood, seeing himself finally for what he was - an old man standing bewildered and alone on that precipice at the end of life, powerless and afraid of the unknown void that lay ahead.

Yet perhaps it was simply the miserable rainy weather that had worsened his mood today, he tried to tell himself, coming after long days of spring sunshine. The Italian garden was still bright with colour but the usually vibrant shades of Lake Geneva were dimmed to streaks of grey in the dawn mist. Even the fortress-like ramparts of the French Alps seemed dark and dismal today.

Or perhaps it was the news from *Zuid Afrika* that had depressed him so deeply. The Boer leaders in the field were now close to collapse, and it seemed only a matter of time before they would have to surrender to Kitchener and the British on the damned *rooineks*' terms. That would be the hardest thing of all to stomach – to see his beloved Transvaal under the thumb of his hated enemy, the British Empire…

Kruger raised his eyes suddenly from the surface of the lake as he heard a footfall behind him. He tried to smile when he saw who it was, despite his grim mood. 'Ah, Hennes, *Goede Morgen. Hoe gaan dit, mijn vriend.*'

Van der Merwe was himself in sombre mood, though. 'Have you seen the new report from Ma'mselle Flammarion in Zurich? She says that an attempt was made on the King's life in Germany on Friday but failed yet again.'

Kruger shook his head. 'No, I haven't seen her report yet. Is our man dead?'

'Perhaps. Ma'mselle Flammarion doesn't know yet for certain.'

Kruger sighed. 'Well, I had heard nothing from him since last week when he sent me that coded letter saying that he was about to make a fresh attempt after his failures in Paris and Zurich. So perhaps he did die trying as he said he would…'

'Maybe it's for the best, Mr President. The British would have punished our people without mercy if their king had died at the hands of an assassin hired by us.'

'Perhaps,' Kruger agreed reluctantly.

'Can I see the letter he sent you, Mr President?'

Kruger shrugged his tired shoulders. 'I believe, Hennes, that I carelessly destroyed it.'

'That is unlike you, sir.'

'Perhaps I'm finally getting old and forgetful, Hennes.'

'Not you, Mr President…'

*

Kruger watched van der Merwe retrace his steps back up the garden to the villa. He thought again of *de Slager's* coded letter: the man had been absolutely convinced that there had to be an informer in Kruger's own entourage. That was the only thing that could explain how the British seemed to have anticipated and foiled his every move...

And Kruger had wanted to say to his old friend, 'Was it *you* who betrayed me, Hennes? Perhaps you thought you had good reason. *But was it you...?*'

Last night he had talked to Hennes during dinner about the old days; he had known van der Merwe so long, he regarded him almost like a younger brother. 'What do you remember the most about Africa?' he'd asked his old friend at one point.

'Oh, the High Veldt for sure, Mr President. The clear air at sunrise, the dust rising above herds of game. And the blue mountains of the Eastern Transvaal, where I spent so much of my youth. And what about you, sir? What memories of *Zuid Afrika* will you take with you at the end of your life?'

But knowing he would never see his country again, Oom Paul had found it hard to pick one particular time and place and memory of Africa. He had so many sweet and evocative memories to choose from - of his youth in the Cape, and during that Great Trek across a continent - that it was impossible for him to separate the overwhelming kaleidoscope of images in his mind. He remembered the smells of herbs and heather in the Cape highlands; and the endless scrub of the Karoo, over whose vast silences the stars hung in majestic splendour. In his mind he saw again the verdant brilliant immensities of the High Veldt, extending limitlessly into the heart of Africa. And Natal, with its mountains, green and warm, its palms and bananas, its wild tropical flowers and magnificent forests of yellowwood and tambuti, falling down to meet the blue line of the Indian Ocean.

And yet one special memory perhaps transcended all others, if Kruger was absolutely honest, and that had to be the vision of his first wife, Anna, her sweet young body lying naked beside his in the pearly light of an African dawn...

And the tears began to flow from Oom Paul's bloodshot eyes as he saw Africa in his dreams for the last time...

.

EPILOGUE

July 1902

Eleanor Winthrop was a happier woman these days, as she sat contemplating her future on the promenade deck of the ocean liner, the *Kaiser Wilhelm der Grosse* of the North German Lloyd Line, bound for New York and home. They were already three days into the voyage, which had been pleasant so far, if marred somewhat by the inclement weather and bracing wind. Leaden skies and a slowly heaving grey ocean filled with whitecaps were not what Eleanor had been expecting in July, even in mid-Atlantic.

She turned and smiled at her companion in the chair beside her. 'Is that a good book, Joseph?'

He was reading *The Invisible Man* by H.G. Wells but seemed less than absorbed in it, she thought, reading an occasional page in desultory fashion, then setting it aside again with a vacant frown. Eleanor was aware that although Joseph had recovered spectacularly well from his physical injuries – restored to the muscular and handsome Joseph of before – yet, spiritually and mentally, he was not quite the same. Occasionally he seemed withdrawn into a deep melancholy that was hard to penetrate.

She had visited him and nursed him religiously during the two months or more of his recovery and convalescence. She knew that he was deeply grateful to her, but still didn't understand if his feelings went deeper than that. She was fully aware, though, with a slight sense of desperation, that she was running out of time in her quest to win his devotion. They would dock in New York in less than four days, and she was by no means sure what the future would hold for them afterwards.

It seemed the shadow of that woman, Miss Amelia Peachy, still possessed Joseph in some way. She was a ghost, after all, and how could she, a mere flesh-and-blood woman, compete with a ghost...?

*

Joe, too, was reflecting on the last few weeks. He and Eleanor had finally returned to Paris in June where he had enjoyed a boisterous if emotional reunion with René Sardou.

The timing of his return had been propitious. That first night back in Paris, René had taken him to the same *boîte de nuit* in a Montmartre backstreet where Corazon was still performing her stimulating routine, despite the terrible disaster that had befallen her island home. The tall and willowy Creole from the island of Martinique was still as lithe, vivacious and exuberant as ever, and - Joe was glad to see - still seemed determined to flout the French decency laws by wearing the smallest female costume imaginable.

René was happy too; the night before he had finally wormed his way into the gorgeous Corazon's bed, and couldn't believe his good fortune. 'I think she only gave in to me because she was in such low spirits after the volcano disaster. But I cheered her up all right. I think I am really in love, Joseph. My God! What an experience! It was like being drowned in a vat of warm dark honey...' René cocked an astute eye in Joe's direction. 'You're still sad for this Miss Peachy woman, are you not, my friend?'

'A little,' Joe admitted. Actually it was still a deep perpetual ache in his heart at the thought that she was no more. The bodies of Amelia and Plesch had never been recovered from the Rhine, only that of Monique Langevin, and Joe had still clung on to a slight hope of Amelia's improbable survival until quite recently...

'She wouldn't want you to mourn her forever,' René said sagely. 'You're too young and handsome for widower's weeds just yet, my friend...'

*

In June in Paris, Joe got a letter from Albert Einstein in Bern. He was now, he said, a Patents Officer Third Class in the Swiss Civil Service, and couldn't have been happier if he was a full professor of physics in Zurich. And now that he had a proper permanent salary, he fully intended to marry Mileva in the New Year, despite his parents' objections.

Joe closed the letter happily, and imagined now that Albert's life would drift into contented obscurity as he gave up dreams of academic fame in favour of the steadier, if undemanding, existence of a complacent civil servant and married man.

Joe had his own future to resolve too. It seemed Eleanor was determined he should re-start his father's business when he returned to America, as he'd dreamed, but she was also clearly just as determined to be part of his personal life from now on, too...

*

That evening in the salon, Joe played Bridge with a varied selection of first-class passengers.

Of his fellow players, Joe was most intrigued by his own Bridge partner at the table: an English diplomat and born raconteur with the improbable name of Sir Gyles Fortescue-McFarlane, who was a rich source of amusing and risqué anecdotes. Sir Giles was sixty or so, with thinning hair and mutton chop side-whiskers like Lord Salisbury, and was, despite his bawdy sense of humour, apparently the British Ambassador designate to Washington.

For all the amusing stories at the card table and the intricacies of the game, though, Joe still found his attention wandering from time to time. He reflected on all the things that had occurred in the last months while he'd been making his tortuously slow recovery. The Boer War had finally ended as the Boer guerrillas capitulated to the British, a treaty being signed at Vereeniging in the Orange Free State at the end of May. Cecil Rhodes, one of the architects of British rule in Africa, had not lived to see the victory, though, dying at the end of March.

And on May 8th, St. Pierre, capital of Martinique, the glorious Corazon's island, had suffered a disaster of epic proportions, wiped out completely by the explosion of Mount Pelee. Thirty thousand had been killed in the town, mostly because of asphyxiation from poisonous gases. In fact only one person had survived, a Monsieur Cyparis, who was imprisoned in a deep underground cell for drunkenness at the time of the eruption.

Having survived an ordeal of his own in the last months, Joe felt a peculiar affinity with this fortunate Monsieur Cyparis...

In June, King Edward VII had been forced to postpone his coronation. It had been scheduled for June 24th but it was reported that the King was seriously ill with appendicitis.

Joe thought of the irony of that, if the man went and died now. Everything that Amelia had done to keep that man alive would be wasted! *Or would she have laughed at the irony of it?*

Perhaps she would...

Joe finally excused himself from the Bridge game after losing yet another rubber, and wandered up on deck. There he found Eleanor looking at the moonlit ocean.

She smiled sweetly at him. 'Have you finished your game, Joseph?'

She did look extraordinarily beautiful in the moonlight, the silvery light enhancing the paleness of her face and turning her hair to a burnished gold colour. *Why should he fight this any more?* he thought. He was only human, after all, and in the face of all this provocative beauty, he did what came naturally to a young man with an ache in his heart and a beautiful girl in his sights.

He put his arms around her slender waist and kissed her as she lifted her face to his...

*

Sir Gyles Fortescue-McFarlane had returned to his suite to read through his papers before bed.

He sipped his brandy nightcap as he read again the secret memorandum on the King's condition from a friend at the Foreign Office.

CONFIDENTIAL PRIVATE MEMO: From the Chief Secretary of the Foreign Office to Sir Gyles Fortescue-McFarlane:

'...*Everyone apparently believes the concocted story that the King has been suffering from appendicitis.*

The story of the attack on him has been kept secret, including the fact that there was a woman with him at the time. This has been done not only for reasons of national security, but also to prevent the scandal that the King's unbecoming conduct would have generated. It would have been deeply embarrassing for the Royal Family and for H.M. Government if the press had discovered that the King had been attacked and nearly killed while frequenting an infamous brothel in Mayfair.

A bold rogue in this establishment apparently tried to murder the King with a knife. The King received slash wounds to his arm and chest. But the young woman who was with the King defended him vigorously, bravely fighting off the assailant until other staff in the establishment came to the rescue.

The assailant escaped however. There is a possibility he was a well-known anarchist and assassin called Johan Plesch. This man was believed to have died in Switzerland in March, but those reports may have been premature.

The identity of the young woman who saved the King's life is also a mystery. She left the premises without being seen. I did suggest to Sir Charles Gorman that she was one of his agents, assigned to protect the King and acting incognito, but Sir Charles only denied this with his customary enigmatic smile and quickly changed the subject...'

THE END

ABOUT THE AUTHOR

Gordon Thomson is a civil engineer by profession, a Geordie by birth, and Sunderland supporter (and therefore masochist) by inclination. His professional engineering career took him all over the world - Africa, the Far East, South America, as well as Holland and the UK - and this experience of exotic places and different cultures is what gave him the urge to try writing.

He has a Japanese wife and two grown up sons, one of whom was born in Holland, so he does claim to be a citizen of the world, if a very English one.

This story is the first of a series of adventure stories featuring the Edwardian secret agent Miss Peachy, which are intended to be, as one reviewer kindly put it ,"…Boys' Own or Girls' Own stories for adults…"

He has previously published the Victorian thriller *Leviathan,* and the Restoration mystery thrillers *Winter of the Comet* and *Summer of the Plague..*

Printed in Great Britain
by Amazon